Tumbleweed

Julia Bramer

Tumbleweed is an uncompromising story of a woman coming of age in a sometimes brutal world. It contains sexually explicit scenes and some violence and is intended for mature audiences only.

ISBN: 0692203877
ISBN-13: 978-0692203873

To the revolutionary youth that hoped for a better Egypt.

Prologue

I wouldn't grovel. I wouldn't submit. Not to him. He could mock me, beat me and burn me, but I knew who he was. A hypocrite using his faith to justify his actions. I was the enemy. I seduced his poor, defenseless son and nephew, so I deserved everything he would do to me. But I was defiant.

That was day one.

The Mohammeds

I arrived in Cairo in January 2011. I was greeted by my personal tour guide, Mohammed, and I immediately knew I wanted him. He was hot. *Perfect.* Tall and muscular, he exuded a quiet confidence, dressed casually in blue jeans and a white dress shirt, the top two buttons undone revealing tufts of dark chest hair. I imagined the curly clusters trailing down to his cock. *A big, juicy cock.* I smiled brightly and introduced myself.

"Hi, I'm Haley."

He replied in perfect American English. Desire churned my insides. He whisked me through passport control and customs to a white SUV where his cousin, another Mohammed, waited. My pulse raced. He, too, was gorgeous, both with almond-shaped eyes, straight noses, high cheek bones and coarse wavy black hair. But while the cousin's skin was pale and eyes a greenish-brown, the first Mohammed's complexion was olive and kissed by the sun, his eyes the color of charcoal.

I wanted both of them, fantasizing about a delicious ménage à trois in the desert. As the second Mohammed drove me to my hotel, I began making plans to seduce them, but I needed to be careful. The Egyptian culture was repressive, especially when it involved sex, and I wanted sex.

First, they needed nicknames. Mohammed and Mohammed was too confusing, especially since the pair would be guiding me around Egypt for a month. I suggested I call the olive-skinned one Momed and the pale-skinned one Hammed, which seemed to amuse them. My pussy twitched. I was off to a good start and began the seduction by asking Momed how he'd learned to speak English.

"From American music and movies," he said. "Mohammed, I mean Hammed, is fluent, too. We learned together so we could start our tour guide business."

I was impressed, their ambition making them even more enticing.

"Are you married?" I asked.

Not that it mattered, except if they weren't, it probably meant they had little or no sexual experience.

"No.

"Girlfriends?"

"Hammed has one."

"What's her name?"

"Nubiti." Momed answered for Hammed, who appeared to be the silent partner.

Or maybe he was simply concentrating on driving me safely to the hotel. The traffic was controlled chaos, a jumble of cars, buses and trucks with five vehicles side by side in what should have been four lanes, swerving from one to the other, the drivers jockeying for position and honking their horns.

Neither man seemed fazed by it, though. I peppered Momed with more questions, learning the two Mohammeds were the same age, 25 years old, a couple of years older than me. Like most Egyptian children they lived with their parents awaiting marriage, their incomes helping to provide for their families.

I'd seen it before, generations of families living together and supporting each other. Memories of Spain and *him* bubbled to the surface. I immediately suppressed them, but I couldn't stop my stomach from roiling. Then Hammed pulled in front of the Hilton and I was drawn into the hotel by another hot-looking Egyptian, distracting me from thoughts of *him*. As I rode the elevator to my room with a differential bellboy ogling me appreciatively, I focused on the sexy Mohammeds, hoping they'd invite me into their homes one day, my fantasy expanding to include an illicit rendezvous at an Egyptian residence.

I was in the country for both business and pleasure. It was a dream of mine to see and photograph the ancient sites. There were also rumblings of a revolution in the making, which I didn't want to miss. Tunisia's dictator had fallen a month earlier and social media was abuzz with young Egyptians planning their dictator's demise. I could feel the excitement and expectation in the air.

A revolution. I'd faced the bull in Spain, an earthquake in Chile and a human stampede in South Africa, and if everything fell into place, I would come face-to-face with an actual revolution. I was ready for it, certain to take a photo that would capture the imagination of the world. *A money shot.* And if I succeeded, my fame as a photojournalist would continue to grow.

The bellboy explained the features in the room, which was a large suite with a 270-degree view of the Pyramids and Nile River to the west, the Egyptian Museum and central Cairo to the east and the old town to the south. The room was expensive, but unlike when I first started out and pinched pennies by staying in homes of the locals, I could afford it now. I was rich.

I'd grown comfortable with the wealth, expecting the best. I didn't even try to mask my annoyance at the boy's halting English and impatiently dismissed him, itching to get back to the delicious Mohammeds. They were waiting in front of the hotel to take me to the Pyramids, and I quickly checked my appearance in the bathroom mirror before heading out to meet them.

I'd dressed conservatively before leaving Europe, wearing capris jeans and a blue-striped knit top that covered my shoulders and arms. The outfit was not my typical attire, preferring to show my cleavage and more leg, but I wasn't in Kansas anymore and needed to fit in.

Yet it was against my nature to succumb to ridiculous rules. The shirt was tight, accentuating my full breasts and slim waist. So were the pants, emphasizing my firm ass. But at least I'd concealed the parts the imams cared about, and I consoled myself with the fact that underneath the clothes I was wearing a sexy bra and thong, ready to seduce the Mohammeds if I were to be so lucky.

Plus, there was no concealing my long blond hair and blue eyes, which were a big part of my sex appeal. And since I wanted to blend in as much as possible anyway, acting like a typical tourist and not a photographer on the hunt for a money shot, I sucked it up.

The drive to the Pyramids took forty-five minutes. While Hammed stayed with the vehicle, Momed showed me around. He placed a lanyard with an official tour guide badge around his neck, guided me through a throng of hawkers selling postcards and other souvenirs, and explained in great detail the history of the ancient structures, interspersing corny jokes into his pitch. Not only was he gorgeous, he was extremely knowledgeable about Egyptian culture and sweetly funny. I couldn't help but smile.

Awestruck by the sheer magnificence of the place, I snapped shot after shot. When I stood at the base of the Great Pyramid and looked up, I imagined the tens of thousands of workers who built it. I even handed my precious camera to Momed so he could take my picture, which I'd do many times during my stay.

After photographing the Pyramids one at a time, Momed guided me to a spot on the horizon where I could shoot the three of them together. Arab men and their camels immediately descended upon us, and before I knew what was happening, a ratty turban was placed on my head and Momed lifted me onto one of the beasts.

Hot desire instantly sizzled up my spine. His breath tickled my neck, his eyes twinkled amusedly. Then the camel lifted its butt in the air and slowly stood on its hind legs, almost sending me toppling over its head. Gripping the creature's saddle horn tightly, I gave him a dirty look. Laughing boisterously, he took pictures of me and teasingly pretending to drop the camera.

My lust spiked. If I could have only one of the Mohammeds, I would choose him. His exuberance was infections. His bright smile lit up his beautiful charcoal eyes. I wanted him. I wanted them both.

Trudging through the sand to the Great Sphinx next, I reminded myself to be patient. I also had a job to do and casually asked him if there would be a revolution.

"Yes, I think there will be a revolution," he said. "The young people are tired of the old ways. Our culture is very repressive and our government pretends to be a democracy, but it is not. We want more freedom and opportunity. I hope the people will come together and make a change. Some of my friends say they are willing to die for it."

It was a dramatic statement, yet I felt little compassion for him, the emotion one I hadn't embraced for a long time. Instead, a rush of self-satisfaction flooded through me, which was an emotion I was very familiar with. It was then I knew I could seduce him, knew there was one freedom I could give him, give him *and* his cousin. It would only be a matter of time before it happened, and at that moment I felt free to reveal my real objective for being in Egypt.

"If there's a revolution, you'll still be my guide, won't you?" I asked. "I'll need your help."

"Yes, of course, Haley."

It's not as if he had much choice. I was paying the Mohammeds a lot of money to be at my beck and call, and they'd soon earn it in more ways than they expected.

I doubted it would be a burden.

Momed chose a restaurant in central Cairo for dinner. It was a place where he and Hammed felt comfortable dining with me, their reticence to share a meal at the Hilton a stark reminder of the repression in their country, a country where it was frowned upon for a tour guide to eat with a client at a fancy hotel.

I ordered the macaroni béchamel and a bottle of wine. The restaurant didn't serve alcohol, which didn't bother the Mohammeds but it pissed me off. I needed a drink and quickly gobbled up the food, demanding they take me back to the hotel before they finished their meal.

"Is something wrong, Haley?" Momed asked.

Hammed shifted from lane to lane, honking the horn and concentrating on getting me back to the hotel as quickly as possible.

"No, there's something I need to take care of," I said. I really needed a drink.

When Hammed arrived at the Hilton, I directed him to park in the lot out of view of the valets and the few guests who loitered outside. After reviewing the itinerary for the next day, I scooted to the middle of the back seat, thanked the Mohammeds profusely for their assistance and gave them each a quick peck on the cheek.

"See you tomorrow!" I said cheerfully, strutting to the lobby and swaying my hips sublimely, sure they were watching my every move.

Except for rows of brightly lit shelves displaying expensive alcohol, the hotel bar was dark. The customers were either couples lounging in plush chairs or businessmen clad in tailored suits leisurely sipping drinks at the glossy bar. I chose a seat in the corner, ordered a rum and coke and took a gulp, sighing happily.

I ordered another drink five minutes later. A bald man sporting an ugly Chaplin-like mustache glanced furtively my way. Annoyed, I ignored him, sifting through the images from the day on my camera, hoping Charlie Chaplin or some other guy didn't try to pick me up. I wanted to be alone but not by myself. Drinking in my room was too depressing.

Not that I was against an occasional sexual encounter with good-looking strangers in bars. I spent a lot of time checking out the action in bars and nightclubs, my need for sex insatiable. But that night I wasn't in the mood. My mind was on the Mohammeds and my next move. Besides, I liked my own company best, finding most people boring. I'd grown comfortable with my solitary lifestyle.

I was young, independent and fearless. I'd taken care of myself for a long time and grown up fast. Now I lived fast, always on the prowl for the next money shot and hot sex. I was also beautiful, which made the search for partners easy. Yet ordinary sex was no longer enough to keep me satisfied. I needed more and meeting the Mohammeds had set my imagination on fire.

I drank until I became sleepy, and that became my routine, touring Egypt during the day and spending the evening at the bar alone. I was patient. With each passing day, the Mohammeds became more comfortable with me and my ways, which included a lot of friendly body contact and innocent flirting, or at least I made them think it was innocent.

And as I set up the seduction, the mood in the country became tenser. Small protests broke out near the hotel and in front of the police station down the street. Yet there didn't seem to be a unified effort among the various groups that were seeking reform. Momed kept me apprised of it all, and he was hopeful about a demonstration scheduled after Friday prayers. I was hopeful, too, but for selfish reasons.

That was Tuesday, the day I broached the subject of sex.

"Do you think your revolution will lead to a sexual revolution, too?" I asked.

The Mohammeds grinned knowingly at each other. Hammed, who rarely spoke, looked at me in the rearview mirror, his greenish-brown eyes serious. "We do not talk about sex in Egypt. It is taboo but hopefully that will change."

"Have you ever had sex?"

"Yes, it is possible sometimes," Momed said. "Men and women think about it all the time. Younger people like us, but we must be careful, especially the women. There is a lot of sexual harassment."

"And people watch your every move," Hammed said. "If you are seen together going into your house, there will be talk, and if your parents find out, you will have trouble."

"But I've seen a few people hugging and kissing in public," I said.

"It is risky to do so," Momed replied.

"So what do you do?" I asked. Another knowing look passed between them. "Come on, guys, tell me," I prodded. "I doubt you can say anything that will shock me."

Momed snorted and said, "We know."

I was sure they were referring to the fact that Americans are more open about sexuality, but then Hammed said, "We saw your Playboy centerfold in the November issue. *Haley's Comet, Young and Upcoming Photographer gets Photographed.*"

"Oh," I muttered, caught off guard. Then I laughed, thrilled by their admission and hoping they were fantasizing about me as much as I was fantasizing about them. "Well, what did you think?" I asked.

"Great! Beautiful!" they responded at the same time.

We all burst into laughter. I shuddered with anticipation. They were ready for me and I decided Wednesday would be the day. The only question remaining was if they'd do it together.

"So, you jerk off to Playboy centerfolds?" I teased.

"And watch porn. We all have computers," Momed grinned.

"Yes, but we like it with women better," Hammed said.

"Hmm, of course you do." Smiling, I wondered if they'd ever jerked off to me.

When they picked me up at the hotel the next day, I had a surprise. I told them I wanted to skip the sites and picnic in the desert instead. The hotel staff loaded up the SUV with a canopy, blankets and coolers filled with food and drink. Momed hastily made calls looking for a more appropriate vehicle for traveling across the sand.

We headed south and stopped at a carpet store to pick up a small, funky off-road bus, the side of it painted with a mural of camels, sand and a big yellow sun. It was well-equipped with multiple spare tires, a satellite phone for communications and a CD player. Momed turned on the music, pumped up the volume, and we sang to '80s rock 'n' roll, which blared from speakers attached to the roof's interior. I was ecstatic, feeling like we'd become friends, enjoying our youth and freedom. And soon, we'd be enjoying each other.

Two hours later, Hammed pulled off the highway and headed into the Western Desert. It was a bumpy ride. Momed and I bounced wildly on our seats, singing and laughing. An hour later, Hammed stopped in the middle of nowhere, sand and barren rocky hills as far as my eyes could see. It was perfect for what I'd planned, finally alone with the Mohammeds and not a soul in sight to watch our every move.

I eagerly hopped off the bus. Sweat immediately pooled on my forehead and dripped down my spine. The desert was uncharacteristically hot for January, giving me the excuse I needed. I stripped off my white cotton shirt and jeans, leaving me wearing only a black lacy bra, bikini panties and sandals.

Gaping, Momed and Hammed stopped setting up the canopy. I stifled a triumphant grin and shrugged. "It's freaking hot, guys. Feel free to do the same."

That knowing look passed between them again. My insides tightened, certain they'd eventually end up naked in my arms. I watched them set up the canopy, spread the blankets under it and lug the coolers into the shade. Perspiration seeped through their polo shirts. They looked miserable. When they finished, Momed said something in Arabic to Hammed, and they quickly peeled off their clothes right down to their white jockey underwear.

It was my turn to gape. They were magnificent, beautiful...

One pale and one golden, their hard bodies glistened with sweat and cocks bulged beneath the jockeys. My belly clenched, my pulse raced. It took all my willpower to stop myself from immediately pouncing on them. Instead, I acted like I didn't notice and sank to my knees, focusing on organizing lunch. Yet I was completely aware of my half-nakedness. My pussy plumped and throbbed. Hot juices accumulated between my legs. As I laid out plastic food containers, I sensed their eyes following my every move, their lust electrifying the stark landscape and me.

There's nothing to compare it to, that feeling of sexual power over men, except maybe taking that perfect shot. I had a strong urge to snap their picture, their silhouettes shifting sensuously in the shadows of the canopy. Their musky scents teased my nostrils and manhood tantalized my libido. A rush of sweet satisfaction surged through me and I forced myself to remain calm.

Men like the Mohammeds couldn't be rushed.

Instead, I grabbed a beer from the cooler, dramatically took a big swig and sat cross-legged on the blanket, intentionally opening my legs. The beer was ice cold. I rubbed the can on the nape of my neck, my body on fire, heated by the desert and hot anticipation.

"Do you want one?" I asked. "There's water and soda, too."

I wasn't surprised when they both chose beer. There were no prying eyes to see them and no one to admonish them. I didn't say anything, their religion their own business. They sucked it down as if it was water, and I passed around the food–flatbread, salads and vegetables marinated in olive oil, little pies filled with meat and cheese, and a semi-sweet nut pastry for dessert.

The meal was delicious, made more so by the crisp desert silence and half-naked Mohammeds. Their cocks strained against the jockeys, a constant reminder of what was to come. When we finished, I gathered the leftovers and crawled on all fours over to the cooler, giving them a good look at my ass and glancing over my shoulder at one Mohammed and then the other.

Hammed stretched out his legs and leaned back on his elbows, lips curling into a slight grin. Momed sprawled out on his side, propped his head on a hand and draped the other over his hip, hiding the swelling inside his briefs.

They regarded me expectantly, waiting for my next instructions. I snaked next to Momed first, laying on my side and kissing him softly. He gasped and tensed. I slipped my tongue inside his mouth, exploring, tasting. With each flick he relaxed more and more until he was kissing me back, his tongue becoming more fervent with each stroke.

White-hot lust shot through my veins. Liquid fire burned my spongy flesh. I coiled my tongue around his, fusing them in a sultry tango, my fingers toying with the curly hair on his chest and moving down to the band of his jockeys. I slid my hand inside and rubbed a thumb across the slit on the tip of his engorged cock. A pleasurable groaned rumbled from deep within him.

My pussy ached. I looked at Hammed. He sat erect, gawking, his eyes glassy and feverish. I slithered over to him and climbed onto his lap. I wanted both the Mohammeds and pressed my lips to his. He moaned as if relieved I would come to him, too, and he crushed me to him, wrapping his arms tightly around me and forcing a demanding tongue inside my mouth.

He kissed me hungrily, hands roaming up and down my back. He fondled my ass and thrust his hips upward, grinding his erection against my sodden panties, making me wetter, hotter, every synapse in my body snapping and sizzling.

We broke away at the same time, gasping for air. His eyes smoldered and I headed south, nipping at his moist skin and the black tufts of hair on his chest. When I reached the base of his hard abs and the spot right above the pubic hair, he lifted his butt so I could tug off the briefs. Licking my parched lips, I watched his granite-hard flesh spring free.

His cock was big and juicy. My heart hammered. I gripped the thick shaft and wrapped my mouth around the crown. He shuddered and I peeked at Momed, his body rigid and eyes black with lust.

My pussy pounded with an almost desperate need, more aroused by Momed's eyes following my every move. I thought about skipping the blow jobs, wanting a cock inside me, craving the delicious contact with my sweet spots. But I knew the Mohammeds would come too quickly, starved for sex by the repressive Egyptian culture. I clamped my mouth on Hammed's engorged flesh and expertly sucked and stroked.

Just as I'd thought he came fast. He collapsed onto his back, sighing heavily as I licked him dry. It was the same with Momed, whose pleasurable groan ran deep, rumbling through me. After he climaxed, I removed my bra and panties and lay between them, shivering in the sweltering heat, waiting for them to come back to earth.

I didn't have long to wait. Momed nestled next to me and draped a leg over mine. He burrowed his nose in the crook of my neck and whispered words in Arabic I didn't understand. He cupped a breast and skimmed his fingers over the nipple, sending fiery sensations to my already burning clit. I let out my own whispery moan.

He twisted and plucked and licked. Hammed soon joined in, clamping onto the other nipple. I shuddered triumphantly. Their warm lips and wet tongues bathed me in sweet torment. A dizzying ecstasy cut through me. It was what I'd fantasized about, what I'd wanted from the moment I met them.

They titillated and teased. My nipples puckered and swelled. Each delicious lick sent me closer to the edge. Then Momed feathered his fingers across my belly and down to the hot folds between my thighs, fixing on my clit.

He rubbed it hard and clumsily. I closed a hand over his and showed him what I wanted. He learned quickly, massaging the sensitive flesh slowly, agonizingly, working me over until I writhed between them, ready to explode.

"I want to try." Hammed pushed Momed's hand aside. I would've laughed if I wasn't desperate for release. I patiently showed him what to do, and while Momed returned to my inflamed nipple, Hammed rested his head on my belly and caressed my sweet spots, massaging my clit and kneading my spongy walls with surprising sensitivity.

The orgasm began as a ripple. I closed my eyes. It mushroomed quickly and stabbed through me with exquisite intensity. When it sputtered and my breathing returned to normal, I opened my eyes. The Mohammeds hovered over me, watching my reaction.

Grinning crookedly, I glanced from one to the other. Momed smiled brightly, gave me a quick peck on the cheek and said, "You are wonderful, Haley Hanson."

"Great," Hammed concurred, eyes twinkling lecherously.

"So are you." I peered at their magnificent cocks, which were as stiff as boards again. My stomach lurched. "You know we're not done, don't you, guys?"

They gave each other that knowing look. I got on my knees with my naked ass in their faces and slowly crawled to my camera bag. I grabbed the handful of condoms I'd packed earlier, crawled back and tossed them onto the blanket. There were at least ten brightly-colored foil packages and their eyes widened.

"What?" I asked playfully.

Momed stuck two fingers into his mouth, the ones that were inside me minutes before, and he dramatically licked them, his lips quirking up into a wicked grin. My pussy prickled with the insatiable need that ruled my life. I glanced at Hammed; his face etched with carnal expectation as he casually stretched out and leaned back on his elbows.

Hot adrenaline shot through my veins. I ripped open a foil, looking from one Mohammed to the other. I chose Hammed for no other reason than he was in the right position at the right time. I wanted to be on top, wanted the control, and I straddled him, kissing the perfectly-formed crown on his cock before rolling the condom on it. Growling with animalistic pleasure, he grasped my hips as I sank onto him and he slowly filled me up. Stretching me, hard stone against moist flesh, *magnificent.*

Taking my time, I grinded against Hammed's thick shaft, each thrust hitting its mark and arousing me anew. My back arched, body steadily building toward climax. I peeked at Momed, who watched intently like before. He liked watching and I liked being watched.

I locked eyes with him and rode his cousin. He edged toward me and grabbed the nape of my neck, drawing my face to his. I thought he might kiss me, but he licked the sweat dripping from my chin, his tongue rolling up my hairline and around. Then he snaked behind me, grasped the long hair that stuck to my back and pulled it off my moist skin. His tongue leisurely moved upward from the base of my spine, lapping up my drenched flesh like a cat.

It was decadent. Two men and a woman greased with perspiration. The sun battered the desert at midday, turning the temperature up a few more degrees. Momed's hands slipped over my wet skin to my heavy breasts. He scooped them up and pinched my nipples between thumb and forefinger, his tongue midway up my backbone. Hammed bucked beneath me, ass clenched as he rammed faster and faster into me.

Clit hotter than the scorching heat, I masked a tortured grunt with a low moan. My pussy swelled and throbbed, ready to burst, but Hammed beat me to it. Shouting one word in Arabic, he clutched my buttocks and detonated. His body went rigid, lips forming an "O" as he exhaled slowly and his cock convulsed inside me.

I rubbed my sodden pussy against him and locked eyes with Momed again. He snatched a condom from the pile, ripped it open with his teeth and hurriedly put it on, cock standing at attention, engorged and ready for me. I grinned wickedly.

Two men were infinitely better than one, an intoxicating combination if I could find it. My greedy self-indulgence was boundless; my sexuality unleashed those many years ago with *him*. His shadow haunted me and shaped my obsession, the depth of my depravity deep and forged in the cafes and nightclubs and back alleys in a dozen countries with dozens of men. Once I'd started down that road, I couldn't stop and couldn't go back. A dark and insatiable impulse propelled me forward, driving me into the sweltering barren desert and into the arms of strangers like the Mohammeds.

I pushed Momed on his back and climbed on top. He groaned that rumbling groan from deep within. An expression of pure pleasure crossed his face as I mounted him. At first he closed his eyes and gripped my ass as Hammed had done. Then he abruptly sat up, buried his head between my breasts and pumped furiously into me, ramming against all the right spots.

I wrapped my legs around his hips and held on. He took me back to the peak, dizzy and quivering with delicious sensations, climbing steadily toward orgasm. Hammed nudged back into the action and clamped onto a nipple, biting and tugging at it with his teeth. The agony and ecstasy triggered my release, sending me into the abyss.

I slumped on Momed's shoulder. Head spinning and blood pumping, the convulsions rocked my womb. I surrendered to them, barely noticing Momed's own explosion, carried along by the powerful vibrations that were mine and mine only.

~~~~~~†~~~~~~

I was sandwiched between them. Hammed thrust into me from behind and Momed massaged my clit. He ravished me with his mouth, moving over my body with deliberation and lapping up moisture as it beaded on my skin. When they switched places, Hammed returned to biting and tormenting my swollen nipples, occasionally releasing them and kissing me hard. I climaxed again, my pussy throbbing with raw pleasure. When the euphoria subsided, I immediately wanted more, drunk with sexual power.

We lay on our backs, sweat dripping down the sides of our skin. Momed's breathing returned to normal, and he gracefully hopped to his feet and strutted to the cooler, returning with bottled water.

"I want a beer," I said.

"No, Haley, you must drink water or you will get dehydrated." He cocked an expectant brow.

Smiling inside, I took the water. I didn't know whether Momed was simply doing his job or wanted to make sure I didn't pass out because of the heat, a few condoms left to use. I gulped the bottle of water and drank another. Then we fucked until the condoms were gone and the sun edged closer to the horizon, giving us a couple of hours to leave the desert before darkness set in.

I used a blanket to wipe the perspiration from my body, watching the Mohammeds as I dressed. They stood side by side under the canopy and gazed at the stark landscape, absorbed by their own thoughts and completely serene, their cocks finally tamed, their hard, naked bodies glistening in the haze of the vanishing daylight.

They were magnificent, the light fracturing their silhouettes into a prism of color as it bounced off their moist flesh. I surreptitiously grabbed my camera and snapped a few shots, my heart clenching with a hint of affection.

It was a weak moment. I rationalized the temporary lapse by telling myself I was a photographer and it was my job to capture the essence of the people I met. That was all.

I'd hardened myself against caring about my conquests years ago. Except for my parents, brother and best friend, Jillian, I couldn't care less about the rest of humanity. Besides, I didn't need a picture to remember the Mohammeds. The day in the desert was forever seared into my memory. It was just a photo, and after we returned to the highway, I ignored them and dozed in the back of the bus, my body sated for once.

While the hotel staff unloaded the picnic gear, I told the Mohammeds it was their turn to surprise me and the next day's tour schedule was up to them. That knowing look passed between them. When they drove away, they looked practically giddy.

I ate dinner at the hotel, skipping Egyptian food and ordering a thick beef filet with fries and an expensive bottle of Merlot. Afterward, I retired to the bar for a couple more drinks before heading to the suite. I was tired. The long hot day, sexual games and booze had finally caught up with me. Yet I couldn't fall asleep. Edgy, I ordered another drink from room service, set the laptop on my lap and loaded the Mohammed photos from our desert rendezvous, hoping I'd captured the spirit of the moment.

I did and gasped. The picture was a stunning portrait of them, the light turning Hammed's silhouette into a shimmering, ghostly figure with one lustrous green eye, and Momed's into a dark, faceless shadow with thick black lashes illuminated by the sun, the contours of their hard buttocks and sinewy back muscles tinted by yellow and burnt orange. The photo was at once erotic and chilling, flush with carnality and provoking the senses.

It reminded me of *him* and I froze. I could hear my heart beating. My stomach twisted in knots. I slammed shut the laptop, leapt from the chair and backed away, as if I'd touched a hot burner on a stove. Memories of another silhouette on a sailboat erupted in my brain, piercing my skull. Overcome with nausea, I sucked in air, trying to control the panic. After a few minutes, I was steady enough to pick up the house phone and order a bottle of wine.

Needing a distraction, I turned on the TV and clicked through the channels until I found a documentary about polar bears. I settled on the chair with the wine and drank from the bottle, falling into a drunken stupor. When I woke the next morning, my head pounded riotously, hurting too much for me to reflect on why.

Relying on a hangover cure I'd used in the past, I drank two Bloody Marys at breakfast and took four aspirin. By the time the Mohammeds picked me up, I was left with a dull headache, a reminder of earlier years when I'd let my drinking get out of control.

I didn't want to think about that painful time in my life and turned my attention to the Mohammeds. They brimmed with eagerness, playfully keeping the itinerary a secret. I relaxed and concentrated on my pussy, which had suddenly perked up. Thoughts of another carnal day with the Mohammeds sent adrenaline surging through my veins. The insipid thud in my head slowly faded.

Hammed drove south again along the fertile Nile River Valley to Egypt's first capital, Memphis. Momed escorted me to view the colossal limestone Ramesses II statue, the Ramesses III monument and an eighty-ton calcite sphinx statue. The ancient effigies were incredible, but I was most interested in the town and its inhabitants.

Police wearing black uniforms with shiny gold buttons directed traffic at clogged intersections. Women clad in colorful skirts and headscarves carried large milk tins on their heads. Camels loaded with bundles of straw and sacks of dates tromped through the streets led by men wearing long white robes and turbans, all of them going about their daily lives against a backdrop of traditional mud brick houses juxtaposed against modern, five-story apartment buildings.

They were the kind of scenes I loved to photograph. And although I didn't make much money from these types of shots, I'd occasionally be at the right place at the right time and snap an interesting event or moment that would be picked up by a newspaper or published in a travel magazine. I spent an hour wandering around covertly taking pictures with Momed. Thrilled, but also hoping it wasn't the only reason the Mohammeds had brought me here.

"Now what?" I asked.

Momed smiled wickedly. My belly clenched. We walked backed to the SUV where Hammed waited, smirking salaciously. He placed his official tour guide badge over his neck and grabbed a blanket stored in the back of the van. We headed toward the river, stopping at a food stand on the way to buy water, sodas and pita sandwiches stuffed with a concoction of fava beans, falafel, babaganoush, eggs and potatoes all mashed together. Then they led me into the greenery along the Nile, taking a worn path used for centuries.

It was cooler among the palm, eucalyptus and sycamore trees. Momed morphed into his tour guide persona, pointing out prickly shrubs sprouting pale flowers and fruit trees with ripe figs and mangos. The people we passed barely glanced our way, just a couple of tour guides with official badges escorting another tourist on an excursion to see the sights along the banks of the Nile.

After forty minutes, we left the path and picnicked under the shade of tall palm trees. Although the pedestrian traffic had thinned at that point, the spot wasn't very secluded. I wondered what we were doing there, hoping the Mohammeds weren't teasing me. I'd left the hotel that morning certain about another rendezvous, certain about their voracious appetite for sex with me, but I began to have doubts. Yet there was a gleam in their eyes and a spring in their step, so I held my tongue, hoping they wouldn't disappoint me.

We finished our sandwiches and packed up. They led me farther away from the river. After ten more minutes, they stopped in front of an abandoned, ramshackle mud brick house half-hidden by overgrown shrubs and trees. There was graffiti sprayed all over it, which was unusual in Egypt, so I immediately took a photo.

Momed shook his head back and forth, lips pinched with disgust. "This is terrible. The house is one of the last from ancient times. I cannot believe it."

Hammed lowered his eyes, looking morose. I studied the dwelling more closely, wondering why people would deface a historical building.

Then they burst into laughter. It took me a second to realize they were teasing me. I punched Momed on the arm.

"Damn it, Momed," I muttered.

He grabbed me by the waist, kissed me hard and swung me around. It caught me off guard. The display was too intimate. More intimate than sex. Affectionate even, but I didn't have time to think about it. He grasped my hand and pulled me toward the house, the wicked gleam back in his eyes.

There was no door and the opening was low. We ducked to get inside. The entryway was dirty and cluttered with garbage. I couldn't imagine what we were doing there. I certainly wasn't going to fuck them in *there*, and then Momed drew me into a side room and my heart skipped a beat.

It was a twelve-by-twelve-foot space with colorful cushions and pillows positioned against three walls. An Egyptian carpet was laid out on the beaten earth floor, and there were hookahs, candles and lighters neatly tucked in a corner.

"My friend told me about it," Hammed pronounced proudly. "Only a few people know it is here."

"Is it okay, Haley?" Momed asked.

"Perfect."

The lengths the youth in Egypt would go to achieve some privacy were unbelievable. Anyone who didn't know about the place wouldn't make it past the entrance, a clandestine hideaway along the Nile hidden in plain sight. My pussy immediately moistened, my pulse raced and my nipples tingled. I looked from Momed to Hammed, licking my lips seductively.

"Would you teach us cunnilingus?" Hammed asked softly.

Every inch of me ignited with white-hot lust. He seemed a little embarrassed and I went to him, kissing him lightly on the corner of the mouth and grinding against the hard bulge in his pants. "I would love to," I murmured.

While Hammed undid my jeans and slid them to the ground, Momed approached from behind and nuzzled my neck. He pulled the shirt over my head, removed my bra and rubbed a cheek across my back.

I'd already determined Momed was the affectionate one. He loved to lick and caress me all over. His cousin, on the other hand, was the perfunctory one, always wanting to simply get the job done. So while Momed fondled my breasts and kissed me hard, Hammed spread the blanket on the carpet. He drew me away from Momed and sat me on it, efficiently removing my sandals and the jeans and panties around my ankles. Then he neatly folded the clothes and set them on a cushion before kneeling between my legs and eyeing me expectantly.

Shivering from head to toe, liquid fire amassed in my deepest recesses, aroused like never before. They wanted me to teach them, maybe even dominate them, and I could do both.

"Get me a couple of pillows," I demanded. Momed quickly obliged, placing three on the blanket next to me. I rolled onto my belly and clasped one to my chest, nonchalantly dangling my calves in the air. Yet I was anything but nonchalant. My pussy throbbed. My heart beat wildly. "Take off your clothes. Both of you."

Momed ripped off his polo shirt and tossed it aside. Hammed hurriedly pulled his over his head, quickly folded it and placed it on top of my clothes.

"Slowly, guys."

Hammed narrowed his beautiful greenish-brown eyes, as if he was unsure he liked the game and didn't appreciate being bossed around. Momed swayed his hips seductively, eager to please. They did what they were told, eyeing me hungrily as they slipped off their shoes and socks and removed their jeans and jockeys.

I stared at them, suppressing the urge to jump up and taste their fat, juicy cocks, my libido going haywire. Instead, I licked my lips sensually, rolled onto my back and spread my legs wide, placing my middle finger in the wet folds of my pussy.

"You want to lick this?" I asked. I stroked my clit. Hammed's jaw clenched and Momed's eyes darkened. Hot sparks shot through me.

"Yes," Momed rasped.

"You first, then."

Momed hastily knelt between my legs and grinned crookedly. I spread the lips of my pussy so he could see my clit amid the small patch of professionally trimmed pubic hair.

"Aim here," I said, touching my most sensitive spot.

"Okay, Haley, I will do my best," he teased.

I leaned back on my elbows. Hammed hovered over us, eyes fixed on my pussy. "Hammed, you hold my legs apart. Don't let me close them," I ordered.

Smirking lecherously, he knelt behind Momed, jerked my legs wide and roughly gripped my ankles. I didn't mind. I liked it rough, too.

I nodded at Momed to start and he planted his tongue where I told him, flicking lightly. A jolt of pleasure ripped through me. I gripped the blanket in my fists and watched him taste me, suck me, moaning softly.

"Stick your tongue inside me," I croaked.

He jabbed and licked, his silky tongue grooming my swollen clit with great relish and then dipping it into me as far as he could reach. I strained against the hands that restrained me, wanting to close my legs but knowing better, knowing the orgasm would be more intense if I rode it out.

The power. The ecstasy. Two hot guys at my disposal, surrendering to my demands and wanting to please me. I bowed into Momed's mouth, reaching the brink, my inner thighs trembling. One more flick of the tongue and I shattered and shuddered. The pleasure rolled from the depths of my core up my spine and down to my toes. I collapsed on my back and lightly patted Momed on the head like a good pet.

He grinned boyishly, pleased with himself, lips glistening with my juices. He slithered next to me, snuggled against my naked body and burrowed his face in my throat. "Was it good?" he asked softly.

"Excellent," I replied breathlessly. The convulsions slowly subsided. I peered at Hammed, who eyed me hungrily and continued to hold my legs apart. "Hammed, get the condoms from the camera bag."

He got up slowly, a bit grudgingly, and strutted to the bag. His cock looked painfully hard and bobbed with each step. Momed's poked me on the hip, their desire triggering my arousal again, the mud room supercharged with sexual energy.

Hammed returned with a handful of condoms and hovered above me. I stretched my legs, sat up and asked, "Do you want to lick me or fuck me first?"

His answer was to drop all the foils but one and rip it open. He rolled the condom over his cock and waited for instructions, the salacious grin back.

"Well, go ahead, take me as you wish," I taunted.

He dropped onto the blanket, maneuvered me on my hands and knees and moved behind me. There was no kiss, no sweet caresses and no foreplay. He gripped my buttocks, spread my legs with his knees and rubbed his cock on my slippery pussy, searching for the opening and ramming into me when he found it.

He let out a low animalistic growl, pushed deeper inside me and rested there for a moment. I wasn't surprised by his indifference to the rest of my body. He wanted his release and he wanted it fast. It didn't matter to me. He felt good. Granite hard. Stretching me.

Grinding and hitting my sweet spots just right.

He picked up the pace, grunting with each thrust. I braced myself against the relentless pounding. Momed moved to sit at my head and watched us, stroking his erection. I motioned for him to come closer.

He scooted up to my face, his cock bloated with blood. I rested on a forearm and swept the hair from my brow, my exposed ass tilting up in the air. Hammed adjusted his attack, drilling into me deeper. I planted my lips on Momed's engorged shaft and sucked it into my mouth. Both men groaned and grunted with pleasure, their gratification heightening mine.

Hammed pumped faster, furiously, his breathing labored. I steadily edged closer to the brink, each scraping stroke multiplying the exquisite sensations. Unable to concentrate on Momed anymore, his dick slipped from my mouth and I hung my head, the peak within reach. Hammed rammed into me one last time and stilled, his cock convulsing riotously against the spongy, wet walls inside me.

I thrust my ass against him, grinding, craving more friction. But it wasn't to be. He deflated fast and pulled out, kissing my behind and dropping onto his belly next to me, his eyes glassy and soft.

Groaning with frustration, I flopped on my back, looking up at Momed. He grinned eagerly, his cock pressed against the back of my head. "Hurry up, Momed," I sighed impatiently.

He reached across Hammed and me, grabbed a condom and put it on in seconds. "As I wish, too?" he asked. I rolled my eyes and nodded.

He scooted between my legs, pushed them farther apart and slowly sank into me, a growl rumbling deep in his chest. His hands and mouth roamed across my body at will. Kissing me hard. Massaging my breasts. Licking and sucking my nipples while plunging in and out of me at a snail's pace, taking his time with long and sturdy strokes.

I wrapped my legs around his hips and thrust upward, urging him to go faster. He refused to rush, savoring me as if I was his favorite dish. When I embraced his muscular back and pressed him to me, he struggled free and pinned my arms above my head.

"Hold her, Hammed," he said.

My eyes widened with surprise. He shrugged and grinned crookedly. "You said I could do what I want," he admonished.

"Of course."

And what he wanted was to ravish me. While Hammed restrained my hands, Momed taunted and teased me until I was practically purring. Every inch of my flesh tingled. My nipples puckered and ached. My pussy dripped with hot need. It was only then his tempo increased, steadily moving faster and harder.

Wound up tight and ready to combust, I met him thrust for thrust, his fat cock raking me over the coals. The faster he went the hotter my clit burned. Then it flashed white hot and a powerful orgasm blistered through me.

It was one of those orgasms that left me blinded, dazed and gasping for air. Hammed released my arms and I wrapped them around Momed, hugging him tightly as the spasms raged and he reached his own climax. He went limp, his body heavy and crushing me, and I couldn't move, couldn't speak, left delirious and shuddering.

I might have fallen in love with Momed after that, but I no longer cared about love. When I could breathe again, I laughed blissfully. He braced his hands on the floor, pushed up and suspended his sinewy body above me, studying me for a moment before kissing me softly on the lips and collapsing onto the blanket next to me.

The Revolution

Friday finally rolled around and I waited in the suite for the Mohammeds to pick me up after Friday prayers. We would be sticking around Cairo with hopes the rumors about a big turnout for the protest were true. If not, I would tour the Cairo museum, which was supposed to be incredible, but museums bored me. For my own selfish reasons, I hoped the rumors would come to fruition.

Drinking my third cup of coffee, I gazed out the large window at the crowded city landscape. Thousands of satellite dishes protruded from rooftops. Freshly washed clothes hung from balconies. Smog blanketed the domes and minarets of mosques, turning the colorless panorama into a hazy desert mirage. My mind turned to Momed and the abandoned mud brick house on the Nile.

It wasn't often a man could fuck me into oblivion and turn me into mush. I remembered only two others, one who I'd chosen to forget and the other who'd died in South Africa saving me from my own death. Now there was Momed. Smart, funny and incredibly sexy, Momed. Any woman would be lucky to have him, and after yesterday, I could officially categorize him as an exceptional lover.

Hammed, on the other hand, was just proficient. Selfish. Distant. Lacking affection. He could make a woman climax if he wanted, and I had to give him credit for his due diligence. After Momed had surprised me at the mud brick house, setting me on fire with his sweet torment, Hammed licked my pussy to orgasm. I couldn't judge him too harshly. His goal was raw sexual gratification.

He was a lot like me…

~~~~~~~†~~~~~~~

Momed called at two o'clock to let me know they were on their way.

"Haley, it is happening!" he announced excitedly.

"Are you sure?"

"Yes, yes, the imams are giving their blessing."

I let out a long sigh. The suite's luxurious king-size bed taunted me. I was suffocating under the repressive regime, wanting the Mohammeds in my bed fucking me in the middle of the night as the need arose. But there would soon be a *revolution* to divert my attention. The impatient, restless gnawing feeling inside me faded.

A revolution…

I watched people stream onto a vacant lot next to the hotel. But it wasn't any vacant lot. It was Tahrir Square. And as the minutes passed, more and more materialized carrying placards and waving country flags. They weren't just the youth, either, but gray-bearded men wearing turbans and families with babies and small children.

I hastily cleaned the camera lens and rushed to meet the Mohammeds outside. The elevator seemed to take forever to pick me up on my floor. As it descended back to the lobby, I listened to a British couple vent their frustration with Cairo traffic. They had no idea it was about to get worse.

Hammed's SUV pulled up to the hotel entrance fifteen minutes later. The Mohammeds emerged from the vehicle, Momed smiling exuberantly and Hammed looking nervous. I found out why when I was introduced to his girlfriend.

"Nice to meet you, Nubiti," I greeted, avoiding Hammed's worried glare.

She wore a traditional long black skirt, long-sleeved yellow shirt and a yellow headscarf, her smile radiant and excited. It was obvious she didn't know what Hammed had been up to.

"Haley Hanson, so nice to meet you, too." Her voice was soft and melodic, her accent British. She said my name as if she'd been waiting forever to meet me.

"Nubiti brought you different clothes to wear. You cannot go in there like that," Momed said.

He was right. The tight shirt and jeans I'd worn along with my blond hair and blue eyes would definitely make me stand out among the natives.

Nubiti offered me a tote bag and I grabbed her elbow. "Come with me," I said, pulling her toward the hotel and looking over my shoulder at Hammed frowning disapprovingly. I knew he was afraid I might reveal our sexual escapades, which I would never do. Yet I liked making him nervous and innocently rolled my eyes.

Nubiti hesitated, looking grim. The hotel security guard scowled at her, obviously unhappy about my Egyptian guest. I dragged her forward and acted like her being there was the most natural thing in the world. Besides, he didn't intimidate me, and after she walked through the metal detector, I clasped her arm and drew her away before they could frisk her.

We rode the elevator with four other guests. As we ascended to my floor, she stood rigidly next to me with her head meekly bowed, seemingly uncomfortable and apprehensive about being inside a fancy hotel in her own country. It pissed me off. I hated the idea she'd been browbeaten by society into submission like that. Yet it wasn't my problem. I was there for a money shot.

Once we entered the suite she relaxed, smiling brightly at the scene outside. The square had become packed, the overflow blocking the road around it. More people spilled from the side streets every minute.

"We are happy you are here, Haley," she said. I raised a brow, confused by the remark and suddenly pensive. "We know about your photographs. The bull at Pamplona, the child in the rubble of the earthquake in Chile, the dead at the stampede in South Africa, the religious gathering at the Ganges. You are very good, Haley. My favorite is the one of Mikel Garro."

I could hear my heart beating. My stomach twisted in a tight knot. I didn't want to hear his name, didn't want to remember.

"You can help us, Haley. You can help our cause. And we want to help you. Your photos of our revolution will document our struggle and be seen around the world."

A wave of nausea gripped me and I turned away. I didn't want her to see me weak, vulnerable. I grabbed a miniature whiskey from the minibar and shakily poured it into a glass, gulping it down in one shot. The fiery liquid slid down my throat, its heat spreading through me and calming me enough to face her again. I put on a fake smile.

"That works for me," I said casually, eyeing the tote. "So let's get started."

She grinned and laid the clothes on the bed. I stripped down to my bra and panties, thinking I couldn't care less about their cause. The world was a cruel, crazy place and I wouldn't let myself feel for it. I was only after another money shot and would let her help me get it.

She'd brought me a black skirt like hers, a purple tee top and a long-sleeved, lightweight purple-and-white jacket. After I slipped on the clothes, she fastened my hair in a ponytail and wrapped a black headband around my hairline to cover the blond wisps on the front of my scalp. Then she draped a silky purple headscarf over it, dramatically flung the ends around my neck and stepped back.

She smiled sweetly and I studied her more closely, wondering if Hammed had ever fucked her. She was lovely, at least the part I could see, her face oval with high cheekbones and a straight nose. Her eyes were a brown sugar color, which she enhanced with dark brown eyeliner and mascara. Her lips were heart-shaped and painted with a glossy pink lipstick. Despite her modest demeanor in the elevator, she seemed very modern.

Suddenly interested in her story, I asked, "What do you do, Nubiti?"

"I studied accounting at the University, but I do not have a job. Most young people do not, especially the women."

"How long have you been dating Hammed, um, I mean Mohammed?"

She chuckled and replied, "Mohammed told me about your nickname for him. I do not blame you. There are a lot of men named Mohammed in Egypt."

"No kidding. It's confusing."

"Yes, but we are used to it. He thinks it is funny. No other tourist has been so creative."

"Hmm... Do you love him?" She looked surprised by the question.

"Did he talk to you about me?" she asked excitedly, *hopefully.*

I don't know why I asked or why I even cared. I should've kept my mouth shut and tried to change the subject. "Only that he had a girlfriend. Are you ready to go?"

"No, not yet, we must do something with your eyes. Do you have black mascara?" I didn't. She pulled a makeup case out of the bag, led me into the bathroom and watched me apply a thick layer of black mascara and outline my eyes using the same dark color. "I think I love him," she said. "My parents approve of him, even though he is from a lower class. But he has a job, and my parents are very modern-thinking."

"Oh?"

"Yes, they have invited him to dinner several times."

"Well, it sounds like things are moving in the right direction," I said. "What color of lipstick?"

She handed me a tube of glossy pink like hers and continued. "Maybe. Mohammed's father supports the Muslim Brotherhood and he does not approve of me."

"Oh."

"Mohammed says he doesn't care. He respects his father but

hates the Brotherhood. Same with his cousin. His father and Mohammed's are brothers. They are stuck in the past."

"So what will you do?"

"It is for Mohammed to decide," she shrugged.

I wanted to shake her and tell her to take control of her life. It was obvious she loved Hammed, so she should find out if he felt the same way. If so, she should demand he fight for her. But again, it was none of my business. I had a job to do.

"Well, what do you think?" I asked. Except for the blue eyes, I had to admit I looked much more Egyptian.

"It is better. There are a few of us with your eye color, and as long as you are with us, you will be fine."

We returned to the large living room, and she strode determinedly to the camera case, picked it up and unzipped the top.

"Wait!" I scrambled over to her and snatched the case from her hands. "No offense, but I don't like people touching my camera."

It was true. I didn't want people handling my equipment, but there were also several condoms packed inside it and I didn't want her to see them. She was smart enough to put two and two together.

"I am sorry," she said, "but you should try to hide the camera. I will show you."

Humoring her, I handed over the camera and quickly zipped up the case and tossed it onto a chair. She placed the strap over my neck and tucked the camera under the jacket so it dangled beneath an armpit. "Perfect," she declared, looking self-satisfied.

I suppressed my annoyance. I was a professional and would have automatically concealed it myself. Yet I kept my mouth shut and gave her another fake smile.

We met the Mohammeds at the SUV, which they'd parked in the hotel lot. Nubiti went immediately to Hammed, eyeing him demurely and smiling sweetly. He visibly relaxed and glanced my way. I rolled my eyes, not caring that he'd spent the last forty-five minutes in purgatory worried I might spill the beans.

"Haley, you look fantastic!" Momed exclaimed.

"Thanks, Momed, but are you implying I usually don't?" I said it irritably. His brows creased anxiously.

"No, Haley, no! It is not what I meant! You are always fantastic!"

I playfully punched him on the arm. When he realized I was teasing *him* for once, he smiled broadly.

"Are we ready?" Hammed asked.

I turned toward the crowd, which had swelled and would soon spill onto the hotel property. At least I could find my way back, I thought, and I reached beneath the jacket and caressed the camera, exhilarated and ready to go.

"Wait, Haley, I forgot! There is something you need." Momed grabbed an object from the car and eyed me seriously. I crossed my arms over my chest impatiently, and he placed a fake mustache on my upper lip and burst into laughter.

If he was anyone else, I might have tossed the stupid thing in the gutter. Yet his exuberance was growing on me, my affection for him hard to ignore. I let him take my picture, and then he draped an arm around me and Hammed took a picture of us together. As if I was his girlfriend.

It made me nervous. I was not Momed's girlfriend and never would be.

Winding my way through the masses, I quickly forgot about it, doing what I do best. I shot picture after picture of whatever caught my eye. A group of old men dressed in robes and turbans smoking rolled cigarettes. Women clad in black burkas huddled next to them. Young men and boys with fists raised in the air. Politicians dressed in suits speaking through bullhorns and young women without headscarves swaying to a beat only they could hear.

At first the atmosphere was celebratory, not at all like a protest. There was singing, laughing and children playing. But as the hours passed and the police presence increased, a tension filled the air. The soulful call to prayer at sunset was ignored, drowned out by chants I couldn't understand. Darkness fell.

And the people kept coming, pushing me farther into the vortex of bodies. Crushing me, suffocating me until it was impossible to photograph anything. Memories of the dead and injured after the stampede in South Africa flashed through my mind. I grabbed Momed's arm and told him I wanted to leave.

He eyed me disappointedly and tapped Hammed's shoulder. That knowing look passed between them. But before they could say anything, a commotion erupted right next to us and the sea of people parted, revealing a young woman being assaulted by several young men.

The attackers groped her breasts and ripped off her skirt. She screamed and flailed, punching and scratching anyone she could. I pointed the camera at her as one man snatched a blue-flowered scarf from her head and waved it in the air. Men cheered. Others stepped into the fray and attempted to fight off her assailants.

Momed tugged at my shirt sleeve. I kept shooting until the people closed in around her again and he roughly gripped my wrist and forcefully dragged me through the crowd toward the tall building with the red Hilton sign, pausing occasionally to make sure Hammed and Nubiti were following.

By the time we reached the hotel, which had been surrounded by police in riot gear, we were all breathless. Momed looked mortified, Hammed's jaw clenched angrily and Nubiti's eyes welled with tears. While they huddled together speaking Arabic in hushed tones, I excitedly examined the photos of the assault in the camera's view screen. It was hard to tell in the darkness, but I thought there was a money shot there. I smiled triumphantly.

The civil disobedience continued into the next week, the populace in a state of nervous anticipation. Crowds grew and dissipated in the square. There were frequent clashes between the protesters and undercover police. Activists burned down several police stations and a curfew was instituted. The demonstrators ignored it and the police couldn't enforce it. Tourists fled my hotel, replaced by journalists from all over the world.

I posted photos of the post-Friday prayer protest on my website. A picture of the assault against the woman was picked up by every media outlet. It was another money shot–the woman's expression one of sheer terror as five distinct hands representing a different skin color present in the Egyptian lineage squeezed her breasts. The feverish sneer on the face of the man who waved her headscarf in the air was ominous, and the spectacle of her lacy white bikini panties caused much consternation and rebuke, initiating a flood of reaction from every side of the issue.

The ultra-religious chastised the woman for being at the protest in the first place, believing she got exactly what she deserved. Women touted the incident as an example of the sexual harassment and discrimination against them. The diehard activists insisted it was an isolated occurrence, wanting to preserve the revolution's true nature.

The Mohammeds were on the side of the women and the activists, but their support was hypocritical. I never saw Nubiti with them after that and they tried to dissuade me from attending future protests. I wouldn't be deterred and ordered them to hire bodyguards to come with me. Every time I entered the crowd, I was surrounded by five, strong young men. I was fearless, not stupid.

The photo turned me into a celebrity at the hotel. The staff, which was reduced to a skeletal crew as the days passed, was at my beck and call. They waited on me before their more prominent guests, like the high-profile journalists who suddenly wanted to be my friend and attempted to include me in their tight-knit circle. I ignored their advances, finding them pompous, ratings-seeking fools.

It was a busy week. The Mohammeds escorted me from one photo opportunity to the next. And since I wouldn't leave Cairo, there wasn't an opportunity to be alone with them again. But I didn't suffer. I hooked up with a handsome Italian cameraman I met one night at the hotel bar. Any time we found ourselves together at the hotel for an hour, we would escape to my room and fuck.

Then it was Friday again and the demonstration was expected to be bigger and more violent. Momed arranged for me to start the afternoon on the balcony of a private residence overlooking the square. It would be a great place to capture the sheer magnitude of protests, but when the Mohammeds arrived to pick me up, they had a better offer.

"The Muslim Brotherhood is joining the cause," Momed announced excitedly. "My father sent my mother and sister to stay with a cousin in Baris. He left the house to join the protesters. There is no one home."

My insides clenched. My libido ignited. Since the day I'd met the hot and handsome Mohammeds, I'd fantasized about an illicit ménage à trois with them at their homes. Momed's was available, so the revolution could wait.

I raced up to the suite, grabbed a handful of condoms and raced back to the guys. As Hammed drove away from Tahrir Square toward the old city, they gave each other *that* look. Smiling, I wondered if their cocks were growing as hard as my pussy was growing wet.

The traffic was terrible, exacerbated by thousands of Egyptians on foot clogging the narrow streets and heading in the opposite direction toward Tahrir Square. Hammed parked in a lot near the old city, and they donned their official tour guide badges and led me into a network of crooked passageways.

The area was eerily quiet. Many small shops and restaurants were closed, a consequence of the mass exodus to the protest. The few people left were the elderly and women with babies in their arms. We passed windowless, irregularly-shaped stone buildings, connected and cramped together and only distinguishable by their uniquely distorted facades. I paused to snap a few photos, seemingly no end to the narrow alleyways, and then we slipped through an entrance portal into a sunlit courtyard.

It was like entering another sphere. Patches of greenery and flowers brought color and life to the otherwise dull background. We walked briskly to an old wooden door that opened into Momed's home. His eyes darted nervously around him.

I didn't know what to expect and was astounded by the house's interior. The first room we entered was a large living area. It was dark, the only light passing through a single window facing the courtyard. Similar to the exterior, it was oddly shaped. Rectangular, except the long walls fanned out an extra foot on one side and a half foot on the other, leaving the short walls asymmetrical.

I'd never seen anything like it. "Can I take a picture?"

"Yes, of course, Haley. Do you like it?" Momed asked.

I did. It was unusual and cozy, decorated with worn brown leather sofas, big throw pillows and soft cushions placed haphazardly on an old wooden floor.

He showed me the rest of the house, every room with the same lopsided walls. Reverting to his tour guide persona, he detailed the structure's history, the exterior wall a historic stone fortification built in the 12th century, which surrounded that particular section of old Cairo.

We finished the tour in Momed's bedroom. It was on the second floor and faced the courtyard. A laser beam of sunshine shot through another small window, hitting the headboard behind his full-size bed. Momed stretched out on it, clasped his hands behind his head and grinned expectantly.

I looked from him to Hammed, who sat at the foot of the bed and removed his shoes and socks. It was strange yet exciting being there. The Mohammeds were men in their mid-twenties. They still lived in their parents' homes and probably would until they got married. I couldn't imagine such a life for myself, having left my parents when I was eighteen. But I guessed if that was all a person knew, it wasn't strange at all.

Momed had made his room into a man cave. He had a flat screen TV and updated computer and audio equipment, hundreds of CDs and DVDs stacked on shelves, and books and magazines piled in corners. The rough stone walls were painted a light brown, the headboard and wardrobe were black, and a black leather recliner rested next to the window. And instead of posters of half-naked women or sports cars taped to the wall like you might find in a young man's room, he'd hung framed portraits of Martin Luther King, Jr. and Nelson Mandela.

"Come here, Haley."

Momed patted the mattress and the burn ignited. I slowly removed the headscarf, the one Nubiti had given me. I'd worn it along with the rest of the outfit expecting I'd be photographing the demonstration from within the crowd, not fucking the Mohammeds. Tossing it at Hammed, I licked my lips provocatively and sublimely swayed my hips, savoring the moment.

The jacket came off next. I took my time with the tee top, languidly sliding it up and over my breasts and head and flinging it at Hammed. I shimmied out of the long skirt and playfully kicked off the sandals, leaving only a pink thong and matching bra, which was the skimpiest one I owned, the sheer fabric leaving little to the imagination.

Momed scooted to the end of the bed and sat next to Hammed. His gorgeous charcoal eyes bulged. Hammed grinned lecherously. I smiled back. I assumed it was a fantasy of most young Egyptian men to watch a real, live Playboy Playmate perform a striptease, and I was happy to do it for the Mohammeds. They'd done everything I'd demanded and more, without complaint. Besides, the gyrations made *me* hot. My pussy pulsed, my nipples tingled. I cupped my tits and caressed them, my body rocking to a silent rhythm.

The ray of light perforated the room. I stepped into it and watched it bounce off my half-naked figure and refract, hitting the side walls. I twirled in it, around and around, stopping with my back to them. I removed the headband and ponytail tie and bent over, jiggling my ass as I raked fingers through my hair, fluffing it up so it cascaded wildly around my face. When I turned around, both men were gaping.

Their reaction sent shivers up my spine. Beads of desire amassed between my legs and turned into liquid fire. I continued to gyrate and touch myself, staying in the beam and inching toward them until they could reach out and touch me. Then I slipped off the bra, dangled it in Hammed's face and provocatively draped it around his neck.

He gawked at my breasts as if he'd never seen them before. I wriggled out of the panties and dropped them on Momed's head. He immediately snatched them up and buried his nose in their silkiness, inhaling deeply. My pulse raced. I straddled his lap and rubbed my drenched pussy against the swell in his pants.

"Haley," he sighed.

He set the panties on the bed and fondled my tits. Warm palms skimmed over my nipples, sending a hot signal directly to clit. I arched into him and untucked the polo shirt from his jeans, tugging it upward. He raised his arms long enough for me to remove it. He licked and sucked my nipples, moaning appreciatively. It took all my willpower to pull away. I wanted him naked. I crouched in front of him and hurriedly took off the rest of his clothes. One shoe and then the other. One sock and then the other. Jeans. Jockeys.

His cock sprang free. Rock hard and thick. Symmetrical, unlike the walls of the house. I softly kissed the tip before moving to Hammed, who was practically squirming. He peeled off his shirt and unzipped his jeans. I stifled a grin, knelt before him and helped him out of the rest of his clothes.

If I could have bottled the raw and raging desire that surged through me, I would have. My skin burned. My pussy ached. Every sinew in my body tightened excitedly. I grabbed a handful of condoms from the camera case and tossed them on the bed.

Momed liked to watch and I like being watched, so I wanted to fuck Hammed first. I hastily slid the latex over his stiff cock. He slid backward and I climbed onto his lap, mounting him quickly and moaning with pleasure.

He dropped onto his back, gripped my hips and closed his eyes. I rode him hard while Momed burnished my flesh with lips and tongue, lapping at my nipples and kissing me hungrily. The sunray beat on my backside. The agonizing ache mushroomed. I moved up and down, angling my body so Hammed's hard shaft pounded against my sweet spots.

An orgasm quickly bore down on me. I let it come, knowing there was another big cock waiting for me. The sensations rampaged through me. I collapsed on Hammed's chest, unraveling as he continued to slam into me, seeking his own relief. He rammed one last time and stiffened, detonating, shuddering.

We shuddered together. Delicious vibrations drummed from one nerve ending to another. His hands fell limply off my hips and fell onto the bed. I scrambled to Momed, who'd already applied a condom and was waiting impatiently. I crawled on top of him, pussy hot and pounding, juices beading in my fleshy folds. He groaned contentedly and reached for my tits.

He didn't want to simply fuck me. He wanted to devour me again, but this time I took control. I pushed him onto his back, braced my hands on his chest and slowly rose, resting the crown of his cock in the bowl of my vagina. He thrust his hips upward and I pulled back.

"Haley, *please*," he moaned hoarsely.

Giving him a warning look, I slowly sank back down. He grinded into me, a plea to go faster. I repeated the move over and over, teasing and taunting him, my slit becoming wetter and hotter with each drop. Then I lifted completely off and leaned forward, dangling my breasts in his face. He attacked them immediately, gripping my back and drawing me closer. Wriggling away, I glanced at Hammed.

He lay on his side, head resting on a hand, eyes locked lecherously on us.

"Hammed, hold his hands above his head," I commanded. Acting offended, he rose lazily and did what I ordered.

I suspended one tit over Momed's face. He feverishly licked and sucked my swollen nipple. That hot signal blazed from it to the deepest recesses of my pussy. My muscles throbbed impatiently. I mounted him again and used his fat shaft like a fine-tuned instrument, strumming and stoking my magic spots.

He met me plunge for plunge, twisting his hips to reach deeper.

The heat converged and spread. I held it at bay, wanting to surf the wave a little longer. I rose off him and leisurely ran my tongue over his hard abs and up to his muscular chest and to the tip of his head, dangling my other breast above his lips.

Groaning impatiently, he bucked and thrashed, his wet mouth clamping onto the nipple. He sucked and tugged on it with his teeth. I whimpered softly, pain and pleasure ripping through me.

The sun shifted. I felt a laser of light hit my naked ass. Warm air tickled my exposed pussy. I spread my knees wider, eagerly baring myself to it, my juices pooling and bubbling, my eyes fixed on Hammed.

He knelt before me, pinning Momed's hands to the mattress, his dick springing back to life and pointed directly at me. I snaked farther forward and engulfed it into my mouth, tasting its sweet succulence.

Hammed growled happily and Momed strained to lick my clit. I sank lower. His tongue lashed at exactly the right spot, just like I'd taught him. The sensations mushroomed and multiplied. I was ecstatic. Fucking two men. Erotic, decadent.

My clit pounded, desperate for relief. I scooted back and dropped on Momed's engorged shaft, riding him hard and fast. The sunlight's hot beam danced up and down my spine with each bob. Our grunts and groans grew louder. He exploded and I let go, my whole body shuddering with–

"Mohammed!"

The harsh, angry cry came from the doorway. I froze. So did the Mohammeds, eyes turning toward the voice.

"Baba," Momed croaked.

Hammed sprang from the bed, Momed rolled off one way and I rolled off the other. The man was obviously Momed's father and he frothed with rage, gesturing wildly and screaming in Arabic at the top of his lungs. A vein that ran from the middle of his hairline to edge of his brow bulged and visibly pulsed, ready to burst.

I scurried to gather my clothes. Hammed pulled on his pants first. Baba slapped him hard on the face and shoved him against the wall, spitting angry words and clenching his fists.

I scrambled into the skirt and tee top, covering my private parts as fast as I could. Momed ripped off the condom before zipping his jeans. Baba pushed him against the wall and slapped him, too, shouting and shaking his fists.

They bowed their heads deferentially. Baba pivoted to me, eyes black with pure, raw hate. Fear sliced through me. My heart skipped a beat, skipped several beats, and my stomach cramped anxiously. I wanted, *needed,* to get out of there as soon as possible, his fury barely contained. I hurriedly slipped on the jacket and grabbed my sandals and camera case.

Snarling, his eyes locked onto the teensy pink thong dangling over the bed's edge and the sheer bra on the floor below it. He snatched them up and crushed them in a hand. I glanced at the Mohammeds seeking guidance. Hammed shifted uncomfortably and hung his head. Momed nodded at the door, his beautiful eyes begging me to leave and hurry. I tried to skirt around Baba, but he roughly grabbed my arm in an iron grip and held me there.

"No, Baba," Momed cried.

Baba scowled. His eyes glazed over. He dangled the bra and panties in my face, cursing, and shoved me toward the door.

"Wait for us at the fruit stand, Haley, the one by the car," Momed said to my back.

Baba jerked me forward. I stumbled down the steps to the first floor. He dragged me outside to the courtyard and pulled me toward the alleyway. He didn't need to strong-arm me. I wanted to go as much as he wanted me to. He abruptly stopped in front of an old wooden gate situated between his house and the one next door, and he shoved me through it and yanked me to a stairway that led underground.

"Hey! Where the hell do you think–"

He smacked my face with such force I tumbled down the stairs, banging an elbow against the concrete. Pain shot up my arm. My ears buzzed. Dazed, I fuzzily watched him fish a key ring out of a pocket of his white robe and open a door.

I struggled to stand, but he kicked me in the ribs. Gasping for breath, I doubled over, clutching my side. He dragged me by my ankles into a dark room. Hinges creaked as the door closed. For several seconds it was pitch black. Then a harsh light beamed from a single bulb on the ceiling and he stood under it, screaming and shaking his fists at me.

"What do you want?" I moaned, unable to believe what was happening. Momed's father actually struck me. He kicked me and pushed me down a flight of stairs. The assault at the protest, the terror in the young woman's eyes as the men attacked her and her utter helplessness flashed through my mind.

A dark, sick feeling swept through me. I looked more closely at Baba. He wore a long robe and turban, his beard and mustache neatly trimmed and sprinkled with gray. He was a traditionalist, not one of those young, repressed men at the protest, drunk on their new freedom. I didn't understand why he simply didn't let me go, especially since he had a daughter of his own.

My eyes darted nervously around the room, searching for an escape. But there was only the door we'd entered through. I was trapped inside an old cellar, oddly-shaped like Baba's house. It had thick stone walls and no windows.

I looked more closely at the items stored there. There wasn't much. A worn, stained mattress propped against a wall, a few crates containing books stacked in a corner, several torn plastic buckets with dirty rags hanging over the rims and a couple of rickety wooden chairs. Nothing I could use as a weapon. My stomach twisted anxiously.

I decided to act deferentially like the Mohammeds. I slowly got on my knees. My body screamed with pain. I humbly lowered my eyes and clasped my hands in prayer. "I'm sorry, Baba, I'm sorry." It didn't matter. He continued to rant. He hurled the bra and panties at me. My stomach knotted more. "Please," I implored.

His face twisted menacingly, his rage palpable. I shrank in its wake, bowing to the ground. I hated doing it, but I had no choice, hoping he would calm down and let me go. He did calm. Or at least he stopped shouting and moved toward the door.

All I could see from my vantage point was his brown suede loafers, treading lightly, noiselessly, the hem of his white robe swishing with each step. He stopped next to my camera case. I must have unconsciously clung to it as he dragged me into the cellar. It was my most prized possession, my comfort. He picked it up and I heard him unzip it. A couple of colorful condom foils dropped to the floor.

My heart sank. The calm turned deadly. I had a fleeting thought I might not get out of the cellar alive, but I brushed it aside and stood shakily. He pulled out the camera and dropped the case, scowling threateningly. The vein on his forehead popped and pounded furiously. He gripped the camera by the strap, swung it back and forth and slammed it against the wall.

"No!" I lunged and shoved him as hard as I could.

He stumbled backward and I attacked, but it wasn't because of the camera. Every instinct told me to fight and I did. I punched and scratched, but he was too strong, too angry. *Very, very angry.* He wrestled me to the ground and ripped off my skirt. He stared at my pussy for a moment, and then ripped off the jacket and tee.

Naked and trembling, I scooted away from him, terrified. The fear practically choked me. He grabbed a clump of my hair and jerked my face to his. Rage seeped from his pores. He smelled like smoke, stale. His face contorted with uncontrolled fury, seething and spitting words I didn't understand. When he finished saying what he had to say, he shoved me aside. I cowered before him and he turned away. I anxiously watched him gather my clothes and the camera, unscrew the bulb on the ceiling and exit noiselessly, taking the light with him.

The Cellar

And then there was darkness. Silence. I sat there shivering and horrified, unable to grasp what had just happened, unable to believe it. The panic built inside me and the blackness closed in, suffocating me. For the first time in my life I felt helpless. Completely helpless.

It was surreal. Only the feel of the cool, hard floor on my naked ass kept it real. I was in trouble. *Big trouble.* My eyes welled with tears, but I held them back. A piece of me was unwilling to accept that I was powerless. I wouldn't submit to despair.

I screamed for help. My shrieks echoed off the thick stone walls. There wasn't a sound on the other side of those walls. No car horns. No voices. Only silence. No one could hear me.

And the Mohammeds couldn't even text me. Baba had my phone. It was in the pocket of my skirt. The panic threatened to overwhelm me, the blackness suddenly harsh, sucking the life out of me.

I stood shakily. The pitch blackness was unnerving, altering my sense of equilibrium. I stepped forward cautiously, extending my hands in front of me and heading toward my last sighting of the door. Blind. Scared. One small step at a time until I bumped into the wall.

I skimmed my hands along the grooved rock, moving sideways until they brushed over a wooden façade. The surface was cracked and splintered, decaying but solid nevertheless. I searched for a handle, hitting a large knob. I pressed and twisted and pulled it, but the door didn't budge. I tried again, praying it would open, but the knob only rattled. I tried one more time, not willing to accept that Baba had locked me in there. But he had and I sank to the floor, the panic returning and sticking in my throat.

It was so quiet. *Eerie.* I could hear my heartbeat. Faster than normal but strong and steady, reminding me I was alive. I was down but not out, and I thought surely Baba would return soon. He simply needed time to calm down and was waiting at the door. I got back on my feet and searched for the keyhole.

It was shaped to fit an old skeleton key. I crouched to look through it, hungering for the light and hoping for a glimpse of Baba. But the wood was too thick. Only a pinprick of light appeared on the other side of it.

Then I had an idea, remembering the creak as he closed the door. I moved my hand to the edge of it and fingered a smooth steel hinge. It was wide with inch-size bolts, anchored securely. Solid. *Impossible.*

I slowly dropped back down to the floor. It was a crazy idea anyway. There was nothing in the cellar to use as a tool to pop out the bolts, and I was forced to accept the fact that I was trapped there. Imprisoned by an angry, irrational man, crazed by finding me fucking his son and nephew in his house, and I didn't know whether he'd come back or leave me there to die.

Yet, I'd been in the cellar only a short time and refused to believe the worst. Baba was bound to return and set me free. He was simply punishing me for my depravity, teaching me a lesson. I told myself to be patient. Besides, Baba was Momed's father. I couldn't believe a man who'd raised his son to be as sweet, intelligent and funny as Momed wouldn't possess within himself the same qualities. He only needed time to calm down.

I leaned against the door a while longer, wishing I had the long black skirt Nubiti had given me. Not that my nakedness bothered me. I'd spent many hours without clothes pursuing sexual gratification. But the brick floor was cold and hard and uneven. Uncomfortable. My thoughts turned to the chairs. I could wait for Baba on a chair. Then I remembered the mattress propped against the wall and I suddenly wanted to lie down. My side hurt, and the standing and sitting only exacerbated the pain.

I used the wall to guide me and moved slowly, thinking Baba was incredibly mean to leave me in the dark. I bumped into a bucket on my way. The dull thud of my bare foot hitting plastic resonated loudly in the silence. When I reached the mattress, I tugged it to the floor and gratefully collapsed on top of it.

I didn't rest there long. It smelled like mildew, wet and sour. When I stood, a sharp pain pierced my ribs. The odor festered in my nostrils, my sense of smell heightened by the lack of other stimuli. I stumbled to the wall and leaned against it, disoriented, trying to remember which way to go to reach the chairs.

It didn't matter. One way or the other and I'd find them. I traced the stone with my fingers, stepping gingerly and finally bumping into one of them.

I gratefully sat and sighed heavily. I'd been holding my breath. The chair rocked. It was wobbly, unstable, and I stilled. My mind raced with questions.

Why had Baba returned home? He was supposed to be at the protest. It briefly crossed my mind I'd been set up. Hammed, Momed or both the Mohammeds had told Baba what we were doing, and since neither bothered to make sure I left safely, they must have planned it.

Yet they seemed as surprised as me by Baba's sudden appearance. And like me, they cowered before his wrath. Besides, I doubted the Mohammeds would ruin a good thing, certain they loved our clandestine encounters as much as me. They were probably headed to the fruit stand right now. And when they didn't find me there, I was certain they would look for me, especially Momed, who really liked me. Plus, I was also paying them well. If I were free, there was a lot more money to be made.

But when they didn't find me at the fruit stand would they look in the cellar? Would they suspect Baba had imprisoned me there?

Where was he? Where was Baba?

The darkness, the silence, was getting to me. I told myself over and over to be patient. I had no choice but to wait for Baba's return. I had no choice.

Why had I tempted fate? Why had I thumbed my nose at their beliefs, their acceptable standard of behavior? I knew full well the repressive nature of the Egyptian culture, yet never in a million years did I expect the drastic consequences, never expected to be locked in a cellar and stripped bare, especially by Momed's father.

For a religious man, his actions seemed hypocritical, but I wasn't all that surprised. Middle Eastern women were treated like second-class citizens or worse. Nubiti and the girl at Tahrir Square, they were at the mercy of men. At the time I couldn't care less. It had nothing to do with me. But now I was in trouble. *Big trouble.*

Yet I refused to believe Baba would harm me further. He was just mad. My thoughts turned to my parents. My weekly call to them was on Sunday. Two days and if I wasn't free by then, they would be worried. I hadn't missed a Sunday call for more than three years. *Never.* No matter what country I found myself in, no matter who I was bedding at the time, I would call them, having learned my lesson after *him.*

But I didn't want to think about *him* and closed my eyes, shutting out the memory and the darkness. I wondered what was happening at Tahrir Square, what I was missing. Since the Muslim Brotherhood had joined the cause, the protest was bound to be bigger and better than the previous Friday. It was certain to be a photographer's dream, and I would have been there if Baba hadn't interrupted us.

Or would I? The Mohammeds were too delicious, their draw too great. I might have stayed in that bedroom well into the night.

I was insatiable. I knew it, yet I couldn't help myself. Sex and photography made me whole. They gave me a bit of happiness. I pursued both as often as I could, greedily and without regret. And I wouldn't regret the Mohammeds, no matter what happened in the cellar.

I must have nodded off, because I didn't hear the hinges creak or see the light come on. Baba jerked me to my feet and roughly grabbed my arm with that iron grip of his. He tied my hands behind my back before I knew what was happening.

He hadn't calmed. His eyes still simmered with rage and the vein on his forehead popped and pulsed. There were noticeable bloody scratches on the back of his hand and on his neck. Gloating, I was glad I wasn't the only one wounded. It gave me courage.

He'd used a purple headscarf to bind my wrists. It was the one Nubiti had given me. He must have found it in Momed's bedroom. I strained against it, trying to loosen the knot with my fingers. It was tight and I kicked at him, my own anger boiling to the surface.

Smiling demonically, he shoved me back onto the chair. It rocked unsteadily, one wooden leg ready to split from it. He leisurely rolled a cigarette, hovering over me. My heart sank. He wasn't ready to let me go, and I realized it wouldn't matter what I said or did. He was on a mission.

Whether he wanted to teach me a lesson or punish me or exact some sort of revenge, I didn't know. Whatever he wanted, he obviously wasn't done with me, and I straightened my spine defiantly. I wouldn't cower or bow anymore. I wouldn't let him break me.

He lit the cigarette and inhaled deeply. I glowered at him and crossed my legs, sitting in a ladylike position although I was stark naked. My bare breasts heaved with each breath. I noticed he was wearing the same robe, which meant a day hadn't passed, but I couldn't be sure. Time was meaningless in the cellar. Maybe he had ten identical ones.

He took another drag, smirked and yanked me to my feet. The cigarette drooped from his lips, his eyes black. A chill tickled over my skin, and in an instant he was on the chair bending me over a knee. The rickety thing rocked and creaked. He held me down with an iron grip on my arm and a strong hand on my buttock. I kicked and screamed. The thrashing and our combined weight was too much for the wobbly wooden leg and the chair broke.

I fell to the floor. My elbow hit brick, the same elbow as before. I screeched in agony. He crawled over to me, flipped me onto my belly and spanked me. Hard. Furiously. *Crack. Crack. Crack.*

Each strike stung more until my ass was on fire. My elbow throbbed and I couldn't stop the tears. Hot cigarette ash pricked the skin on my back. After he smoked it down to a stub, he extinguished it on my ass.

The burn barely registered, my behind smoldering anyway. The smell of singed flesh filled the air. Then he abruptly stood, unscrewed the lightbulb and left.

Stunned, I rested there for a while, catching my breath. The darkness and silence were a relief. I went to work on the headscarf, tugging at the knot and stretching the fabric until I was able to wriggle free. Choking back more tears, I carefully crawled around until I found the mattress. I gingerly lay on my uninjured side, ignoring the odor.

My elbow pounded painfully. A large lump had formed on it, but it wasn't broken. I touched the spot on my buttock where Baba had burned me. Something wet oozed from it, but it was a small wound. The beating could have been worse.

I could handle the pain but not the hopelessness. It simmered in my gut, threatening to take over. If it did, Baba would win. He would break me.

I forced myself to think about ways to escape. I wouldn't succumb. Baba had gone too far.

Amid the fog of pain a plan slowly evolved. I would surprise him. The next time he came to beat me I would hide by the door and hit him with the broken chair leg or a book from one of the crates.

I crawled to the crates. The uneven brick floor chafed my knees. My ribs protested with each small advance. My head bumped against the wall, and I haltingly got to my feet and used the grooved stone to guide me to the corner. The crates were there, and I searched for the heaviest book, dropping them one by one onto the brick. The dull thuds echoed in the stark silence.

I found a fat one and moved cautiously to the door, setting it nearby. I crawled around, found the wooden chair leg and lay it next to the book. By the time I made it back to the mattress, I was exhausted. I didn't want to lie on it again, but I couldn't sit, my ass burning. I maneuvered onto my good side. The pungent odor immediately engulfed me.

Now all I had to do was stay awake and hope the next time the lock clicked I could make my way back to the door quickly enough. Then I thought I should simply drag the mattress to the door and I wouldn't have to worry, so I did.

Although banged up and wretched, I felt better. At least I had a plan. I ran various scenarios through my mind and prayed Baba returned soon, craving the light, craving my freedom.

It was hard to know how much time passed. The darkness and silence were at once unnerving and comforting, lulling me into an unsettled lethargy. When I thought I might fall asleep, I leaned on my good elbow and tried counting the seconds.

One Mississippi, two Mississippi, three Mississippi…

I gave up after five minutes. Time moved too slowly, making me more anxious. Then the thirst took over and my stomach growled angrily. My last meal had been breakfast. A cheese omelet and fruit. My last drink had been coffee with frothy milk. My last sip of water had been at breakfast. I'd never gone without food or water unless it was by choice, which had happened a few years before. But I wouldn't think about that miserable time. I wouldn't think about *him,* and I suppressed the memory as I'd done many times.

Then I needed to pee, *bad,* which was good at first because it kept me awake. But without any other stimuli except the pain and thirst and hunger to occupy my mind, the need to relieve myself built and inundated my thoughts until I scrambled to the buckets, stood over one and let it come.

I woke shivering. It must have been the middle of the night, because it had become cold in the cellar. I wrapped the scarf around my feet and rubbed my arms, thinking at least I could keep track of the days by the temperature in the room. But it wasn't much comfort. My body shuddered uncontrollably.

The lock clicked and I froze. I could hear my heart pumping. Strong. Steady. Fast. *Baba was coming.*

I grabbed the chair leg and scrambled to my feet. Adrenaline raced through me and I focused on the task at hand. It was time. *A chance to free myself.* The hinges creaked, fresh air filtered into the cellar and I raised the wooden stick above me, swinging with all my strength. But there was nothing there, only a whooshing sound as the makeshift weapon sliced through the air. I swung again and again and then the light came on.

He was standing under the bulb, smirking condescendingly. My heart sank like a stone. He was wearing a different robe, a powder blue one, so I knew it was a new day. But it didn't matter what he wore. His eyes were black, venomous, the vein on his forehead still pounding angrily. It was then I knew I might die down there, alone and naked in the black cellar.

There was nothing left to do but attack. He easily overpowered me, wrestled the chair leg from my hands and struck me hard on the forehead with it. The blow sent me stumbling backward onto the mattress.

A sharp pain ricocheted through my skull. I instinctively covered my head with my arms as he continued to strike me, pummel me, the stick's hiss slicing through the silence. A hazy film closed over my eyes. I drifted in and out of consciousness, the pain barely registering. Images blurred. Time warped.

Baba rolling a cigarette. A smoky smell. A nebulous wisp floating and curling upward toward a harsh yellow light. Rough hands. Flipping me onto my back. Spreading my legs. Burning flesh. Baba sitting. Baba's black eyes. Glazed black eyes. Erratic breathing. Baba's blue robe. Rippling. Rippling. Something's under the robe. Baba's hand. Pumping. Jerking off. Hot coal down there. Burning flesh...

~~~~~~✝~~~~~~

The fog in my head dissipated. My entire body throbbed. My skull pounded. I didn't want to open my eyes, didn't want to think or feel.

I tentatively rolled onto my side and raised my arm, reaching for my forehead. Pain exploded through my elbow. There was a large bump on my temple and fleeting images of Baba ricocheted through my brain. Black, glazed eyes, uncontrolled fury unleashed as he beat me to an inch of my life.

I licked my parched lips. My mouth was so dry I couldn't summon a bit of saliva. My pussy burned. So did the inside of my thighs. I hesitantly reached down there and ran my fingers over the inflamed areas.

Baba had used my flesh as an ashtray again, this time marking my genitals. I reflexively checked the burn on my buttock. It was swollen and dripped with puss, probably infected by the dirty mattress. The darkness closed in once more, the silence turning deadly.

I was in bigger trouble than I'd imagined. The harsh reality of what he'd done to me while I lay half-conscious slowly became clear. Baba had wanted to make me suffer, humiliate me, and he'd chosen to scar the area on my body that gave me the most pleasure, gave men the most pleasure. It was symbolic, but it was more than that. He was sadistic, suddenly free to torture a woman like me. *Inferior. Deviant. A whore.* I'd become unworthy of even the most basic human rights. At that moment, I accepted my fate.

I would die in that cellar.

I could hear my soft breath and heart beating. *Steady and*

surprisingly calm. I didn't want to die, but there was nothing I could do about it. I was exhausted. Weary. Worn out by the silence and complete darkness. The pain. The helplessness. It would be a relief to die. The realization gave me unexpected peace.

My eyes fluttered open only to face the nothingness again. A prism with no color, no light. I no longer cared. The light had disappeared inside me years ago, gradually replaced by cynicism and indifference.

I didn't know how long I'd been in the cellar. Two days, maybe three, but it hadn't taken long for Baba to break me. Baba had won. Baba had broken me, but in truth, I was already broken. My heart had grown stone cold, the happy 18-year-old girl who joyously pursued her dream a distant memory.

I'd become selfish, unsympathetic and ruthless in my pursuits. I'd accomplished a lot, my photos seen on a myriad of magazine covers and in newspapers and galleries across the globe, but it wasn't enough.

Never enough. I was always hungry for more. As my success grew, so did my hedonistic desire for all the pleasures life offered. The best wines, gourmet foods, fashionable clothes, and most of all, sex. A decadent obsession for sexual gratification had crept into my soul, taking over and leaving me alone and melancholy and searching for even more.

All because of *him.* I'd tried to forget him. I'd tried to move forward, tried to find a kernel of happiness among the living, but I was dead inside without him. For the first time in years, I said his name out loud.

"Mikel…"

Then the floodgates opened and the memories I'd repressed for so long gushed to the surface. I let them come. I wanted to remember him, needed to remember him. The excitement, the love, the joy.

And I did. Every detail. Every nuance. There in the dark, silent cellar. Alone, beaten and broken, I relived the best time in my young life.

Pamplona and the Running of the Bulls

I met *him*, Mikel Garro, three-and-a-half years ago in Pamplona, Spain.

I was eighteen. The magic year. My parents sent me into the world with a camera and a dream, their free spirits letting me go because a college education was too conforming and our small town too confining.

It was raining the day I left. It was a gentle rain, the sun peeking in and out of the clouds. As my father drove to the airport and my mother chattered nervously, the lush green hills and cornfields of my youth went unnoticed. My hair frizzed and my face moistened with humidity. It was like any other day.

My father, who was the smartest man in the world and could have won Jeopardy if he'd tried, and my mother, who was the most kind-hearted person I knew, nudged me to the end of the security line at the airport. They kissed me goodbye with misty eyes, and a lump formed in my throat as I slipped through the metal detector and disappeared to the gate.

I was excited yet nervous. As I waited to board the plane I checked my wallet for the millionth time to make sure the prepaid credit card bearing ten thousand dollars was still there. The plastic card held my entire savings, accumulated during my high school years from the meager tips I'd earned waitressing at the local diner. It was to be my lifeline for as long as it lasted or until I was noticed. It was my ambition to become a world-famous photographer.

My journey began in Pamplona. After an arduous trip from the Midwest to New York to Madrid and then to my final destination, I was tired, annoyed and in need of a shower. The man next to me on the short flight to New York was too large for his seat, squishing me against the window. The long leg to Madrid was worse. I was sandwiched between a guy who was drunk by the time we landed and a woman wearing too much perfume. I spent too much money on food during the layovers, money that would've been better used for a taxi ride into Pamplona. But I needed to be frugal and took the bus, which dropped me off at the square in the old part of town.

It was hot that July, sweltering, and I hid beneath the shade of an old oak tree, trying to get my bearings. I would be staying at a private residence in a vacant bedroom for forty euros a week. I knew the place was close to the plaza, but I was disoriented, half-numb with jet lag. I sat on a park bench and protectively clutched my suitcase and backpack, scanning the passing faces for a friendly local who might speak some English.

I must have looked desperate, because it didn't take long for an elderly man wearing a wool flat cap to offer his assistance. He kindly walked me to my destination a few blocks west of the town square, chatting amiably using halting English while I replied using my limited Spanish.

He led me to a three-story Gothic structure with pointed arches, large windows and an ornate façade. The first two floors of the building were taken up by a hardware store. The man took me through a side entrance and accompanied me up thick stone steps to the third level, where I was greeted enthusiastically by my host family, the Zabaletas.

It was siesta time and my arrival interrupted the midday meal. The entire family was present. Mrs. Zabaleta immediately offered me a hearty plate of spicy lamb stew with smoked cheese and bread. I gratefully wolfed it down, the food delicious, especially after the junk I'd eaten during my journey. Then I concentrated on remembering their Basque names.

The family's patriarch was Zorion and Mrs. Zabaleta was Tote. A jolly couple in their mid-fifties, Zorion barked orders and smoked a hand-rolled cigarette while Tote scurried around the kitchen wearing an apron, fussing over me and piling food on my plate.

Their daughter, Catalin, and her husband, Edur, had two gregarious young boys. They chased each other around the flat until Catalin rounded them up and dragged them to a room for a nap. Zorion and Tote's other child, Gabirel, was a tall, good-looking 15-year-old. He sat next to me at the big dining table watching me eat and enthusiastically practicing his English.

I was grateful at least one of the Zabaletas spoke some English. My year of Spanish language instruction in high school had hardly prepared me for a simple conversation, not that it mattered. I was immediately treated like one of the family, and it didn't take long for me to feel comfortable there.

After lunch, Gabirel ushered me to a small corner room with a window overlooking a cobblestone street. The space was clean and stark, offering a single bed, a rocking chair and an antique wardrobe. I didn't need much. Like many families in Spain, the Zabaletas lived together above the business they owned, and with five bedrooms and only one bathroom to be shared by all, it was a cozy arrangement.

The rent was low and it included meals. It had everything I needed to survive for a couple of weeks except air-conditioning. The room was stifling hot, the large fan set below the window useless. After the Zabaletas retreated to their rooms for the afternoon siesta, I took a lukewarm shower in the old claw-foot tub in the bathroom. Then wearing only a bra and panties, I crawled on top of the thin bedspread and closed my eyes.

I was exhausted. The jet lag had finally caught up to me. The heat made me more tired. Yet with Catalin and Edur groaning and sighing in the next room, obviously making love and not even trying to hide it, it was impossible to fall asleep. As the squeak of mattress springs grew louder and faster, I wondered if most Spanish couples used the siesta to do the same. It was only when the last sigh was sighed and the mattress springs went silent that I was able to drift into a restless, sweaty sleep, dreaming about my future as a world-famous photographer.

~~~~~~✝~~~~~~

I was in Pamplona that hot July to photograph Los Sanfermines, the famous "Running of the Bulls" and the weeklong party accompanying it. After a brief phone call to my parents to assure them I'd arrived safely, I set out the next morning to start with the picturesque old town. The city was packed with people from all over the world, and I secured the camera strap around my neck and joined the rest of the tourists wandering from site to site.

By noontime the heat was blistering. Sweat accumulated on my forehead and my long blond hair stuck to the nape of my neck. I took a break, settled at an outdoor café and ordered a Coke, paying a ridiculous amount for it. My thoughts turned to the next day when I would run with the bulls.

I'd promised my parents I wouldn't do it, but it was a lie. I wanted to experience all of the festivities, especially the running. I hoped to be lucky enough to snap a unique photo from the inside that was worthy of publication, and unless I was gored to death they'd never know. Besides, if I wanted my dreams to come true, I needed to take chances and I could take care of myself, just like they wanted. Yet, I couldn't help but feel a little guilty.

My parents worked hard to make a living and the world a better place. My father spent fifty hours a week teaching science at a community college and another twenty or thirty as an agitator, advocating for environmental issues and attending protests. My mother worked just as many hours as a parole officer for the county and as an elected town council member. They loved me, but they expected me to be self-sufficient.

Consequently, by the time I was eight I was laundering my own clothes. If I didn't do it, no one would. I packed my own lunch for school and perfected using the microwave. When I was thirteen and my brother, Kyle, joined the Marines, there was nothing I couldn't do for myself or learn to do.

I was alone a lot during the week, but my parents reserved the weekend for me, unless there was a protest, a parolee crisis or a city council meeting. The moments we did spend together were always enjoyable and filled with love, made more precious because of their absence. And since I'd proven I could take care of myself, they gave me a lot of freedom, which my friends always envied.

I'd grown up fast because of them, raising myself while they pursued their passions. Now it was my turn. I brushed aside the guilt. After all, it was only a little white lie. Of course they'd forgive me. But as I sat alone at the café slowly sipping the expensive Coke and watching strangers pass by, I was suddenly overcome with love for them and a little bit homesick. I missed them.

I nursed the Coke until the café began filling up with diners. When I returned to the flat for the midday meal, the entire Zabaleta family had congregated at the large dining table again. I felt better in their company. Their devotion to each other was comforting, and since they continued to treat me like one of their own, I was back to my old self by the time I retreated to my room for the siesta.

Catalin and Edur went at it again on the other side of the thin wall. While I waited for them to finish, I edited and catalogued the photos from that morning on my laptop, emailed my best friend, Jillian, and ironed the white capris pants, midriff shirt and red scarf I would wear for the bulls the next morning.

Later, I accompanied Gabirel to a party at a friend's house. The streets were crowded, the atmosphere supercharged with excitement and expectation for tomorrow's running. I felt it, too, and when we ducked into a private courtyard behind tall doors, I was pleasantly surprised by the gathering, finding people of all ages jammed together drinking free beer, laughing and dancing to Spanish hip hop, pop rock and reggae.

It was great to let loose. The locals were fun and flirty. As midnight approached, more youth packed into the courtyard and the music grew louder, the dancing more frenetic. When a nameless guy fondled my ass and poured beer on my head, I realized it was time to go. The bulls were waiting for me at eight in the morning.

It took me a while to find Gabirel amid the crowd. He was with a young girl, drunk and hanging all over her. As I navigated slowly through the throng to him, a hush came over the courtyard. The music stopped and all eyes turned toward the tall doors.

That was when I first laid eyes on *him*. My heart skipped a beat. He was glorious, *hot*. Like many of the girls there, all I could do was gape. I almost stuck around hoping for the chance to meet him, but he was engulfed by the mob and I lost sight of him.

On our way back to the flat I asked Gabirel about the sexy stranger. He walked crookedly and slurred the answer. "He is Mikel Garro."

"Is he famous?"

"Sí, he is the striker for Osasuna."

"Osasuna?"

"Osasuna is our soccer club."

"Do you know him?"

Gabirel snorted and tripped on the cobblestone. I clutched his arm and held him upright. I hoped his parents wouldn't blame me for his condition, and I wondered if there was a soccer game scheduled in the near future.

I arrived at the police barrier the next morning at seven-thirty and joined the other runners. It was easy to blend in. Everyone was wearing some sort of traditional white shirt and pants with a red waistband and neckerchief. Excitement churned my stomach, yet I couldn't help but be anxious.

Running with the bulls was reckless, hundreds of people injured every year. If I wanted, I could photograph the event from behind the wooden barriers out of harm's way. Maybe I was being foolish. Maybe my ambition was getting the better of me. But then the singing of the benediction began, nervous excitement filled the air and adrenaline shot through me.

The opportunity to jump start my career was within my reach. I toyed with the compact digital camera hidden in the crevice between my breasts, fully aware it was against the rules to take pictures while running with the bulls. Yet competing drunk was also forbidden, and I was sure several participants were already loaded. No one was stopping them.

Besides, if a person was crazy enough to run with the bulls in the first place, then the few rules hardly mattered. My plan was to set the camera speed on "sports" to freeze the action and shoot randomly. If I had the chance, I would also stop and take a few shots.

The choral ended with a shout of "Viva." A rocket fired and then another. Bulls and steers thundered down the cobblestone street and runners screamed and scattered. A surreal fog enveloped me. Time stood still one second and moved at hyper speed the next. I ran forward and sideways, pressing the shutter button over and over. Then a thousand pound beast charged straight at me and the world stopped.

It was just me and the bull. The creature rumbled forward in slow motion. I was struck by the look in its eyes. Rather than seeing red, they were filled with fear and panic. My insides clenched anxiously. I lifted the camera to my face, desperate to capture the moment. I snapped one shot, two shots and three shots before it was almost upon me. I leapt from its trajectory, but not before the bull's horn slashed my calf. Scrambling through the gap in the barrier, I made it to safety, skinning my elbows and banging my knees against the brick. Exhilarated, ecstatic, my heart pounded wildly. I clutched the camera in a fist, gasping for breath.

"Dios mío!" I was hoisted to my feet by a man with strong hands. Another man rattled off a string of Spanish words, his tone laced with rebuke.

I glanced at their faces. A young man's eyes danced with amusement while an older man glared at me disgustedly. I burst into hysterical laughter, thrilled by my audacity and grateful to be alive.

"Come with me, cariño, I 'elp you," the younger one said. He wrapped an arm around my waist, grinning from ear to ear.

He was shorter than me, and I draped an arm over his shoulder and allowed him to lead me down the narrow street. People clapped and whistled and took photos, but I was too overexcited at the time to realize they were reacting to me.

The older man threw up his hands and walked away. The younger man looked me up and down and stated, "You very brave, cariño, and loco. My name is Danel."

He guided me into a crowded café, nudged a man from his seat and gently set me on the chair. I breathed deeply, trying to catch my breath and stop laughing long enough to respond. "My name is Haley. I need to catch my breath."

Danel narrowed his eyes and stared at my leg. "You 'urt," he said. He nodded at the guy behind the bar, and he rushed to my side with a wet towel.

It was then I noticed the gash on my calf. Blood seeped from it and dripped onto the floor. My elbows and knees throbbed. I couldn't stop smiling.

Danel eyed me curiously. He bandaged the wound, wiped the blood from my elbows and nodded at the bartender again. "You American?" he asked.

"Yes."

"You 'ere alone?"

"Yes."

The bartender passed him a wine glass filled halfway with an amber liquid. He placed it in my hand and ordered, "Drink, cariño."

I didn't ask questions and guzzled it. The strong, earthy drink slid down my throat and warmed my insides.

"You 'ere to kill you?" He crossed his arms over his chest and raised a brow expectantly. When I feigned offense, he laughed boisterously, his big smile revealing crooked teeth.

"I'm a photographer or at least want to be." I said it proudly, *defiantly,* because I wanted to be taken seriously. Then I realized I'd completely forgotten about the camera. I loosened my grip on it. The device was wet from the sweat on my hand. I wiped it on my shirt and stuffed it back into my bra.

"It why you face down the bull, cariño?"

"Yes." I stood up gingerly, suddenly anxious to leave. I wanted to return to the apartment and review the photos on my computer, hoping I'd captured the true nature of the running, especially the beleaguered bull.

Danel insisted he walk me back to the flat. For some reason he'd taken an interest in me, and he bombarded me with questions about my background and aspirations. He was friendly and easy to talk to, and when we arrived at the apartment, he asked to see the photos.

We stopped in the hardware store first. I didn't feel comfortable inviting him into the flat without permission from the Zabaletas. Tote was at the market and Zorion fussed over my injuries. I should have known he'd be concerned. After fifteen minutes of offering assurances, Danel and I headed upstairs.

While we sat at the kitchen table waiting for the pictures to load on my laptop, he invited me to the bullfight after the siesta, to dinner after the bullfight and then to a party at his brother's house. I didn't know how to respond, uncertain about his intentions. An uncomfortable silence fell between us.

I hoped he wasn't asking me for a date. He was nice and well-dressed and seemingly well-educated, but he didn't appeal to me in that way. I didn't want to hurt his feelings. Fortunately, he was also intuitive.

"No, cariño, no! It not like that!" he exclaimed, chuckling and shaking his head back and forth. "I taken by another. 'e not like Los Sanfermines and left town until it over. I bored and need company."

Danel was gay. It was the best news I could have heard. He

leaned close and we viewed the photos one by one. When the money shot appeared on the screen, I excitedly threw my arms around him and hugged him hard.

The photo was amazing, the last one I'd shot before diving out of danger as the massive animal charged toward me. It was a sharp close-up of the bull's head, horns and eyes. Two white-clad runners with red neckerchiefs could be seen clearly in the background. But it was the bull's eyes that caught my attention, its emotions at that singular moment crisply displayed in them. Panicked and confused, a creature forsaken, and it tugged at my heart.

Mikel

Danel picked me up in a sleek black Mercedes at three-thirty. I wasn't expecting the expensive ride and wondered what he did for a living. I didn't know much about him. We talked only about me that morning, and while it was nice to be the center of attention for a change, I wasn't a self-centered person back then, although I eventually came to be one.

I wore a simple blue sundress, which showed my skinned elbows, the bruises on my knees and the bandage on my calf. It was too hot for anything else, but before we left the apartment I asked if I was dressed appropriately for the evening. Danel was also dressed casually in black jeans and a polo shirt, yet I wasn't sure what to expect.

"You beautiful, cariño," he said.

The bullfight stadium was packed to capacity. We squeezed together on a long bench with the other fans, our seats at the arena's edge and close to the action. I'd brought my large SLR camera to document the drama, but I stopped taking pictures after the first lance was thrust into the poor bull's shoulder. I closed my eyes when it was finally killed with a spear. I found the so-called "fight" to be a savage display. My father's activist temperament bubbled inside me. There were five more bouts, all the bulls from the morning's run on the chopping block. I avoided the rest of the spectacle by turning my attention to Danel and asking him countless questions about his life.

He was 30 years old, a lot older than I'd thought, and a successful sports manager. He promoted several major athletes in Spain, including the matador at the bullfight. He loved the fights, enthusiastically describing the various moves, but his partner, Carlos, hated them. Danel explained it was the main reason why his "amor" had skipped town that year. He didn't want to spend another Los Sanfermines with blood-thirsty tourists. I could relate, the spectacle unsavory, but I held my tongue. Bullfighting was a part of Danel's culture and centuries in the making.

We ate dinner at a trendy restaurant in the suburbs at nine o'clock, which was early by Spanish standards. By the time we arrived at his brother's house, the party was in full swing. The house was stunning. Large and modern, it was situated in the hills outside the city, and it was obvious Danel's brother was very wealthy.

He explained he lived there, too, and led me through the main level to the garden and pool in the back. I'd never seen so many hot guys and girls in my life, some wearing skimpy swimsuits and hanging out by the pool and others congregating around an outdoor bar.

Danel grabbed my hand and pulled me forward, shouting at a guy with his back to us. "Hermano, she 'ere!"

The man was talking to two attractive women, who were giggling flirtatiously and eyeing him salaciously. At the sound of Danel's voice, he spun around and smiled broadly. I stopped in my tracks, gaping. Danel's brother was *the* Mikel Garro, the famous soccer striker from the party the previous night. My heart hammered wildly.

Hollering something in Spanish, Mikel Garro strode purposefully toward me. He was dressed in tight blue jeans and a loose linen shirt, his smile dazzling. He kissed me on each cheek. His guests crowded around us.

"My name is Mikel," he greeted warmly, more glorious up close.

Shaggy dark hair, tan rugged face, and he had the most beautiful eyes, the color of chocolate, fringed by thick long lashes and twinkling mischievously. He clutched my hands and exclaimed, "It 'er!"

Cheers erupted. People chattered excitedly. I didn't know what was happening or why I was being welcomed with such enthusiasm. Mikel gripped my hand tighter and stood close.

My stomach churned. His scent tantalized my senses. Overwhelmed, I glanced nervously at Danel. He burst out laughing, withdrew a phone from his back pocket and deftly set the display to YouTube.

"She does not know," he said conspiratorially to his brother, grinning from ear to ear.

He handed the phone to Mikel and Mikel leaned closer, his arm brushing mine. A shiver raced up my spine. He started the YouTube video, and my jaw dropped. It was a recording of *me* at the Running of the Bulls, standing my ground, taking photos as the bull charged and then diving to safety. And there were already thousands of views.

Speechless and mortified, I'm sure I blushed from head to toe. "You bonita, cariño. Beautiful and brave," Mikel whispered.

I swallowed hard, dumbstruck by the turn of events. I'd risked my life to snap a money shot and I *did,* although no one would probably see it. Instead, they'd see *me.* I'd become the story's subject, the YouTube video going viral. It was disconcerting, crazy, not my plan at all.

Yet it had gotten Mikel's attention and he was sweetly impressed. Thinking back, it was then that I fell in love with him. That soon. His silky voice and mesmerizing chocolate eyes awakened my libido, and although I didn't know it at the time, my love for him would change me forever.

The chemistry between us was immediate. A hot electrical current ricocheted from me to him and back to me. It didn't matter that we were from different countries and spoke different languages. Words weren't necessary, but we said them anyway, his halting English and my patience with it enough to communicate. He didn't leave my side the entire evening. While the others partied, we huddled in our own little world on the end of a deck chair, talking freely about everything.

He spoke enthusiastically about his soccer career and spot on Spain's team for the next World Cup. I couldn't believe I was in the presence of a *real* World Cup player. My mother loved the World Cup, and she'd take rare time off from work to watch it and I'd watch it with her.

He talked about his family. Like most Spaniards, they were the center of his life. His parents lived in southern Spain on the Costa del Sol. They'd moved from Pamplona after Mikel started making money and bought them a condo on the beach. At that moment, they were on a cruise in the Caribbean for their thirtieth wedding anniversary.

He told me Danel was his best friend and business manager. He'd supported Mikel's soccer dreams from a young age. He revealed they'd had a sister, Esti, who died of leukemia when she was sixteen. When he talked about her, his sensuous eyes saddened, his voice hushed. It was obvious he'd adored her.

He loved many sports, including American basketball, his favorite team the Miami Heat. It surprised me. He also enjoyed sailing, disclosing he owned a sailboat moored at the coastal town of San Sebastian.

I was fascinated, hanging on his every word. But he didn't talk only about himself. He peppered me with questions about my life. I uncharacteristically opened up. I felt totally at ease in his presence and spoke candidly about the boring small town in the Midwest where I'd grown up, and my parents and brother, and my dream to become a photographer.

He praised me for my courage at the Running of the Bulls. Giving me a stern, playful look, he also recounted the number of people who'd died from such foolishness. And he demanded to see the money shot, which Danel had already told him about.

The fact that he was interested at all made my heart flutter. He grabbed my hand and led me inside the house to his office, which was filled with soccer memorabilia and trophies. He casually sat on the chair in front of the computer and pulled me onto his lap. It was an intimate gesture considering we'd just met, and my hands trembled as I accessed my website.

The site was Jillian's idea. She insisted it was a necessity, worshipping anything internet-related. She'd created it herself, setting it up so people could see my work and purchase the photos directly online. If she would have been there at that moment, I would have kissed her feet, because Mikel wrapped his strong arms around me, pressed his cheek to mine and took control of the keyboard, slowly scrolling through the photos and muttering "fantástico" over and over.

It was almost three in the morning when the last party guests departed. Mikel insisted I stay, saying it was too late to drive back to the flat in Pamplona. He guided me upstairs and led me into his bedroom. I was happy and nervous, thinking he wanted to make love to me. But he rummaged in the closet and handed me a red-and-blue-striped Osasuna t-shirt for me to sleep in.

I grinned weakly, enchanted by his thoughtfulness but disappointed. A desperate desire lodged in my gut, and I eyed his bed with a longing I'd never felt before. His eyes followed mine, his brows furrowed. Then he pulled me into his arms and smiled mischievously.

"You want make love, cariño?" he asked. He pressed close, pinning me to his body with a hand on the small of my back. His cock was hard.

My heart skipped a beat, not expecting the blunt question or provocative display. His seductive brown eyes lured me in, and I was thankful I'd prepared for such a moment, losing my virginity several months ago, which was Jillian's idea, too.

She was sure I'd encounter some hot guys during my travels. Wanting me to have some fun, we formulated a plan for both of us to finally get laid. We took birth control pills for a month and purchased sexy bras and underwear. The boys in our small town were too immature and too boring for the task, so we wormed our way into a college fraternity, introduced to the guys by an upperclassman from our town. I chose Blake for my first sexual experience and Jillian chose Lucas.

Blake was good-looking, cocky and all too happy to give me what I wanted. We had sex four times, yet I never enjoyed the big "O" and I ended it. I consoled myself with the fact that at the very least I'd learned the mechanics, becoming familiar with condoms and blowjobs, and more importantly, I discovered how easy it is to please a man.

Jillian was luckier. She experienced an orgasm the second time. We compared notes and giggled, and like all our new experiences such as drinking beer and smoking pot for the first time, we did it together.

While I considered what to do, Mikel's scintillating eyes smoldered lustily. I briefly wondered if he'd think less of me for submitting, but it was a day of risk-taking and my desire was overwhelming.

"Do you want to make love to me?" I asked shyly. It was a stupid question. I felt his answer digging into me.

"Yes, cariño, very much but I not force."

His gentlemanly response cemented my decision. I gave him a crooked smile and responded, "I want you, too."

What happened next would change me forever, and although I'd tried to erase him from my memory, in the end it was impossible. Even as I lay beaten and broken in the cellar, I could still taste him, feel his hot flesh on mine and smell his special Mikel Garro scent, a mixture of fabric softener and a hint of oranges.

He cupped my face, eyes darkening into thunderclouds. His hands were smooth and warm on my cheeks, and he kissed me with a tenderness that inflamed my senses, his velvety lips tantalizing me, lips that would eventually touch every part of me and make me want more.

The kiss became more demanding. His tongue slipped into my mouth, scraping and teasing mine. He held me tighter, hips swaying seductively, grinding his cock against me. A liquid fire amassed between my legs and all my inhibitions faded into oblivion.

My preparedness, practical as it was, had left me unprepared for the fire kindling inside me. He trailed soft kisses along my neck and deftly unzipped the sundress, slowly sliding it down my body and leaving it piled around my ankles on the floor. I trembled, his light touch agitating every fiber in my being.

"Bonita."

His voice was low and husky. His palms skimmed my bra, teasing my nipples beneath the silky lace before gliding down my bare back to my behind, sneaking inside my panties and gently squeezing my buttocks.

My pussy burned. He inched the panties along my thighs and over my knees and over my calves to the floor, leaving them wrapped around my ankles with the dress. He crouched there, unbuckling the sandal straps, removing the shoes and nipping at my toes one by one.

Peeking up at me with those seductive chocolate eyes, he trailed his soft lips up my leg to my clit, burying his nose there and sniffing and rubbing the moist flesh. Then he stood and expertly released my breasts from the bra and pulled me toward the bed. Leaving the clothes in a pile behind me, I quivered naked before him. His eyes grew stormier.

He studied me from head to toe and unbuttoned the top two buttons on his shirt. He pulled it over his head and quickly stripped bare. I gawked appreciatively, his body ripped with a rock solid abdomen, toned muscles and powerful soccer legs. His skin was perfectly tan except for a pale ass and pelvis, and his cock was hard and fat, pointing straight at me.

I must have looked shocked because he smiled devilishly and chuckled. He drew me into his arms. "You virgin?" he asked.

"N-no," I stammered. Hot flesh seared me. He tipped my chin up and regarded me curiously, expectantly. "No, I'm just, um, you're just, um, fantástico."

Grinning crookedly, he buried his nose in my neck and whispered words in Spanish I didn't understand. Then like with the bull time stopped. He laid me on the bed and slithered on top of me. His cock skimmed my exposed skin. He kissed me with a passion I'd never known or expected, his tongue demanding and searching every corner of my mouth. I melted beneath him as he headed south, lips branding me with soft kisses, hands caressing my breasts, tongue attacking my nipples, licking and teasing them with such sweet abandon I moaned and whimpered, my deepest, darkest parts aching with an almost unbearable need.

I opened my legs and bowed into him. He slipped a finger inside me, churning my juices and continuing to taunt my swollen nipples. My insides burned with an agonizing yearning, quaking with each deliberate stroke. When he rolled onto his back and quickly slipped on a condom, I gasped for breath, goose bumps bubbling on my flesh from the sudden heat loss.

His sultry eyes scorched me, blazing with unabashed hunger. Hot blood blistered through my veins. Every synapse in my body fired chaotically as he knelt between my legs and slowly plunged into me. His groan was long and drawn out. His pleasure echoed through me. I wrapped my legs around his hips and gripped him tightly, my clit on fire.

It wasn't long before his leisurely offensive quickened. He thrust harder and faster. His engorged cock pounded against my sweet spots, each delicious plunge pushing me higher and higher. I closed my eyes, surrendering to the delicious sensations. There was only me and Mikel, our flesh wedded with raw desire.

The orgasm bore down on me. I'd never felt anything like it. It took over and spiked through me, sizzling white hot. I spiraled out of control, shuddering and crying out his name. I felt him still and opened my eyes. His handsome face was taut with tension, reaching his own climax. He pumped into me a few more times and collapsed on top of me. I wrapped my arms around him and sighed contentedly, my clit convulsing and body quivering.

~~~~~~~†~~~~~~~

I lay on his chest, enfolded in his arms and basking in the afterglow of my first orgasm. He'd unleashed my sexuality and I wanted to do it again and again, wanted to do it with him. He affectionately kissed the top of my head and murmured, "You catch my 'eart, cariño."

My pulse raced. I understood the gist of what he'd said and briefly wondered if he was declaring his love. Yet the idea was preposterous. I didn't know how to respond, my feelings jumbled. It didn't matter. In seconds he was asleep, his breathing soft and regular, his body cooling beside mine.

I snuggled against him. My nipples swelled and tingled, my pussy pulsed and beaded. I shifted so I could view the full length of him. He was magnificent, a Basque Adonis. I craved more of him, his taste still on my lips and his unique scent teasing my nostrils.

I traced my fingertips across the small tattoo on his rib cage, where his sister's name had been inked in black, a red heart used for the dot above the letter "I." I continued slowly over his taut abs to the dark pubic hair surrounding his slumbering shaft, and I rubbed my thumb over the tantalizing, moist crown.

It twitched ever so slightly. He rolled onto his side, burrowed his nose in my throat and unconsciously threw a muscular leg over my thighs and draped an arm over my belly, pinning me on my back and effectively preventing further probing.

I stifled a groan. Once was not enough. I closed my eyes, willing myself to think about something else, like what I should photograph next. There were parades, processions and other sports events scheduled throughout the weeklong festival. I wanted to document as much as I could. The last image in my mind before I finally fell asleep was of the bull and the panic in its eyes.

I woke the next morning in Mikel's bed, a soft cotton sheet draped over my naked flesh, my skin cool for the first time since arriving in Pamplona. I lay there for a moment, enjoying the air-conditioned room. It was a treat after the suffocating heat in the small bedroom at the Zabaleta apartment.

The sun streamed brightly into the bedroom through glass balcony doors. I rose slowly then froze, gaping at the pillow next to me. A long-stemmed yellow rose and an orange with a smiley face drawn on it were perched on top of it. My heart swelled happily. I couldn't believe it, the gesture incredibly sweet.

Excited to see Mikel again, I scrambled out of bed. I hurriedly slipped on my panties and the Osasuna t-shirt and raced out the door into the foyer before coming to my senses. I didn't know who or what waited for me downstairs. I quickly retreated back into the bedroom and paced nervously, flushed and out of sorts like never before.

I'd left my camera on the chair in the corner and picked it up. To calm myself, I took a photo of the yellow rose and smiley-faced orange. A slow burn rolled through me. I took a few close-up shots, practically shuddering with longing.

Scolding myself for acting like a lovesick moron, I wandered onto the balcony and pointed the camera at the countryside. The view was breathtaking, lush with orange trees, olive trees and grapevines hugging rolling hills, the colors suddenly bolder and brighter. Camera in hand and doing what I loved to do, a soothing serenity enveloped me. My practical side took over.

I had a dream to realize and a bright career ahead of me. My reaction to Mikel was simply lust, nothing more, falling in love not an option. Besides, Jillian would scoff at my silliness. We had a pact. We'd never allow men to distract us, no matter how hot and charming.

I scampered into the en suite bathroom, stripped naked and studied myself in the mirror. I looked the same, blessed with natural blond hair and blue eyes from my Scandinavian ancestors. Except for the skinned elbows, bruised knees and a gash on my leg, my body was flawless, a 36-26-35-inch curvaceous hourglass.

I hesitated before stepping into the shower, awash in Mikel's scent. Fabric softener, oranges and sex. It taunted me all over again, threatening my resolve. My stomach somersaulted at the very thought of him. I couldn't wait to see him again, and I knew I would. The yellow rose and orange with a smiley face was a sure sign of his interest, and there was no denying mine. I quickly showered, donned the sundress, applied a little makeup and raced downstairs.

~~~~~~†~~~~~~

Following the sound of voices, I strode into the kitchen and found Danel talking excitedly on the phone and a heavyset, gray-haired woman watching a small, flat screen TV set on the counter.

Danel smiled brightly, quickly wrapped up the call and exclaimed, "Buenos días, cariño! 'ow you? You sleep good? 'ow leg?"

His excited concern was endearing. He crouched to examine the bandage on my leg, slowly peeled it off and shouted at the woman, who scurried away and returned seconds later with a large Band-Aid.

"Gracias, Xenia. Aley, this is Xenia. She take care me and Mikel. Do you like breakfast? Coffee?"

I grinned, still not used to the Spanish pronunciation of my name. "Aley" without the "H." Again, before I could respond, Danel sat me on a chair at the kitchen island and Xenia placed sweet rolls, jam, cheese and coffee with frothy milk before me.

"Mikel, 'e at football training. 'e come 'ome soon." Danel gently applied the bandage and lightly kissed my bruised knees. "You like my brother, yes?"

He eyed me mischievously, his lips curled into a crooked smile. Before I could answer, his phone rang and he was immersed in another excited conversation.

Xenia hovered over me, studying me and waiting for me to eat. I sipped the coffee and smothered cheese on the sweet roll. Compared to my usual solitary breakfast at home among the cornfields in the Midwest, the scene was chaotic, a flurry of activity and fussiness. Still, I loved the attention. A warm glow spread through me.

I savored the roll and Xenia rewarded me with a motherly smirk.

She sliced several oranges in half, squeezed the fresh pulp into a juice glass and set it before me. It was the first time I'd tasted fresh orange juice, mine usually coming from a plastic carton. It was the most delicious drink on earth, its subtle sweetness refreshing. As I swallowed the last flavorful drop, Mikel bounded into the room, a boyish smile plastered on his handsome face, his hair damp from a shower.

"Aley!" He rushed to me, his exuberance electric, lighting up the room.

I jumped off the chair and flew into his outstretched arms. He kissed me hard and fondled my ass. I was swept into his vortex, my heart pounding wildly, pulse racing.

"I miss you, cariño," he said softly in my ear.

My pulse raced faster. I'd never met anyone like him. He left me breathless, his cheerfulness infectious. When I looked back at that time, before I was broken, I was spellbound by him. Despite his rock star status, he was unpretentious, guileless and sweet. I couldn't resist him nor did I try.

Xenia set a plate with a large ham and cheese sandwich on the kitchen island and squeezed more orange juice. Mikel guided me back to the stool next to him, took a big bite of the sandwich and set his dazzling brown eyes on me.

"What you do today?" he asked.

I told him I wanted to return to the old city and continue photographing the activities at Los Sanfermines. He intimately brushed strands of hair from my face and tucked them behind my ear.

"I go with you, sí?"

The idea of wandering Pamplona's streets with him was a seductive proposal. My heart fluttered. "Sí," I responded softly.

He smiled happily and turned back to the sandwich. Danel sidled onto the chair next to him and they huddled together, talking in low voices and occasionally glancing in my direction. I was sure they were discussing me, which made me uncomfortable, although whatever Danel was saying seemed to excite Mikel.

"Bueno," Mikel said. He patted his brother's back and faced me. "Danel say I must see movie premier tonight. You go with me, sí? And you give me phone number, sí?"

I didn't have a cellphone. It cost too much. I lowered my eyes, suddenly embarrassed.

"What, cariño?" His brows furrowed with worry and confusion.

I felt ridiculous, probably the only 18 year old in the modern world without a cellphone. But they were expensive and I didn't think I'd need one during my travels. I'd planned to use email instead, and since it was imperative I make my meager finances last as long as I could, a phone was not an option.

Because Mikel was Mikel, a man who wore his heart on his sleeve, I told him about my situation and was rewarded with a crooked grin and a sweet kiss. "No problem. I buy you one," he said.

"No, Mikel, I can't let you do that," I responded adamantly. There was no way I was going to let him buy me a phone.

"But it impossible, Aley. 'ow I contact you when I need you?" I set my lips in a stubborn line. He chuckled and pulled me into his arms. "I loan you phone, sí? You must do what I say or you must be with me always."

I snuggled against him and smiled to myself, preferring the option to be with him *always* instead of lending me a phone.

He drove me back to the flat in a black Ferrari Spider. It was another hot day and we rode with the top down. My long hair whipped freely in the wind. I felt on top on the world.

He squeezed into a parking space on a street a couple of blocks from the Zabaleta apartment. The area was crowded with people and several stopped what they were doing to stare at the car and us. He quickly donned sunglasses and a Miami Heat ball cap, explaining they were necessary to avoid the paparazzi and the attention from his many fans. We quickly walked down the sidewalk, hand in hand, and as we passed the hardware store window, Tote dashed outside, shouting in rapid Spanish. She grabbed my arms and glowered disapprovingly.

Mikel crossed his arms over his chest, lips curling with

amusement. "She say she care you not go 'ome last night. It why you need phone," he said.

I should've known the motherly señora would be worried. I apologized profusely using both English and mangled Spanish. She grabbed my elbow and pulled me into the store, berating me loudly and standing me before Zorion, who kissed me on both cheeks and hugged me hard.

I continued to apologize. Mikel removed the hat and sunglasses and their attention turned to him. Their jaws dropped. There were kisses and handshakes and appreciative glances my way, and they dragged us to the flat where I took photos of them with Mikel, who was very gracious and took it all in stride.

While Zorion and Tote gladly kept Mikel entertained, I retreated to my room and hurriedly changed into jean shorts, a blue tank top that highlighted my eyes and flat sandals. When I returned, my Spanish parents suddenly realized they'd left the shop unattended. Tote raced downstairs, flustered and prattling to herself.

Mikel draped an arm over my shoulders, lips quirking up amusedly. "I say to Zorion you go movie tonight with me. 'e say it okay you not go 'ome tonight."

My insides tightened. Hot desire immediately pumped through my veins. I ached for the darkness, too many hours of sunshine left in the day. Then I panicked. I had no idea what to wear to a movie premier in Basque country.

Mikel donned the cap and glasses, kissed Zorion on each cheek and grabbed my hand to leave.

"Wait." I told him my problem, and he led me to my bedroom and casually sifted through my limited wardrobe.

"You make picture, then we shop for phone and good dress. We siesta my casa today and then go movie. Sí, cariño?"

Sí, sí, sí. If Catalin and Edur were the example, I wouldn't have to wait for darkness to be with him. I quickly stuffed makeup and underwear into my backpack. My pulse raced faster, flushed with anticipation. I didn't make a fuss about buying a dress either, because I'd budgeted for new clothes anyway, knowing it was impractical to bring everything I might need with me.

We strolled through the old town for a couple of hours, hand in hand as if we'd been together forever, old souls connecting again. Like with the bull, the world stopped and time stood still. The range of colors became brighter and more intense, the laughter louder and every nuance of life was amplified by ten degrees.

Giant figures with big heads wandered around after the morning parade. Street performers danced and sang. A mass of regular people moved to and fro, enjoying the festivities against a backdrop seeped in history. I snapped shot after shot, molding each scene into one of my own. Throughout it all, Mikel was attentive, adding narrative to the picture, his enthusiasm bringing light to the story.

And he constantly touched my already overheated body. He nipped at an earlobe, softly kissed my forehead and fondled my ass. I'd never felt more alive and cherished.

He bought a phone and "loaned" it to me, and we programmed numbers into it together. His first, then my parents, then Jillian, then Danel and finally the Zabaletas. He dragged me into a high-end women's boutique store and I dragged him back out. I wouldn't let him buy me a dress, too, so we scoured the bazaar where I found a shiny blue one that showed off my curves. I proudly bought it along with matching high heels for only thirty euros.

We ate the midday meal at his favorite restaurant, where he took off the cap and sunglasses, confident he wouldn't be bothered there. We feasted on paella, cheese, bread and a decadent dessert accompanied by a bottle of wine and cappuccino. Afterwards, I had a deeper appreciation for the daily siesta. I was ready for a nap.

Yet when we arrived back at his house and he flopped onto the bed and grinned mischievously, sleep was the last thing on my mind.

I crawled on top of him. He encircled me in his strong arms, kissing me tenderly. His cock hardened and I rubbed against it, my clit instantly plumping. I wanted him badly and hurriedly unbuttoned his shirt. He sat up so I could peel it from his magnificent skin. He deftly pulled the tank top over my head and removed my bra, sinking his face between my breasts and sighing loudly.

"Fantástico…"

His soft lips skimmed my naked flesh. He lavishly licked and sucked my nipples. They were a direct line to my clit, and the more they puckered and swelled, the more my pussy plumped and burned. I squirmed with need and grinded against his growing erection.

His beautiful eyes gleamed seductively. He crushed his mouth to mine and I responded fervently, a hint of white wine and cappuccino lingering on his tongue. His taste drove me crazy. I wanted to sample more of him, craved more of him.

Drawing back, I lightly kissed the corner of his mouth and hot skin. I licked his nipples and journeyed from one end of his muscular torso to the other, fumbling with the button and zipper on his jeans until I set his cock free.

It was big and beautiful, throbbing and making me wetter. I sucked it, stroked it and relished the taste of him. He gripped my hair in his fists, prodding me to go faster. His buttocks clenched. He moaned loudly. I engulfed it in my mouth, the head ramming against the back of my throat.

He was all mine, hot, juicy and bloated. I tantalized and teased until he shuddered and detonated in my mouth. Warm creaminess pumped down my throat. His body went limp. His fists dropped to the side. I licked the come from my lips and his shrinking shaft, savoring each drop. When I was done, I slithered next to him and rested a cheek on his chest.

Panting softly, he wrapped an arm around me, lightly kissed my forehead and closed his eyes. I groaned inwardly, hoping he wasn't going to fall asleep again. My deepest, darkest parts ached with an almost painful need. I squirmed against him. His breathing became softer and steadier, his body still.

The seconds passed. I chastised myself for pleasuring him without receiving my own. I didn't know what to do and nudged him with my hip, softly saying his name. "Mikel?"

More seconds passed. Then he suddenly flipped me over and pinned my hands above my head, grinning wickedly. "You want me, cariño?" I cussed and struggled against his hold. "I not let you suffer," he chuckled.

His playfulness was charming and provocative. I burst into laughter. I could tell he enjoyed teasing me and I didn't mind as long as he gave me what I wanted. He did to me what I did to him, except he worked me over slowly, bringing me close to an orgasm and then backing off, torturing my nipples before returning to my clit and licking it lavishly. His cock grew harder with each round until it was fat and juicy again.

Then he rolled onto his back and rolled me with him. I rode him hard and fast, loving the position and the control it gave me. I could set my own pace and angle my pussy so his cock hit exactly the right spots, scraping against my swollen flesh, pushing me to the edge. When I finally climaxed, the orgasm ripped through me and curled my toes. It pulsated and persisted until he detonated and encircled me in his arms.

I was jolted from a deep sleep by pounding on the door. Mikel swore under his breath, hauled me to my feet and dragged me forward. "'Urry, Aley, 'urry…"

I wasn't used to napping. I stumbled to the bathroom. He guided me into the shower, giving me a crooked, impish smile. Water streamed over his naked flesh. My stomach somersaulted, back flipped, went completely haywire. I shook the cobwebs from my head.

He kissed me softly, maneuvered me under the spray and ruthlessly turned on the cold water. I could've killed him, but it was a quintessential Mikel move, lighthearted, playful. I squealed and cursed and woke up.

So did he. His cock sprang to life. I reached for it and he grabbed my wrists. "We late, cariño. Please be good and do what I say."

I begrudgingly did, the shower brief. Afterward, I quickly dried my hair and applied makeup while he dressed in the other room. There wasn't a robe, so when I was done I scampered naked into the bedroom and immediately stopped in my tracks, gaping.

He was spine-tingling hot. He'd dressed in a tailored black suit and red tie, his chocolate eyes sultry behind thick lashes. My heart pounded wildly and pulse raced. He hurriedly helped me into the dress and high heels and stood back and gazed appreciatively at me.

"Bonita, " he said.

My reaction was visceral. My nipples hardened and pussy moistened. His reaction was the same. When he drew me into his arms and kissed me passionately, I could feel his cock bulging.

Danel accompanied us to the premier. He drove his Mercedes, leaving me alone in the backseat to reflect on the last couple of days. They'd been the most exciting days of my short life. It was a thrill to run with the bulls. I'd snapped a great photo, although I doubted anyone would see it. But the highlight had been meeting Mikel. I squirmed every time he looked at me, a turning point in my otherwise boring life.

As we waited in the theater lobby for the movie to start, Mikel kept a protective hand on the small of my back. I felt special, cherished. For a small-town girl like me it was intoxicating. Everything was new and exotic, especially him, and he acted like he was enchanted with me, too. When I gawked at the exquisite fresco on the ceiling of the fifteenth-century Gothic theater, wishing I'd brought my camera, I swear he knew what I was thinking, his sexy brown eyes twinkling affectionately.

The place was packed. He proudly explained the film was directed by a Basque, and for the first time I truly understood their kinship. Their heritage was a cornerstone of life, an innate connection that brought comfort and acceptance. It was ingrained in everyone who identified themselves as Basque. They were excited to see Mikel there, too, and he graciously held court and signed a few autographs, keeping me close and smiling affably.

We sat in prime balcony seats with Danel, a teammate of Mikel's and his wife, and two glamorous models, who glowered at me from behind. I wondered if they'd expected Mikel to show up alone, hoping for a chance to flirt with him. But he only had eyes for me. He held my hand during the entire movie and periodically leaned in my ear to explain a scene. He nuzzled my hair, which didn't go unnoticed by any of them.

Afterward, we went to dinner. Mikel's teammate and wife joined the three of us, and it was a lively affair. Mikel entertained us with funny stories. Danel impersonated Spanish celebrities I didn't know. We drank a bottle of champagne before dinner and wine during the meal, which wasn't served until eleven o'clock. By the time we finished it was one in the morning, and I was yawning and tipsy.

Danel wanted to hit the nightclubs, but Mikel sensed I was tired and begged off. I would learn he was like that, always considerate and wanting me to be happy. Danel left with Mikel's teammate and his wife, and Mikel drove the Mercedes back to the house, intimately caressing my thigh the entire way back. By the time we arrived, I was no longer tired but wired with desire, which was probably his plan all along.

As soon as we stepped inside the house he attacked, as if he'd been waiting a million years to fuck me again. He didn't bother with foreplay, either, pushing me against the nearest wall, hiking my dress up and ripping off my panties. He stroked my bare ass and grinded against me, pinning me to the wall and hastily removing his jacket and tie.

Ecstatic and mesmerized, I quivered excitedly. He lifted me by the butt, fixed my legs around his hips and carried me to the kitchen, grabbing a condom from a cookie jar on the counter before setting me on the island.

It took him only seconds to free his cock and slip on the condom. Then he was inside me. He buried his nose in my neck and groaned with pleasure, thrusting hard and deep. I wrapped my arms and legs around him, closed my eyes and let the delicious sensations take over.

~~~~~~~†~~~~~~~

Afterward, we snuggled in bed and talked in low voices. When I woke the next morning, he was gone again, a red rose placed on the pillow this time.

I burrowed under the sheet. His scent lingered on it and me. I tingled just thinking about him, daydreaming about waking up next to him, his cock huge and ready for me. But it made me crazy, and I dragged myself from bed and scampered to the shower.

Knowing what to expect downstairs this time, I put on jean shorts and the Osasuna t-shirt and headed to the kitchen. Danel paced in the living room and talked on the phone. It looked like he'd just gotten up, too, his hair disheveled and feet bare. He smiled brightly at me and returned to the call. Xenia placed the same breakfast before me and didn't hover this time, turning away to watch TV. I slowly sipped coffee and ate the sweet roll, reflecting on the rhythm of life in Spain. The last couple of days with Mikel were an eye opener.

With the substantial midday meals and late night dinners and partying, it was no wonder Spaniards needed a siesta. And after having my own siesta with the sumptuous Mikel, the afternoon nap held even more significance.

I squirmed on the chair and eyed the cookie jar, wondering why he had a container full of condoms in the kitchen and what Xenia must think about it. Then he swept into the room and the atmosphere sizzled with excitement.

"Aley!" He bounded over to me, kissed me hard and tossed several newspapers on the counter. "You must see!"

Smiling proudly, he presented the Pamplona morning paper. My bull photo was featured prominently on the front page next to news about several injuries at the running the day before. My byline was printed below it. The Bilbao and San Sebastián papers carried it, too, but not on the front page. It was even carried in the big city Madrid and Barcelona papers in the entertainment section.

I was speechless, looking from one paper to the next and at Mikel, my eyes as wide as saucers.

"You 'appy, cariño?" he asked. I flew into his arms, beaming. He laughed, swung me around a few times and gently placed me on my feet, nodding at Danel. "Danel make call for me. It picture all Spain must see."

My heart constricted. Danel smirked. I hugged him hard and dashed back into Mikel's arms, suddenly overcome with love for him. It radiated from every pore, consuming and frightening me. I knew then I'd fallen in love with Mikel Garro, and it wasn't supposed to happen. It wasn't part of my plan, a major complication. A large lump formed in my throat.

"Thank you, Mikel. Thank you, Danel," I managed to say.

"We must see you website," Mikel said eagerly.

He grabbed my hand and pulled me into the office. I sat shakily at the computer and he leaned over me. His breath warmed my skin, his scent drove me crazy. Heart beating wildly, I accessed my website and gasped.

There were eight purchases of the bull photo, including one by an animal rights organization and one by the venerated Associated Press. It meant my bull would be seen around the world. I couldn't believe it. My future as a famous photographer suddenly looked brighter than ever.

And since I'd priced the photo at one hundred euros, I'd also made eight hundred euros overnight, a substantial sum considering my finances. My belly pitched and churned, partly because of the money and partly because Mikel made it happen. I didn't want to love him and I didn't know what would happen next.

Loving Mikel

Carried along by the rhythm of life, the next few days were a blur. Lazy afternoons fucking and napping and late nights partying. And because I was with Mikel most of the time anyway, I left the Zabaleta apartment and stayed with him.

I continued to photograph Los Sanfermines, usually accompanied by Mikel. When it was over, I didn't know what to do next, my plan stalled because I'd stupidly fallen in love.

Fortunately, Mikel's coach gave the team a few days off from practice and he took me sailing. We were on our own without Danel and friends for the first time. He taught me about jibs and booms and tacking, and we skimmed across the vast Atlantic, stopping to deep sea fish or skinny dip in the warm coastal waters. We made love and made love some more, and there was little time left to think about my dilemma.

On the third day, the wind was still and the water calm for hours. The boat drifted in the sea, and we spent the afternoon basking naked in the sun on lounge chairs set at the bow.

"It good, sí, cariño?" he asked.

"Wonderful, peaceful," I said.

He reached for me and I went to him. Every nerve ending ignited with that delicious anticipation only he could provoke. He drew me onto his lap and embraced me lovingly.

"You love me, sí?" His luminous eyes flickered solemnly. An astonished gasp stuck in my throat and I stiffened. "Please, Aley, it important," he prodded, narrowing his eyes worriedly.

To say I was confused is an understatement. He looked sad, as if he already knew the answer. But I wasn't sure which answer would make him sad, and I wished he wasn't so damn guileless, wearing his heart on his sleeve, although it was his best quality.

I didn't want to reveal my true feelings, especially since I didn't know his. My mind raced. Shouldn't he be declaring his love for me first? Or maybe he wanted to know because he *didn't* love me. He'd somehow sensed I'd fallen in love with him and didn't want to hurt me. It would be just like him, and the more I thought about it, the more I was sure that was the case.

My heart sank. Yet if he didn't love me, my problem would be solved. "Yes," I confessed softly, wanting to get it over with.

He smiled a spine-tingling smile and kissed me hard. "Bueno. I love you, also, mi amor."

It was the best and worst moment of my life. I didn't know it was possible to feel two desperate conflicting emotions at once, but they didn't last long.

He kissed me passionately and maneuvered me so I straddled his belly. His cock grew hard and thick between my ass cheeks. He molded my tits in his hands and licked and nipped at my nipples until they were swollen and stiff and my pussy dripped with desire.

He took me without using a condom, which suddenly didn't matter because we were in love. I was on the pill anyway and he knew it. And without the latex barrier, sex with him was even more amazing. His shaft was rock hard, *hot*. I felt the slit on it grazing my clit as he entered me. It pulsed as it pounded into my spongy flesh, and we exploded together, convulsing and moaning as one.

The world stood still as the orgasm ripped through me. I collapsed on his shoulder, nuzzling my nose in his throat. We lay like that for a long time, his hand caressing my hair and fingers skimming up and down my spine. At that moment I knew love and it was all that mattered.

Then the wind picked up and we fixed the sails to the west. The sun slowly disappeared into the sea. Streaks of radiant reds and yellows and pinks saturated the horizon. Mikel stood gloriously against the backdrop setting the jib, his disheveled hair flopping in the breeze and naked silhouette cloaked in a colorful aura.

My eyes welled with tears. He was magnificent. I loved him. His lightness had seeped into my soul, brightening my ordinary life. I'd placed my camera under the lounge chair thinking I might photograph the sunset, but I pointed it at him instead.

He paused and gazed at the horizon, lost in thought, majestic, the seams of his sinewy muscles dancing in a prism of brilliant hues. I quickly snapped six shots, wanting to capture his exquisite beauty and preserve it forever. When he noticed what I was doing, he lunged at me, grabbed the camera and playfully tossed me into the Atlantic.

We returned to his house in the wee hours. While I brushed my teeth at the bathroom sink, he approached from behind and rubbed against my ass, swaying his hips from side to side. Slowly, deliberately, rock hard.

I grinned at him in the vanity mirror. Foamy toothpaste seeped from the corners of my mouth and beads of desire immediately pooled between my legs. His eyes locked onto me, turning into seductive dark chocolate. I hurriedly rinsed and watched his hands travel up and down my body, teasing me as I swished and spit.

"It good you and me," he said. When I set the toothbrush aside, he quickly stripped me, glaring hungrily at my reflection as each item of clothing dropped to the floor.

He reached for my tits, cupping them, squeezing them and brushing his palms over the nipples. I glared in the mirror. I was beautiful, my skin kissed by the sun and breasts firm and round. He twisted and tugged on my nipples and they puckered and stiffened. I couldn't look away, transfixed, fascinated by my body and my response to his caresses. My pussy pounded with an almost desperate need, turned on by the erotic woman in the mirror who was me.

He slowly slid a hand across my belly and placed two fingers on my magic spot, fluttering, massaging and dipping inside me. The ache expanded and intensified. He followed my reaction as he tormented my flesh, entranced like me.

It made me hotter, seeing myself as he saw me. Then he stepped back and hastily removed his clothes and liberated his cock. I gawked at it in the glass, granite-hard perfection, throbbing. As he moved behind me, it vanished from sight. His hands skimmed over my skin, one landing on a breast and the other on my clit again.

Sweet, sweet agony. I glimpsed my entire body shudder. A magnificent orgasm bore down on me, but I held it at bay, watching him gently bend me over the counter. He spread my legs with his knees. His fat shaft bobbed over my ass, then disappeared inside me with one hard jab.

He sighed a long, dramatic pleasurable sigh, briefly shut his eyes and quickly opened them again, locking onto mine. His cock stretched my plump, pulsing wetness. I braced myself on my forearms, my swollen nipples scraping against the sleek vanity surface. I kept my head up, mesmerized by every move.

He pulled back slowly and rested the crown of his dick in the bowl of my pussy before ramming into me again. His jaw clenched and muscles rippled. He taunted me over and over like that until I was whimpering and grinding against him. He steadily increased the pace, gripping my hips harder and moving faster and faster. I positioned myself so every stroke hit my sweet spots.

The heat rolled through me. Each thrust turned it up a degree. I continued to monitor our reflection in the mirror until the orgasm overtook me. Unable to focus on anything but the convulsions sweeping through me, my head lolled, my eyes closed. He detonated powerfully and our spasms merged. He slumped over my back, breathing heavy, soft lips nipping at my ear. I couldn't imagine ever leaving him.

~~~~~~✝~~~~~~

Mikel left early for practice again the next morning. This time he left me a bouquet of pink roses in a crystal vase. I lazed in bed, the image of him fucking me in front of the mirror stuck in my head. I was *hot,* sexy. I'd never thought about myself like that before.

I knew I was beautiful. I'd been ogled by men since I was fifteen. But I'd never focused on my looks or used it to my advantage, preferring to be respected for my brains and talent. Besides, my mother had made sure I understood beauty didn't last, pointing out the gray hair that tinged her temples and the tiny wrinkles forming around her eyes as she edged toward fifty. Still, after watching myself in the mirror, I felt incredibly sexy and thought together we were amazing, *electrifying*, capable of becoming famous porn stars if we wanted, my imagination running wild.

Chuckling, I doubted we would ever go *there*, and I turned my attention to the flowers. Somehow he'd secured them in the middle of the night. I didn't know how he did it and rose early for soccer practice and still had the stamina to fuck me a couple of times a day. I loved every delicious second with him, but I couldn't forget about my plan. I couldn't just sit around.

After breakfast, I retreated to the office to search online for information about upcoming events in the area. Fortunately, there was a major union protest planned in Madrid in three days, which I thought would be interesting to photograph. Plus, it wouldn't take me away from Mikel for too long. I'd also planned to visit Barcelona and photograph Antoni Gaudí's works while I was in Spain. His famous masterpiece the Sagrada Família church had opened for Sunday services, so I added Barcelona to my plan. A *new* plan, one that allowed me to follow my dream and love Mikel at the same time, at least in the short-term.

It was a relief to set a schedule, and I loaded the pictures from the sailing trip onto the computer next, scrutinizing them one by one. The Romanesque church spire set against the Pyrenees, the quaint village hugging the shoreline and the goofy pic of us in bed after making love, our faces plastered with cheesy grins. Then I clicked on the first shot of Mikel on the sailboat and shuddered.

The image was hauntingly beautiful, his silhouette suspended in the dusky light with yellow and pink bands flashing across his naked flesh, an array of pastels bouncing off his tight butt, powerful legs and sinewy backside. And as he gazed into the distance, his sculpted muscles and rugged facial features appeared to dance in the sunset, the thick, long lashes stemming from one eyelid magnified by multitudes of color.

Awed by the sheer splendor of him, my heart skipped a beat, my breathing stopped. It was another money shot, sensual and provocative yet poignant. It teased my emotions. I stared at it for a long time before scanning through the other five photos and returning to study it closer.

There was no need to edit the shot. Its perfection was evidenced by the reaction it provoked. I was at once thrilled and disappointed. No one would ever see it. It was personal. And although there was no frontal nudity, only a statuesque male form reminiscent of eighteenth-century Baroque nudes, I was sure Mikel wouldn't want his naked body exposed to the world.

I sat there for a while gazing through the window at Danel by the pool. As usual, he was conducting business on the phone. My stomach churned. I was desperate to show the photo to someone, and I raced outside and dragged him to the office.

"Check this out," I said proudly. My pulse raced excitedly.

Like me, he stared at it for a long time. "Magnífico, Aley, magnífico…" he finally said.

I beamed. A warm glow mushroomed inside me. Then Mikel bounded into the room and swept me into his arms, smiling broadly and kissing me hard.

"I miss you, mi amor," he said. The glow ignited into a flame and burned through me, his mere presence electrifying.

Danel showed the picture to him and I stood nervously behind them. They spoke animatedly in Spanish for several minutes. "It fantástico," Mikel declared. "It must be see, but not see on you website. Danel 'ave good idea. You send Danel, sí?"

He used too many "sees" and "sís" in those sentences, and at first I didn't understand what he was saying. Then I realized they had a plan and I hugged him. The photo would be "see."

I quickly emailed it to Danel. I sent it to my parents and Jillian, too, with a note that read "for your eyes only." Whatever Mikel and Danel had planned, I had a feeling it would be good.

Mikel had an appointment in town with a reporter, who was interviewing him about the upcoming Osasuna season. There was nothing for me to do until the midday meal, and I decided to wash my clothes. But Xenia insisted it was her job, so I lounged by the pool and called my parents and Jillian.

Mom and Dad loved the sailboat photo but not as much as the bull one. Smiling, I was sure they were wondering why I was taking a photo of a naked man. But they'd never judge and went on and on about how proud they were of me.

Jillian was proud of me, too, and went on and on about how hot Mikel was.

"How many orgasms?" she grilled.

"Christ, Jillian, it's not like I've counted them," I chuckled.

"What's your favorite position?"

Her questions became more and more outrageous until we dissolved into a fit of laughter. My heart lurched, missing her desperately.

Then she interrogated me about my feelings for him and warned me to enjoy the sex but not fall in love. When I hesitated with a response, she knew right away I already had.

"Damn it, Haley, stick to your plan," she admonished.

She ranted for ten minutes, insisting I keep our pledge to each other. I made promises I didn't know if I could keep. When Mikel returned and swept me into his arms, I forgot about everyone except him.

We had lunch at the house that day. Danel's partner, Carlos, joined us. He was much older than I'd expected, at least forty, and he had a shiny bald head and didn't say much. Not that he had an opportunity, overshadowed by Mikel and Danel's constant banter. Xenia prepared a feast—Serrano ham and cheese for an appetizer, grilled asparagus for the first course, baked snapper with tomato sauce, garlic, onion and peppers for the main course and chocolate cake and ice cream for dessert, which I learned was Mikel's favorite.

As usual, I was stuffed and sleepy afterwards, but it wouldn't be a siesta without screwing around. Mikel was particularly attentive, making sure I knew how much he loved me. But as we lay together enjoying the afterglow, he narrowed his brows worriedly. He told me he was leaving for Madrid to practice for a World Cup qualifying match that would occur there in five days, and he asked me to go with him.

He needn't have worried. I was ecstatic. The timing couldn't have been better. I told him about my plan to photograph the protest in Madrid and the church services in Barcelona after that. He embraced me tightly, looked relieved and soon fell asleep. As I drifted off, I wondered what he'd been anxious about.

We left for the city after the siesta and talked about everything during the four hour drive. I loved his openness and the easy camaraderie between us. When he laughed, I lit up inside. I had fallen hard and fast for Mikel Garro, every moment with him better than the last, and

I looked forward to our time together in Madrid, intoxicated by thoughts of a romantic getaway in the beautiful Spanish capital.

"Where you go, mi amor?" His eyes twinkled happily.

I smiled brightly. "Just thinking."

"You think of me, sí?"

"Sí," I giggled, amazed by how quickly he'd learned to gage my inner thoughts.

"I think of you always, also," he grinned. He grasped my thigh and squeezed it affectionately. "My parents, they come back. They come for Cup. I excite you meet them."

The announcement freaked me out. My insides lurched. Meeting his parents was big deal, a sign our relationship was taking a more serious turn. And although I'd accepted my fate, accepted the fact that I'd fallen in love with him, I wasn't ready to meet them.

Then I realized they must have planned to attend the match long before Mikel met me. They were his parents, after all, and the World Cup was a big deal. I relaxed. It was just a friendly introduction and nothing more.

We arrived in Madrid at sundown. Mikel had reserved a hotel in the suburbs. I was surprised by his choice, expecting to stay in the old city, and I grimaced at the outside of it, the building an ugly, ten-story brick box.

But the interior was anything but ugly. The lobby was stunning. There were high ceilings painted with old-world murals of buxomly women and naked cherubs dancing in a flowery garden, opulent crystal chandeliers descending dramatically from the rafters, and nineteenth century art nouveau furniture placed cozily on shiny marble floors.

An attractive front desk clerk efficiently checked us in. She smiled flirtatiously at Mikel and eyed me warily. A solicitous bellman showed us to our room, which was a suite on the top floor with views of the enormous Santiago Bernabéu soccer stadium a few blocks away and the old city in the distance.

Like the lobby, the suite was also decorated in the old-world style. There were ceiling murals and crystal chandeliers in the living room and one in a dining room, which hung over a large mahogany table. The bedroom was fitted with a customized, king-size poster bed, which Mikel immediately stretched out on, grinning crookedly, his dazzling brown eyes sparkling mischievously.

He looked delectable. I loved the idea of playing house with him in the massive suite for the next five days, just me and Mikel. He opened his arms for me and I crawled on top of him, eager to taste him again, eager to love him. He pulled me against his chest and tenderly kissed the top of my head. I melted in his embrace, my favorite place in the world.

"You 'appy, cariño?" he murmured.

"Sí, mi amor, very."

"Me, also," he sighed. He held me like that for a while, a burgeoning erection expanding promisingly beneath his jeans.

It drove me crazy, demanding my attention. I slithered down to his cock, quickly released it and greedily engulfed it into my mouth, focusing on his sweet spot, the crease between the crown and the shaft. I stroked and sucked until he was moaning and bucking with pleasure.

I loved his response, loved his engorged, succulent cock throbbing in my mouth. When he exploded, he growled my name, a low, husky animalistic hum that sent shivers up my spine. Then he pretended to fall asleep, only this time I didn't fall for it. When he was ready to go again, it was a wild ride.

We flipped back and forth, me on top, him on top and back again until I couldn't take it any longer. My pussy sizzled and clit ached. I grinded on his slippery cock and bobbed on his hard flesh, faster and faster, the orgasm igniting quickly, burning hot and raw and leaving me shuddering in its wake.

Arrested

We didn't bother with dinner that night and fell right to sleep. When I woke the next morning, Mikel was spooning against me, an arm draped over my belly and nose burrowed in the nape of my neck. I sighed contentedly, flushed with the most delicious feeling. Waking up next to him was much better than a perfect rose.

Love had arrived unbidden and unexpectedly, a powerful paradox I couldn't control or neglect. It scared yet invigorated me, and I understood instinctively there was nothing I could do but accept it and nurture it and hope it was true. Once it had snagged me, there was no going back.

Yet as I lay against his heated flesh and inhaled his delicious Mikel scent, I couldn't help worrying, our future uncertain. Then he woke and kissed me hard and the rhythm of life began again. Carried along by its unique beat, I assured myself there was nothing to fear, certain love would conquer all.

There was no time to make love. Mikel was running late and rushed to soccer practice, which lasted until one o'clock every day.

The training was intensive, players from the various Spanish clubs vying for an all-important spot on the World Cup team. While he trained, I spent the mornings wandering around Madrid photographing palaces, basilicas, markets and street performers, the old city steeped in history.

It was a magical time. Excitement and hot anticipation gripped me constantly, my stomach in perpetual flux. We fucked a lot, and during the hours between siesta and late night partying, Mikel played tour guide, wanting me to experience it all, from flamenco dancing to tapas and to modern Spanish art.

On the third day, protesters packed the old city's streets from Plaza Major to Plaza Puerta del Sol. The mood was somber and defiant. I merrily snapped pictures of faces and signs, darting from one perch to another searching for the best shots.

I'd been to rallies before with my father, but they were small gatherings compared to the mass of people who turned out that day. The narrow streets were filled from end to end. It was impossible to portray the sheer volume of humanity from the ground, so I conned my way onto the balcony of a third-floor flat in Plaza Mayor and documented the action from up there.

Everything was peaceful until a gang of young men carrying bats and spray paint tore through the square. They smashed windows and defaced seventeenth century buildings. The anarchy was newsworthy, and I snapped shot after shot. When the vandals turned a corner and passed out of view, I raced back to ground level and chased them down. Riot police swarmed to the scene, batons drawn.

In the zone, the world stopped again. A hooligan with a bat wildly swung it at two helmeted officers. I held my breath. A policeman hit one of them on the back with a baton, forcing him to the ground. A glint of pepper spray streaked through the air.

I captured the moments one by one until I was grabbed from behind and two cops roughly dragged me away. Before I knew what was happening, I was locked in a paddy wagon with a dozen young delinquents, clutching the camera and wondering why *I* was being arrested.

~~~~~~✝~~~~~~

I was taken to the central police station at Plaza Puerta del Sol. It was located in a rundown, eighteenth century red-brick building. The cops had rounded up a lot of people, including old men and women, the six large jail cells aligned against the far wall already teeming with protesters. As I sat quietly on a bench waiting for a multilingual officer, I wondered what they could have possibly done to warrant arrest.

When a policeman finally got around to interviewing me, I explained my situation but to no avail. I didn't have identification, carrying only my camera, cellphone and a few euros in my pocket. He immediately confiscated the camera. It pissed me off, worried he might see Mikel's sailboat photo, and then he reached for the phone.

"No, please, can I call someone first?" I pleaded.

We were interrupted by more protesters. They complained loudly and scuffled with the guards. The cop muttered something under his breath, lips pursed. But he nodded his assent, and I quickly called Mikel and left him a message, meekly handing over the phone when I was done.

He locked me in one of the overcrowded cells. Since Mikel was at practice and wouldn't get my message for several hours, I squeezed onto a wooden bench between two old men and bided my time.

Time moved slowly. I wasn't afraid. On the contrary, it was exciting. I wished I had my camera to document it all. Angry faces, soulful hugs and encouraging smiles. It was all there, the trials and tribulations of the dissenter. Then Mikel finally arrived and the mood in the building immediately shifted.

I heard him before I saw him. He stormed through the place like a tornado, pushing aside anyone who stood in his way. His normally cheerful voice boomed angrily, the other prisoners gaped. I jumped off the bench and met him at the steel bars. He peered worriedly at me with his beautiful chocolate eyes and my heart clenched anxiously.

"Mi amor," he said softly.

My pulse raced at the mere sight of him. He was glorious, his floppy hair still damp from a shower and shirt half-tucked, as if he hadn't taken the time to finish dressing. I grasped the bars and he wrapped his hands around mine. His intoxicating scent rolled over me, overpowering those of my cellmates and tantalizing my senses. He kissed my knuckles tenderly, eyes turning dark. My gut knotted, thinking he was mad at me, but he spun around and marched through the station, shouting and cursing and glancing at the names on office doors.

Recognizing him as the great Mikel Garro, my fellow inmates cheered. He ignored them and disappeared into a room. A few minutes later, a policeman opened the jail cell and led me to the same door Mikel had gone through. And there he was, waiting for me with outstretched arms.

I flew into them and he embraced me warmly. Relief washed over me. My insides clenched. Mikel would take care of me.

"What is your concern with this matter, Mikel?"

Mikel held me protectively by the waist and glared at the man in the room with us. He'd found the person in charge, the Police Chief, and the man eyed me warily, his arms crossed over his chest and lips set in a grim line.

I didn't know whether they knew each other or everyone knew Mikel, but it didn't matter. Mikel was pissed and responded icily. "This very good friend, Aley Anson. She Americana and do no wrong. She photographer."

The Chief raked a hand through his gray hair, rubbed a thumb and forefinger along his thick mustache and looked me up and down. "This señorita, a photographer?" he asked sarcastically.

I didn't appreciate his tone and straightened my shoulders. "Yes, and you took my camera and I want it back," I snapped.

"You think you are in charge, young señorita?" he scoffed.

Mikel tightened his grip on my waist and gave me a warning look. "What you want and give her free?" he asked.

The Chief smirked, sank onto the chair behind his desk and gestured for us to sit.

"I need to see her passport," he said, "and if the señorita is really a photographer, I want to see her photos."

"My passport's back in Pamplona," I groaned, knowing if I had to produce it, I'd be there awhile.

"Where, cariño?" Mikel asked.

"It's in the nightstand drawer in your bedroom," I replied softly, peeking at the Chief.

The Chief raised a brow and grinned smugly. Mikel pulled out his phone and called Danel.

"My brother make copy and email me. It proof, sí?" Mikel offered.

The Chief toyed with his mustache and eyed me somberly. I couldn't believe he was wasting time on me when there were real deviants to harass, like the thugs who smashed store windows and defaced the beautiful buildings in his city. Then it hit me.

"I have pictures of the guys who destroyed property at Plaza Mayor," I said. He bolted upright, eyes flickering with interest. "I'm sure I caught some of their faces."

He was on his feet and out the door in a flash.

I was torn, not wanting the Chief to see the provocative Mikel photo, yet I didn't like violence. If there was one thing I'd learned from my father, it was that only peaceful protests worked. I admired the protesters but not the hooligans, who were definitely not at the Plaza to serve the cause.

Lips curling into a mischievous grin, Mikel grasped my hand and asked, "What you do, Aley?"

My heart swelled. There was so much I loved about him. His carefree spirit and joyful exuberance for life, and of course, he was gorgeous and sexy. He also appreciated my talent, having gone out of his way to promote the bull photo. I think he also admired my fearlessness, never trying to reign me in. And that day he also revealed his protective side, immediately coming to my aid and ferociously defending me.

"Nothing, Mikel. I was on a balcony at the Plaza Mayor shooting the rally from up there. These guys came out of nowhere and began smashing windows and spray painting buildings. I started photographing them, and then I went back to the street and shot the action from there. Then the cops showed up to arrest them, and I guess I got too close, because they arrested me, too."

"Aley, Aley, Aley," he sighed, shaking his head back and forth. "You nosy and you get trouble."

He wasn't chastising me. He was concerned about my well-being and kissed me affectionately on the forehead, murmuring "mi amor…"

The Chief barreled back into the office carrying my camera and cellphone. He ignored us and quickly loaded the pictures on his computer. Fortunately, his software program sorted the photos by days and he only reviewed the ones from the protest, taking his time and muttering "hmm" and "interesante" as he clicked through them. When he was finished, he leaned back in the chair and regarded me appreciatively.

"I believe you, señorita," he said. "I will copy these for our records, and when I see your passport, you may go."

"I say she very good," Mikel declared. He smiled broadly, looking pleased with himself. My heart sang, the flux in my stomach churning into a tidal wave.

Mikel Garro was a force of nature and impossible to resist. And he really did love me.

I was sure I would have eventually gotten out of the mess on my own. But the fact that he loved me enough to spring me from jail meant a lot to me, reinforcing our commitment to each other and strengthening our bond.

We waited a half-hour for Danel's email. I glowed happily as Mikel cheerfully signed autographs, starting with the jailed protesters and then the cops. "Buena suerta, Buena suerta!" they cheered. Even the Chief wanted one, and then he let me go.

Mikel grasped my hand. The streets were still filled with protesters and his fans immediately recognized him. We raced to the car. As we drove away he squeezed my thigh affectionately.

"Now you jail chicken," he teased.

I burst into laughter, charmed as always by his tendency to confuse words, the mixed-up reference his best one so far. When I could speak, I politely corrected him.

"Jail bird," I said, kissing him on the cheek.

"Sí, jail bird," he repeated. His sexy brown eyes twinkled and my stomach lurched. The love I felt for him was sometimes almost too much to bear.

It was late afternoon when we got back to the hotel. We ordered big steaks and fries from room service and ate off the intricately carved coffee table, stretching out on the Moroccan rug beneath it. We'd missed the siesta, but there was always time for lovemaking. After we'd cleaned our plates, he pulled me onto the sofa and set me on his lap.

Eyes soft and sensuous, he tenderly cupped my face, kissed me lightly and murmured, "You catch my 'eart, Aley."

He'd said the same thing to me the day we first met. My heart sang, realizing he'd fallen in love with me then. It was love at first sight for him, too.

"I'm so happy I met you, Mikel. I love you."

We desperately grappled to remove shirts and shoes and underwear, fucking on the couch. Afterward, he held me close, rhythmically stroking my hair as we lay entwined in each other's arms and I drifted to sleep.

"You will leave me," he sighed.

His soft lips brushed against my cheek, his words barely registering. It was his use of the future tense that caught my attention, and I burrowed my head in his throat and sluggishly muttered, "What?"

"You will leave me, cariño."

This time I clearly heard him. I eyed him nervously. "What do you mean?"

"You talent, mi amor. You go make picture of world."

He was worried about me leaving him. I swallowed hard, torn between him and my dream. "No, I mean yes, I mean no," I stammered. "What I mean, Mikel, is I'll go away, but I'll come back. I'll go to Barcelona next week, stay one night and then I'll come back. I want to go to France next, but I'll be gone only a couple of days and then I'll come back. I will *always* come back, mi amor."

Mi amor. He was my love, my first love, and I meant what I said. I was young, fearless and determined. There had to be a way to have both.

Searching for reassurance, he gazed deeply into my eyes. I smiled brightly and kissed him passionately, expressing all my love in that kiss. His eyes turned soft and warm again. It was all I needed. I was sure if he loved me as much as I loved him, we would work it out.

~~~~~~†~~~~~~

Later, there was a party at his coach's house. He dragged me off the couch and into the shower with him. This time he wasn't concerned about the clock. He leisurely washed my hair and the rest of me. We were late for the party.

We weren't the only ones. The mañana way of life guaranteed no one was ruled by a time clock. We arrived at eleven o'clock and the place was packed with Mikel's teammates and their wives, girlfriends, family and friends. I recognized a few of them from the night we'd first met at his house. They greeted me enthusiastically, like I was part of the clan. I was kissed on each cheek at least fifty times before Mikel pulled me away to talk to his coach.

Mikel's World Cup coach was a handsome widower in his fifties. He was fit and muscular, gray wisps of hair streaking his temples, and he lived in a stunning apartment in Madrid's Bourbon area at the gateway to the city.

He grasped my hand and eyed me affectionately, like a daughter. "Young señorita, you are as lovely as Mikel described."

"Thank you, Señor Puma," I replied, impressed by his impeccable English.

"You are brave, too. Mikel showed me the bull video. I wish all my boys had your courage."

I smiled to myself. At first I was embarrassed by the YouTube video, thinking it would overshadow my photography skills. Yet it seemed to give me street cred among Mikel's friends, and I had a change of heart.

"She jail bird, also," Mikel quipped. He gave me one of his playful, crooked grins and relayed the story of my arrest, embellishing the facts to make me look like a hero. Rolling my eyes, I nudged him with an elbow and amended the story. His coach laughed and Mikel protested half-heartedly.

Danel and Carlos showed up unexpectedly a couple hours later. Danel beamed with news about the sailboat photo, but he wouldn't reveal it at the party. We quickly said our goodbyes and headed to a restaurant nearby. As we gathered in the lounge, my pulse raced with anticipation. He ordered a bottle of champagne and toasted to our good fortune. Then he excitedly disclosed the plan. Although I didn't know it at the time, the idea would be the genesis of my ascent to fame and wealth.

As manager of Mikel's brand and company, Danel wanted to purchase the photo and use it for both charitable and commercial purposes. Mikel had agreed to be an ambassador for the United Nations World Hunger program six months before, a fact he'd omitted about himself. My heart fluttered. It was just like him, always modest about his accomplishments, his kind and generous spirit endearing.

As a result, Danel had been working with the U.N. on a campaign to raise awareness and increase donations. Nothing resonated until he saw Mikel's sailboat picture. While Mikel and I were in Madrid, he and U.N. representatives had spent many hours creating a campaign using the photo, which Danel said was sure to set the world on fire.

Eyes gleaming impishly, he pulled out an oversized manila

envelope from his briefcase and teasingly caressed it with his fingers. Mikel lightheartedly scolded him to get on with it, and Danel presented an eleven-by-fourteen-inch poster of the photo with words in English that stated "Let the Sun Set on World Hunger."

The idea was brilliant in its simplicity. The sensual yet poignant silhouette of Mikel combined with the heartfelt sentiment stirred me. I admired Danel's business acumen, thinking he was a star in his own right.

He explained that people who donated one hundred dollars or more to the World Hunger program would receive a sixteen-by-twenty-inch poster and a t-shirt, compliments of Mikel Enterprises. Plus, Mikel's company would donate an additional twenty-five percent for each individual poster and t-shirt purchased by fans at retail price.

"It fantástico!" Mikel exclaimed. He jumped up and hugged his brother enthusiastically.

"There more," Danel said, eyeing me hopefully. "I need buy photo rights. You will sell, sí, Aley?"

I hadn't expected the picture to see daylight, let alone be used in a global advertisement. Of course I would sell it to him. He handed me a contract written in English, which gave me a ten percent royalty for every sale.

Trusting Danel completely, I eagerly signed it, deliriously happy with the turn of events. We celebrated with another bottle of champagne at dinner, and when Mikel and I returned to the hotel, both a little drunk on champagne and life, we made slow and passionate love, the world our oyster.

World Cup Mania

Mikel's parents arrived the next day after the siesta and checked into the hotel. It was the eve of Spain's World Cup qualifier against Germany and excitement filled the air, yesterday's gripes forgotten and the country unified behind their team.

Satordi and Ysenia Garro were delightful. Similar to the Zabaletas, they immediately treated me like one of their own. Ysenia, Mikel's mother, was a lot like him. Beautiful with chocolate eyes and long lashes, she was gregarious and playful. She doted on her sons from the moment she arrived, bringing fresh oranges and olives from Spain's Andalusia region and complimenting them for every little thing they said or did.

Satordi, his father, was average-looking like Danel. Crooked teeth, receding hairline, he was reserved and quiet, probably from a lifetime of being overshadowed by his wife and sons. Yet he took it all in stride, eyes gleaming with obvious pride.

To avoid Mikel's legions of fans, we ate dinner in a private dining room in the hotel restaurant. Ysenia entertained us with amusing stories about Mikel and Danel as children. The wine and laughter flowed.

"Danel, 'e push Mikel to climb big tree in plaza," Ysenia said. "Mikel no can climb down and cry and cry. 'e 7 year old. Many policía come and carry ladder. Big commotion."

"Mama," Mikel groaned, pretending to be mortified but kissing her cheek affectionately.

My heart clenched, the adoration he had for his mother sweet and endearing. Ysenia graciously included Carlos and me in the conversation, too, asking us questions about our childhoods, and the evening passed quickly, even though the dinner lasted four hours and it took another half-hour to say our goodnights.

When Mikel and I were finally alone again, I wrapped my arms around his neck and rubbed against him. "I like your parents," I said.

He gently removed my arms and stepped back. Never expecting him to rebuff my advances, I must have looked confused and hurt, because he drew me close and planted a tender kiss on my forehead. "We not make love tonight, cariño. I must keep strength for match."

I stifled a giggle, certain the "no sex before competing" edict was a myth. Yet, I'd do anything to support his dream, as he'd done for me.

From the moment Mikel woke on game day, he was nervous and preoccupied. There was nothing I could do to distract him. He ordered breakfast for everyone from room service. When his parents showed up early, Ysenia dressed stylishly in a red shirt and yellow neckerchief and Satordi donning a Garro jersey and grinning like a kid, it was a relief.

Danel and Carlos appeared soon after, grinning conspiratorially. They brought several newspapers with them and triumphantly presented one to each of us. Danel had been busy. There were already full-page color advertisements for the Hunger promotion placed in Madrid's El Pais, El Mundo and ABC newspapers as well as the Marca and Diario, which featured sports.

I was ecstatic. My beautiful shot of Mikel was being seen across the country and on World Cup qualifier day, no less. I was so excited I almost didn't notice the small picture in El Pais opposite the Hunger photo. It was one of my photos from the protest, a dramatic shot of a hooligan smashing a café window.

Pulse racing, I scurried to my laptop and checked my website. El Pais had purchased it the previous night. I also noticed a shop in Pamplona had purchased six pictures of the old town I'd taken during Los Sanfermines, probably to make postcards. Slowly but surely my dream was coming true, and the cherry on top was I had more money in my pocket than the day I'd arrived in Spain.

Mikel didn't comment and I didn't say anything. It was his day and my turn to support him. While we hung around the suite, Ysenia kept the mood lively. She lovingly praised Danel for his business acumen. When she realized I didn't have red-and-yellow soccer apparel, she ordered Danel to get me something. He rushed out and brought back a tank top with Garro lettering embroidered on the back, scolding Mikel for not doing it himself.

Mikel only shrugged. My belly knotted. I missed his constant affection. I ached for him to hold my hand and stroke my hair. Thankfully, Ysenia coaxed him from the room for a quick lunch in the private dining room, which at least gave us all a change of scenery.

There was no siesta afterward. The tension built. When he finally left for the stadium, I breathed easier. We all breathed easier. An hour later, we walked to the stadium in lock step with the other soccer fans making the same trek. The mood was electric.

Ysenia guided me through the crowd to our seats. The stadium quickly filled to capacity and pulsed with chants and cheers and a sea of national flags. Awestruck, I photographed the wave of red and yellow Spanish fans at one end of the field and the German faithful stuck in the worst seats of the house in the far corner. They were dressed in their national green color and looked conspicuous among

Spain's primary hues, a colorful contrast beneath a darkening sky.

I snapped photos of Satordi and Ysenia together, Danel and Carlos together, and then the four of them. When Danel insisted I be in a picture, too, I hesitantly handed my camera to him, my prized possession. It was carelessly handed from one person to another to a lady several rows below us. I held my breath. My stomach knotted. She fiddled with it for a few seconds, looking for the shutter button. She took a few shots of the five of us and the camera was carelessly handed from one person to another back up to me. When it was finally in my possession again, I exhaled a thankful breath. Then the players took the field and the crowd jumped to their feet, roaring their support.

I zoomed in on Mikel. He stood in a line with his teammates, mouthing words to the national anthem, his usual cheerful expression now serious and determined. My heart hammered anxiously, wanting him to do well and come back to me smiling and happy. For the next two hours I was a nervous mess.

I wasn't the only one. Ysenia gripped my hand tightly and gasped each time Mikel was tripped to the ground or took a goal shot. The normally quiet Satordi was on his feet most of the match, cursing his approval or displeasure depending on the call.

I put the camera back in its case and set it under my seat. I didn't want to miss a second of action, my eyes fixed on Mikel. He was incredibly fast, his footwork amazing. In the twenty-third minute, he stole the ball, raced down the field and passed it to a teammate, who kicked it in to score the first goal. The fans went wild and there was a collective sigh of relief, a win within the Spanish team's grasp.

When the Germans scored in the forty-second minute, the volume in the stadium decreased tenfold. But not for long. Mikel stole another ball and dashed toward the goal. Cheers erupted. He took a shot. The ball ripped toward the goal, right on target, but it was tipped by the goalie and soared over the net. The crowd roared a collective groan.

During halftime, I raved about Mikel. He was not only talented but the star of the team. Ysenia nodded her agreement and hugged me affectionately. A warm glow settled in my gut, happy Mikel had included me and grateful I was with his family and not alone at the hotel watching the match.

"Aley, look!" Smiling mischievously, Danel nudged me and nodded at two young women seated directly in front of us. They huddled together, giggling and eyeing a smartphone. I heard them say Mikel's name and the word the word "caliente," which was one Spanish word I understood. I peeked over their shoulders and smiled back at Danel. They were looking at the Mikel poster.

It was Danel's turn to hug me. "You rich," he said.

He revealed there were already six thousand orders for posters and t-shirts and 250,000 euros donated to the U.N. since the morning papers came out. Speechless, I calculated the royalties in my head. Although I wasn't rich yet, I'd made almost thirteen thousand euros in less than twelve hours, and the ad hadn't even been published in North and South America yet.

While I absorbed the numbers, his phone rang. He quickly answered it and held up an index finger to my face. "Un momento," he said into the phone. Turning his attention back to me, he clutched my hand. "It reporter from El Mundo. She want interview you for 'unger photo at ten o'clock tomorrow. It good, sí Aley?"

Still speechless, I nodded my assent. The players took the field for the second half and I quickly forgot about the money and the interview. Mikel ran back and forth across the pitch. The teams traded possession. Both defenses were strong and the minutes passed slowly, everyone on edge, the suspense excruciating.

In the eighty-seventh minute, Mikel moved toward the goal with the ball, darting from left to right. A German defender kept up with him step for step. Mikel faked a pass and skirted around him, leaving him in the dust. He took a shot, angling the ball to the corner, and it whizzed past the goalie and into the net.

Eighty thousand fans went wild. The decibel level was so high the stadium vibrated. Mikel's team members jumped onto his back and hugged him. He ran along the sideline and raised his hands victoriously. When he made his way to my side of the stadium, he grinned crookedly. *At me.* My heart skipped a beat.

Six minutes later the game was over. The collective euphoria washed over me and the tension drained from my body, replaced by a constant flux churning my insides. I would be in Mikel's arms again soon. He would be back to normal, *happy.* I couldn't wait.

The five of us waited for him outside the locker room. Ysenia wiped happy tears from her cheeks and Satordi grinned from ear to ear. When Mikel emerged forty-five minutes later, they wrapped their arms around him and embraced him for a long time. When he turned to me, his brilliant brown eyes twinkled mischievously. He grabbed me by the waist and joyously swung me in the air, kissing me hard before setting me back on my feet.

My heart swelled with love and pride. "You were fantástico, mi amor," I said.

He grinned boyishly and quipped, "The German, 'e fool by my move."

His constant butchering of the English language made me laugh. I hugged him hard around the waist. He winced and I quickly stepped back, eyeing him worriedly.

"It good, mi amor. No worry," he said, lightly kissing my forehead.

I was worried, but he brushed it off. He wrapped one arm around me and the other around his mother and casually escorted us out of the stadium through the player's entrance.

Just like the night before, it took a half-hour to say goodbye to his family. After making arrangements to meet for a late breakfast the next day, Satordi and Ysenia left for the hotel and Danel and Carlos took off to party with friends in old Madrid.

I wanted to go back to the hotel, too, but Mikel drove us to a teammate's house outside the city. Although the players were normally rivals, clashing every week during the regular soccer season, they set aside their animosity for World Cup competitions, and it was customary to celebrate big wins together at a place where fans couldn't mob them.

This time they congregated at a house owned by a guy from the Real Madrid club. It wasn't just a house, though. It was an opulent mansion with eight bedrooms, a marbled-floor ballroom, an ornate grand staircase and a luxurious swimming pool overlooking a golf course. A valet parked the car and a maid escorted us to the ballroom, where we sat at a long mahogany table with twenty other early arrivals gorging on shrimp, lobster and filet mignon.

The mood was raucous, the women beautiful. Mikel was the center of attention, his last-minute goal making him the most popular and envied man in the room. He took it all in stride, modestly complimenting the other players, and as the first arrivals finished their meal, they left to party at the pool and were replaced by latecomers.

Mikel and I didn't go to the pool right away. Instead, he pulled me into a dark corner in the foyer beneath the staircase and drew me into his arms.

"I miss you, mi amor," he murmured. His eyes blazed lustily. He cupped my face, lips finding mine, tongue demanding, hands roaming over my ass and up to my breasts.

Missing his touch and his Mikel scent, I responded hungrily, grinding against his growing erection. Every part of me ignited with desire, the last twenty-four hours without him leaving me more wanton than ever.

"I no wait. Come with me," he said.

He nuzzled his nose in the crook of my neck and led me to the staircase. We paused at the bottom step, watching another couple descend. Their hair was mussed up and clothes disheveled. They acknowledge us with a grin and a nod. The man patted her behind as they walked away.

Eyes gleaming wickedly, Mikel grabbed my hand. I smiled knowingly. There were eight bedrooms in the mansion and my pussy ached for him.

We started up the stairs. He groped my butt and kissed my neck. We almost made it to the top when a voice boomed from behind us.

"There you are, Garro!"

Mikel groaned and turned around. He guided me back to the bottom of the staircase and grudgingly greeted the man.

"Hola, Ernesto."

Ernesto was our host. He embraced a voluptuous woman in each arm, his thin lips set in a smug line.

"Hot babe," he smirked, nodding at me, his grin salacious and accent British.

Mikel grinned and pulled me close. "This Aley Anson. She my girlfriend."

"Right, *girlfriend*," Ernesto replied sarcastically, oozing arrogance.

I instinctively didn't like him. Not only was he unattractive, his nose crooked, face flat and eyes squinty, I was certain the only reason the ladies were with him was due to his wealth and status as an elite soccer player.

"Tell Danel I want to talk to him about becoming my manager. The Hunger poster is brilliant. You'll make a fortune," he said.

Mikel kissed my cheek and proudly replied, "Aley take photo."

Ernesto looked surprised. The cocky smirk crossed his face again. "I should hire you to do the same for me," he snorted.

He was mocking me, taunting me, insinuating he wanted me to take a photo of him naked, too. The thought disgusted me. Ernesto could never come close to Mikel's beauty and grace. I had the urge to punch him in the face.

"You be lucky, but she for me," Mikel laughed. He couldn't care less about Ernesto and swept me off my feet. He effortlessly carried me up the stairs, smiling and shouting something over his shoulder in Spanish. When we reached the landing, he carted me down the hall past closed bedroom doors until he found one that was open.

He playfully tossed me onto the bed and I quickly forgot about Ernesto, gawking as Mikel turned on a light, locked the door and stripped. An excited shudder rolled through me. He was as glorious as ever, cock stiff and fat, body toned and rippling with muscles.

Then I noticed the bruises. There was a nasty one on his abdomen and several on his thighs. I shot up and reached for him, kissing the one on his belly.

"Does it hurt bad?" I asked, peeking up at him.

"It normal, cariño. I good."

I gently rubbed my nose on the contusion, feathered kisses on it and moved to his cock, licking the tip and stroking the sensitive area below the crown with my thumb and forefinger. He inhaled sharply, closed his eyes and gently grasped my head. Loving his response, loving the taste of him, my clit instantly plumped and pulsed.

I took it slow, submerging his shaft deep into my mouth. I sucked hard, drawing back to lavishly lick a drop of come from the slit and returning to the sensitive crease and leisurely massaging it. The closer he came to orgasm, the tighter he gripped my head. He was almost there when someone pounded on the door.

I pulled away, startled. Mikel groaned with frustration. He shouted at the door and a man on the other side shouted back. They yelled back and forth in Spanish and I burst out laughing. With the euphoria over the win, a host of beautiful women offering themselves for the taking and eight rooms available for fucking, the testosterone level in the house was off the charts. Plus, if the other players had avoided sex like Mikel had done the night before the match, they were ready to make up for it, as was Mikel with me.

I reached for his cock, still giggling and eager to finish the job. He narrowed his eyes, pushed me onto my back and pounced. He hastily wriggled my jeans and panties down to my ankles, tugged off my sandals and stripped me below the waist. I worked on my top half and hurriedly peeled off the tee, kissing the Garro lettering on the back of it before dramatically lobbing it and my bra toward the clothes piled at the end of the bed.

Smiling his dazzling smile, eyes twinkling devilishly behind thick long lashes, he dove between my legs and immediately found the perfect spot, titillating my wet flesh with extravagant licks, his velvety tongue plunging inside of me for a taste and moving back to my clit.

Heat waves radiated in my deepest core. I leaned on my forearms and watched his broad shoulders flex and ripple. His floppy hair tickled the inside of my thighs. I savored every sensation and every hot lick, riding the waves for all they were worth, surging and swelling, building and cresting. I wanted to ride them forever, holding on to them for as long as I could. When there was no other choice, I let go, the surf breaking and crashing, an intense orgasm roaring through me.

Embracing the sweet ecstasy, I collapsed onto my back. He slithered on top of me, nuzzled his nose in my neck and whispered, "You like, sí."

I managed to nod and felt his smile on my skin. He rolled me over, knelt between my legs and skimmed his lips up my spine, hands grazing the contours of my breasts and moving beneath me, pulling me up so I was on my knees with my ass in the air.

Leaning on my forearms, I looked over my shoulder. His cock was fat and throbbing. My pussy convulsed, still wet and ready. He gripped my hips and slowly plunged into me. Groaning and grunting, he fucked me hard and fast and climaxed quickly. With a heavy sigh of pleasure he dropped onto the bed and drew me into his arms. *My favorite place in the world.*

We both dozed. For how long I didn't know, trapped in a time warp all our own, a rhythm all our own. I tried to keep my eyes open, thinking it would be rude to hang out there too long, but my body wouldn't cooperate. Then shouting in the hall jarred us awake, and Mikel grudgingly crawled from bed, stiff and wincing with pain.

I went to him and traced my fingers across the bruise on his belly. It had swelled and turned blacker. Frowning, I eyed him worriedly. Before I could say anything, he smiled his adorable crooked smile and tenderly kissed me, taking his time and slipping his tongue into my mouth.

I melted in his arms. Words weren't necessary. He was sore, but it was part of the game. The commotion continued and we dressed groggily. When he opened the door, all hell broke loose.

Three guys lunged toward the bedroom. They jockeyed for position, shoving each other from the doorway before any one of them could enter. Their drunken girlfriends stood to the side and egged them on. The yelling grew louder and the wrestling turned into punching.

Mikel grabbed my hand, tugged me forward and hustled me downstairs. "They stupid drunk. They not my team," he grumbled.

We headed outside, where the party was also out of control, a face-off between rival players from different Spanish leagues and their friends. Most were drunk and half-naked, the guys stripped down to their jeans and the women clad in skimpy bikinis or topless. Shouting insults, they brawled by the pool, trying to push each other into it. I wondered what had set them off.

Glowering, Mikel gripped my hand tighter and turned to go. Ernesto dashed over to us and blocked our exit, smirking, the women still hanging on each arm.

"Leaving, Garro? The fun's just beginning." Seemingly enjoying the mayhem, he sloppily kissed one of the ladies on the crest of her breast.

"Yes, we go. Thank you for party," Mikel replied politely.

We tried to skirt around him, but Ernesto didn't move. Mikel stepped back and straightened his shoulders, eyeing him warily.

"My girls want to know why you don't like Spanish girls," Ernesto taunted.

For whatever reason, Ernesto was intent on picking a fight. This time I tugged on Mikel's hand and barreled forward, bumping into one of the women as we passed. She called me "puta." I knew what the word meant from sitting in jail. *Bitch.* I kept walking, hoping to escape as soon as possible.

Thankfully, Mikel didn't take the bait, and we hurried inside the house and headed for the front door.

"Fuck, Garro, you on a leash?" Ernesto goaded.

His booming voice carried into the room. Mikel stopped and

spun around, accidentally knocking a fishbowl off a plant stand. It shattered into pieces, colorful condom foils scattering everywhere. Distracted, Mikel's expression turned from angry to surprised.

I was surprised, too. A fleeting image of the cookie jar on the kitchen counter at his house flashed through my mind, thinking there must be a lot of fucking going on with these soccer players. But at least they were playing it safe, and I grabbed Mikel's elbow and pleaded with him to go.

"It's not worth it, Mikel. You're not like him," I said.

Visibly relaxing, he draped an arm over my shoulder and guided me to the car, not looking back.

We returned to the hotel after midnight. I immediately drew him a hot bath, adding bubbles from the upscale toiletry collection. He sank slowly into it and let out a long sigh, gazing at me expectantly. "You come, cariño?"

He gestured for me to join him and my pussy immediately jumped to attention. I sat on the toilet and hurriedly removed my sandals and ripped off the tank top, my pulse racing as it always did when his luscious eyes turned seductive and mischievous.

"You do naked dance, mi amor?" he asked.

"Striptease," I corrected, laughing.

He flicked bubbles at me and grinned boyishly. "You do striptease?"

The suggestion made me hotter. I slowly slid the jeans over my behind, turned away from him and bent over, giving him a good, long look at my ass in the skimpy thong.

"Fantástico," he murmured.

Fluffing my hair so it fell wildly around my face, I spun around to face him and traced my fingers along the band of the thong. When I slipped them inside and stroked my clit, his eyes practically bugged out of their sockets. Smiling, I licked my lips seductively. My pussy dripped and plumped and pulsed. My first striptease turned me on as much as it did him, and if I'd wanted, I could have made myself come in an instant.

Instead, I moaned softly, deliberately. I moved my hands up to my tits and skimmed the lacy fabric on the bra. I unhooked it and held it close to my chest, swaying my hips suggestively before flinging it at him.

He snatched it out of the air, his coordination perfect just like him. The bubbles swirled around his rib cage. He gazed hungrily at me with his beautiful chocolate eyes. He was enjoying himself and so was I.

Making a show of it, I shimmied my tits in his face. When he reached for them, I backed away.

"Mi amor, come to me," he appealed.

It was impossible not to want him, love him, and I quickly peeled off the thong and slid into the tub, straddling him. Grasping the nape of my neck, he gently drew me in for a kiss, tongue passionate, loving and intense, a slow sultry dance. I drowned in that kiss, swept under by a—

The lock clicked. Baba was back. I silently cursed him, wanting to remain in the past, wanting to stay with Mikel. I felt him looming over me, sensed the stark light streaming from the ceiling and smelled cigarette smoke. I remained immobile and kept my eyes closed, knowing what would happen next.

He nudged me with a foot. When I didn't move, he kicked my belly. I didn't make a sound, a part of me still defiant. He muttered something in Arabic and extinguished the cigarette on my hip.

As the cherry burned my flesh, it took all my willpower not to scream. He grabbed my ankle, turned me over and spread my legs. It was quiet for a while. Then the panting started and grew raspy and more erratic. The hazy image of our last encounter flashed through my mind. I knew what he was doing.

I wanted to fight back. Call him a hypocrite and a sadist. How dare he judge me when he sought pleasure from my bruised and battered naked body, jerking off like a teenager? And then there was a long, drawn out sigh and a flick of a lighter. Squeezing my eyes tightly, I waited for him to burn me again.

It seemed to take him forever to finish the cigarette. He snuffed it out on the sensitive crease between my thigh and genitals. I gasped sharply, unable to control the reflex. Rolling onto my side, I prayed he would leave.

He hovered above me for a moment, mumbling a few words. I held my breath. My skin crawled with fear. He kicked my backside, cursing, and then left, taking the lightbulb with him. I burst into tears, certain he'd be back seeking more pleasure and exacting his sadistic revenge until I was dead.

My only hope was he'd bury me in the desert where no one could find me. I didn't want my parents to see me like that. Tortured and mutilated. It would kill them, yet so would vanishing from the face of the earth.

Either way, it was the worst punishment Baba could enact. They didn't deserve such horrible pain, and I wept until I drifted into a restless, tormented sleep.

Forsaken

I woke shivering and feverish. My body ached all over, but I'd grown used to it by then. I'd grown used to a lot by then, stuck in a time warp, the darkness becoming a safe cocoon, a welcome black prism.

Colorless. Easy. No bright hues to distract me, no refracting light to shift and dance, and no highlights. I was suspended in nothingness. No beauty. No ugliness. There was only a gnawing hunger and thirst. My mouth turned into an arid wasteland, my lips cracked and bled, leaving a lingering iron taste on my parched tongue.

My only hope left was Momed. I was sure he was still looking for me, sure he wouldn't give up. He was the only man on a long list of them after Mikel who'd penetrated my defensive shield, the only person in Egypt who I was certain truly cared about me.

Yet if he didn't rescue me soon, I'd be dead. With nothing left but memories, my thoughts returned to the time in my life when I was happiest. Back to Mikel and his moist lips on mine. So moist. The taste of him, the smell of him and the passion.

~~~~~†~~~~~

We made love that night sloshing around in the bubbly bath. Afterward, he tenderly dried me off with a fluffy towel and dried the wet tips of my hair with a hair dryer, treating me like the most precious gem on earth.

The next morning, I was startled awake by pounding on the door. Mikel buried his nose in my throat, grumbling with displeasure. He kissed me softly and rolled out of bed. Groggy, I watched him slip on his jeans commando-style and grin crookedly as he left the room, closing the door behind him.

Glowing inside, I burrowed under the covers, hoping whoever was disturbing us would go away. I'd fallen hard for Mikel Garro, every fiber in my being craving his delicious touch, the last few weeks the best of my short life. Yet I couldn't give up my dream. I prayed for a way to have it and him, too. There was no going back.

He burst back into the bedroom smiling excitedly. "Aley, get up! El Mundo! They 'ere!"

I'd forgotten about the interview. I scrambled from bed, suddenly nervous. It was after ten o'clock and I was sure I looked a mess.

"You dress, mi amor. I talk and you make you more beautiful, sí?" He swept me into his arms and kissed me hard.

My heart swelled with love. I knew then he would support my dream no matter what. We'd find a way.

"Go, Aley, go!" He pointed me toward the bathroom and affectionately swatted my ass.

His excitement was infectious. He quickly put on a shirt, kissed me one more time and left me to get ready. Smiling, I hurriedly washed my face and brushed my teeth. I took my time with my hair and makeup, wanting to look beautiful for him and make him proud. And since it was the day after the big match and I was his girlfriend, I dressed in jeans and the Garro tank top.

Straightening my shoulders, I stepped confidently into the living room. Mikel came to me immediately, beaming with his usual exuberance. He kissed me lightly on the lips and grabbed my hand.

The gesture didn't go unnoticed by the reporter from El Mundo. She arched a perfectly-threaded brow, set her coffee on the table and rose gracefully from the sofa to greet me, insisting I call her by her first name, Pilar.

"Our readers want to know *everything* about the woman who took the Mikel Garro Hunger photo," she explained in excellent English.

A well-dressed woman in her forties with a stylish cropped haircut, Pilar was accompanied by a photographer, who lingered by the window, an expensive camera in his hand. Danel was there, too. He rose from a cushy chair, gave me a quick nod and took charge, saying we would start with pictures. The photographer had another assignment and was in a hurry.

Mikel retreated to the bedroom while the photographer set up. Not expecting to be photographed, I was glad I took the time to look presentable. The pictures took fifteen minutes. When Mikel returned, freshly shaven and smiling, he lit up the room like he always did. He plopped down onto the sofa next to me and casually draped an arm on the backrest.

Pilar gazed curiously at us. I was sure she was dying to know about me and Mikel, but she started with an innocuous question. "How did you become interested in photography?" she asked.

Since I hadn't prepared for the interview, I was grateful for the easy question.

"It was after a studio photographer came to school to take school pictures," I started. "I was in the first grade and thought it was cool. I asked him a million questions and he made me his assistant for the day. After that, my parents taught me how to use their 35mm camera. I could use it whenever I wanted as long as I paid for the film and pictures.

"It was an expensive hobby back then. I'd spend my allowance and any money I made from extra chores on it. Since it was so expensive, especially for a kid, I was really careful about the pictures I took. I guess it helped me develop an eye for a good shot."

"She good eye," Mikel quipped, squeezing my thigh affectionately.

"Thanks, Mikel," I chuckled. "Then, for my thirteenth birthday, they bought me my own camera. Mr. Mason, the man who owned the photo studio in my hometown, taught me how to develop the film in his darkroom.

"I loved doing that, especially the part when I'd dunk the contact sheet into the chemicals and the images would magically appear. Then digital cameras were invented and I went crazy. They're the best invention ever."

Mikel laughed and kissed the top of my head, smiling proudly. I'd already told him the story but not Danel, who leaned forward on the chair listening intently.

"So I experimented with every feature on the camera and took thousands of pictures of anything and everything. I won a couple contests and started saving money so I could travel. It's a big world and I want to photograph it all, so here I am."

"How old are you, Haley?" Pilar asked.

"Eighteen. I'll be nineteen in a few months."

"And you are here in Spain on your own?"

"Yes."

"Your parents let you go off on your own?"

She raised that eyebrow again, her tone tinged with disapproval. I couldn't have cared less. "Yes," I said proudly. "Since I already knew I wanted to be a photographer, there was no reason to get a regular job or go to college, so I might as well get started. My parents have always supported my dreams."

"I see..." she murmured. "It is different in Spain. Our children stay closer to home."

She paused to allow me to explain further, but I remained silent. I understood the cultural differences, but I was American and not the only American kid who had taken off on their own at eighteen. And I was perfectly capable of taking care of myself.

At least that was what I thought then.

When I didn't elaborate, she smiled politely and asked the next question. "Okay. Let's talk about the Hunger photo. How did it happen?"

I glanced at Mikel. His eyes twinkled with amusement. There was no way I'd tell Pilar the whole story, and I focused on the photo's elements instead.

"The sun was setting and the light perfect, so I snapped a few shots," I said.

"How did you get him to pose naked?" she asked.

I had to give her credit. She was fishing for juicy information about our relationship. I didn't know what to say, didn't know how much Mikel wanted me to reveal. Fortunately, Danel interrupted.

"She take bull photo, too," he said.

"It my favorite," Mikel piped in.

Pilar had no choice and shifted the questions to the bull photo. Then she asked about my future plans.

"I'm going to Barcelona to photograph the Sagrada Família church."

"You are staying in Spain? In Pamplona?"

"Yes." I peeked at Mikel from the corner of an eye. He looked happy. I was, too, certain he'd support my dream.

Then Pilar couldn't help herself and asked the question.

"What is your relationship with the great Mikel Garro?"

Danel interrupted again. This time his voice had an angry edge to it. They talked in Spanish and I looked to Mikel for help.

"Danel say interview you not me," he shrugged.

He kissed me sweetly and Pilar stopped mid-sentence. She glared irritably at us and Mikel chuckled. He wrapped me in his arms and said, "Aley my girlfriend, sí, mi amor?"

"Sí, mi amor…"

After the interview, we ate a late breakfast at the hotel restaurant with Mikel's parents, Danel and Carlos. As soon as Mikel entered the room, there was a collective gasp from the other patrons. Many stepped forward to congratulate him and ask for an autograph. He accommodated them with his usual modesty and charm. Then we said our goodbyes to his parents and drove back to Pamplona.

It was an enjoyable ride, just me and Mikel on the road with the top down on the Ferrari, whizzing past one picturesque town after another, the hot sun beating down on us. We talked about my trip to Barcelona and whether I should take the morning or afternoon train.

Besides the church, I also wanted to see a few of Gaudi's other works while I was in Barcelona. The earlier I left, the more time I'd have to explore and photograph. But if I took an earlier train, Mikel would be at practice. Danel would need to take me to the station. I wanted Mikel to send me off.

"You must take Ferrari. Then you go and come like you want," he said.

I thought he was teasing me. But his expression was serious and I exclaimed, "No way! I'd be worried the whole time something might happen to it!"

"It mend."

I loved how he mangled the English language, always choosing a word that didn't quite fit, yet finding one close enough that I understood his meaning. We bantered back and forth until we reached a compromise. I'd leave in the afternoon and take an evening train for the return. That way Mikel could drop me off and pick me up. The fact that he wanted to take care of me made my heart soar.

After returning to Pamplona, we went out to dinner and partied with his Osasuna teammates, who wanted to congratulate him on his World Cup performance. When we returned to the house, he made slow, passionate love to me as if it would be the last time we'd be together for a while. I couldn't help but think maybe my career had an upside, because if Mikel Garro made love to me like that every time I took off for a few days, I might leave more often.

When I woke the next morning, he'd left another yellow rose and smiley-face orange for me on his pillow. My flesh tingled with images of him. *His moist lips on my nipples. His tongue titillating my clit. His hard, juicy cock stretching me, and his gorgeous, warm chocolate eyes gazing lovingly into mine.*

I could still taste him, smell him and hear him murmuring in my ear. "I love you, te amo, I love you, Aley."

Suddenly, I didn't want to leave. Not even for a day. I missed him already. My mind, body and soul were completely coupled to his. But I needed to go. If I gave up my dream, I would stop being me. I would regret it. So I dragged myself from bed and packed my backpack. On the off chance I was arrested again, I stuck my passport in an inside pocket.

I ambled downstairs carrying my dirty clothes from the last five days, hoping Xenia had time to do my laundry before I left. I wanted to take the Garro top with me, planning to sleep in it and keep him close. A lump developed in my throat. Feeling ridiculous, I swallowed hard and reminded myself I'd be gone for one day. *Just one day.*

Xenia was at her station in the kitchen. She placed the usual sweet rolls, jam, cheese and coffee with frothy milk before me. She grabbed the clothes and took them to the laundry room, smiling warmly, as if pleased I was letting her take care of me. The usual pile of newspapers was stacked on the kitchen island. I flipped through El Mundo looking for the story about me, thinking it must not have been published because otherwise Danel would have marked it prominently.

But it was there on page twelve with a nice picture of me next to the Hunger photo. I didn't understand much of what was written. What I did understand was what I'd expected. A biography. Mention of the "toro foto." Mikel's name a couple of times. I set the paper aside and leisurely ate breakfast, certain Danel must be pleased by the free Hunger campaign publicity.

~~~~~~†~~~~~~

When Mikel returned, he found me at the computer in his office checking my bank account, which had grown to $173,260 since the Hunger merchandise went on sale two days ago. I was stunned, for a second wondering how the money got there. Then I remembered I'd given Danel my bank account information, but I didn't know he'd included a clause in the contract that provided for a daily direct deposit of my share of the royalties. I couldn't believe all that money was mine.

Excited, I rushed into Mikel's arms.

"I miss you, mi amor," he murmured in my ear, nipping at the lobe.

A delicious shiver raced up my spine and I forgot about the money. "I missed you, too."

"You pack?" he asked.

"Yes."

"You go two hour. I tire and need siesta."

His luminous eyes twinkled mischievously. I knew what he wanted. I wanted it, too, always hungry for him, my body in a state of constant sexual tension. He kissed me softly and grabbed my hand.

"Mikel!" Danel barreled into the room, eyed me coolly and pulled Mikel aside. They huddled together and spoke in hushed tones. Danel's eyes darted from me to Mikel. Mikel frowned and quickly became agitated, voice raised angrily.

I didn't know what they were saying, but it was obviously about me. I couldn't imagine what I might have done. Danel tried to talk over Mikel, which only made him madder, their exchange turning heated.

I'd never seen them argue, the brothers usually in sync about everything. My gut knotted anxiously.

"Estúpido!" Mikel yelled. He threw his hands in the air, marched over to me and pulled me into his arms, glaring irritably at Danel.

"What's the matter?" I asked.

Mikel kissed the top of my head reassuringly. "It nothing," he replied crossly.

"It not nothing," Danel retorted adamantly.

Mikel gave him a stern, warning look. Danel ignored it and growled, "You do not listen, hermano. It serious."

Whatever had happened to pit brother against brother made me nervous. I needed to know. "What's serious? Tell me," I demanded.

"It nothing," Mikel sighed.

He held me tighter and moved to leave, but I stood my ground, glowering.

"There bad talk of you interview," Danel stated. He glared at Mikel defiantly. "Many do not like Mikel with chica Americana."

"What?" I gasped.

"They stupid," Mikel said. "It no one business."

"You make business," Danel scoffed. "You say Aley you girlfriend. Aley say she stay in Pamplona for you."

"But, but, why does it matter? Don't the Spanish like Americans?" I asked.

"Americana okay, but Mikel, 'e España champion. Fan want Mikel Garro with España señorita."

"How do you know?" I asked.

"They say online. On El Mundo website."

"Everyone feels that way?"

"It fifty-fifty."

"Estúpido," Mikel sighed. "Come, Aley, I no worry."

I agreed with Mikel. The entire controversy was stupid, *manufactured*, and I was sure I knew who was behind it.

Ernesto.

I went with Mikel, grimacing at Danel, who suddenly couldn't look me in the eye, as if I was the enemy. I didn't understand. It pissed me off. Sure, he was Mikel's manager and probably thought he was looking after his best interests, but he should be supporting Mikel as a brother. Anyone with eyes could see how happy Mikel was with me, how happy we were together. It was almost as if he expected Mikel to dump me because of some misguided xenophobes.

Mikel took me to his bedroom and kissed me, his beautiful eyes soft, warm and scintillating.

"No worry, mi amor. It blow under," he said.

Giggling, I threw my arms around his neck and whispered "blow over" in his ear. He swung me around, laughing, and tossed me onto the bed. We made love, taking our time and savoring every morsel of each other. Afterward, Mikel sped to the train station in the Ferrari, and I almost changed my mind about Barcelona, never wanting to leave his side.

~~~~~~✝~~~~~~

But I got on that train. As I lay on the stinky mattress in the cellar–alone, naked and shivering–I wondered, as I had many times back then, what would've happened if I'd changed my mind and stayed with Mikel, stayed with mi amor.

I didn't want to remember the rest of the story. I wanted to remember the good times, start over in Pamplona and the night I met him, and I recounted the story of me and Mikel in my mind again.

He spun around and smiled broadly. I stopped in my tracks, gaping. Danel's brother was Mikel Garro...

After I reached the moment when he kissed me goodbye at the train station, I started all over again, because if I didn't, I would have to reflect on my life after him and how I ended up in the cellar. I wasn't ready to go down that road. I wasn't ready to take responsibility for what I'd become. Besides, thinking about all those moments with Mikel before the train warmed my heart. It stopped me from fixating on my dire circumstances, keeping the hunger and thirst and pain at bay.

The lock clicked. I paused mid-story and opened my eyes, waiting for the light, desperate for the light even if it was only for a short time, the darkness no longer a safe cocoon but a black hole with no end.

Baba loomed large and glowed hazily beneath the yellow bulb. I looked away, the bright beam too harsh. I struggled to sit up. A sharp pain pierced my ribs, my head pounded and my ass burned with infection. I supported myself on my good buttock and peered up at him, hoping for a kind look, a change of heart. But he had that same scowl, his eyes black with scorn.

"Please, Baba, please let me go." My voice was gravelly and barely audible. It was strange hearing it, as if the sound was coming from a distant place.

He glared at me and puffed on a cigarette. I got on my hands and knees and slowly crawled to him, my body screaming with pain. I wrapped my arms around his ankles, praying he would take pity on me. "Please, Baba," I begged.

It was not to be. Recoiling from my touch, he roughly booted me aside. The half-finished cigarette dropped to the floor, and he stomped on it and quickly unscrewed the lightbulb.

"No, Baba, no!" I cried. Then he was gone. "Nooooo!"

I slumped onto the hard floor, not caring about the pain, not caring that he'd given me a reprieve and left without using my flesh as an ashtray again.

I wept, sobbed, what little hydration I had left pouring from my eyes. I wept for all I'd lost, wept for my parents, wept for the world with men like Baba in it. Then I crawled back to the mattress, curled into a tight ball and faced my demons.

Wearing the Miami Heat baseball cap and sunglasses, Mikel escorted me to the train platform. He held my hand and squeezed it affectionately. A lump formed in my throat again.

"You be good, mi amor. No trouble, sí?"

He grinned his boyish, crooked grin and kissed me long and hard before helping me onto the first-class car. I gazed at him on the platform until I could no longer see him through the window and the train zipped out of sight.

It was strange being on my own again. But while my throat constricted with longing, already desperately missing him, my stomach strummed excitedly. There was so much I wanted to see, so many amazing photographs to take. For years it was all I'd thought about, traveling from one exotic destination to the next, and I'd almost forgotten that feeling.

The simple plan I'd made for myself was no longer simple. My love for Mikel had become all-consuming, distracting me from my aspirations. I no longer felt free to come and go as I pleased. Nor was I compelled to, drawn to him like a bee to honey, and I was certain he felt the same.

A service attendant passed with a snack cart. I ordered a Coke, indifferent to its cost this time. I had more money than I could've ever imagined, the Hunger photo an immediate success and the royalties adding up daily. And although riches were never part of my plan, my unexpected wealth added a new dimension to my life with Mikel.

I could hop on a plane anytime to anywhere without worrying about the ticket price. I could even take first-class like with the train, which I would've never done before. And I didn't need to carefully schedule my travel to save money, moving regionally by bus or train from city to city. Suddenly my future became clear.

I closed my eyes and envisioned it. A soothing calm enveloped me. I would live with Mikel. At first I would go on short excursions and stay a night or two, like the Barcelona trip. Then, when he became accustomed to the lifestyle and no longer worried I might leave him, I would take longer ones. During off-season he would come with me and we would make love on the beach in Tahiti and in a chalet in the Himalayas. Maybe we would marry someday. Have a child. Be happy.

It was a relief to have a new plan, my practical side demanding resolution to my disparate desires. I opened my eyes and soaked up the Spanish landscape, enjoying my freedom again. I couldn't wait to experience Barcelona.

~~~~~~✝~~~~~~

It was strange taking a taxi from the train station to the hotel in Barcelona, as was staying at a hotel instead of a hostel or a private home. I let the bellman take my backpack to the room, and he hung around introducing me to its features, which included a flat screen TV, minibar and plush bathrobe.

"I am at your service, señorita," he said. He clasped his hands in front of him and eyed me expectantly.

"Gracias," I replied politely. Unaccustomed to my new circumstances, I edged him toward the door. Then I realized he was fishing for a tip and hastily handed him three euros, having no idea if it was too much or too little. He smiled brightly, which didn't help. As soon as I shut the door behind him, I plopped down on the king-size bed and called Mikel.

"Aley, mi amor, I miss you," he said.

My heart skipped a beat. I imagined him smiling crookedly, his sultry brown eyes soft and sexy. I missed him, too.

We talked for a half-hour. He teased me about my tip dilemma, berated himself for not being by my side and warned me not to get arrested again. When I left the hotel, my stomach returned to a state of constant flux, high on life and loving him even more.

Camera in hand, I strolled along the lively Las Ramblas, feeling like the luckiest girl in the world. The tree-lined pedestrian mall was crowded with tourists, locals and street performers. I enthusiastically photographed it all, back in my element. There were musicians, acrobats and colorful souvenir kiosks. Since I was flush with money, I allowed a street artist to draw my caricature, which I thought would be a perfect souvenir for Mikel.

As the day drew to an end, the mall became more lively, illuminated by old-fashioned street lamps and thousands of twinkling fairy lights. I found a seat at an outdoor café, ordered tapas and wine and watched the people pass by. With nothing else to do until morning, I ordered another glass of wine. It was then I noticed an old man sitting on a wooden stool under a tree, a street lamp casting a soft light on him.

Clothes mismatched and tattered, face covered with a scruffy gray beard, fingers crooked and swollen, he looked like a vagrant. Yet he was painting a beautiful portrait of a fluffy white poodle, a gnarled hand moving with quick, precise strokes, his eyes darting back and forth between the canvas and a café across the way.

Following his gaze, I spotted the dog. It waited patiently at the feet of its master. I wondered if its owner had commissioned the man for the painting or if the man was hoping to sell it to him. My heart constricted compassionately, an overwhelming desire to help the old artist settled in my gut.

There were more of the painter's works propped against the tree, and I looked more closely at them. A fierce-looking, brown-and-white bull with scraped horns caught my attention, reminding me of *my* bull. An idea on how to help the artist crept into my brain. I would pay the man to paint my bull on canvas and give it to Mikel instead of the caricature of me. And since I had the money to do it, I quickly paid my bill, raced back to the hotel and used the printer in the internet room to make a color copy of my bull.

But when I returned to the tree he was gone. My heart sank. I looked across the way. The dog and his master hadn't moved and I didn't see a canvas in their possession. I don't know why it meant so much to me, but I vowed to return to Las Ramblas before I left town. I wanted to help the man and I wanted my bull on canvas.

I returned to the hotel around midnight and called Mikel. He was at a party. Loud hip hop music blared in the background and he sounded a little drunk, which was unusual considering he had soccer practice in the morning.

"I'll call you tomorrow," I said. "I love you."

A roar of laughter erupted on the other end of the line. Mikel shouted something I didn't understand and the line went dead. I waited for him to call me back, but he didn't. It worried me a little, but it was late and he was obviously having fun. Besides, I'd talk to him tomorrow after practice and be back in his arms shortly thereafter.

I slipped on the Garro top, crawled into bed and hugged a pillow to keep me company. It was strange not snuggling against Mikel's hot flesh, yet I quickly fell into a deep sleep. When I woke the next day, I was excited and ready to photograph Antoni Gaudí's brilliant works.

I started at his most unconventional, the Sagrada Família church. While the front exterior was garish, a mass of ornamental sculptures and rippling shapes that made it seem as if the church was melting in the sun, the interior was awe-inspiring, especially the nave, which looked like a magical forest filled with colorful, fluted columns.

I spent too much time there, but I couldn't help myself. The unique curves, geometric shapes and bell towers were compelling images. It was the same at Gaudí's Casa Milá, its wave-like, white stone façade creating an unusual rippling effect, and at Casa Batlló, the curved iron balconies and heavily tiled walls bizarrely beautiful.

There was more to see, the city speckled with his creations. But I wanted to return to Las Ramblas before my train left at six. I raced back to the hotel and picked up my backpack, suddenly realizing I'd been so absorbed in my work I'd completely forgotten about Mikel.

I checked my phone and he hadn't called. My stomach churned anxiously and I dialed his number. When he didn't answer, my first thought was something bad had happened to him. He'd been drinking too much at the party the previous night. Maybe he'd been in a car accident.

I called again and left a voice mail, speaking haltingly, my voice cracking emotionally. "It's…it's me. Um…um…I'm leaving in a couple of hours and haven't heard from you. I miss you. I love you. Call me."

I dialed Danel's number next. He picked up immediately. "Si, Aley, 'e okay. 'e meet U.N. now," he said.

Sighing heavily, my insides unknotted. "Thanks, Danel. Tell him I called and I'll see him tonight."

"Sí, sí."

He hung up abruptly. I stared at the phone, his curtness unusual. I hoped he wasn't still upset about Mikel and me, but I didn't have time to dwell on it. I dashed to Las Ramblas and the tree where I'd last seen the old artist. He wasn't there. I grimaced disappointedly. I really wanted to surprise Mikel. He loved the bull photo and I knew he'd love it preserved on canvas. I also really wanted to help the poor man. But there was nothing I could do. My stomach growled.

With time to spare, I ate seafood paella at the same restaurant as the night before. It was only a 10-minute walk to the train station, so I lingered awhile longer. When the painter appeared carrying a stool in one arm and an easel, canvas, paint and brushes in the other, I could barely believe my luck.

Clutching the copy of the bull photo, I approached him excitedly and communicated using my halting Spanish and sign language. He eyed me warily until I flashed four hundred euros in his face. Smiling broadly, his mouth practically toothless, he furiously went to work, somehow understanding I needed him to finish fast.

I don't know why that painting had become so important to me, so important I risked missing the train. It was just a gift. But at the time I really wanted to give Mikel something special, a token of my love that would always remind him of me. The fact that I could help the old artist made it more special.

Still, I didn't want to miss the train. As the man's gnarled fingers deftly added paint to the canvas, I nervously studied him. It was hard to tell his age. The scruffy beard and long hair hid his face, and he reeked of poverty, a pungent musty odor wafting from his thin body. I took a few pictures of him, one hand holding the camera to my eye and the other the bull photo. I checked the time on my phone every few minutes, my nervousness growing, praying he would finish on time.

Twenty minutes before the train was scheduled to leave, I almost gave up. Then the old artist suddenly stopped painting, peered at the canvas for a few seconds and dramatically took another swipe at it with the brush. He studied it for a few more seconds, added a few color splashes and peered up at me. Smiling broadly again, he flipped over the canvas for me to see.

"Completo," he said proudly.

Amazed by his talent, I gaped. He'd gotten it exactly right, especially the bull's eyes. I threw my arms around his neck and hugged him enthusiastically. He looked stunned, probably not used to people touching him, but I couldn't help it. He'd finished just in time.

"Gracias, señor, gracias," I said.

He handed me the painting and humbly took the money. When I turned to go, he lightly grasped my forearm, took the canvas from me and turned it to face away from my body, gesturing at the paint. It took me a moment to understand what he was implying. The oil was still wet.

Heart beating excitedly, I rushed off. I was on my way back to Mikel. I would have gotten on that train, too, if I hadn't encountered a mass protest two blocks from the station. I attempted to skirt through the mob without someone bumping into the painting, but it was impossible. I had to go several blocks out of my way, and when I reached the track, the train had departed.

Slumping onto a bench, I cursed the Spanish for their incessant demonstrations. The next departure was scheduled two hours later. I trudged dejectedly around the station chastising myself, and then I spotted the car rental booths at the far end of the terminal.

The last thing I wanted to do was drive in a foreign country, but I didn't want to wait two hours for the next train either. I could be halfway to Pamplona by the time it left, so I stiffened my spine and approached an American company.

Twenty minutes later, I was behind the wheel of an Audi, the GPS set to my final destination. I called Mikel and he answered immediately.

"Mikel! I missed the train!" I said excitedly. "But I rented a car, so you don't need to pick me up at the station. I can't wait to see you! I really miss you."

"Aley, I must say–"

The line went dead and I stared at the phone. It was out of power. I hadn't noticed the battery status before then, never paying attention to it because Mikel had always charged the phone for me. I didn't think to pack the charger either, and since the Audi wasn't equipped with one, I couldn't call him back.

It didn't matter. At least I had time to tell him about my new plan. My stomach churned with that delicious anticipation only Mikel Garro could summon, and I started the car, searched for a good radio station and hit the road.

~~~~~~~✝~~~~~~~

Driving in Spain was easier than I'd expected. The highway was a well-maintained toll road and it was hard to keep to the speed limit. I stopped once to pee and buy coffee, and I arrived in Pamplona in less than four hours.

The GPS guided me to Mikel's, the streets became familiar. As I pulled up to the house I groaned. There were several cars parked outside. Either he or Danel were having a party. Setting aside my fantasy of Mikel sweeping me into his arms and carrying me upstairs to his bedroom, I grabbed my backpack and camera from the trunk and the painting from the back seat, and I scampered inside.

Loud music and laughter filtered into the kitchen. I dropped my stuff on the island and peeked outside. There were about twenty people hanging out by the pool, but Mikel wasn't with them. I checked the office and headed upstairs. With each step my heart raced faster. I couldn't wait to see him again. I couldn't wait to give him the bull painting.

When I reached his room, the door was partially closed, a sliver of light filtering into the hallway. I pushed it open and stopped in my tracks. A gasp stuck in my throat. A couple of the partiers were fucking on Mikel's bed. They lay sideways across the mattress, the woman on top. She moved slowly up and down, eyes closed in the throes of passion, the crack in her plump ass broadening with each drop.

I didn't know what to do. I couldn't move. She was dazzling, exotic. Her skin was flawless, bronzed from head to toe. Her long black hair cascaded over his face. The soft lamp light illuminated her large breasts and swollen pink nipples. I watched the man reach for them, fondle them, and she sighed softly and languidly opened her eyes.

It took her a moment to focus and lock onto me. Her lips twitched into a satisfied grin, seemingly unfazed to see me there. She even nodded in my direction. Shuddering with embarrassment, I lowered my eyes and turned to leave, glancing up one more time to express my apologies with my own nod. Then her lover turned his head and looked my way, and my stomach twisted into a tight knot.

I could hear my heart beating.

The man was Mikel.

He looked directly at me. I thought I saw his beautiful brown eyes flash with sorrow before turning blank, emotionless. The world stopped. My mind and body went numb. He slowly turned away, grasped her waist and thrust upward, driving into her with deliberate intensity. I dropped the painting and fled.

Just like then I could hear my heart beating. My stomach twisted in knots. I'd repressed the memory for so long it was almost new, more painful than Baba's beatings, more painful than a slow death.

The next few days were a blur, but I remember Danel in the kitchen. While hot tears streamed down my cheeks, he peered at me indifferently and lowered his head. For a fleeting moment I wanted to demand answers, but deep down I knew there were none. I grabbed my backpack and camera, desperate to run from there as fast as possible, and I left.

I couldn't understand any of it. In the span of one day my love, *mi amor,* had turned into a cruel monster. My sweet, exuberant, loving

Mikel had betrayed me, my preparedness to conquer the world a joke, a wasted exercise, my self-esteem, self-confidence and intrepid spirit destroyed in an instant. And he didn't even bother to run after me, didn't seek forgiveness. He stayed in his bedroom, the room we'd shared for many nights, and he fucked that woman. He stayed with her, pleasuring her.

I was nothing to him.

I was nothing.

Shattered, I escaped to Les Eyzies, the next destination on my quest for fame. I didn't know where else to go and didn't remember the journey there, trains, maybe a bus or two. I found refuge at a Bed & Breakfast, where I immediately crawled into bed desperate to forget, desperate for sleep, the constant, excited flux in my gut growing into a dull ache, inhabiting me body and soul.

Nothing made sense.

I scoured my memory for any sign, any reason why Mikel had scorned me. Maybe the public backlash over him dating an American had become worse. I was certain the woman in his bed was Spanish, so was he trying to save his tarnished image, his brand?

But he'd said it didn't matter. He'd said he loved me. Maybe the controversy was hurting the Hunger campaign. He'd been meeting with U.N. people when I'd called that day, and it would be just like him to be concerned about the campaign's success. But it didn't explain the cruel way he'd rebuffed me. He knew I would be returning around the time he was fucking that woman. *He knew...*

I couldn't erase the image from my mind. *Her ecstasy. The blank look in his eyes.*

Maybe he'd decided he couldn't accept our unspoken arrangement. He didn't want me leaving him, even for a day, but couldn't he have talked to me? From the moment we'd met it was as if we had known each other all our lives, our connection immediate. It didn't make sense.

Nothing made sense.

Maybe we were simply too young. I was almost nineteen and Mikel was twenty-two. Maybe he'd gotten scared or maybe he'd been stringing me along the entire time. He was a famous European soccer player, after all, worshipped by millions with thousands of gorgeous women at his beck and call. I'd witnessed the shenanigans. The testosterone. The condoms in the cookie jar and fish bowl. Maybe I'd been just one of many.

No matter how hard I tried, I didn't want to believe it, didn't want to accept that I'd misjudged him. I'd been certain he loved me, certain we had a future. My mother always said I was perceptive, gifted in that way, probably because I listened more than I talked. But even that part of me had been shattered. I'd been incredibly naïve and gullible.

I couldn't turn off my mind, couldn't sleep. I dragged myself from bed and robotically walked to a shop near the B&B. I don't remember what day it was or whether it was day or nighttime. I returned with a bottle of wine, but I couldn't open it, so I went back and bought a corkscrew.

I drank all the wine and passed out. When I woke, I bought another bottle. Then I bought Courvoisier. The days passed. Other than the clerk at the corner store, my only contact with the outside world was the B&B owner, who pounded on my door every morning to announce breakfast. If I was conscious, I would tell him to go away and leave me alone, and he would.

Then he didn't. He barged into the room carrying a telephone. "Mademoiselle Hanson, your mama wants to talk to you," he said.

He hovered over the bed, looking at me through vintage wire-rimmed spectacles, his wrinkled face etched with concern and determination. I thought I heard him say my mother was on the phone, but my mind was foggy from alcohol and it was impossible. No one knew where I was.

"Mademoiselle, please talk to your mama."

"Go away," I said, my voice raspy and barely audible.

"No, Mademoiselle, it is your mama. She is worried."

He thrust the phone in my face and I knew from his dogged expression he was telling the truth. Yet I was confused. I didn't understand how my mother had tracked me down. Then I bolted upright, suddenly concerned that something bad had happened to my dad or brother. My stomach twisted guiltily.

"Mom," I croaked into the phone.

"Thank, God," she sighed. "Haley, honey, what's going on? Mr. Lachance said you've been staying with him and haven't eaten or come out of your room for days."

I realized my mother didn't track me down. Monsieur Lachance had tracked *her* down. I glared angrily at him. He raised a brow and nodded at the phone. There was nothing I could do.

"Haley, are you all right, honey?" Her voice cracked with fear.

A slew of raw emotions bubbled to the surface. My eyes welled with tears. "I'm fine," I squeaked.

"You don't sound fine," she said. "Are you sick? Are you hurt? What happened, honey?"

"Really, Mom, I'm okay. I haven't been feeling well, but I'm better," I lied.

"Did you go to the doctor?" Dad piped in. His tone was laced with alarm.

It took all my resolve not to burst into tears. My father was always the one who panicked and turned into mush the rare times I'd been sick or sad.

"It's not like that," I replied softly.

"Did someone hurt you? Did that Michael guy hurt you?" he growled.

Although he pronounced Mikel's name wrong, he'd hit the mark. His perceptiveness was remarkable. The dull ache in my gut throbbed.

"No, Dad, no. I've been feeling a little overwhelmed, blue I guess. Maybe I'm a little homesick, that's all."

I knew I could tell them about Mikel, but I wasn't ready. I could barely suffer his name said out loud.

"Come home then, honey. You don't have to conquer the world right away," Mom said.

"I'll be okay, *really*," I assured.

"We're catching the next flight to France," Dad declared.

"No! Mom, Dad, I'll be fine. I promise. I'll call you tomorrow."

"Try to eat something, honey. You'll feel better."

"I will, I will," I said, scanning the room.

It was as tidy as the day I arrived except for the empty wine bottles and an almost empty Courvoisier bottle on the nightstand next to the bed. I peeked at Monsieur Lachance, certain he'd be watching me from now on.

"You be sure to thank Mr. Lachance for his concern. He's a nice man. He has four daughters of his own," Dad said.

"Sure, Dad, I'll call you tomorrow…"

Jillian

I wasn't sure how many days had passed, maybe three. I combed my greasy hair, tied it in a ponytail and brushed my teeth. I hadn't bothered to change my clothes since I showed up in Les Eyzies, and I dumped my meager belongings from the backpack onto the bed. Except for some cosmetics, what I had on, and the jeans, shirt and underwear I wore when I'd gone to Barcelona, I'd left everything else at Mikel's. I morosely picked through what was left.

Then I saw it, the Garro tank top folded neatly beneath a crumpled shirt. My heart lurched. I wanted to simultaneously rip it to shreds and caress it lovingly. I'd never felt so alone.

Fighting back tears, I grudgingly trudged downstairs. Monsieur Lachance was waiting for me with a bowl of soup, a baguette and a big glass of milk. I mechanically ate what he put before me, slurping, chewing and forcing it down my throat. I wished he hadn't felt the need to butt into my life. I wanted to hate him, but I couldn't.

Along with the wire-rimmed glasses, he had shaggy, chin-length hair, a curly beard and full mustache, all stark white. He looked like

Santa Claus. And with four daughters of his own, I couldn't fault him for his concern for me, probably tracking down my parents using my passport information, which all European hotels copied for their records. He'd gone to a lot of trouble, and I knew if I didn't make an effort, he'd call them again.

Fortunately, once he'd fed me, he didn't feel the need to chitchat. When I finished, I politely thanked him and left the B&B in search of a cellphone. In my haste to leave Mikel, I'd left the one he loaned me on the kitchen island at his house. He couldn't contact me except by email, and I briefly thought about my laptop perched on the chair at the B&B. A glint of hope bubbled in my gut.

I ignored it. Fucking the exotic woman in his bedroom had said it all. I morosely slogged forward. Even if he wanted to contact me, there was nothing he could say to mend my broken heart. It hit me that we were really over.

I would never see him again, never feel his soft lips on mine, never smell his intoxicating scent and never taste his delicious flesh. I wanted to turn around, run back to my dark hollow and crawl back into bed. If it hadn't been for Santa Claus' interference, I would have.

But I promised my parents I would call them the next day and I needed my own phone, needed the privacy. I steeled myself against the harsh sunlight and moved to the street's shady side, barely noticing the people I passed or the quaint scenery, a deep sadness settling in my soul.

I'd instinctively escaped to Les Eyzies, planning to go there anyway, my next quick trip and then back to Mikel. And if it hadn't been for Mikel, I'm sure I would've been bursting with excitement, the charming village surrounded by four ancient cave sites containing some of the best examples of prehistoric paintings estimated to be 20,000 years old.

I'd planned to photograph the art in one of the caves. It was closed to the public, but because of my father, who'd become good friends with the French Minister of Culture during an environmental conference, I'd received rare permission from the government to enter it, yet I no longer cared.

I couldn't think about my work, my solace. I wandered down the street in a trance. I managed to buy the phone plus a couple of t-shirts and panties, and I bought another bottle of Courvoisier in case I ran out.

I would indulge Monsieur Lachance and dutifully eat, maybe even leave my dark hollow for a short time every day, but I couldn't manage without the alcohol, my heart broken and my mind on overdrive, continually wrestling with questions I couldn't answer and images I couldn't forget.

~~~~~~†~~~~~~

I thought I heard pounding on the door and the lock click. Baba hovered over me, only he had white hair, a beard and spectacles. The vein on his forehead pounded furiously, his black eyes glazed with hatred. I hid under the bedcover at the B&B, praying he wouldn't see me.

My eyes snapped open. Darkness greeted me. Silence. I was in the cellar, feverish, sweating and shivering at the same time. My mind was playing tricks on me.

I struggled to sit on my good buttock. The other one was swollen the size of a soccer ball and hard with infection. I braced myself on my good arm, weak and shrinking from dehydration and hunger. If I'd known back then in Les Eyzies what real suffering was like, maybe I wouldn't have been as self-indulgent. The self-imposed exile, the self-pity, all of it.

I was dizzy and couldn't sit long. I lay back down on the mattress, wondering if Baba would return or if he was done with me, his final punishment leaving me to die a slow death in the cellar. I didn't dwell on it too long, at peace with my fate.

I'd grown up fast. Fell in love fast. Lived fast. Maybe it was supposed to happen that way for me, compressing a lifetime of happiness and sadness, excitement and despair, love and heartache into just twenty-three short years.

I wanted more, though. I wanted all the good and bad life had to offer. But it was too late. Baba had broken me. I used the last of my grit to finish the story, recounting the years after Mikel, hoping to understand my free fall from grace, hoping to come to terms with my misdeeds and seeking some sort of redemption for my failings before I died.

After the brief shopping trip, I returned to the B&B and drank Courvoisier until I passed out. When Monsieur Lachance pounded on the door the next morning, I groggily donned one of the new t-shirts, quickly made myself look presentable and dragged myself to breakfast.

There were two couples there already, sitting at small tables in the alcove of the large eighteenth-century manor. Bright sunshine filtered into the cozy room through arched bay windows. Head hammering with a merciless hangover, I silently cursed Monsieur Lachance and hunkered at a table in the darkest corner, forcing down a croissant and juice.

It seemed to satisfy him, and I lethargically slogged up the stairs and went back to my room. I considered calling my parents, but they wouldn't be home from work until later, so I drank a shot of Courvoisier and slipped into bed.

The hangover fog and alcohol was sufficient to allow me to drift into a restless sleep. My dreams oscillated between images of Mikel's sensuous brown eyes twinkling mischievously, his crooked smile, his hands gripping bronze hips, the tips of a woman's long black hair skimming his flesh, an emotionless blank stare.

An unending loop, a rush of bliss that mutated into deep sorrow and back to bliss, the internal struggle that tormented my waking hours reflected in my dreams.

I was dreaming within a dream.

I struggled to wake. Escape the loop—

"Haley! God damn it, Hales, open the door!"

Jillian?

Jills?

My eyes shot open.

"Come on, Hales, you're freaking me out here. Open the fucking door…"

It took me a minute to believe she was really there. It had to be her. She was the only one who called me by the nickname "Hales," just like I called her "Jills."

I rolled out of bed, stumbled to the door and shakily unlocked it.

"What the fuck!" she exclaimed. "Jesus Christ, Hales, you look like shit!"

It was really her, perfectly made up, her heart-shaped lips painted a glossy red and frowning grimly. Except for a ridiculous beet-red beret, she was dressed stylishly in a sleeveless red sundress and matching shoes, her long brown hair feathered and curly and flowing luxuriously over her shoulders.

She was beautiful and I rasped, "Jills?"

"Holy shit, Hales, what the hell happened?" The floodgates opened. I burst into tears. She drew me into her arms and hugged me tightly. "Jesus, Hales," she muttered softly.

Melting in her embrace, I let go of the pain, the heartache, weeping hot tears on her bare shoulder. She held me like that for a long time whispering soothing words. When my sobbing turned into gulps for air, she guided me to the bed and gently sat me on it.

"It's that guy, Mikel whoever," she grumbled. She knew me better than anyone. *My best friend.* "Jesus, Hales, what did he do?"

I told her everything from beginning to end. It was a relief to say it out loud, my stomach unknotting with each word. She remained silent throughout, patiently comforting me until I finished.

"I don't understand, Jills. It was as if I never existed…"

She hugged me hard, grasped my hands and eyed me seriously.

"So how do you want to do it?" she asked. I didn't understand and raised a brow. Her lips quirked into a devilish grin. "Should we kill him with a gun? A knife? How about poison?"

It was quintessential Jillian. I erupted in hysterical laughter, crying and cackling at the same time. All the bottled-up emotions gushed out of me.

She made me take a shower and waited on the toilet as I wearily washed from head to toe. The knot in my stomach was gone but not the dull ache. It was part of me, would gnaw at my gut for months, but with her there, at least I was functioning.

"You better call your parents and then I want to explore," she said. "Isn't this where the caves are? The one you want to photograph?"

Shrugging, I toweled off and she set her lips in a stubborn line.

"Shit, Hales, you knew the guy for a few weeks. I know you fell hard for him, but you can't give up your dreams. Remember our pact?"

Of course I remembered it. We promised not to let guys distract us from our goals, but it was easier said than done.

"I'm not leaving France until you're back to your old self," she declared.

I knew she meant it and groaned inwardly. She was a force of nature, always bold and dogged. I vowed to get my act together or at least fake it. School would be starting soon and I didn't want my best friend to miss her first college semester because of me. She'd been accepted at MIT, her dream to become a computer engineer, and she was ecstatic about it.

"You don't have to babysit me, Jills. I'll be okay."

"Yeah, right," she smirked. "Look at yourself. You've got big dark rings under your eyes and I swear you've lost ten pounds."

I glanced in the vanity mirror and quickly turned away. It was like looking at a ghost of me, but it wasn't the sunken eyes or the few pounds I'd lost that were ghostly. It was as if I wasn't there, a shadow of myself.

She dried my hair for me and chatted about her flight to France, underscoring the fact that my parents had bought her an open-ended ticket for the return trip. Then she helped me apply makeup. I didn't see the point, but I went along.

When she was done, she pointed me at the mirror and said, "That asshole doesn't know what he's given up." I cringed, wishing I could hate Mikel as much as her. She didn't notice and joked, "You know you're hot, Haley. Lots of guys are going to want you, love you, but promise me you won't fall in love again until you're at least thirty." She didn't need to worry. I wouldn't be falling in love anytime soon. I still loved Mikel and knew I always would. "Now get dressed and call your parents. You'll feel better after some sunshine and good food in you. I'm starving and can't wait to try some fattening French food."

My lips twitched into a weak smile. Jillian had always bossed me around and I never minded. She was the leader and I was the follower. It was one of the reasons we got along so well.

I eyed my clothes and did what she said. Since the jeans I wore in Barcelona were the cleanest, I pulled them on and redressed in the t-shirt.

"Shit, Hales, is that all you got to wear?"

I flashed back to Mikel fucking the woman in his bed in his bedroom. My stomach lurched. It wasn't as if I had a choice to leave my stuff there. After all, I couldn't pack while he fucked her and I couldn't stick around until he was done.

"Yes, I left everything else behind," I replied softly.

She bounded from the room in search of Monsieur Lachance. While I called my parents, he lugged two large suitcases to the room, smiling broadly. He didn't mind being ordered around by her either, already charmed.

My parents were relieved to hear Jillian had arrived, and they told me to pay for everything while she was with me.

"We'll reimburse you, honey," Mom said. "We're just really glad she's there with you."

"It's okay, Mom, I have money."

I'd forgotten about my windfall, a reminder it had been Mikel who'd promoted the bull photo and allowed the Hunger picture to be published. He'd backed my dream and encouraged me. He'd loved me. I was sure of it.

"We love you, Haley. You girls have fun," Dad said.

Their love and understanding meant everything to me. They instinctively knew I needed my best friend and sent her to me, and she would be a godsend.

~~~~~~†~~~~~~

Jillian and I had always shared clothes and she'd brought plenty. I donned a jean skirt and midriff top and we went to town. She devoured a full lunch of soup, duck and dessert and I managed to eat half of a crepe. Then we visited the Prehistoric Museum on top of the cliff overlooking the town and took a leisurely stroll along the river.

I appreciated her efforts to distract me. I laughed at her jokes and responded to her questions. But dulled by a raw, cutting sadness I couldn't shake, my heart wasn't into it and she knew it.

Still, she wouldn't give up. We ate dinner outdoors at a quaint restaurant located next to the river. In typical French fashion we spent three hours consuming a five-course meal accompanied by two bottles of wine, which I drank thirstily. By the time we returned to the B&B, I was half drunk and exhausted.

The room had been cleaned during our absence, the sheets changed and fresh flowers left on the sitting table under the window. Jillian yawned dramatically and slumped in a chair.

"I'm beat," she declared.

"Me, too," I replied, eyeing the bottle of Courvoisier.

Her eyes followed mine and lips quirked into a quick grin. She grabbed the bottle, poured a healthy shot into two glasses and handed one to me.

"I don't blame you, Hales. After what you've been through, I'd be drinking, too," she said.

I was vulnerable, disillusioned. She knew that, too. She understood me better than anyone, and I was overwhelmed with love for her. She wouldn't judge me, no matter what I did to feel better or to forget. And like we'd done many nights back home, we crawled into bed together, planted our heads on the pillows and faced each other.

"I'm sorry you got hurt," she said softly.

"Thanks, Jills, and thanks for coming. I'm glad you're here."

"Me, too."

"I wish I understood what happened. I thought he loved me..."

My voice cracked. She scooted closer and tenderly rubbed my back.

"Maybe he got scared."

"He could've told me he wanted to break up. He didn't need to–"

I couldn't finish, the horrible image of Mikel fucking that woman suffocating me.

"That was cruel," she sighed.

"And that's–that's what I don't understand." I gulped down tears. "It's not like him at all. At least that's what I thought. He knew I was coming, knew I would be there at about the same time as... It was as if he planned it. He wanted me to see them."

"Do you think he thought you wouldn't care? Maybe it's a groupie thing. You know, you're his main squeeze but not his only girlfriend. He *is* a soccer player, after all, and they're bigger than rock stars in Europe."

"I don't know. Maybe..."

Remembering Ernesto, I doubted Mikel was the groupie type. It didn't matter anyway. I was sure Mikel knew I wouldn't be receptive to that lifestyle.

"Maybe you should call him. Get an explanation and then you'll know."

There was no good explanation. Nothing he could say would ease the pain or give me peace.

"No, it's over," I said, and saying it out loud made it real, *final.*

I couldn't hold back the tears any longer. I wept softly until I couldn't weep anymore. Jillian waited patiently for me to finish, murmuring soothing words and handing me tissue after tissue.

"Thanks, Jills."

"You don't have to thank me. We're best friends forever, right?"

"Yeah, best friends forever."

"Then as your best friend, I'm going to spend the next few days fattening you up and dragging you around until you're so exhausted you can sleep through the night and get rid of those dark circles under your eyes. And once you're presentable again, you're going into that cave and do your photography thing. I'm not going to let a mere man take down my best friend. And then we're going to Paris. I'm not leaving France without seeing Paris, and we'll see it together."

I grinned, suddenly flooded with relief. *A plan.* And even though the dull ache in the pit of my gut persisted, I had no choice but to move forward. Jillian would see to it.

"Okay," I said, "and we can do Paris in style. I've made a ton of money from the Hunger photo."

"You did? How much?" she asked excitedly.

"Last time I checked almost two hundred thousand dollars."

"Holy shit, Hales, at least something good came from that no good asshole."

It took four more days of sightseeing, canoeing and three square meals before Jillian was satisfied with my health and appearance. The laptop taunted me and I eventually checked my email. I couldn't help it. Hands trembling, I waited until Jillian was in the shower to open it. There wasn't a message from Mikel and my heart sank.

And while she shopped for yet another decadent treat at her favorite corner pastry store, I surreptitiously scanned the Spanish papers at the newsstand outside, dreading yet hoping for one more glimpse of him. When I spotted the Osasuna team photo in El Mundo, a deep sadness pierced my soul, the image of him too small to relish his beautiful chocolate eyes or determine his mood.

I stopped looking. The exercise was useless and too painful. Jillian insisted I document her trip to France, and I began taking pictures again, finding some solace in it. I continued to drink heavily, wine at dinner and Courvoisier before bed, but I still couldn't sleep through the night, my dreams interrupted by dark images of Mikel's blank stare and long black hair skimming over his naked skin.

Then Jillian deemed that it was time for me to go back to work. Concerned I was a young degenerate with friends in high places, the museum curator demanded a meeting before I could enter the cave. Jillian dressed me in a crème pantsuit from the extensive wardrobe she'd brought with her and escorted me to the door.

"Go get 'em, Hales," she encouraged. "I'll wait for you at the café across the street."

My heart wasn't in it, but I had no choice. The woman judged me as acceptable and scheduled the private tour for the next day. Jillian was more excited than me. The following morning she trudged up the path through the heavily forested hillside with us, determined to see the entrance to the cave at the very least. I wished I had her enthusiasm. But the thrill, the tingle that ran up my spine when faced with a once-in-a-lifetime opportunity was gone. I wondered if it would ever return.

Still, even at a young age I thought of myself as a professional. The camera had been part of me for so long that taking pictures was second nature, and I didn't simply take pictures, I made them. Yet the cave art was already well-documented. It would be hard to shoot a new image. As I traversed the passageways and shafts, I focused on the sections of fungal growth instead. They were the reason for the cave's closure, the thousands of animal figures painted on the walls needing protection from the light and exhalations from tourists.

The curator guided me from one cavern to another, turning on and off lights as we passed through the different halls. When we entered the Hall of the Bulls, one of the illustrations stopped me in my tracks. It was a seventeen foot-long black bull and appeared to be in motion.

I was at once drawn to it and nauseated by it. Its stark simplicity was exquisite and a reminder of my bull and Mikel. The cave closed in on me. My heart pounded wildly. Despite the cool atmosphere, sweat pooled on my forehead. I panicked. I couldn't move. I struggled to breathe.

My eyes snapped open. *Darkness. Silence.* I was in the cellar not the cave, but I was having a panic attack like in the cave those many years ago. I inhaled deeply and slowly exhaled, forcing myself to concentrate on Paris, shopping in Paris and the bright lights on the Champs Élysées. I continued to breathe deeply until my heartbeat steadied.

That was how I learned to repress the memories of him. I focused on something else. I couldn't keep falling apart at the sight of a bull or a sunset. Or a scent that reminded me of him. He was poison to me now. A simple image of our short time together made me physically ill.

It was also in the cave I decided to swear off men for good. I was obviously a terrible judge of character. I wouldn't make the same mistake again. I would focus on my career and be just fine.

Jillian and I arrived in Paris the next day and checked into an upscale, thousand-dollar-a-night hotel in the St. Germaine district. Our first order of business was shopping, and she immediately dragged me into a boutique clothing store near the hotel.

Jillian couldn't have been happier, bossing around the astonished clerk and locking me in the dressing room for hours. I bought so many chic clothes, sexy undergarments and stylish shoes for both of us that the clerk had to call a taxi to deliver the packages to the hotel.

Afterward, she decided we would dine at the four-star restaurant in the hotel. She ordered me to wear a sleeveless blue mini-dress with a plunging V-neckline and black high heels

"You look hot, Hales," she said, grinning mischievously.

I knew I looked great. Jillian's tender care had brought me back to the living. My blue eyes were bright, the dark circles under them gone. My skin glowed and blonde hair shimmered luxuriously. I wasn't just hot but sophisticated and seductive. I rolled my eyes. I knew exactly what she was doing.

She wanted men to ogle me, hoping more than one would hit on me and bolster my self-esteem, which had been severely damaged after Mikel dumped me. But that dull ache in the pit of my stomach continued to percolate. The idea of hooking up with another guy any time soon revolted me.

Yet I played along. She had my best interests at heart. We strutted into the restaurant, me wearing the titillating blue mini and Jillian dressed in a skintight black one with a low-cut neckline and open back. The hostess escorted us to a prime table in the middle of the room. Heads turned and eyes followed us. We were a provocative pair, Jillian with her dark hair and features and me with my blonde hair and blue eyes. We weren't the only beautiful women there, but we were the only ones unaccompanied by men.

After another leisurely five-course meal, Jillian wanted to hit the clubs. It was Friday night. The concierge recommended one near the Champs Élysées, but it didn't start hopping until after midnight. We moved to the bar and ordered martinis. It didn't take long for two guys to approach us.

They were wealthy Englishmen in the city for the weekend looking for a good time. I don't remember their names, already a little drunk from wine and after-dinner snifters of Courvoisier. But I remember Jillian accepted their offer to buy us a drink and I played along and indulged my friend, who was charmed by their English accents and boyish good looks.

The redheaded, rugged-looking one latched on to Jillian. The one with the short brown hair keyed on me. He didn't seem to care that I barely acknowledged his presence as he arrogantly droned on and on about his business ventures. I could've killed Jillian when she invited them to go clubbing with us.

We rode together in their rented limo. He sat too close, draping an arm over the seat back. He never stopped talking, his breath hot and stale, and I couldn't wait to escape the car. When we arrived at the nightclub and Jillian and I were finally alone, I glared irritably at her.

"What?" she asked innocently.

"Christ, Jillian, did you have to invite them?"

"Lighten up, Hales. Have some fun, will you? It's not like you have to sleep with him."

"It's not funny," I glowered.

Her luscious heart-shaped lips puckered into an indignant pout. I set mine in a determined line. She grinned devilishly and said, "Okay, let's ditch 'em. Come on, I want to dance."

It wasn't hard to lose the Englishmen. The place was packed with the young and restless. We pressed up to the bar as far away from them as we could get and I ordered my third martini. The more I drank, the more I danced, gyrating to the pounding bass in front of a mirrored wall that encased the dance floor.

I barely recognized the woman reflecting back at me. She was sensuous and carefree, hips swaying seductively, her voluptuous body rubbing against a train of faceless guys.

Time warped. The disco lights spun faster and faster. The acoustics boomed louder and louder. A dizzying fusion of hot flesh added to the sensory overload and the room blurred into a kaleidoscope of color. Lightheaded and nauseous, I stumbled over to Jillian and threw an arm over her shoulder.

"I'm going outside," I slurred.

"Are you okay?"

"Fine. Need air."

I staggered through the crowd. The crush of bodies kept me upright, the grins and dirty looks distorted as I pushed people aside, everything out of focus. When I finally made it outside, I gratefully sucked in the cool evening air, trying to offset my drunkenness.

It didn't help. I leaned unsteadily against the building, feeling sick. People lingered on the sidewalk talking and smoking. With each deep breath I inhaled smoke, making me sicker.

I'd drunk a lot at the B&B, but when I was woozy I would sink into bed. There was no hiding on the streets of Paris, and I furtively looked up and down the tree-lined boulevard desperate for an escape.

"There you are." A man propped his hand on the wall and bent close. "You disappeared."

There were two of him and I recognized the accent. He was the Englishman and his breath was sweet. *Sugary sweet.*

My stomach somersaulted even more. "I'm not feeling well," I managed to say.

"You've been terribly naughty." He buried his head in my neck and nipped at my throat.

His lips were leathery and dry. The panic and alcohol rose in my throat. Gagging, I shakily stepped farther down the wall away from him, but he moved with me and grabbed my waist in a tight grip.

I feebly tried to push him off me. "Leave me alone. I said I was sick."

He slipped a hand inside the neckline of my dress and squeezed my breast. "You look fine to me. *Real fine.*"

"Please, stop," I whimpered.

I struggled against him, but I was too weak, too drunk.

"What the hell do you think you're doing!"

The cry came from Jillian. She shoved him off me. I doubled over and heaved, vomiting spectacularly on his leg. Cursing loudly, he jumped back and stomped angrily away.

"Asshole! Rapist!" she shouted after him. Then she gently swept the hair from my face and held it in a ponytail while I puked profusely on the sidewalk until there was nothing left in my stomach to expel.

"Sorry, Jills," I muttered between dry heaves.

"It's okay, Hales, you're going to be okay…"

I don't remember returning to the hotel. When I woke the next day, Jillian was sleeping peacefully next to me.

I rolled out of bed, expecting to feel worse than I did. There was a rancid taste in my mouth from vomiting, but it probably prevented me from having a killer hangover. The shame was the worst part. I hated feeling out of control and unable to defend myself. If it hadn't been for Jillian protecting me, the filthy Englishman might have really harmed me.

My heart swelled with love for my friend. She took care of me when I needed her most. I vowed to behave. Drink less, try to be happy and prove to her I could take care of myself again.

The next few days flew by. We visited the major sites during the day and partied at a new club every night. I barely had a moment to think about Mikel, which was exactly what Jillian wanted. Still, I couldn't shake the feeling a part of me had died the day I'd left him.

Then the Swedish national soccer team arrived at the hotel and stirred up the memories again. They'd come to Paris to play the French national team in a World Cup qualifying match, trickling in one and two players at a time. Strutting their stuff and taking over.

I couldn't believe it. Of all the hotels in Paris, they'd chosen to stay at mine. The dull ache in my gut swelled into full-fledged panic. My first instinct was to check out, but Jillian would be worried and devastated if I fled. I remembered my vow to her and masked my trepidation by telling myself they were just guys who happened to play soccer. But they were hard to ignore, two in particular.

Jillian and I had been sightseeing all day. We ate dinner at a bistro and killed time at the hotel bar waiting for midnight. It was there they approached us. Olle and Viktor, both hot as hell and on a mission.

"Hello, ladies," Olle greeted. "May I buy you a drink?"

His emerald eyes sparkled beneath thick dark lashes, his smile devastating. If Jillian was the swooning type, she would've tipped off the bar stool. Instead, she eyed me questioningly, pleading for permission.

After everything she'd done for me, I sucked it up. "Sure," I replied indifferently.

She enthusiastically stuck out her hand and purred, "I'm Jillian. This is Haley."

Olle grabbed her hand and grinned appreciatively. "My name is Olle and this is my friend, Viktor. It is a pleasure."

The sparks flew between them. I groaned inwardly, glancing at Viktor. He peered curiously at me, hands shoved into his jeans pockets and hip jutted cockily to the side. He was gorgeous, too, with forest-green eyes, sandy blonde hair and a scruffy two-day-old beard that gave him a roguish allure. After Olle shook my hand, Viktor politely offered his.

"Where are you from?" he asked.

He sidled up to the bar next to me and gestured to the bartender. Olle hopped on the barstool next to Jillian. She gave me a crooked, conspiratorial smirk and turned to him. Resigned, I gulped the rest of the martini and smiled weakly at Viktor.

"America. A small town in the middle of the country," I replied.

I'd learned during my short time in Europe that most Europeans were familiar with only the big U.S. cities like New York, Los Angeles and Miami, so I stopped providing details about my tiny town's location.

The bartender served me another martini and Viktor a beer. He drank half of it in three big swallows and said, "I am from Sweden, a small town, too. Falkenberg, do you know it?"

My jaw dropped. "Did you say Falkenberg?" I squeaked.

"Yes, you know it?"

"On the Kattegat?"

"You know it!" he exclaimed, his eyes widening with disbelief. I lowered mine, sipping the martini and immediately suspicious. "You know Falkenberg?" he prodded.

I peeked at him. He seemed as astonished as me. "Yes, I know it," I said softy, amazed by the coincidence. "My great-grandparents emigrated from there. My great-grandfather was a fisherman."

"Skit! You are Swedish!"

He looked at me differently, eyes warm and welcoming. It hit me he might be as uncomfortable as I was with the forced encounter.

"Full-blooded," I said. "My grandparents and parents are all Swedes. It's weird, but it just happened that way."

"It is incredible, beautiful Haley," he said. He bent around me and talked excitedly to Olle in his native language.

"What's going on, Hales?" Jillian whispered.

"He's from the same town in Sweden where my great-grandparents are from," I replied.

"No shit! Hmm…"

I sensed she had more to say and rolled my eyes. "What, Jillian?"

She giggled and leaned close. "Olle invited us to a party upstairs at a teammate's suite. Can we go? Please, Hales?"

It was the first time since Mikel I experienced a twinge of happiness. She was so excited and I laughed. "Sure, Jills. You want to sleep with him, don't you?"

"Hell, yes! I had no clue soccer players were so hot."

I lowered my eyes. My belly clenched. I knew exactly how she felt, but Mikel wasn't simply a soccer player. He was *Mikel,* mi amor.

"Shit, Hales, I'm sorry. I didn't–"

"It's fine," I interrupted.

She'd be going back to the States soon. I wouldn't let Mikel come between us and was determined to support her like she'd supported me.

"Seriously, I didn't–"

"Stop, Jillian, I'm fine. Besides, Viktor is cool. I don't mind hanging out with him."

"Really? Oh my God, Hales, I hope Olle wants me, too."

"I'm sure he does," I muttered, wondering if there was a condom bowl set prominently on a table in the suite.

~~~~~~†~~~~~~

The party was loud and lively. There were at least thirty people dancing to American hip hop or making out on the sofa and chairs. There was even a bartender dressed in a tuxedo.

Viktor and I stood by the window, which opened to a six-story, eighteenth-century apartment building across the street. Since I could easily find my way back to my room, I sipped another Martini, swaying to the loud music.

"Isn't your teammate worried about the noise?" I asked. Not that I cared. I was simply making conversation.

"No, the team has every room on the floor."

"Oh."

"How long will you be in Paris?" he asked.

"I don't know. Jillian is leaving in a few days, and I don't know where I'll go next." The thought of Jillian's imminent departure made me anxious.

"You are not returning to the United States? Are you touring Europe?"

"No, well, maybe. I'm a photographer. Just starting out."

"Really? Have I seen any of your pictures?"

"Um, well..."

If it hadn't been for the fact that Mikel had betrayed me, I would have been proud to mention the Hunger photo, but it still hurt too much to say his name.

"Wait a minute! Are you Haley *Hanson?*" His lips curled into a satisfied grin and he eyed me expectantly. I was dumbstruck, unable to comprehend how he knew about me. "Skit! You are her! You took the Garro photo!" I wanted to flee, but my legs turned into rubber. "Beautiful, brilliant," he sighed.

"How-how-how do you know me?" I stammered.

"Every soccer player in Europe knows about you. Your picture is in the United Nations Hunger campaign summary. We all envy the Garro photo and the fact you are his girlfriend. When you see him, tell him he is a lucky man."

My eyes welled with tears. I visibly trembled. Gin spilled from the martini glass and splashed on his shoe.

"Skit." He gently removed the glass from my hand. "What did I say?"

I didn't want to cry. I *wouldn't* cry. I wouldn't make a fool of myself because of *him*. I took a deep breath and thought about Jillian at the Eiffel Tower. She'd beamed happily, the world at her feet. I'd taken an amazing photo of her. I'd put it on the cover of the photo album I was going to make for her.

"Are you okay, Haley?"

I cleared my throat and stiffened my spine. "I'm good, and I'm not Mikel Garro's girlfriend anymore."

He raked a hand through his hair and eyed me curiously. "Garro's a fool. Let's get drunk."

"Let's." I grabbed the martini and downed it.

Viktor and I hung out near the bartender until a seat opened up on the sofa. He entertained me by poking fun at his teammates, making up hilarious names for them as they paired up with the other ladies who'd been invited to the party.

"Charles and Diana," he said, pointing at a horse-faced player and his beautiful, blue-eyed companion.

I laughed, the alcohol working its magic. It didn't take long for Jillian to leave with Olle, which was my cue to leave, too.

"It was nice to meet you, Viktor." I meant it. He'd managed to distract me from further thoughts about Mikel. "Good luck with the soccer match."

His brows furrowed and he buried his nose in my throat. "Let's party in my room." I stiffened and shivered at the same time. He nipped at my earlobe and softly rubbed his scruffy face on my cheek. "Come on, Haley, let's have some fun."

He gently squeezed my bare thigh and moved under my

miniskirt, his long fingers lightly skimming toward my pussy inch-by-inch. Maybe it was the four martinis. Maybe I was desperate for affection. Maybe I simply enjoyed sex and missed it. Or maybe I wanted to get back at Mikel by fucking another soccer player. Whatever the reason, my libido came back to life. I suddenly wanted Viktor, *bad*.

My clit throbbed hungrily. Desire accumulated wet and hot between my legs. I forgot about my promise to swear off men. "Let's," I said. Smirking, he stood and reached for my hand. I tipsily got to my feet. "No strings, okay?"

"No strings." His eyes locked onto mine, dimming and morphing into a dark moss. He kissed my knuckles, wrapped an arm around my waist and led me to a room at the end of the hall.

It had been forever since a man had touched me, at least it seemed that way. As soon as we entered his suite, his lips crushed mine. He forced his tongue into my mouth, demanding a response, and I answered fervently, throwing my arms around his neck and bowing against him.

I didn't know how hungry I'd become, my body starved for attention and desperate for the sexual gratification I'd become accustomed to. As my tongue thrashed back at his, I fumbled with the button and zipper on his jeans and boldly shoved a hand into his underwear.

His cock was fat and hard. I grasped it firmly and pulled it out of his jeans, caressing the crown with my thumb. He moaned appreciatively, gripped the hair on the nape of my neck and jerked my head back.

"Fuck…" he sighed, lips twisting into a lusty grin.

"Let's."

His grin turned wicked and he led me into the bedroom. He brushed his lips over mine and rubbed his cock against my belly. "How do you like it?"

"Naked," I said

Grunting his agreement, he stepped back and watched as I wriggled out of the skintight mini-dress, shimmied out of the skimpy thong and kicked off the high heels.

He smiled appreciatively and stripped quickly, eyes fixed on my nakedness. My insides tightened and churned as each section of his ripped body came into view, every part of him hard and chiseled with muscles. A dragon tattoo ran from one hip to the center of his sculpted chest, the mythical beast breathing red and yellow fire. His skin was creamy white from head to toe except for his thick shaft, which was a juicy caramel color and engorged with blood.

I wanted to taste it. I wanted to sink my wet pussy down on it. Viktor had his own plans. He pushed me onto the bed and crawled on top of me.

"You're fucking hot," he growled.

He fondled my breasts, squeezing and massaging and planting his lips on a nipple to lick and suck. I groaned with pleasure and gripped his ass, drawing him closer.

Flesh on flesh. Raw sexual desire. He slipped a hand between my legs and caressed my clit with one finger then two. My pussy plumped and beaded. Liquid fire blazed from my nipples to my deepest crevices and back again. Viktor the Swedish soccer player knew what he was doing. For the first time since Mikel, I felt alive.

"I want you to fuck me on top." His voice was low and husky. He rolled onto his back, grabbed a condom from the nightstand drawer and ripped it open with his teeth.

I slithered onto him, wanting to taste him first, and I eagerly engulfed his swollen cock in my mouth.

He let out a long groan and thrust upward, pushing his juicy shaft farther into me and slamming against my throat. "Garro is a fool," he said hoarsely.

I bolted upright and glared murderously at him. "Christ, Viktor, shut up."

If I wasn't so horny, I might have left. Viktor's comment annoyed me. A lump grew in my throat. I ignored it and snatched the condom from him and deftly applied it, focusing on my throbbing pussy as I sank down on him.

My sodden flesh stretched to accommodate his bloated erection.

He grinded against my wet folds, hitting my clit exactly right. Until that moment I hadn't realized how much I missed the fiery sensations that pulsed through my veins and the exquisite, almost painful ache that burned white-hot as I rode him. I angled my sex so his cock scraped the sweet spot inside me, and he clutched my tits, his palms tantalizing the stiff buds and titillating me more. I moved faster.

"Come for me, Haley, come on, baby…"

Viktor thrashed beneath me, grinding and thrusting as I feverishly moved up and down. The euphoria began as a ripple, building, swelling and finally cresting, the orgasm crashing over me. I threw back my head and stilled, holding my breath and relishing the warm waves rolling through me.

I'd almost forgotten. I'd almost given up on men, on sex, on the ecstasy. Viktor stiffened next and gripped my hips. He detonated, cried out my name and our convulsions merged. A sudden surge of power blasted through me, transforming me. I didn't know how and couldn't sort it out right then. I collapsed on his chest. A soothing calm enveloped me. A sense of self-satisfaction I hadn't felt for weeks settled in my gut. And I was overwhelmed with gratitude. Viktor the Swedish soccer player had awakened my libido and fucked me *good,* and it was just for fun.

No strings…

After Viktor began snoring, I slipped out of bed, dressed quickly and scampered to my suite. It was three in the morning and Jillian hadn't returned. I was relieved to be alone for once and crawled into bed and nestled under the covers. My flesh tingled, my pussy pulsed happily and something inside me interminably shifted.

I'd fallen in love with Mikel, deeply, unconditionally and with all my heart and soul. Yet love was elusive and our love wasn't true. I couldn't, I *wouldn't* go down that road again anytime soon, learning my lesson. Yet our time together wasn't wasted.

Mikel Garro had awakened my sexuality. I hadn't realized how much it had become a part of me, how orgasmic I'd become. Being with Viktor was a revelation. I suddenly understood I was a sexual creature. I needed sex more than I needed love and there was nothing stopping me. I was beautiful, *hot*, and I would use it to my advantage.

When I woke the next day, Jillian was snuggling against me with her head burrowed in my throat and an arm draped over my waist. It was the first time since Mikel that I'd slept soundly, not even awakening when she returned to the room.

I didn't want to disturb her, but I needed to pee. I gently removed her arm and scooted to the bed's edge.

"Hales," she muttered groggily.

"Morning, Jills," I whispered. I hastily retreated to the bathroom and took care of business. When I came back, she was sitting and grinning conspiratorially. I crawled back into bed and eyed her expectantly, my heart brimming with love for her. "So? Did you have a good time?"

"Holy shit, Hales, holy shit," she sighed. "He's great, I mean, I don't know how to put it in words. And his cock… I mean, it's huge! I thought he'd rip me apart. I'm amazed it fit, but it did. And I had two orgasms, and he's really very sweet, and he invited us to the match tomorrow night. And dinner tonight. I can't wait! Oh, God, Haley…"

I didn't want to burst her bubble, but if Olle was like Mikel, she wouldn't be having sex with him the night before the match nor would I be attending it. And although I'd come to terms with my new reality in the wee hours of the morning, I doubted I'd ever go to another soccer game, my feelings still too raw.

I would tell her later and instead asked, "How big is big?"

~~~~~~†~~~~~~

We ate dinner with Olle and Viktor at an expensive restaurant near the Louvre. As I'd expected, sex for her that night was not to be. Jillian was disappointed. She whipped out her phone, got online and cited statistics, chastising Olle for believing in a myth. But he stood his ground, promising he'd make it up to her, and she turned to Viktor for help.

"Do you believe that crap, too?" she asked, smiling knowingly at me.

I'd told her about Viktor and me. I think the news made her happier than fucking Olle. It was a sign I was mending and she didn't need to worry about me anymore.

"Skit, yes! I know from experience. I did it once before a match and had weak legs. It is not a myth," he insisted.

She scoffed and we went clubbing instead. The next night, she grudgingly went to the match without me. France beat Sweden, and both men were glum when they returned to the hotel. But they weren't too depressed for consolation sex.

Jillian went to Olle's room and I went to Viktor's. While she spent the night with Olle, I slipped back to our room after Viktor fell asleep, not caring about being with him unless he was screwing me.

We compared notes the next day, giggling and joking as we dressed for lunch with them. Then they checked out of the hotel and returned to Sweden.

"That was fun, wasn't it?" she quipped.

I hugged her warmly. I admired her sunny disposition and the fact that she'd kept her feelings in check, enjoying Olle's company and not becoming infatuated with him. I wished I'd done the same with Mikel. But I couldn't turn back the clock, and since I had only one day left with her, I wasn't going to waste it by obsessing about him.

"Anything you want to see before you leave, Jills?" I asked.

"Is there anything left?" she teased.

"I don't think so," I laughed. It was true.

She saw Paris like she'd wanted and we did it together and in style. It would've never happened if Mikel hadn't rejected me.

"Okay, then shopping it is! I need more suitcases for my new clothes."

My heart swelled with wonderful memories of her. My eyes fluttered open. Then my heart sank, confronted by the darkness and silence again. And there was something else. A foul smell. Worse than the putrid mattress, which I'd become used to. It smelled like rotting meat.

As I struggled to rise, my hip squished a creamy substance. I gingerly touched it. Bile rose in my throat. I'd reflexively defecated sometime during my reverie.

Completely humiliated, I fought off the despair and rolled shakily onto the hard floor. My infected buttock throbbed painfully. My anus was raw and caked with feces. My skin was clammy and hot. I had no idea how long I'd languished like that or how long it had been since Baba's last call. Hours? Days?

"Don't give up, Hales, and don't let anyone or anything stand in your way. I love you and go get 'em!"

It was Jillian shouting encouragement as she ran to the gate and disappeared around a corner at the Charles de Gaulle Airport. She was there with me. In my head. Encouraging me.

But I was dying. It was too late. I'd done what she'd said. After she left, I'd taken control of my life again and fearlessly forged ahead. I'd become famous, but to what end?

To die in a dark, silent cellar?

"Jills…"

"Go get 'em, Hales!"

"Jills…"

"Don't give up, Hales!"

I couldn't change my fate, but it was suddenly important that I die with a modicum of dignity. I would die but not in my own shit.

Staggering to my knees, I tried to remember the right corner, the corner with the crates of books. I fought the dizziness and agony. I willed my broken body to move, forcing one hand forward then the other. Then a knee. Then the other knee. One more time. One more time…

My head hit the wall and I gasped for breath. I was terribly weak and feverish. Perspiration trickled off my nose. Infection had invaded my body and there was no antibiotic to purge it. But I wasn't dead yet and Jillian was there with me, reassuring me.

I pressed on, crawling slowly and deliberately until I reached the crates. I braced my hands against the stone and painstakingly tottered to my feet. I immediately felt faint, but I managed to tip over the top crate and the one below it before I spiraled into unconsciousness. When I woke, I was on the floor surrounded by books.

I'd landed on my ass. The pain burned through me. I teetered to my knees, inhaling deeply and trying to stay alert. It took me several minutes before I was steady enough to fumble for a book. I ripped out its pages two and three at a time until there was nothing left but the binding.

The minor exertion left me breathing heavily. My flesh dripped with sweat, which I used to moisten some pages. Then I stretched an arm behind me. My muscles protested as I wiped my ass.

I crumpled the soiled paper and tossed it as far away from me as I could, and I repeated the process again and again until my anus was clean. It felt good to accomplish something, even though it was pointless considering I'd be dead anyway. Yet I forged ahead and used the sweat and paper to wipe the puss from my buttock and finally the grime from my hands.

Then I collapsed from exhaustion and rested on my good side. I wanted to sleep, wanted to return to the past, wanted peace, but the brick floor was uneven and cold. When I was able, I wobbled to my knees again, tore out more pages from the books and spread them over the brick until there was a half inch of padding to lay on.

I wished I'd thought of it before. Maybe the burn on my butt wouldn't have become infected and my death wouldn't be as painful. But it was too late, too late to change many things, and there was one regret that overshadowed all others.

I wished I'd asked Mikel why he'd forsaken me.

The Billionaire and His Wife

I waited at the airport until Jillian's plane left, selfishly hoping the flight would be delayed or canceled. One more hour with her was better than nothing. But it wasn't to be, and I dejectedly returned to the hotel and crawled into bed.

I missed her terribly and couldn't rest. She'd been my rock, my distraction and my inspiration. After she was gone, I didn't know what to do or where to go next.

"Don't give up, Hales, and don't let anyone or anything stand in your way. I love you and go get 'em!"

She wasn't there to see me depressed again and hiding under the covers in the dark. Still, I sensed her presence and felt ashamed, as if I was betraying her trust. It would have been so easy to drift back into despair, the loneliness creeping up on me. But I fought it and angrily scrambled from bed, deciding I might as well go downstairs and have a drink.

The hotel closet was full of clothes Jillian had insisted I buy. In a loving salute to her, I chose a slinky, backless mini-dress with a scooped neckline that accentuated my breasts. It was five o'clock, the bar teemed with customers, and I slid onto a stool next to an elderly man and his wife and ordered a martini.

It didn't take long for a handsome young Frenchman to approach and offer to buy me a drink. Glowering irritably, I ignored him, not in the mood for companionship of any kind. In retrospect, I shouldn't have dressed so seductively, because before I could finish my first drink two more guys hit on me. When the man and his wife left and vacated the seats next to me, I signaled for the bill.

"You know they can't help themselves." The voice was soft and melodic and came from a striking woman who gracefully slipped onto the stool beside me. "Where's your friend?" she asked.

She was stunning, exotic, with smooth, dark cocoa skin, large, slightly-tilted eyes that were an unusual grayish-green, and coppery hair streaked with blonde highlights, styled in a trendy pixie cut.

Taken aback by her familiarity, I eyed her warily.

"Oh, sorry," she chuckled. "I'm Celine. My husband and I have been staying here and we couldn't help but notice you and your girlfriend. You're American, right?"

"Yes," I responded curtly. I hastily signed the check and stood to leave.

"Wait, I didn't mean to offend you," she said. "Please, stay. Let me buy you a drink. My husband is busy with business and I hate drinking alone. If you like, I'll fend off the guys, although I don't know why you'd want me to."

Her luminous eyes danced with amusement, and I was suddenly curious. I also wanted another martini and didn't want to start drinking alone in my room again.

"Sure, I'm Haley."

She extended a slim hand. "Nice to meet you, Haley."

I politely shook it. Her grip was warm and confident and she gestured at the bartender and ordered martinis for us.

"Cheers!" she toasted. "Where are you from?"

I didn't want to chitchat. I didn't want to do anything except drink. Yet I needed the distraction and grudgingly replied, "The

Midwest."

"Los Angeles. Is your friend sick?"

She was a nosy distraction and I muttered, "Um, no, she left today."

"Oh, that's too bad. It looked like you girls were having fun." She sounded almost motherly. I wondered how old she was. "Where did she go?" she asked.

I took a big gulp of the martini, feeling like I was stuck with her until I finished it. "Back to the States. She's starting college in a few days."

"And you? Are you a college student, too?"

Before I could answer an attractive man wearing an expensive tailored suit leaned in between us. He set a hand on the bar and smiled lecherously at me. "Ma chérie, vous—"

"Excuse me!" Celine exclaimed. She grabbed him by the waist, moved him aside and chastised him in perfect French.

He was as shocked as I was. He cursed under his breath, glared murderously at her and stomped off.

Grinning mischievously, she sipped the martini and quipped, "That was extremely rude."

My lips quirked into a weak smile. Just as she'd promised, she deflected the unwanted advance. I relaxed a little.

"They can't help themselves," she smirked. "You're really quite lovely, Haley. Young and fresh. You can't blame them for wanting a piece of you."

"Thank you." The way she was looking at me made me uncomfortable. "You're lovely, too."

I don't know why I said it, except I was nervous and it was true.

"You're very kind, but I have a few years on you, *ma chérie,*" she said sarcastically, making fun of the guy in the suit by emphasizing the French words. "So, where were we?"

I decided to humor her and replied, "No, I'm not a student. I'm a photographer."

"A photographer! How wonderful! What kind? Portraits? Landscapes?"

I'd expected the usual patronizing reaction, but her interest seemed sincere. "Various. Some landscape, some travel, some street and some action, but I like photojournalism best."

"Very nice, Haley, I wish I'd had a goal when I was younger. Anything published?"

I didn't want to tell her about the Hunger photo. It would always be a reminder of Mikel. Then I realized I was being stupid. I was proud of it and needed to use it to my advantage if I wanted to get ahead in my career. "Um, yes." I replied guardedly.

"Good." She pulled out a phone from her purse. "Where are they published? I'd like to see them."

I didn't know why she even cared, a stranger. I couldn't put my finger on it, but there was something about her that was unsettling. Still, I liked the attention and asked, "Have you seen the new United Nations campaign for the hunger program?"

"Yes, of course. It's sensational, isn't it? And that boy, the soccer player, is to die for. God, I would love a–" She stopped mid-sentence and nervously toyed with the huge diamond on her ring finger. "We donated a boatload of money. Why do you ask?"

"I took the photo," I blurted out.

I expected her to be shocked. Instead, she smiled brightly and said, "That's wonderful. Very impressive." She didn't ask about Mikel, which was a relief and somewhat surprising considering her initial reaction to him. "You must have dinner with us tonight. My husband would love to meet you. He thinks the photograph is amazing, and here you are, the photographer..."

After the third martini, I accepted the dinner invitation. It was to be the beginning of my descent into decadence.

Celine's husband was Jack Luck, *the* Jack Luck, the billionaire, 3-D software designer turned movie producer and maker of one of the most popular movies of my generation, an irreverent satire of sexual dysfunction in the modern age titled *Vicious.*

"Haley Hanson, you're as beautiful as you are talented." He gazed at me with dark sultry eyes and grasped my hand.

My jaw dropped. Everyone in the world knew Jack Luck, and to meet him in person was a stroke of *luck,* or at least I thought so at the time. He exuded a sexy, seductive power that commanded notice, still incredibly handsome for a man in his fifties. Fit and toned with a full head of salt-and-pepper hair clipped stylishly, he was dressed casually in jeans, a black shirt and black sport coat, which enhanced his sex appeal.

"Um, nice to meet you," I replied nervously.

He placed a hand on the small of Celine's back and then mine. "Ladies," he said silkily, and he escorted us outside the hotel to a waiting limousine.

As we drove away, I tried to remain calm and cool. But I was in the presence of American royalty and stammered, "I-I-I love *Vicious.*"

He smiled politely and I groaned inwardly, feeling like a foolish little girl.

"Jack's working on a new movie, which will be even better," Celine said.

She chatted about the new film and the potential actors until we arrived at the restaurant, which was a small, off-the-beaten-path Italian bistro in the Montmartre district. The maître d' hovered at the table, refilling our wine glasses the instant they were half full. Jack delved into my life and ambitions while deftly making me feel at ease, or maybe it was the wine. Either way, by the end of the meal, I agreed to join them for an Aegean Sea cruise on board their private yacht for my birthday, which was two weeks away.

It was a snap decision. I needed to keep moving forward and Jack promised to sail to any ports of my choosing–Athens, the Greek Isles, Istanbul–wherever I wanted. The offer was too tempting. Or maybe the alcohol had something to do with it.

"It's very generous." I concentrated on not slurring my words. "But why? You barely know me."

Even in my drunken state I was suspicious about their

motivations. I was nobody. It didn't feel right for them to make such an extravagant offer. Yet I would've been crazy not to accept. After all, he was *the* Jack Luck, and besides, if I still felt uncomfortable in the morning when I was less intoxicated, I could always change my mind.

Jack glanced at Celine. A knowing look passed between them. "I like your drive, kid, and your pluck," he said. "You know what you want and you have talent. Plus, Celine insists and I can't deny her."

He liked my "pluck." Maybe that was the attraction. Or maybe I reminded him of Celine, who'd shown her own pluck at the bar.

She leaned across the table and grasped my hand. "Jack is always so busy and I get bored. It'll be fun having you around."

The explanation was as good as any, the idle rich looking to be entertained. I let go of my reservations and asked, "When do we leave?"

Celine and I spent the next two days shopping and preparing for the trip. She took me under her wing, starting with a stop at a salon, where I had my hair trimmed, eyebrows threaded, nails buffed and polished and pubic hair clipped and shaped so it wouldn't show in the skimpy bikinis she would buy for me, despite my strong objections.

"Don't be silly, Haley, I'm filthy rich," she smirked.

"I have money, Celine. I get royalties from the Hunger merchandise."

"That's all well and good, but when you're with me, I pay. I don't want to hear another word about it."

She was not only spunky but stubborn. I soon learned there was no use fighting her. She also seemed to really enjoy herself, and I wondered if she was the same with everyone or just me.

Other than the fact that she was beautiful and married to Jack Luck, I didn't know much about her. When we stopped for lunch, I took the opportunity to find out more.

"How long have you and Jack been married?" I asked.

"Eleven years."

"How did you meet?"

"Hmm… At a birthday party."

I waited for her to elaborate, but she took a bite of salad and averted her eyes.

"Do you have children?"

"Me? *God, no*. Jack has two from a previous marriage and one from an old girlfriend, but you probably already know that. They're all boys, well, men now."

I still couldn't gage how old she was and was dying to ask. But I didn't feel comfortable asking her outright, so I kept peppering her with questions and hoped the answer would reveal itself.

"Were you married before, too?"

"No, Jack's my first."

"What did you do before you met him?"

"This and that."

She didn't seem to have a problem talking about Jack, but she was acting very mysterious about her own background. The nagging feeling she was hiding something bubbled inside me.

"What about you, Haley? You're too young to have been married, but have you ever been in love?"

Mikel's crooked grin flashed through my mind. I pushed it back, suddenly appreciating Celine's reticence to talk about herself. Maybe there was someone in her past she wanted to forget, too.

"Um, no," I lied.

She gazed curiously at me. I lowered my eyes, certain she knew I'd lied. But two could play the game. I wouldn't feel guilty nor did I care what she thought about me. I poured myself another glass of wine and took a big gulp.

"Tell me if I'm overstepping, Haley, but do you like boys or girls?" The question came out of the blue. I spit wine back into the glass. "It doesn't matter one way or the other," she chuckled. "I'm only curious. You seem down since your girlfriend left, and you didn't give those guys at the bar the time of day."

I gaped at her. The question wasn't offensive. I was simply surprised she would ask it. Yet two could play the game and my lips curled into a slight smile. "I'll tell you if you tell me how old you are."

Celine chuckled some more and sighed. "That's why you've been so inquisitive today. Please, Haley, don't be shy with me. If you want to know something, then ask. If I want to tell you, then I will. I'm thirty-nine."

"Boys," I smiled brightly.

She raised her glass for a toast. I clinked mine to hers, enjoying the game. She grinned mischievously and said, "If you've never been with a woman, you should try it sometime, too."

When I checked out of the hotel two days later, the bill had already been paid by Celine. That nagging feeling simmered in my gut. Jack and Celine hadn't come downstairs yet, so I waited in the lobby with my five-piece designer luggage set filled with my new wardrobe. Restless, I called Jillian.

"How's school?" I asked.

"Harder than I expected, but there's a cute guy in my physics class and we have a study date tomorrow."

"Sounds promising. What's his name?"

"Marcus. He's really hot, and I think he's smarter than me."

I smiled inside. Jillian would never take a guy seriously unless he was as smart as or smarter than her.

"What have you been up to? You're not moping around, are you?" she asked.

"No, I'm fine. You'll never believe where I'm going and who I'm going with," I said.

"Spill, Hales."

"A cruise on a private yacht with Jack Luck."

There was a silent moment while she digested the news and then she squealed, "*The* Jack Luck!"

"Yep, *the* Jack Luck and his wife."

"You're shitting me! How did that happen?"

I quickly filled her in. When I finished, she bombarded me with questions.

"Is he as hot in person?"

"More."

"What's the wife like?"

"She's interesting. Gorgeous. Kind of strange, mysterious. She thought you and I were lovers."

"What? She did?"

"Yep. She'd been watching us and said I should try it with a woman sometime," I chuckled.

"It's a date!" she teased.

The comment was classic Jillian and my heart swelled affectionately. She was my best friend and I trusted her completely. Suddenly, I was nervous about my decision to go off on my own with a couple of strangers.

Sensing my anxiety as only she could do, she asked, "What, Hales?"

"I don't know. Don't you think their invitation is a little odd?"

"Jesus, Haley, don't overanalyze it. He's Jack Luck, not a serial killer. Go. Have some fun. If you're not enjoying yourself, you can swim, can't you?"

"Yes," I laughed. Then Jack and Celine appeared. "Gotta go, Jills. Call you soon."

The world I entered that day was one few would ever see. *Surreal. Amazing.* The life of the rich and famous and I had a close-up shot of it.

We took a limo to Orly Airport and sat side by side in the back seat, the remaining roomy interior stacked with luggage that wouldn't fit in the trunk. Then we jetted to Athens in Jack's private plane. The luxurious accommodations and service provided by a hunky male flight attendant were beyond anything I could have imagined, the three-hour flight seeming to fly by. A martini, then a delicious Niçoise salad for lunch accompanied by wine, then another martini and we were there.

When we landed in Athens, I had a good buzz going. The hunk solicitously escorted me off the plane and to a Mercedes minivan parked on the runway. After the luggage was transferred into the back of the vehicle by two men wearing orange safety jackets, we were transported by a uniformed driver a mile across the tarmac to a waiting helicopter.

"Ever been on a helicopter, kid?" Jack asked. Amusement lit his green eyes.

I eyed him irritably, wishing he'd stop calling me "kid." He barely knew me. He said it affectionately, though, which I didn't understand or think I deserved.

"No," I replied softly. I watched him climb into the copter and my jaw dropped. He was the pilot. The blades began to spin noisily. My hair whipped around my face and my stomach somersaulted.

"He's been flying them for years," Celine shouted over the whoosh of blades.

He hopped out of the craft and escorted Celine and me to it. He guided me to the seat in front, strapped me in and placed headphones on my ears. He did the same for Celine, who sat behind me. Once the luggage was piled in the craft's rear, he lifted off and headed south, reaching the sea in five minutes.

He flew low over the water. The dull ache in the pit of my stomach disappeared, replaced by a rush of excitement. We whizzed above the blue ocean and I grinned from ear to ear, mesmerized by the waves and whitecaps that surged below me.

"You okay, kid?"

His normally deep voice sounded tinny through the headphone speakers. I heard my own tinny voice shriek "it's great, Jack!"

Celine chuckled. "I told you she'd love it."

Smiling a rare smile, he warmly squeezed my thigh and glanced knowingly at Celine behind me. Then the boat came into view and my jaw dropped again.

It was huge, a long, sleek mega yacht with an oval pool at one end of the deck and a heliport at the other. Jack deftly set the copter on the helipad, shut off the engine and waited for the propellers to still before unstrapping himself and me.

Three crew members rushed to the craft. A tall, skinny man dressed in trim white pants and a blue polo shirt gave me a toothy smile and helped me on board.

"My lady," he greeted. He bowed his head deferentially and led me to a covered verandah to join Jack and Celine. They stood next to two crew members, one a grizzly-looking man with a leathery tanned face wearing a uniform and a captain's hat, and the other a muscular guy clad in trim white pants and a red polo shirt instead of a blue one.

"Haley, this is Captain John Black and the ship's purser, Reginald," Jack introduced.

"Miss." The Captain removed his hat and bowed his head.

"My lady," Reginald greeted, bowing his head, too.

I shifted nervously, uncomfortable with the formality and royal treatment.

"Reginald manages the crew. If you have any problems or complaints, tell Reginald," Jack said.

Then two women appeared dressed in tight white miniskirts and blue tank tops. Celine took over the introductions.

"Haley, this is May." She nodded at a petite Asian girl, her creamy white face framed by a stylish bob hairdo. "She's your personal assistant while you're with us."

May smiled shyly and bowed her head like the others.

I gaped. "Personal assistant?" I had no idea what a personal assistant did on a yacht and why I would need one.

"Yes, Haley, she'll take care of all your needs while you're here," Celine replied irritably, as if I was from a different planet.

"But, I don't need a—"

"May is very discreet," she interrupted, waving a hand in the air dismissively. "This is my PA, Maria."

Skin smooth and coppery, her long black hair pulled back in a tight ponytail, Maria was a Spanish beauty. The image of another Spanish beauty with long black hair fucking Mikel flashed through my mind. My gut wrenched.

Maria acknowledged me with a slight nod. I couldn't look at her and turned away, gazing into the sea and forcing myself to think about something else, like the luxurious jet and thrilling helicopter ride. I wished I'd taken photos to send to Jillian.

"Maria, May, go unpack for us." Celine's curt, demanding tone jolted me back to the present. As Maria and May walked away, I asked if I could take pictures of the boat.

"Be my guest, kid," Jack said. "If you'll excuse me, I have work to do. Celine will show you around."

"I need my camera. I packed it in the carry-on."

"May!" Celine shouted. May turned on her heels, scurried back to us and eyed me expectantly. "Well, tell her," Celine snapped, obviously frustrated by my unworldliness.

Glowering, I straightened my spine, annoyed that she assumed I'd be familiar with using a personal assistant, which I didn't need or want anyway. I took a deep breath and said, "Please bring me my camera case. It's in the carry-on."

The encounter with the personal assistants was the beginning of a love/hate relationship with Celine, although I couldn't say I ever really loved her. Like was more accurate, and the longer I stayed on the yacht, the more I simply tolerated her. Yet as I lay dying in the cellar, I realized that much of her petty, condescending and despotic behavior, which had initially turned me off, had in reality rubbed off on me.

But at first I was awestruck by the mega yacht and the lifestyle.

She gave me the grand tour, proudly pointing out its lavish features, starting at the top deck, where the master suite, four VIP suites, a private dining room and lounge were located.

I was given the VIP suite situated next to the master bedroom at the rear of the boat. May was waiting for me there, camera case in hand. I removed the camera and immediately started snapping pictures. The suite was double the size of the hotel room in Paris. The entire exterior wall, including the one in the luxurious bathroom, had large windows with spectacular sea views, giving it a light and airy feel and making it seem even larger.

The décor was stunning, too, a contemporary art deco design with abstract geometrical shapes and bold colors. And amid the modern furnishings was the latest technology, including flat screen TV's, a toilet seat warmer and electronic window shades. The dressing room was even equipped with light settings that matched the illumination in the public areas so women could apply makeup in the perfect light.

Celine guided me to the deck below next. Besides the helm, heliport and pool, there was a discothèque and bar, large salon, dining room, state-of-the-art kitchen and gazebo lounge. When we finally got to the other end of the boat where the pool was, my jaw dropped once more, surprised to see another guest sprawled out on a comfy deck chair.

Glistening with oil, he was an amazing specimen of manhood with a bronze torso teeming with tattoos, toned muscles that rippled into a perfect "V," and a generous cock that bulged provocatively inside a snug speedo.

A gasp stuck in my throat. My pussy twitched. I glanced at Celine.

"That's Kostas, your birthday present. You said you like guys," she smirked.

Kostas gracefully sprang to his feet and strutted over to me. Celine introduced us, and he smiled a dazzling, friendly smile, eyes a striking crystal blue that seemed bluer against his tanned skin and thick black hair. Wanton desire churned my blood.

"You are as lovely as Celine said you would be," he murmured silkily.

A good six inches taller than me, he bent his head and kissed me on both cheeks. There was a trace of an accent, and because of his name I assumed he was Greek. An excited tingle tickled up my spine.

Kostas, my *birthday present.*

A hot guy for a birthday present. The personal assistant. I didn't know what to think, feeling like I'd entered an alternate universe. Yet at that moment I really liked Celine. Kostas was delicious, the gift audacious, and I was floored, speechless.

"You can get to know each other later," she said. "Let's finish the tour and change into our suits. I haven't been in the sun for ages."

We quickly toured the bottom two decks, which contained the engine room and smaller suites and staterooms for the fifty crew members. When I returned to my suite, May was waiting for me.

"May I help you, Miss?" she asked meekly.

I immediately felt uncomfortable. "No, I'm going for I swim," I replied politely.

I strode into the dressing room to look for my swimsuits. She scurried after me, headed straight for the walk-in closet and grabbed the eight new bikinis Celine had purchased for me. After aligning them neatly on an art deco divan set below a large wall mirror, she stepped back and eyed me expectantly. Astonished, I stared back at her.

"Um, thanks, you can go now," I sighed.

"No, Miss, I will help you dress." She lowered her eyes timidly and I rolled mine.

"Look, May, I can dress myself. No offense, but I don't need a personal assistant."

"But I am assigned to you. This is what Mr. Jack pays me to do," she croaked nervously.

I shoved aside the bikinis and dropped onto the divan, wondering what to do. May was already driving me nuts, but it was not her personally. It was the idea of her. I was out of my league and found the entire PA situation ridiculous. Celine was acting like a queen and I was her princess. I had a nagging feeling she had an ulterior motive, as if she wanted May to keep an eye on me, although I couldn't fathom why.

Since there was nothing I could do about it right then, I stripped and slipped into a blue-and-white-striped suit with a thong bikini bottom. May fussed with the top, straightened the straps and asked, "Do you want sunscreen, Miss?"

"Yes," I replied.

She scampered to the bathroom and I studied myself in the mirror. The bikini was simple and skimpy, three triangles covering my full breasts and pussy. I looked hot and wondered if Kostas would think so, too. Then the memory of Mikel fucking me in front of the mirror in the bathroom at his house invaded my thoughts. I turned away from my reflection, forcing myself to focus on something else, like where May had stored the matching sarong and the smoking hot Greek Adonis waiting at the pool.

May returned with the lotion and offered to apply it. I snatched it from her hand and asked about the sarong. In seconds she was wrapping it around my hips.

I didn't thank her, not wanting to encourage her. I retreated to the bathroom, closed the door and washed my face and applied sunscreen. I left the rest of me for Kostas, hoping he'd be happy to rub it all over me. Then I fluffed my hair, added pink gloss to my lips and headed to the pool, ignoring May as she followed at a distance.

I found Kostas in the pool. When he saw me, he grinned appreciatively and gracefully climbed out of the water.

"Haley!" he exclaimed.

His body glistened and dripped with water. He was mouthwateringly hot and I imagined licking him from head to toe. He swaggered provocatively over to me, and I was relieved Celine hadn't shown up yet, wanting to find out more about him without her interference.

"Hi," I greeted, smiling.

"Please, sit with me," he said. He dragged a lounge chair next to his and patted the cushion.

I removed the sarong, draped it over the back of the chair and stretched out, gawking as he toweled off. He started with his handsome face and moved to his muscular arms, his chest, his hard abs, across the bulge in his speedo, between his legs, around to his back and down to his feet.

When he finished, he gazed directly at me with his crystal blue eyes. My lips curled into an appreciative grin, my libido on high alert.

He lay on the chair next to me, grabbed a drink from the small table set between us and took a sip.

"Would you like ouzo?" he asked.

I wanted *him*, but I couldn't say it out loud and instead asked, "What's ouzo?"

"It is the most popular Greek drink."

"Is it alcohol?"

"Yes. It tastes like licorice."

"Sure."

The buzz had worn off from earlier, and after suffering another memory of Mikel and May's hovering, I needed more liquid courage. I also had a powerful desire to get laid by the delicious Greek Adonis, who I was sure could help me forget about both of them.

He nodded at May and she scurried away. I rolled my eyes and asked, "Do you have a PA, too?"

"No," he scoffed. "That is Celine's way. It is very…how you say…elite."

I couldn't have said it better. "I don't want one either. It makes me uncomfortable."

"You must talk to Jack. Celine will not listen, so you must go to him," he said.

I opened the sunscreen tube and applied lotion on my arms, vowing to take his advice and talk to Jack as soon as I could. Then just as I'd hoped, he flung his legs over the side of the chair, nonchalantly sat on the edge of my lounger and grabbed the sunscreen. "Let me help," he said.

He squirted sunscreen on his palm and rubbed it over my leg. A hot shiver raced up the limb to the top of my spine. I lay back, savoring the feel of his strong hands on my flesh. It was a beautiful day, not a cloud in the sky, the sun's rays turning the ocean into a vast shimmering aqua pool. It sizzled on my white skin as it gradually lowered in the late afternoon sky, turning up the heat.

"How do you know Jack and Celine?" I asked softly.

He moved to my other leg and worked up to my belly. "My agent and Jack are friends. I am an actor. I *want* to be an actor, but right now I model. I have a meeting with the director of Jack's next movie in a few days. I will audition for him. Turn over, please."

I languidly flipped over, mind racing. When Celine had called Kostas my *birthday present*, I'd assumed he was there to have sex with me if I wanted. But she was obviously being facetious, not that it mattered. It just made him even more desirable.

He released the clasps on the bikini bra, swept the straps from my skin and started on my shoulders. Sighing happily, I asked, "Is this your first time on the boat, too?"

"No, I was here in June for–"

He was interrupted by May. She returned with another crew member dressed in the official white pants and blue polo shirt. He carried a serving tray and efficiently set my drink and one more for Kostas on the table along with a plate filled with snacks, white linen napkins and tiny silver forks. He fussed over their proper arrangement on the small surface for a minute. When everything was perfect, he bowed to Kostas and asked, "Anything else, sir?"

"No, thank you."

The waiter silently left and May sat under an umbrella at a table within hearing range. Kostas' hands roamed to my sides, his fingertips grazing the contour of my breasts. I stifled a gasp. He moved to my bare ass cheeks, rubbing and taking his time before advancing to the back of my legs. Moisture beaded in the folds of my pussy and I parted my legs, giving him access to my inner thighs.

He started on one leg, massaging using both hands, the tips of his fingers skimming the tiny strip of fabric covering my clit. I suppressed the urge to moan and squirm. Every nerve ending inside me screamed with need, and I squeezed my eyes shut, trying to find the right words to invite him to my suite without revealing my utter desperation.

"I see you two are getting along."

Celine's voice reverberated in the background. Kostas abruptly stopped, bent over me and murmured, "Don't move. I will be back."

He patted my bottom and sprang to his feet. Annoyed, I watched him swagger over to Celine and warmly kiss her cheeks. Maria stood silently by her side, carrying a large designer beach bag. I eyed Celine up and down, hating her at that moment, hating her smug expression.

Yet I also couldn't help admiring her. She was still beautiful for a woman nearing forty, her body slim, firm and curvaceous. And she looked amazing in a white string bikini, floppy blue hat and matching high heels.

"Maria, move that chair next to Haley," she ordered. Stifling a groan, I watched Kostas grabbed the lounge chair and drag it next to me before Maria could set down the tote. Celine dropped onto the chair, kicked off her shoes and complained, "Christ, Kostas, that's what Maria's for."

I rolled my eyes and he grinned knowingly. "It's my pleasure," he quipped, returning to my side. He squirted lotion on a palm and returned to where he left off, but the thrill was gone.

"What are you two drinking? Ouzo? I hate that stuff. Maria, get me a piña colada," she demanded. "And take this and help me get this off."

She removed the hat and handed it to Maria. Maria placed it on her head, and she quickly untied the strings on Celine's bikini top and pulled it off her.

Caught off guard, I gawked. Her sizable breasts drooped without a bra propping them up. Her nipples were really large and the color of dark chocolate. I averted my eyes and stifled another groan, not expecting to sunbathe topless. But since she was doing it, I felt I had no choice. When Kostas finished with me, I flipped over and set the bikini top out of the way at the end of the chair.

Kostas grinned and fixed his eyes on my tits. He licked his lips seductively and nodded at them. "You should finish, Haley, with your...unless you want me to do it for you."

I hadn't applied lotion to the part of my breasts covered by the suit. I would have preferred he do it for me, but not in front of Celine and the PAs. Irritated, I snatched the tube from his hand and finished the job, locking eyes on him and slowly rubbing the lotion on my pink nipples.

His cock twitched beneath the tight speedo. My pussy pricked and beaded. He was a perfect distraction, incredibly sexy and solicitous. Other than that, he was plastic and vacuous, his personality bland and attention lavishly dutiful. A shiny object to play with and he was exactly what I needed.

The ouzo was delicious. I downed the first, ordered another and then another, half-listening to Celine babble about whatever popped into her head.

"Dinner's at eight. We dress for it, Haley," she said.

"Hmm..." The ouzo delivered a mellow high and made me sleepy.

"Did you hear me, Haley?"

"Yes, Celine. Eight o'clock. Dress."

"Good. I'll leave you two alone. I need to talk to the chef and see what Jack's doing."

It took several minutes for Maria to gather her stuff. Nothing the poor woman did seemed to satisfy Celine.

"Damn it, Maria, I told you..."

Blah, blah, blah. I blocked out her voice. It grated on me, dripping with arrogance and condescension. I watched Kostas stand and graciously kissed both her cheeks. When she was gone, I sat up and stretched, relieved to have a quiet moment alone with the sexy

Greek Adonis.

But I wasn't alone with him. May was still there, eyes meekly lowered and waiting. I ignored her and focused on Kostas. He strutted back to the lounge chair, his vivid blue eyes twinkling with amusement.

"You need to be careful with ouzo. It sneaks up on you." He offered me the snack tray, which included sliced cucumbers, olives, small feta cheese chunks, a white dip and pita bread.

I popped a piece of cheese into my mouth, eyeing him hungrily. "What time is it?"

"About six. The sun will be setting soon."

There was plenty of time to be with him before dinner. I ached for him, for sex. It made me feel alive. It made me feel something other than the insipid dull ache that was always beneath the surface no matter whom or what was there to distract me.

"I need a nap," I said. "Do you want to come with me?"

It was easy to be blunt with ouzo flowing through my veins. He smiled broadly and grasped my hand. "Yes, Haley, but I am not sleepy."

Grinning salaciously, he helped me to my feet and draped the sarong over my shoulders. A coconut-vanilla oil scent rolled off him. Heat radiated from his delicious body.

I shivered excitedly, clasped the wrap and pulled the ends together over my bare breasts. He placed a hand on the small of my back and nudged me forward. May hopped up from her perch, and I groaned with annoyance, glancing over my shoulder as she snatched up the bikini top and my sandals and followed us at a discreet distance.

When we reached my suite, I looked from Kostas to May and back to Kostas, grimacing. He chuckled softly, pulled me across the hall into the room opposite of mine and shut the door behind us.

"You need to talk to Jack," he grinned.

"I will." I dropped the sarong and lunged, jumping onto him and wrapping my legs around his hips and arms around his neck.

"Oh, baby, I love a woman who knows what she wants." He

clutched my ass and crushed his lips to mine, shoving his tongue inside my mouth and lashing fervently as he carried me to the small bar in the corner of the room and set me on it.

"Your tits are amazing," he murmured. He groped them, squeezing and twisting the nipples between thumb and forefinger, his tongue thrashing mine.

The lingering licorice taste melded with mine. I gripped him tighter with my legs and grinded against the rock hard swell between his. He responded with a low moan, clasped the hair on the nape of my neck and pulled my head back.

He kissed my throat and moved down to my nipples. An exquisite tremor rippled through me and spiked when it reached my pussy. Whimpering softly, I became lost in the sensations, the muted sadness inside me quelled by a simple lick of the tongue.

He sucked and teased until the pink nodes were red and swollen and I couldn't take it anymore. "Please, Kostas," I groaned, my skin sizzling and thong soaked with need.

He wriggled it off me. His delicious tongue quickly found my clit and he licked lavishly. Leaning back on my forearms, I watched his broad shoulders flex as he worked his magic. I came fast. My spongy flesh convulsed furiously, the heat spreading through me like wildfire.

"Holy shit," I gasped.

His head popped up and he grinned triumphantly. He wriggled out of the speedo and his cock sprang free.

"Holy shit," I gasped again.

It was bigger than Viktor's, bigger than Mikel's. The liquid fire between my legs burned anew.

He reached for my shoulders, pulled me upright and leaned in for a soft kiss. I licked my warm juices from his lips and he hoisted me off the bar. Standing shakily, I used his hard body to keep me upright. My pussy still throbbed. I slithered down his muscular chest and nipped at the lightning-bolt tattoo on his breast, then the starry constellation on the other one and then the red die with snakes eyes on his abdomen.

When I grasped his cock, it was hot, pounding. I engulfed as much of it into my mouth as I could, sucking and whipping my tongue around it. He moaned a low guttural growl. I worked him over until he was clenching his buttocks, ready to explode.

"It is getting late. I want to fuck you." His voice was raspy, deep, edgy. He effortlessly hoisted me back onto the bar and caressed my bottom lip with an index finger. "Do not move."

He sprinted into the bedroom, cock rock hard and bobbing with each step. I grinned appreciatively and contentedly swung my legs back and forth, looking around the suite.

It was similar to mine with a wall of windows facing the sea and a bar in the corner of the living area, but it was decorated with dark leather furniture and masculine brown and blue tones.

I stared out the window. While Kostas had expertly pleasured me, the sun had set. Crests of gentle waves shimmered in the moonlight. A deep melancholy slowly wormed its way through me. Memories of Mikel bubbled to the surface. Before they could swallow me whole, Kostas sprinted back into the room and ripped open a condom foil with his teeth. He'd returned just in time and wasted no time, scooting me forward and shoving his fat cock into me. The melancholy evaporated. He rammed against my sweet spots. I forgot about Mikel.

After a quick shower, I lethargically dressed for dinner, wishing I could crawl into bed and sleep instead. The last thing I wanted to do was socialize, and it crossed my mind I shouldn't have accepted the invitation to cruise the Aegean.

I liked being alone and unscheduled, but staying on the yacht with Jack and Celine came with obligations. I hurriedly applied makeup, donned a slinky black dress with a plunging neckline and headed down the corridor with May in tow.

Everyone was already at the bar drinking cocktails, including the Captain. Kostas immediately strutted over to me, looking hot in black jeans and jacket and an open-collared white shirt.

"You look fantastic," he said softly. He grabbed my hand and kissed my knuckles. His dreamy blue eyes danced seductively.

The image of his fat, throbbing cock perked me up, suddenly wide awake. He escorted me across the room to the others. Jack eyed me approvingly and clasped my hands.

"Are you enjoying yourself, kid?" he asked.

He was dressed similarly to Kostas except in gray, which highlighted the streaks of it in his thick hair. I smiled brightly.

"Yes, thank you, Jack," I said.

He was always very friendly to me. I still couldn't fathom why, but it would make it easier to talk to him about May. Glancing at her out of a corner of my eye, I vowed to talk to him about her before the evening ended, hoping he'd understand and make her go away.

"Love the dress, Haley," Celine cooed.

"I love yours, too," I said.

As usual, Celine looked elegant and classy in a floor-length, white halter dress that accentuated her curves. Her grayish-green eyes twinkled mischievously.

She reintroduced the Captain, who wore a formal white uniform with shiny gold buttons. He'd left his Captain's hat behind, revealing a tan bald head that matched his face.

I had two martinis before dinner. The alcohol spread through me and loosened me up again. We moved to the dining room and Jack sat at one end of a long oak dining table. Celine and I were placed on each side of him, and Kostas sat next to me and the Captain sat next to her. Six crew members circled the table, serving a lavish six-course meal with a different wine that complimented each dish.

The conversation flowed easily and brushed on current events. Then Jack steered the subject to me.

"I've studied your work on your website. You're very talented and the site is also impressive," he said.

"Thank you." A warm glow settled in my gut. The compliment meant a lot coming from a man like him, but I couldn't take all the credit. "My friend, Jillian, who was with me in Paris designed the website and maintains it. She's attending MIT and studying computer engineering."

"She's very talented, too. Tell me, how did you manage a private Lascaux tour? I've attempted to access the cave with no luck."

It was hard to believe a man with Jack Luck's fame and wealth couldn't have anything he wanted. I silently thanked my father, half-gloating. "My dad is an environmentalist and knows the French Minister."

"Hmm... I'd like to talk to your father sometime," he said. "You did a good job documenting the decay. I noticed the photos were published in a couple of scientific journals."

"Yes."

"And the bull photo at Pamplona. Very nice. Do you get off on danger, Haley?"

I laughed, remembering that day. It was thrilling, but it wasn't the danger that excited me. It was the opportunity to take a money shot.

"No, not really," I said. "I just wanted to document the event, give people a sense of it, you know."

"I see. And the Mikel Garro photo? What sense were you trying to portray with that one?"

I took a sip of wine, trying to mask my dismay at the simple mention of *him*. Steeling myself, I concentrated on keeping my voice light and even. "That one was a fluke," I replied.

Both Jack and Celine chuckled. A knowing look passed between them.

"I read somewhere you were Mikel Garro's girlfriend," Celine commented. My stomach knotted.

Even though her remark seemed innocent enough, it was one more moment when I hated her. It took all my willpower to maintain my composure.

"Not really," I lied. "We were just hanging out together while I was in Spain."

"He's a really handsome man. *Yummy.* I would've stuck around," she teased.

Jack affectionately kissed her cheek. He gazed at me expectantly, as if she'd asked a question and wanted to know my answer.

"Um, well, I couldn't." Despite my best effort, my voice cracked. I took another sip of liquid courage. "I needed to go to my next photo opportunity. I've just started my career and can't afford to stay in one place for too long."

They seemed satisfied with the answer. After that, the explanation became my mantra. Whenever someone asked me about Mikel, I would repeat it word for word.

Jack clasped my hand, eyed me kindly and said, "I admire your drive, kid. Celine has no self-control." He was joking, but it was a strange thing to say. "I've been thinking while you're here I'd like you to take a portrait of us."

"Sure." My insides immediately unknotted.

"Good. Also, once your portfolio is larger, you'll want to consider showing your work in galleries. We'll be docking at Santorini tomorrow. It's a beautiful island. Think about where you want to go next and let me know."

It was almost eleven o'clock when the last dish was removed from the table. Blissfully drunk, I nudged Kostas and said, "Go talk to Sheline. Keep her busy while I talk to Zack." The words came out slurred, but I couldn't care less.

He grinned slyly. I boldly sidled up to Jack and grasped his arm. "Can I talk to you?"

"Sure, kid."

"I don't want a PA."

He frowned, eyes narrowing. "Is there a problem with May?"

"May, um, no, she's fine. I don't want a PA. It makes me uncomfortable."

His jaw clenched. "Can't you learn to like it? Indulge my wife? She only wants you to enjoy all we have to offer."

I straightened my spine defiantly. I wouldn't be dissuaded, the alcohol giving me courage. Besides, except for the sex with Kostas, there wasn't much that interested me on the yacht. I could leave whenever I wanted.

"No," I replied defensively.

He pursed his lips and glowered. Then they curled into an indulgent smile. "I can see you're as stubborn as Celine. Fine, Haley, no PA."

I jumped up and down, clapped my hands like a kid and kissed him sloppily on the cheek. "Thanks, Zack."

Kostas was waiting for me on a comfy leather sofa in the lounge. He looked sexy as hell, and I tottered over to him and giddily plopped down, snuggling against his hard body.

"May's gone," I said softly. He nuzzled his nose in my neck, my libido jumped to attention. "Take me back to your room and fuck me, okay?"

Smirking, he glanced at Jack and Celine and pulled me to my feet. I leaned drunkenly against him. "I will escort Haley to her room," he said.

A surreptitious look passed between Celine and Kostas. For a second that nagging feeling bubbled inside me. But there were no long goodnights and no sign of May. I happily ignored it.

When we were finally alone in his suite, he crushed his mouth to mine. The heat immediately pooled between my legs. Every fiber of my being hammered with an unquenchable thirst, the booze intensifying the longing rather than numbing it. I kissed him back greedily. His hands raked me, squeezing my ass and fondling my breasts. I grabbed the lapels on his jacket and tugged it off his shoulders.

He broke away and we both gasped for breath. While he hastily removed the sport coat I fumbled with the buttons on his shirt. All thumbs, he helped me unbutton it, eyes boring hungrily into mine.

It was what I wanted, what I needed, to be coveted by men and bring them to their knees with uncontrollable desire. I could see in his eyes that he'd do anything to fuck me, *possess me*, if only for a moment.

I yanked the shirt tail out of his pants and kissed his chest. He grinned mischievously and led me into the bedroom, turning on the recessed lighting and setting it to a soft glow.

Anticipation crawled over my flesh. He sat on the bed and hurriedly removed his shoes and socks. I quickly examined the room. It was laid out exactly the same as mine with a row of windows on the exterior, a bed positioned against the interior corridor wall, and a floor-to-ceiling mirror on the wall that separated the guestroom from Jack and Celine's.

When his feet were bare, he locked his brilliant blue eyes on mine and stripped off the rest of his clothes. I licked my lips as he seductively approached and spun me around to face the mirror.

"You are so hot," he whispered in my ear.

His smooth cheek rubbed against mine, his hard cock dug into my back. I watched him slowly unzip the dress, slip the straps off my shoulders and wriggled it over my curves and down to the floor. The heat between my legs spread. My pussy ached. He snaked his hands around to my tits and skimmed his palms across the nipples.

Just like with Mikel, there was something about watching him, watching me and watching us in the mirror that really turned me on. The liquid fire burned white hot in the crevices between my legs. He slipped a hand into my panties and tantalized my clit. Moaning loudly, I leaned against his naked flesh, widening my stance and swaying my ass to the rhythm of fingers dancing on my pussy. When he removed his fingers to slide the panties down to the floor, I protested with a soft whimper.

He grasped my hand and pulled me toward the bed. I robotically kicked off my high heels and stepped out of the clothes wrapped around my ankles. Leading me like a queen, his crystal blue eyes gleamed lustily. He paused to grab a condom stored in the nightstand before stretching out on the bed. Lying with his head to the mirror, he drew me on top of him.

"You do it." He ripped open the foil and handed me the condom.

I took it from him and stared at my naked reflection in the glass.

His rock hard cock throbbed before me. I licked the tip of it, rolled on the condom and braced my hands on his ripped abs, watching his thick shaft slide slowly into the farthest reaches of my slippery core, stretching me to the limit.

He gripped my hips and stab upward. I leisurely rode him, angling so he hit my sweet spots with every plunge. My tits bobbed and swayed with each delicious drop. The ache in my pussy intensified. He met me thrust for thrust, bolting upright and burying his head in the crevice between my breasts. "I love your tits..." he murmured.

"I love your cock," I murmured back.

He bucked into me and attacked my nipples, sucking and licking and nipping at them with his teeth. Closing my eyes, I clutched his shoulders, savoring the pain and pleasure. The orgasm came for me, but I held it at bay. He thrust and grinded and nipped harder, his attack more frenzied the closer he came to climax. I opened my eyes, wanting to witness the erotic finale.

But what I saw in the mirror wasn't what I expected. My jaw dropped. I blinked several times to make sure I wasn't seeing things.

"You don't mind if I join you," Celine purred. She slipped off a silky robe, tossed it onto the bed and slid naked onto the mattress.

"Celine," Kostas rasped breathlessly.

His mouth left my nipples and he kissed her. I gaped at the scene in the glass, shocked and fascinated as he continued to pound into me while kissing her. Then he returned his attention to me, tongue tormenting one of my nipples and Celine's mouth clamping onto the other one.

I didn't know what to think, didn't have time to think. My body took over. A powerful orgasm ripped through me. I slumped on Kostas' shoulder and gasped for breath, shaken to the core. He stopped bucking and gently stroked my hair while Celine rubbed my back.

When the tremors subsided, I turned to Celine and croaked, "Does Jack know you're—"

"He doesn't mind," she interrupted, grinning slyly. "He likes to watch and he likes the scent of another man's come on me. Slide off, he's waiting for me."

I glared at Kostas. He shrugged sheepishly, not surprised at all. Confused, I scrambled off him, tempted to leave. But I couldn't, transfixed as Celine peeled off the condom and sank onto his bare shaft.

I gawked, completely mesmerized by the sight of them fucking two feet away from me. She rose above him so his cock poked into the rim of her pussy. His fat shaft throbbed and glistened with her essence and disappeared inside her.

"Ooh, baby, that feels so good," she cooed, eyeing me salaciously. "Haley, sweetie, don't be shy. Come here. I like a little love from a woman, too." She fondled her breasts and toyed with her nipples. "Come on, sweetie, suck on them. You'll never know unless you try."

She knew exactly the right button to push. It was my nature to be adventurous. Adding alcohol to the mix only fueled the fire, and I was overcome by curiosity. My clit plumped and pulsed. I tentatively crawled over to them and rested on my knees. I reached for the tit closest to me, caressed it with both hands and planted my mouth on the dark node.

"Fuck," she moaned.

Kostas gripped her hips and fervently rammed into her. Her eyes closed and head sagged. I peeked at our reflection in the mirror. All my reservations disappeared, my pussy dripping with longing. I stretched to suckle her other nipple, and Kostas grabbed my ass. He slipped his hand between my thighs and fixed a long finger on my clit. The ache in my deepest recesses pounded painfully. I moved a knee to the side, opening wider for him.

He bucked into her and fiddled with me. Celine moaned and cursed while I squirmed and licked. Then she stiffened and threw back her head. Kostas tensed.

The hand between my legs fell limply onto the bed. I sat back and watched them orgasm. Kostas clenched his jaw as he poured into her, continuing to thrust upward. Celine collapsed onto his chest, gasping for air. Before he was completely spent, she lifted off his cock, grasped his slippery shaft and rubbed the crown on her waist and nipples, smearing herself with his creamy come.

The scene was decadent, erotic. My clit burned. I dropped onto my back and slid my middle finger over the sensitive strip of flesh, stroking and circling, desperate for release.

"Oh, sweetie, let me do it." Celine sank her head between my legs and lapped at my soaked slit with her tongue. Kostas joined in and nipped at my nipples.

Every synapse in my body sparked, every sinew tightened. I peeked at the mirror again and watched them pleasure me. Kostas' muscular body stretched out beside me, hands and mouth on my tits. The soft light bounced off Celine's round and dark buttocks. My curvaceous form writhed and rocked.

Soaring with exquisite sensations, I closed my eyes and exploded. The orgasm blasted through me, shattering me into a million pieces, leaving me breathless and my ears ringing.

Famished

I slept dreamlessly and woke the next morning alone and curled up naked between soft sheets in the bed in my suite. My head drummed with a pounding headache, harsh sunlight flooded the room and the scent of sex was all over me.

Groaning, I flung the covers over my head. I couldn't believe what I'd done. Yet my only regret was I didn't know how I was going to face Jack and Celine. Their sexual predilections were pretty kinky, and I suddenly understood what Celine had been hiding.

The knowing looks between her and Jack. Celine's seemingly innocent remark about trying sex with a woman. The generous offer to stay on the yacht and Kostas' timely presence. They'd set me up, seduced me for their own pleasure, and it hit me.

He likes *to watch.*

I shot upright and stared at the long mirror on the wall between my room and theirs. It was similar to the one in Kostas' suite and had to be two-way. Jack watched the whole affair. I was so caught up in the sex I didn't connect the dots, and I clutched the sheet to my breasts, wondering if mine was two-way, too.

Trembling angrily, I slumped back under the covers. I'd been an easy target, alone in Paris and seeking my own distractions. They'd used me, their wealth and fame giving them license to do whatever they wanted. Yet I had to admit I was using them, too.

I'd ignored the nagging feeling about Celine and was glad I did. The sex was incredibly hot, *mind-blowing*, and I'd learned a lot about myself because of it.

Both men and women could turn me on and get me off. I also liked watching myself and others doing it. *Just like Jack.* I couldn't fault him and suddenly couldn't care less. *To each their own.* As for me, I wanted *more*.

The days and nights flew by. I spent the days photographing the sites at the various ports we docked at and the nights drinking and fucking. Kostas got his chance to audition for the movie and disappeared, replaced by another hot Greek and then a Turkish one and then a Nigerian one, all of them deemed "clean" by Celine so they could come inside and all over her.

Yet I never completely trusted her, always insisting the guys use a condom with me. And Jack continued to watch through the two-way mirror, a fact Celine glibly confirmed when I confronted her.

Then my birthday rolled around and my hosts threw me a big party, which was attended by more than a hundred rich and famous people I didn't know. But Jack and Celine made sure they knew me.

They set up a small gallery of my photos in the gazebo lounge. The Hunger photo was the centerpiece. I couldn't look at it. Still, I managed to graciously accept the numerous compliments, and I deftly turned the attention to my latest project, the portrait I'd taken of Jack and Celine, which I'd surreptitiously shot during a lighter moment when they thought they were alone.

After touring Istanbul with the Turkish hunk, I spotted them huddling together at the rail on the top deck. They were dressed informally, him in stonewashed jeans and a loose-fitting, open-neck shirt and her in a flowery halter dress with a pleated skirt.

Suddenly, the wind kicked up. Her flowery skirt wafted to the side and his thick hair whirled around his head. She intimately swept it from his handsome face and he smiled a rare smile. The light was perfect. The setting sun highlighted their facial features. I quickly snapped a few shots and quietly retreated to my room.

The photos turned out better than any stuffy formal portrait. I'd captured their love for each other during an unguarded and personal moment. When I presented my creation, Celine cried and Jack hugged me hard.

Along with the gallery of my work, they gave me extravagant gifts—a diamond bracelet from Celine and a top-of-the-line camera from Jack. Later, after the guests had left and Celine smeared the Turkish hunk's sperm all over her body and mine, she took me with her to fuck Jack.

Her unique grayish-green eyes danced excitedly. "I don't like to share my Jack and he only likes to fuck me, but we've grown to love you so much, Haley, we want to include you on your birthday," she explained.

Nothing about the pair could shock me anymore, yet my stomach twisted apprehensively. I was curious, turned on by the opportunity to be with the great Jack Luck. But I also was a bit repulsed, the man my father's age.

I hesitantly followed her. He was waiting for us in front of the two-way mirror, smirking and lounging naked on an oversized, lemon-colored leather chair. Despite his age, his body was fit and cock large and hard. My libido took control, pussy immediately pulsing and beading eagerly.

Celine slithered onto his lap and faced him. He leisurely sniffed her come-coated body. I couldn't help but gawk, fascinated by his fetish and the fact that a man like Jack Luck not only tolerated his wife fucking other men but encouraged it. And I wondered how they'd ever negotiated such an arrangement.

He took his time, rubbing his nose across her dark flesh and licking her nipples. I waited patiently for instructions and studied the Turkish hunk on the other side of the two-way mirror. He stretched out on the bed, still naked, his cock limp and sated. He grinned slyly and closed his eyes. I was sure he was imagining what we were doing in the next room.

"Come here, kid." There was a hint of amusement in Jack's voice. I stepped lightly to the chair. He drew me close, squeezed my ass and brushed his nose across my belly. "Mmm," he murmured. "Let's go to bed."

The bed was in the middle of the suite, which was decorated with impressive, mid-century modern furniture in lemon, smoky blue and dark orange colors. There was a circular mirror on the ceiling, and I smiled to myself. Jack and Celine certainly liked their mirrors, and I wondered if it was two-way, too.

He drew me into bed and immediately went to work, burrowing his nose in my neck and trailing a hand over my belly and breasts and between my legs. Celine slid in next to me on the other side and did the same thing. Then her mouth clamped onto a nipple and his clamped onto the other one and their hands were everywhere.

"Happy birthday, kid," he murmured.

"Happy birthday, sweetie," she purred.

I watched in the mirror. His fingers slipped into the liquid fire and then hers. I spread my legs wide. My clit pounded, ready to combust.

"You like it on top, don't you, kid?" He wasn't asking a question but stating what he believed to be fact. He'd seen me through the two-way mirror enough times to know it was true. I liked it on top and straddled him. But when he gripped my hips and lifted me so I hovered over his cock, I tensed and pulled back.

Celine glowered and rolled her eyes. "You don't need a condom with Jack."

She knew me well by then, too, and I looked at Jack for support. He burst out laughing and snickered, "I haven't used a condom in twenty years. Come on, kid, you'll be fine."

I didn't quite trust Celine, but I trusted him. I slowly sank down on his cock, loving the feeling of flesh on flesh, which was the first time I'd experienced it since Mikel.

My stomach clenched at the mere thought of him. I concentrated on the thick shaft hitting my sweet spots and looked upward, watching in the ceiling mirror.

"Christ, you're tight," Jack sighed. He grinned and grinded into me. Celine's eyes narrowed worriedly. "It was your idea," he scoffed, and he roughly grasped my hips, closed his eyes and bucked into me, moaning and grunting with each deep thrust.

Jack had stamina. After the Turkish hunk and a couple of hours with Jack and Celine, I was exhausted and slipped away. I slept peacefully, as I'd done most nights since arriving on the yacht, and I woke with a smile on my face, pleased with myself.

I'd fucked the great Jack Luck. For a brief moment, I even made Celine jealous. Not that she had anything to worry about. It was a one-time encounter, a great capper to my nineteenth birthday celebration, although admittedly weird.

Stomach growling hungrily, I dressed hurriedly and sauntered into the private dining room for a late breakfast. Jack was there alone eating an omelet and sipping coffee. He smiled his rare smile and patted the chair next to him.

"Morning, kid," he greeted warmly. "It was quite a birthday, wasn't it?"

"Yes," I replied softly, suddenly shy. It was the first time we'd been alone together, and after the ménage à trois, I didn't know what to say to him.

The waiter was at my side in seconds. I ordered an omelet, bacon, sausage, banana pancakes and a Bloody Mary.

"Quite an appetite, kid," Jack teased.

His eyes twinkled with amusement and I immediately understood the double entendre. The joke put me at ease and I replied, "Yes, I'm famished. Where's Celine?"

"Worn out," he smirked.

We chatted amiably about the party and my new camera. Then I hesitantly asked a question I'd been dying to ask since Paris. "How did you and Celine end up together?"

I knew they'd met at his birthday party years ago, but that was all. After screwing both of them, I hoped he would tell me.

"Celine hasn't told you?"

"Told you what?" she asked.

Celine showed up looking as beautiful and exotic as ever, dressed in fashionable white capris pants and a tight-fitting blue camisole. She kissed him lovingly and gave me a quick peck on the cheek.

"How we got together," he said.

"Oh, sweetie, you're a curious young thing, aren't you?"

Groaning silently, I lowered my eyes. I'd gotten to know her well, too. Her tone was laced with condescension. She gracefully sat on the other side of Jack and turned to me, smiling smugly.

"It's no secret, Haley. I was his birthday present."

"She popped out of a cake," he grinned.

It was hard to imagine the chic and sophisticated Celine popping out of a cake. I masked my astonishment by taking a bite of bacon.

"A friend of Jack's spotted me at the club."

"Club?" I asked.

"A brothel in Nevada," Jack corrected.

"Oh."

"What do you mean by 'oh?'" she asked defensively.

"Nothing," I quickly replied. I thought I detected a hint of embarrassment in her eyes. My heart swelled with compassion, her vulnerability much more appealing than her condescension and often cartoonish behavior. "I didn't know you were–"

"A whore?"

"No! I mean, yes, I mean, it doesn't matter to me," I stammered, looking contrite.

"Considering what you've been up to, I should think not," she chastised.

"Celine..." Jack's brows creased warningly.

"I didn't mean to offend you, Celine," I said.

"It's fine," she sighed. "When I met Jack, I'd left the life and co-owned the club. Jack's friend, Tony, was a regular and offered me a lot of money for the special request. I wanted to make some upgrades to the place, so..."

"Best decision she ever made," Jack quipped.

Celine smiled brightly. The rancor faded with it. "It was," she chuckled. "When I did the cake thing, completely nude in front of twenty of Jack's closest friends, I had no idea I'd end up with Jack. Of course, I had no idea what he wanted either."

That knowing look passed between them. I remained silent, pretty sure I knew what he'd wanted.

"I fucked Tony and perfumed myself with his come. Jack watched through a crack in the connecting door between the hotel rooms. Then I fucked Jack. It was the most erotic experience of my life. Jack was amazing."

"You, too, Celine. It wasn't easy finding a woman who can pleasure me the way you do. My ex-wife thought I didn't love her because I wanted her to fuck other men. Celine likes it, don't you?"

"Yes. And add a sweet young thing like Haley to the mix and I'm in heaven."

After a few days more on the yacht, the thrill was gone. I skipped the nightly romp with the latest gigolo and Celine, holing up in my room instead and searching the internet for somewhere exciting to go next.

I didn't sleep well that night. My dreams were filled with fleeting images of Mikel screwing Celine while Jack leered at them and laughed at me. I woke before sunrise, which hadn't happened since I'd left home.

Home. There was no home for me anymore. My life was a mess.

Each day that passed left me sadder and lonelier, a dying leaf in September, ripped from its branch by a gust of air and swirling aimlessly in the wind. I didn't know where I'd land, and I kept being blown in the wrong direction, distracted by love and seduced by fame.

No more. It was time for me to move on. I shook off the night's dream, ignored the dull ache in the pit of my stomach and groggily headed to the verandah with my camera. The sun was rising.

~~~~~~†~~~~~~

"No, you can't go, Haley! Stop her, Jack!"

I hadn't expected Celine would be upset by my announcement and looked at Jack for help.

"You can't expect her to stay with us forever," he sighed.

"But it's too soon! She's my favorite!"

My jaw dropped. She was talking about me as if I was her pet.

Jack glowered and grasped her hand. "Careful, Celine," he said coolly.

She jerked her hand away and spit, "You can make her stay, Jack. *Do it.*"

I rose shakily from the table. Anger and resentment bubbled inside me. I opened my mouth to bite back and quickly clamped it shut. They couldn't stop me from leaving, and like Jillian had teased, I could swim. Not that I'd need to. The yacht was docked at an island port and I could walk off it whenever I wanted.

"Sit down, Haley," Jack snapped. "Finish your breakfast."

"I need to pack," I responded icily.

"Come on, kid, sit. At least tell us where you're going."

"Jack," Celine whined. Her lips curled into a defeated pout. I hid a triumphant smile with a weak grin and calmly sat.

It was one of those times I hated Celine. I avoided her angry glare. Jack patted my hand affectionately, like a father would do to a daughter, which was ridiculous considering he'd fucked me. I took a deep breath and eyed him warily.

"We'll miss you, kid, that's all. Tell us where you're headed."

"Burma."

~~~~~~†~~~~~~

I was tired of photographing stationary Greek and Roman ruins. I needed drama, action. There was an uprising going on in Burma led by tens of thousands of bald-headed monks dressed in red, and the image of them defying a junta-led government captured my imagination.

I packed most of the dresses and high heels in large suitcases, planning to ship them to the hotel in Paris where I'd stayed with Jillian. The "City of Light" would be my new home base, and since my bank account had grown to $620,480 from the Hunger photo sales, I could afford it. Jillian had been right. At least something good had come from my affair with Mikel Garro.

As I stuffed my more casual clothes–the designer jeans, shirts and skimpy underwear into a carry-on and backpack, my stomach constricted with a twinge of excitement, a feeling I thought I'd left behind. I quickly checked the bathroom and closet for remaining items, leaving the dresser drawers for last. Then I froze. A lone item was folded neatly inside a bottom drawer and it was the Garro tank top.

I could hear my heart beating. My stomach twisted in a tight knot.

I'd forgotten about the shirt. I'd almost left it behind in Les Eyzies, but I couldn't go through with it. Instead, I'd buried it in the bottom of the backpack and loaded my toiletries and makeup on top of it. It had been stored in there until May unpacked my things.

My eyes welled with tears. I tried to hold them back, tried to concentrate on the image of a bald-headed, red-clad monk, Celine's jealousy as Jack bucked into me, Jillian's contagious smile. But the tears rolled down my cheeks. I picked up the top and pressed it against my chest.

I wished I could stop loving him. I prayed for deliverance from the memories of him. Yet no matter how hard I tried, I couldn't make him go away. There seemed to be no escape for my tortured soul.

"The plane's ready when you are, kid."

Jack's voice seeped into my consciousness. I quickly wiped away the tears and placed the shirt back into the drawer. Turning to leave, I straightened my spine determinedly. Then I spun around and retrieved it.

I told myself leaving the Garro keepsake on the yacht would spark Celine's curiosity. I didn't want her to sense my weakness and didn't want to give her the satisfaction of knowing I cared about him. Who knew where that could lead? Yet what difference did it make? I was leaving her and her obsession with me behind. It didn't make a damn bit of difference, but I stuffed the shirt in my backpack anyway, vowing to dispose of it later. I *would*.

Celine pouted and refused to accompany Jack and me to the jet. But she did give me a quick kiss on the lips before we left for the airport. I couldn't care less, unable to shake the profound sadness worming through me after finding the Garro shirt.

Jack was busy on the phone conducting business during the short trip and didn't notice. He escorted me onto his plane, and once I was settled, he grasped my hands and eyed me seriously.

"You know you can't tell anyone about what happened on the yacht," he said.

"Sure, Jack, I know. It's not like anyone would believe me anyway."

"I'm serious, Haley, no one. Not even your friend, Jillian."

His jaw tensed in that way that made me take notice. "I promise, Jack."

"Because if you do, I'll have to destroy you. I don't want to hurt you."

A shiver raced up my spine and the hair on the back of my neck stood on end. "You don't have to threaten me. I won't betray you."

He visibly relaxed and squeezed my hands. "I know, kid, but a man like me has to be careful."

"I understand."

"I know you do. You're a lot like me when I was your age. Curious. Adventurous. Driven. And spunky like Celine. I want you to realize your dream and be successful. If you ever need anything, anything at all, let me know. This is my private number."

He handed me a white business card with a printed phone number on it. There was no picture or logo or other text, only the number. It seemed familiar.

"Thanks, Jack, and thanks for everything," I said softly.

He drew me into his arms and affectionately kissed the top of my head. "Go get 'em, kid."

As I watched him go, a warm glow momentarily peeked through the dull ache. In the end the fork in the road had been worth it. Jack Luck and I had become friends, and although I doubted I'd ever see him again, it was nice to have a guardian angel.

The plane started down the runway and the same hunky flight attendant who'd attended to me during the trip from Paris served me a martini. I curled up on the comfy leather seat and stared at the number on the white card. Jack's private number contained the three-digit area code for Los Angeles and the following seven digits were 1-2-1-1-9-6-0.

Then it hit me. The number was familiar because December 1, 1960 was the day my mother was born. The coincidence was unbelievable and I chuckled. If I ever did need the great Jack Luck in the future, it wouldn't be hard at all remembering his phone number.

My eyes fluttered open. For a second I thought I was on the jet, the stark cabin light bearing down on me as I lay in the arms of the hunky flight attendant, Maurice, who'd enthusiastically fucked me on the way to Burma.

I was naked, but there wasn't a warm body next to me. Two pair of brown suede loafers beneath a white halo appeared a few feet away. It was a dream, a mirage. Muffled voices murmured gibberish. My eyes followed the halo upward.

It wasn't a halo but a billowy cloud. It wasn't a cloud but a vanilla ice cream cone topped with a cherry. It wasn't a cherry but almonds. *Almond eyes.*

Baba was back and there was someone with him. Then the mirage vanished and there was only darkness and the harsh silence.

I was hallucinating, yet if I was hallucinating I wouldn't know I was hallucinating. Baba must have returned with someone and they'd been looking at me.

It didn't matter. I was still in the cellar, shivering and sweating and slowly dying. There was nothing for me to do but finish the story.

~~~~~~✝~~~~~~

For the next two years I drifted from country to country seeking money shots and sex.

Jack's pilot dropped me off in Bangkok. I headed to the border but never made it into Burma. The Burmese government blocked entrance to the country as they raided monasteries, censored the media and beat and killed the protesters. The monks fled to China and Thailand, and I ended up photographing the chaos from Mae Sot, an outpost for the black-market trade between Burma and Thailand.

My photos were picked up by the Associated Press and widely distributed. Then I headed to Pakistan for the elections, to South Africa and Kenya and to one country after another, documenting catastrophes and turmoil with my photos, a witness to death and destruction. Throughout it all, I remained detached and emotionless. Not even the wretched faces of dying and starving children were enough to stir me anymore. The compassion I'd once felt for the old painter at Las Ramblas was no longer a part of me.

My contemporaries began calling me Haley's Comet, *a shooting star*. Just as I'd dreamed, I became a world-famous photographer, my meteoric rise happening fast for someone so young. Yet despite my fame, rather than feeling like a shooting star, I felt more like tumbleweed dispersing my seeds one photograph at a time and my hot beads of desire one man at a time.

I abandoned love for simple, honest sexual gratification. I hardened my heart against any further disappointment, my experience with Mikel teaching me the "love conquers all" concept was bullshit. The changes crept up on me, my youthful zest for life tempered in every way because of him, and I became a woman to be reckoned with, the only trait left from my previous life a fearless determination.

And once my sexual appetite was unleashed by Mikel and the kinky games with Jack and Celine on the yacht, there was no stopping me. I easily seduced the hunky flight attendant on Jack's plane, the ten-and-a-half-hour flight to Bangkok turning into a carnal marathon. The surprised front desk clerk who spoke English at the hotel in Mae Sot was more than happy to accommodate me. So were a prominent soccer player in Brazil and countless other nameless men in dozens of countries.

There were more ménage à trois with both men and women. I coasted through life, the sex and alcohol and endless pursuit of money shots my salvation, making me feel alive and whole.

But there were bumps in the road, too. Like the morning I woke in bed next to a Mexican telenovelas star and I couldn't remember how I'd gotten there. I vaguely recalled drinking a couple of tequila shots and dancing with a half-dressed man wearing a crown of feathers, and that was it. Terrified I'd blacked out, I began regulating my alcohol consumption, drinking just enough to ease me into a dreamless sleep.

And it was easy to fool people and fool myself. I *was* a shooting star, relentlessly and fearlessly chasing a unique shot, my talent masking the deep depravity that invaded my soul.

I called my parents every Sunday and saw them once a year. The first year I took them on a Caribbean cruise. The next year my brother was on leave from the Marines and I rented a villa on Italy's Amalfi coast for a week.

It was the first time we'd been together as a family in three years. My parents were ecstatic. They beamed proudly the entire time. Yet like me, Kyle had changed. When I looked into his eyes, I could see his torment, hardened by too many tours to Iraq. He sensed a change in me, too, but we never talked about it, honoring an unspoken understanding we were there for our parents.

Words weren't necessary anyway. He'd been my mentor and protector and I'd been his adoring little sister all those years we raised ourselves. That would never change. We weren't raised to be whiners either. He'd never burden me with the horrors of the war and I'd never compare my plight to his.

It was harder with Jillian. She spent spring breaks and a few weeks during the summer with me in whatever country I landed in. And being Jillian, she never held back, knowing me better than anyone.

"Fuck, Hales, it's been two years," she lamented.

She'd been unpacking one of her many suitcases and noticed my old backpack in the closet. I'd kept it for my excursions to impoverished areas, and she found the Garro top in the bottom of it.

If I would have laughed, she wouldn't have continued. But I hadn't seen the shirt since Jack and Celine, always stuffing whatever I needed on top of it, and the memories of Mikel suddenly overwhelmed me. My eyes welled with tears.

"Have you been obsessing about him all this time?" She held the shirt accusingly to my face.

I couldn't look at it and averted my eyes. "No," I croaked.

It was a true. I hadn't been obsessing about him, indulging in plenty of other diversions. But I hadn't gotten over him either.

"Then why do you still have this?" she frowned.

"I forgot it was there."

It was a half-truth. I knew the shirt was there, but I didn't dwell on its existence.

"You should get rid of it," she grumbled.

My stomach clenched anxiously. I snatched it from her hand and stuffed it into the backpack. "Maybe," I replied softly, "but I think it gives me good luck. Don't worry, Jills, I couldn't care less about Mikel Garro."

She set her lips in a grim line and studied me for a long time. I knew she didn't believe me, but she let it go. "Okay, Hales, whatever you say. Let's party!"

~~~~~~†~~~~~~

My nomadic existence continued into the third year, the year of the World Cup. As the games approached, the news coverage intensified and the fans became more fanatical. Mikel was in the spotlight a lot, and the royalties from the Hunger photo surged. I retreated to the United States, where most people couldn't care less about soccer. If they did, they'd have to search for news about it.

I went to West Virginia first to photograph the aftermath of a coal mine explosion. Then I headed to New Orleans to document the massive oil spill in the Gulf of Mexico. It was there I picked up Johnny, a sexy and effusive fashion photographer, who also happened to be on Playboy's payroll and was always on the lookout for the next hot Playmate.

"I know they'll want you, Haley. You're a perfect Playmate. Fucking gorgeous and talented and the girl next door," he said.

Sated and a little drunk after a late night romp in his suite, I lazed in bed next to him, flattered but not buying it. "There's no way I'm going to let you take pictures of me naked. I barely know you," I chuckled softly.

"Come on, Haley, you know I'm who I say I am. It's a great opportunity and could really help your career."

"I doubt it. No one would ever take me seriously again."

"Are you kidding me? Your photos speak for themselves. A centerfold will only add to your fame."

Johnny was easy to get along with and a great lover. But by our fourth night together I was ready to kick him to the curb. He wouldn't give up, and then he said it.

"Isn't there a guy from your past you'd like to get back at? Show him what he's missing? Throw it in his face?"

It was childish to even consider it, to believe Mikel would even care after all this time. Yet the idea fomented in my mind that maybe he *would* care. Maybe he'd realize he made a mistake and rush back to me.

It was a foolish thought, especially since I couldn't take him back even if he wanted me to. He'd betrayed me, betrayed our love. As the years passed, I came to believe it was a one-sided love anyway, yet I couldn't stop wondering.

I spent the next day photographing oil-coated brown pelicans on the coastal islands and wetlands. Afterward, I wandered into a bar on Canal Street for a couple of drinks before returning to the hotel.

"What can I get you, hon?"

The bartender wore a Hunger t-shirt and I stared at it, my throat tightening. "Um, um, a martini," I stammered.

"You like the shirt? Isn't he the hottest thing you've ever seen? He's a soccer player from Italy or somewhere over there."

"Spain," I muttered.

It was then I decided to become a Playmate. Not because I expected Mikel Garro would care, but because I wanted to prove to him my life was great without him, or at least that's what I told myself.

Johnny had been right. Playboy jumped at the chance to make me a Playmate. A week later I found myself in a Los Angeles studio dressed in sexy lingerie, nervously waiting for the first shoot and wondering what I'd done.

I'd told my parents about it the day before. They were surprised but not judgmental.

"I'll buy a copy but only for your mother to see," Dad said.

Mom laughed and piped in, "I'll rip out your photos so he can look at the rest of the magazine."

Jillian, on the other hand, was speechless.

"You there, Jills?"

"Christ, Hales, I can't believe it. You, a Playmate? Not that you aren't beautiful, but it's not your style to put yourself out there like that."

She was right, but there I was, dressed in sexy underwear and surrounded by a myriad of backdrops and props scattered throughout an old converted warehouse. The photographer, Raymond, told me right away he was gay, probably as a way to make me feel more comfortable. While we waited for his mousy, morose assistant, Gloria, to position the lights, he fluffed up my hair and handed me a camera.

"Let's start with the jungle scene, shall we, Haley?"

I dutifully followed his directions and bent over a fake tree stump and pointed the camera at a fake jungle backdrop.

"Fantastic, beautiful." Circling, he snapped shot after shot from his own camera. "Pull down your undies. Not so far. There. Perfect. Good." A warm ache pulsed in the folds of my pussy. "Ass up. Close your legs. Good... Now widen your stance. Good... Now take off your undies and sit with the camera between your legs. Good... Slide the bra straps off your shoulders. Good... Pull yours breasts out of the cups. Nice, very nice..."

Like watching myself in the mirror, posing naked turned me on. I became more provocative with each position. But as the morning wore on, the warm ache grew hotter and more insistent, making me crazy.

"Arch your back. No, too much. A little more. Legs wider. Wider. Perfect…"

By the time we broke for a quick buffet lunch, I was wound up tight. I hungrily eyed the beefy guy wearing a muscle shirt as he wheeled a cart full of food into the studio. If there wasn't a strict policy against sexual contact of any kind during the shoot, I would have fucked him then and there.

I didn't have a private moment to myself, either. Raymond or Gloria or the makeup lady were always by my side, fussing over me when I changed getups or standing outside the bathroom door when I peed. What began as a harmless endeavor turned torturous. My pussy pounded painfully.

"That's it, Haley. Not so wide and bend your left leg. Good… Move your hand down like you're going to touch yourself. No, don't actually touch yourself!"

It was the last staging of the day and I was completely naked, sprawled out on my back on a bed of colorful maple leaves fingering my clit. Groaning and glaring angrily at him, I hastily stopped.

"That's not the look I was hoping for," he grimaced. "What's the matter?"

"Nothing," I snapped.

He glanced knowingly at Gloria. I got the feeling I wasn't the only Playmate who became hot and bothered during a shoot. I wondered if he preferred it that way, the photos more erotic and provocative because of it.

In the end it didn't matter. There was nothing I could do except walk out, which would have been childish. Instead, I sucked it up, looked seductive and did as I was told.

~~~~~~✝~~~~~~

I left L.A. the next day and headed to New York. My latest solo exhibition was opening at the prestigious Museum of Modern Art in a couple of weeks, and I wanted to add a photo from the Gulf oil spill and oversee the preparations.

The exhibition was entitled "Catastrophe" and included a photo collection documenting natural disasters—an earthquake in Chile, a drought in central Africa, flooding in India. It would be the first one my parents would see, my other shows opening in Amsterdam, Sydney and Tokyo.

I'd never been to New York and was instantly captivated by the city's energy and amusements. I stayed through the summer. Jillian and a host of other distractions were enough to keep my mind off the World Cup, and since the U.S. didn't make it to the finals, the coverage was minimal.

Yet I couldn't avoid the games entirely. The day after the final I woke to news of Spain's win. A big photo of the team was plastered on the front page of the newspaper that was slipped under my door every morning. There was also a smaller picture of Mikel, who'd scored the only goal.

Except for the occasional sight of him on a Hunger t-shirt, I'd only glimpsed a photo of him once since the day I walked out of his life. My heart skipped a beat and stomach knotted. He looked happy, grinning his sexy crooked grin, his luscious brown eyes moist with jubilant tears.

I was relieved Jillian had left to visit her parents the day before, because I burst into tears and wept for a long time. No matter how hard I'd tried, I couldn't stop loving him. My only consolation was the fact that he'd see me soon, too, in the November issue of Playboy.

Dark Depravity

"I am sorry, Haley, so sorry..."

Mikel?

He held me in his arms. His warm flesh heated my cold, shivering body. He'd come back. He'd found me.

"Forgive me, Haley, I am sorry. Forgive me..."

I forgive you, Mikel, I forgive you.

He enveloped me in a soft blanket, lifted me off the ground and cradled me like a baby.

"Sorry... Sorry..." he whispered in my ear over and over.

I couldn't open my eyes. I couldn't open my mouth. The consciousness hovered just out of reach, yet I could hear him and smell his unique scent. I wanted to wrap my arms around his neck and hold him tightly, but my body refused to cooperate, my limbs heavy and aching.

There were strange sounds in the distance. Voices, words I couldn't understand. We moved forward. Into the fresh air. Sun hit my cheeks.

The sun…
He brought the sun…
Then the fog closed in and he slowly vanished.
Don't go, Mikel, don't go!
And it mercilessly reclaimed me.

~~~~~~†~~~~~~

I stayed in New York one more month and attempted to evade Mikel's shadow with a host of new faceless men. My need to be desired became more desperate than ever and my dependence on alcohol and sexual gratification continued to be my only admission to sleep.

It wasn't enough, never enough. A pervasive restlessness set in. I needed to move on, but I didn't know where to go next. I considered returning to Chile, where thirty-three miners had been trapped underground and awaited rescue. Yet every news outlet in the world was covering the tragedy, churning out a daily grind of inconsequential stories until I completely lost interest.

Then the iconic Nelson Mandela was hospitalized and social media buzzed with rumors of his near death. Images of mournful South Africans dancing and singing and celebrating his life tickled my imagination. It was perfect. There was also enough turmoil in the country to keep me occupied until he died, and if I became really desperate, I could always go on a safari and add some wildlife to my portfolio.

I left that afternoon, taking a direct flight to South Africa. A lot had changed since I'd set out on my own. No longer condemned to cramped economy class, I was escorted to my first-class seat and quickly served a martini, the first of several before I stretched out on the flatbed and tried to sleep.

As usual sleep eluded me. But at least I was comfortable. I'd become accustomed to the luxuries in my life, expecting them and taking them for granted. When the flight attendant accidentally dropped a magazine on me, I bolted upright and glared irritably at her.

It wasn't as if she'd woken me up from a great dream. I was simply annoyed. A lot annoyed me in those days. I'd completely forgotten my roots, my waitressing days a distant memory. I didn't realize it at the time, but I'd become a lot like Celine, demanding perfection from the minions.

A limo driver was there to pick me up at the Johannesburg airport. The restlessness continued to eat at me. I waited impatiently while he stacked my luggage on a cart. On the way out of the terminal I noticed an advertisement at a rental car booth for a BMW convertible. The idea of traversing the vast country independently sparked a rare excitement, and I impulsively dismissed the driver and rented one.

As I zipped along the highway with the top down, a feeling of liberation settled over me. The temperature was a mild 70 degrees. The wind whipped hair in my face, the sun blazed. When I arrived at the hotel, I parked at the entrance and jumped out before the valet had a chance to open the door for me.

That was when I met Andries. He exuded a raw sexuality, powerfully built, skin a dark lava color and eyes practically black. Dressed impeccably in a dark suit, white cotton shirt and shimmering blue tie, he was too princely to be a valet. Yet the hotel was the most expensive and luxurious in Johannesburg and he stood curbside smirking at me, so I handed him the car keys.

"Try not to dent it," I said flippantly.

His lips twisted into a menacing smirk. I glared at him. His impudence was annoying although a little intriguing. I strutted into the hotel, certain I could seduce him if I wanted.

The hotel room was another luxurious suite in another expensive hotel, indistinguishable from the others except for the décor. This one was decorated with sleek modern furniture and artwork and accents using the red, yellow, green and black colors in the South African flag.

As soon as the bellman left, I changed into a slinky, low-cut dress and high heels and headed straight to the hotel bar. It, too, was indistinguishable. High-end. Dotted with attractive strangers. Exactly how I liked it. I took a seat at the end of the horseshoe-shaped counter and ordered a martini. The spot was perfect, giving me a great view of the clientele, and I inconspicuously peeked around the room.

Five minutes passed. My pussy prickled, knowing it wouldn't be long before I was approached by a man who'd give me what I wanted. Then I saw him.

The valet, but he wasn't a valet. He was with a stunning woman dressed in a yellow backless dress. Realizing my mistake, I smiled to myself and watched him escort her to an empty booth in the corner. Once seated, he draped an arm over her shoulders and she flinched, her face grim and angry.

They looked like they were having a fight, or at least she was. She lit into him. He set his hard-edged face impassively. When the waiter arrived, she scooted out of the booth, haughtily stomped across the room and disappeared down a hall.

I sipped the martini and glanced at him from the corner of an eye. He briefly talked to the waiter and ran a hand over his cropped hair, a gesture of frustration or maybe weariness. Then he turned his head and looked directly at me.

I stared into space and trailed an index finger along the rim of the martini glass, feeling his black eyes studying me. The hair on the nape of my neck stood on end. Seconds later, he was at my side.

"You are lucky I did not steal your car," he said smugly.

His accent was British, his voice a rich baritone. He exuded an immeasurable sense of power and arrogance, and my nerve endings ignited with a chemical reaction that was at once daunting and exhilarating.

"It's not my car," I shrugged.

Normally, I would have apologized for the mistake, but he was way too cocky and I didn't want to give him the satisfaction.

His black eyes bore into me, jaw clenched angrily. My heart skipped a beat, detecting danger, which added to his mystique. I glared back at him, unwilling to give him the apology he seemed to seek.

The world momentarily stopped. Me against him, a contest of wills, neither of us prepared to back down.

"This is what I am talking about," a woman snarled.

We broke eye contact at the same time and turned toward the voice. His attractive girlfriend stood before us, trembling with fury. I suppressed an amused grin. My brief contact with her boyfriend was enough to elicit a twinge of sympathy for her, yet I couldn't wait to find out what happened next.

"You are a fucking perv, Andries. I leave you for one minute and you are already sniffing up another slag."

His jaw clenched tighter. He glowered menacingly, rage pulsating from his robust frame. "Go back to the table, Zeena," he seethed.

"Prick. I do not take orders from you. I warned you, Andries, one more time and I chip."

"Then go," he responded icily.

She hesitated, the pronouncement seemingly unexpected. Yet once it sank it, she raised a hand to slap his face. He grabbed her wrist before she made contact and sneered, "I said go. I am done with *you*."

He released her wrist, turned away and gestured for the bartender. She gaped at his back, visibly shaken. I turned away, too, peeking at her from the corner of an eye and gulping down the rest of the martini.

"My father will not be happy. Do you hear me, Andries? He will not be happy." Andries ignored her. She straightened her spine, turned on her heels and muttered, "Right slag, that one."

I exhaled softly, burying a smile as she stomped off. Her abrupt departure created an opening for me. And although arrogant men usually turned me off, Andries was sexy as hell and the whiff of danger excited me.

"Can I buy you another drink?" he asked.

The fire in his black eyes cooled. I chuckled softly. "Sure. I'm Haley Hanson."

His large hand grasped mine and a rush of hot anticipation surged through me.

"Andries Wolff," he said. The bartender set a shot of whiskey before him and he sat on the bar chair next to me and downed it. He ordered another one, a double on the rocks this time, and gazed impassively at me. "Are you American?"

"Yes."

"Traveling alone?"

"Yes."

"On business?"

"Yes."

"What do you do?"

"I'm a photographer."

"Hmm… Here for a safari?"

"Maybe."

I'd never admit my true purpose for being there. People would think I was callous. Yet after the scene with his girlfriend, I suspected he was as coldhearted as me.

"And you? I know you're not a valet," I said.

His lips curled into an amused grin. It was the first time he'd shown a trace of an emotion other than annoyance and anger. I knew I had to have him.

"I am an Assemblyman," he replied somberly.

"What's that?"

"A member of Parliament."

"Oh." I was surprised to say the least. His demeanor wasn't very friendly, and I couldn't imagine how he'd managed to woo the public into electing him.

He narrowed his brows. His black eyes turned menacing again. "You are surprised?"

A shiver raced up my spine. He'd read my mind. His abrupt

mood change was unnerving.

"Yes, I'm surprised," I admitted. "You're too hot to be a politician."

The statement was a deliberate attempt to see if he'd bite. Otherwise, no matter how much I was attracted to him, I was wasting my time.

And he bit.

"Do you want to have dinner with me?" His black eyes gleamed wickedly.

We ate at the posh hotel restaurant and drank a lot. But whereas he was at least eighty pounds heavier than me and barely seemed affected, I was feeling no pain. My questioning became bolder, my curiosity piqued. He impatiently allowed me to probe into his life, his mood shifting with each revelation.

Andries Wolff was 28 years old. He'd grown up poor in Soweto and had become a popular rugby player, his star status the impetus for his election to Parliament.

"Ever been married?" I asked innocently.

His eyes briefly flickered with sadness and quickly morphed into black ice. I lowered my head, knowing instinctively he'd been hurt like me, a kindred spirit of lost love, masking his pain with a brash and menacing manner.

"Are we going to fuck or what?" he responded coldly.

Andries Wolff was definitely a lot like me. Smiling, I let him escort me to the suite. He unceremoniously followed me inside and coolly sauntered around the living room, examining the South African artwork while removing his jacket and tie and unbuttoning his shirt.

I quickly kicked off the high heels and wriggled out of the dress. He paused three feet away and scrutinized my half-naked body from top to bottom, rolling his tongue seductively over his full lips. Hot anticipation pumped through my veins, a delicious shiver raced up my spine. I immediately became wet.

He grinned smugly and tugged the shirt out of his pants, undid the cuff buttons and slowly took it off, locking eyes on me as he draped it over the arm of a chair. I froze, gawking at his smooth dark skin and the contours of his rock-hard muscles. He leisurely stripped off the rest of his clothes and stood before me, his cock swollen and pointed straight at me.

Sensual, powerful, he swaggered over to me. "You're a fit one," he smirked, eyes flashing greedily, dangerously.

He leaned close, bit my earlobe and reached around to grasp my ass, rubbing his cock provocatively on my belly. Swallowing hard, I stepped back. His lips twisted into a menacing grin. I provocatively unclasped my bra and tossed it on the floor, enjoying his lecherous glare as I caressed my tits and sublimely licked my lips.

His growl rumbled through me. I slid a hand into my panties and stroked my slippery clit, closing my eyes. A bolt of pleasure ripped through me, and I sensed his heat before I felt his hot flesh encircle mine. He lightly caressed my hair. My eyes flickered open. He gathered tufts of it in a fist, roughly tugged my head back and kissed me savagely, forcing his tongue into my mouth and biting my bottom lip.

"I will shag you," he groaned. He dragged me by the hair to the sofa and forced me to bend over it.

Hot blood rushed to my head. Every muscle below my waist twisted with an insatiable hunger. I placed my hands on the upholstery and braced myself. He stepped away and I heard rustling of fabric and the rip of a condom foil. He pinned me against the couch, tore off my panties and buried his face in my ass, kissing and biting and rubbing his cheek on it.

"Fucking honey." He slithered up my back. His breath was hot on my neck, his hard shaft grinded against my behind. "Spread your legs for me now," he hissed.

I did as he asked. He nudged them farther apart with his knees, roughly fisted my hair again and slammed into me.

"Argh!" His cock filled me up and stretched me to the limit. My heart beat wildly. The liquid fire amassed and simmered in my pussy. I moaned loudly.

"Right, gorgeous, let me hear you," he growled. He withdrew slowly and rammed into me again, gripping my hips and grinding and twisting, thrusting hard and deep. I closed my eyes, relishing the friction and fullness, his fingers snaking around to my clit and stroking my sweet spot.

Every sinew in my body coiled tighter. He fucked me harder and faster, frantically pounding and gyrating and tugging on my hair. "Fuck, gorgeous, fuck," he panted.

The tension built, an agonizing hot ache seared through my loins. Squeezing my eyes shut and gritting my teeth, I let go, a powerful orgasm racking my body.

Andries continued to pound into me, groaning and grunting and finally stiffening. When he exploded, he released my hair and I collapsed limply over the backrest. The orgasm pulsated through me.

"Fucking cracking," he rasped.

I opened my eyes and slowly returned to earth, savoring the aftermath of a quick, hard fuck. When he pulled out, I immediately wanted more. He caressed my ass and slapped it hard.

"Hey!" I shrieked.

He grabbed my knees and flipped my legs over the back of the couch. I fell onto the cushion and languidly stretched my limbs, scalp stinging and pussy deliciously sore. He regarded me appreciatively, his black eyes gleaming with uncharacteristic warmth.

"You're fucking mint," he said.

I wasn't sure what he meant, but I was sure it was good. He effortlessly hurdled over the sofa, grabbed my knees and threw me over his shoulder.

"Whoa!" I yelped.

He strode quickly toward the bedroom, snatched up his tie on the way and dropped me onto the bed. Before I knew what was happening, he roughly gripped my hands, stretched my arms above my head and weaved the tie around my wrists and through the slats on the backboard.

"Wait a minute," I gasped. I struggled against the restraints, hating to lose control. I'd never allowed anyone to tie me up. "Damn it, Andries, untie me!" He loomed over me. A fire ignited in his black eyes. His powerful body frightened me. "I'm serious, Andries, untie me!"

He shrugged cockily, climbed into bed and knelt between my legs. I kicked wildly at him. The blows bounced off his hard body and he easily restrained me, grasping my knees and holding them down on the mattress.

Then his mouth found my magic spot. He circled and stroked my clit with an expert tongue. The fight left me. I squirmed and bowed against him, my pussy burning once more.

"You taste good," he said softly. He reached for my nipples and rolled them between thumbs and fingers.

"Mmm…" I moaned, thinking maybe I'd been too quick to dismiss bondage. The ache in my deepest recesses escalated quickly.

He looked up and grinned wickedly, lips glistening with beads of my pleasure. He slithered up my body and his mouth landed on my nipples. He sucked and mercilessly bit them, sending currents of pain and pleasure to the depths of my groin.

I gripped the posts on the backboard and closed my eyes. His cock hardened. The crown skimmed my pussy and bounced off my inner thighs, taunting me with what would come. He rolled off the bed and strutted out of the room, returning in seconds with another condom. Burrowing between my legs, he slipped in on and eased into me, moaning loudly as he filled me up.

I squirmed beneath him, craving friction. When he lifted off me, I missed his heated flesh pressed against mine. I opened my eyes. He hovered over me, hands braced on the mattress, the contours of his muscular arms rigid. Smirking, he lowered his head, plunged into me and watched himself fuck me, taking his time.

I bent my knees and spread them wide. Every sinew and synapse in my body smoldered, ready to combust. He thrust harder and faster, driving deep. His teeth clenched and eyes glazed over. I angled my hips and matched him thrust for thrust. His thick shaft pounded against my magic spots and his strokes became more frenetic.

The sweet ecstasy mushroomed. I gripped the posts tighter. A waterfall of hot sensations cascaded over me, and as I tumbled into a welcome oblivion, he stiffened and came with me, his heavy body collapsing on top of me.

"Fucking wicked," he hissed.

He lay like that for a long time, slowly shrinking inside me, his weight crushing. But I didn't have the energy to move. My nipples and pussy were sore. So were my scalp and wrists, which were still stretched above my head and tied to the headboard.

After he finally rolled off me, he smiled for the first time. Bright white teeth gleamed against his dark skin, and he gently loosened the tie and set me free. I managed a slight grin and massaged my wrists. He sprang from the bed and eyed me appreciatively, his black eyes almost gentle.

"You're a cracking fuck, Haley Hanson," he said.

I watched him strut into the bathroom. When the shower came on, I closed my eyes. Unlike Andries Wolff, who seemed energized by the evening's strenuous activities, I was completely drained. I slid under the covers, barely aware of him kissing my cheek before I fell into a dreamless sleep.

Mandela didn't die. I stuck around for a few more months, anyway. Being with the powerful and seductive Andries Wolff was easy and liberating, freeing me from Mikel Garro's shadow.

When I looked back at that time, I realized our strange relationship was the longest of my young life, a camaraderie built on broken hearts, although neither of us ever talked about it. I didn't love him and he didn't love me. And unlike Zeena, I couldn't care less if he fucked someone else, which he sometimes did and so did I.

Andries also introduced me to nipple clamps and leg spreaders.

He got off on dominating me sexually, and I let him, enjoying it, too. He didn't stick around after we were done, either, preferring to sleep alone like I did. The restlessness I'd experienced before arriving in South Africa subsided, replaced by a relative calm, my mind constantly clouded with fantasies about what he'd do to me next.

We did more than fuck, too. He took me to Soweto, where I shot some amazing photos. Instead of a group safari, we spent a few days driving around Kruger National Park in my rented convertible. He traveled with me to Cape Town and Durbin and arranged tours of the Venetia Diamond mine and the East Rand gold mine. He was a good companion, an insider. And because he'd done so much for me, when he asked me to help him blackmail an enemy in Parliament, I agreed.

His enemy was Zeena's father. He was blocking an important initiative Andries cared about because he'd dumped his daughter. As Andries set up the tiny video cameras in my suite, he told me to dress more conservatively than I usually did, his black eyes dancing excitedly.

I donned a lavender suit with a pencil skirt, an outfit I liked to wear when I found myself in a business situation. Then I headed to the hotel restaurant to meet Duncan Dobbie, a powerful member of the finance committee and owner of a small chain of high-end restaurants.

He was already seated at a table. I subtly swayed my hips as I approached and smiled brightly during the introductions.

"Thank you for meeting with me, Mr. Dobbie," I said.

He was an attractive man, fit and dressed impeccably in a gray suit with a pink rose boutonnière.

"Call me Duncan," he responded. His eyes gleamed with interest, looking right through me. The November issue of Playboy had hit the stands a few days before, and I had a feeling he was visualizing me naked.

My smile grew bigger. Andries had told me Duncan Dobbie was known for his staunch beliefs in marriage and monogamy. He was also a collector of the popular magazine, preferring to look and not touch. But he'd never met a real-life Playmate and that was to be the hook.

"I have a proposition for you, *Duncan*." His eyes lit up excitedly. I could see the wheels turning in his head. "I'm a photographer. Maybe you've seen some of my works–the United Nations Hunger Campaign photo or the one of the little girl in the rubble in Chile?"

"Yes, yes, I know who you are," he grinned. "Champagne?"

He ordered a bottle of champagne. I waited until he toasted to my good health and continued. "I would like to expand my reach, Duncan. Currently, my photos are only shown in galleries, and I'd like to start hanging them in select restaurants around the world. You are known to have some of the finest restaurants in South Africa with the richest clientele, so I'm approaching you first."

He puffed up like a puffer fish. I smiled triumphantly.

"I am *highly* interested, young lady. Do you have any particular photos in mind?"

He chuckled. There was nothing funny about what he'd said, and I was sure he was picturing a photo of me from Playboy hanging in his restaurants.

"Yes, as a matter of fact I do." I grabbed the phone from my jacket pocket, opened the photo gallery app and leaned close. I presented one of Iguazu Falls and magnified it. "You can't appreciate its full impact on this tiny thing," I sighed. "Why don't you come up to my suite after dinner and I'll show you the real ones."

He practically drooled and rushed through dinner. Considering his reputation, I was shocked he was so easy to lure into my trap. I hooked my arm in his and chatted about his beautiful country as we made our way to my room. Once inside, I immediately removed my jacket. His eyes bugged out. I wasn't wearing a bra beneath the silky white camisole.

"Are you okay, Duncan?" I asked innocently.

"Yes, yes, sorry, yes. Please show me your works," he stammered.

I sashayed to the sofa where I'd placed several tube mailers containing sixteen-by-twenty-inch prints of my photos. I casually bent over and rifled through them, giving him a good look at my ass in the tight skirt.

"This one is perfect for your restaurant." I picked up a tube and turned to face him.

His eyes nervously darted around the room. Beads of sweat formed on his forehead. I suppressed a grin.

"Are you okay, Duncan? You don't look well."

"Fine, fine, I'm fine," he mumbled.

"Let me help you." I dropped the tube and grabbed his jacket lapels. "You look hot. Let's get you out of this."

"No, no—"

Giving him no choice, I tugged off the jacket. He shifted uneasily. I neatly folded it in half and set it on the sofa back, taking my time and smiling sweetly.

"You know I'm not just a photographer, don't you, Duncan?" I purred the words, attempting to imitate Celine's breathless utterances.

"Yes, I mean, no, well yes, but—"

I closed in on him, loosened his tie and slid it from the collar. "You saw me in Playboy, didn't you?"

"Yes."

I started on the shirt buttons, popping the top two. "Did you like?"

"Yes."

He didn't move, didn't fight me, fixating on my lips.

"Hmm… You know, Duncan, you're very handsome and I'm very lonely."

"Yes," he said robotically. I pressed closer and rubbed against the hard bulge inside his pants. He cupped my breasts and buried his nose between them. "Yes," he sighed.

I loved his response, loved his unconcealed desire for me. It turned me on. My pussy twitched. If it wasn't for the tiny cameras sprinkled around the suite documenting our every move, I might've gone all the way.

But I didn't want a video of me fucking floating around the South African Parliament, and Andries didn't need proof of the actual act. I kept to the plan. I stripped, pulled Duncan Dobbie's cock out of his pants and let him suck my tits.

I couldn't care less about Duncan Dobbie or if he deserved to be blackmailed. I didn't worry about what might have happened to him either. For weeks Andries had distracted me, keeping Mikel's ghost at bay most of the time, and my star continued to rise.

A popular travel magazine paid a high price for my South African photos and the Playmate spread went viral. Mikel was sure to see it, and I couldn't help feeling smug, imagining he regretted his loss. Yet I didn't dwell on him long. Every time I did the dull ache in the pit of my gut resurfaced.

And despite my initial reservations, the nude photo spread didn't hurt my career in the least. Instead, it boosted my brand. I was Haley's Comet, a fireball, my name and special talent world famous.

I'd become a fireball in another way, too. I couldn't get enough sexually. I blazed through men and new experiences, my needs unending. As long as I had both the hot sex and the recognition, I was relatively content. And as Andries removed the cuffs from my ankles and I lay sated in bed in my suite after another satisfying encounter with him, I was certain that was all I would ever need.

"Mandela will be attending the Black Manduka concert on Friday," he grinned.

I bolted upright. A Nelson Mandela photo would be icing on the cake. I was there for him in the first place, expecting him to die. Alive was much better.

"And?" I pressed.

He smirked and dropped down beside me. The mattress buckled under his powerful body. "*And*... I have tickets. VIP section."

"Close to Mandela?"

Only hot sex and the promise of a money shot excited me, and I was excited.

"Gorgeous, you are incorrigible."

"Damn it, Andries, tell me!"

He shrugged and slipped a finger into my pussy. "Close enough. He will be on stage for a few minutes."

I hugged him hard. *Close enough*. It was better than nothing, and he flipped me over and picked up the cuffs.

~~~~~~†~~~~~~

The stadium was packed, the crowd sporting Black Manduka t-shirts, hats and face paint. As we weaved through the crowd, I saw another side of Andries. He was lighthearted. Smiling. With his people.

He brought his video camera, which he'd started carrying a lot after the blackmail business. While he panned the horde, I photographed individuals. A guy dry humping a girl, both wearing South African flag-colored berets. An emaciated man with a toothless smile clutching an apple. A large woman with a puffy afro streaked red, blue, green and yellow.

It took us twenty minutes to reach the VIP section, which was cordoned off by moveable metal barricades. It, too, was packed. We squeezed as close to the stage as we could, and I immediately wished I'd worn shoes instead of sandals, my feet stepped on more than once. It was that crowded.

A warm-up band played first. Andries jammed with the rest of the people, hips swaying and feet hopping, his jubilation another side of him I hadn't seen. After thirty minutes, I was antsy and frustrated. I wondered if Mandela would show up. Even if he did, I didn't see how I'd ever get a shot of him, barely able to see the musicians with all the fans standing in front of me.

"I can't see anything," I complained.

"No worries, gorgeous, you will get your pictures," Andries grinned.

When the warm-up band finished, the crowd cheered and chanted "Madiba, Madiba." The MC took the stage, and Andries squatted low to the ground.

"On my shoulders, Haley, hurry," he said.

I didn't hesitate and scrambled onto his broad shoulders. He grabbed my knees and stood effortlessly, lifting me over the bodies in time to see Mandela shuffle to the microphone. He was dressed in loose-fitting white pants and a brightly-colored, hand-painted silk shirt. He smiled and waved. I snapped shot after shot, zooming in and zooming out. When he spoke, the mob went silent. When he was done, they erupted in cheers again.

"Turn around, Andries," I shouted.

He slowly rotated and I gasped at the crush of people. There were too many of them for the size of the arena. My heart skipped a beat. Dread bubbled in my gut. I dismissed it and captured the moment. Then it was over and Andries set me on the ground. I hugged him hard and couldn't wait to return to the hotel and look at the pictures, certain there was one more money shot among them.

But like the rest of the South Africans at the stadium, Andries was a big Black Manduka fan. One of his cousins' cousins was the vocalist. I braced myself for a long evening, wishing at the very least I could sit on the grass.

The band finally sprinted onto the stage a half-hour later. The roar from the fans was deafening. When the first chord was strummed on the electric guitar, they pushed forward and the chaos began.

The VIP barriers were useless and those of us in the front were pressed toward the stage. Piercing screams filled the air.

"Fucking prats!" Andries shouted. He grabbed my elbow before we could be separated. "Hold on to me, Haley. Fucking fools!"

I linked my arm in his. Gunfire erupted. It was hard to tell from where, but everyone panicked and headed for the exits. Even Andries couldn't stand his ground, and we were pushed away from the stage.

I woman fell in front of me. I tried to sidestep her, but my sandal crunched on her hand or foot. I didn't know which one, and I stumbled forward, clutching Andries' arm as if my life depended on it, which it did. When I tripped on the metal barricade, he held me up. But when he faltered and tumbled to the ground, I went with him, landing hard.

The camera lens gouged my abdomen. A sharp pain shot through my belly. I tried to get to my knees, but someone stepped on my wrist and calf. I covered my head with my hands. Andries snaked his way on top of me and shielded me with his powerful frame. Screams and anguished moans echoed from somewhere beyond. At first Andries held himself up enough so he wouldn't crush me. Then he collapsed.

His bulk smothered me, but at least people weren't trampling me. I rested my cheek on the grass, glimpsing pairs of feet clad in every shoe style scrambling for safety. Every time someone stumbled and fell on top of him, the camera gouged my belly, the air sucked out of me.

Time stood still. When the pandemonium faded to a low hum and a minute passed without a single foot stomping by, I wheezed, "Get off me, Andries."

He didn't move. I tugged the camera out from under me and set it next to us. I wriggled and pushed against him, finally managing to slither into the open, gasping for air and clutching my abdomen.

"Get up, Andries, it's over." I nudged him with a foot, but he remained motionless. I scooted closer and examined his inert body.

He clutched the video camera in one of his large hands. There were shoe imprints on his arms, a crushed cigarette pack between his legs, and a small, dirty South African stick flag lying next to his head.

"Andries?" There was nothing to indicate why he wasn't moving. Then I saw it. The tip of the spear on the flag had punctured the side of his neck. The little cotton pennant was soaked with blood and dirt. "Holy shit."

I crawled over to his face. His eyes were open. Tiny red lines streaked and fractured from his black pupils. My pulse raced. Andries was dead.

I stood shakily and looked around. The stadium was littered with the injured and dead and people crying for help. Sirens blared in the distance, growing louder as they neared. I picked up the camera, my belly protesting with pain. Ignoring it, my pulse raced faster. I began shooting the scene.

I took a photo of Andries first. A twinge of sadness nipped at my soul. I didn't love him, yet he'd been my steadfast sidekick for months and he'd saved my life. For him to die like that was a waste.

I turned away and roamed the arena, documenting the stampede's aftermath. *More dead eyes and more blood.* Before heading to the exit, I briefly stopped to study Andries one more time. He was still dead and it hit me. I'd never know anything about his lost love. There was nothing I could do about it, and I pried the video camera from his lifeless hand and left him with the rest of the unfortunate, carrying proof of man's incredible stupidity in my camera, never looking back.

It was almost eleven when I returned to the hotel. I immediately posted the stampede photos on my website and notified news agencies about their existence. The notification application was created by Jillian, who continued to regularly update the site and find ways to promote me. After I'd gained a solid reputation for photojournalism, the media were more than happy to receive the announcements.

Then I gathered my stuff, planning to return to Paris on the early morning flight. It was time to move on.

I dragged my bags from the closet and set them against the bedroom wall. With each slight twist and turn, my abdomen throbbed. Concentrating on the routine I'd developed to make the packing process easier, I robotically folded my wardrobe into neat piles before placing the stacks into their designated bags.

Dresses into one case, casual wear into another, shoes into another. I saved the backpack for last, stuffing it with makeup and toiletries. It was the same backpack I'd started out with, the Garro top still hidden in the bottom of it.

Mikel's ghost knocked at the edges of my consciousness. I

distracted myself by turning on Andries' camera. I viewed the video he took at the concert and curiously watched the rest of them, moving backwards in time.

The next one made me chuckle. He'd recorded a policeman beating a man in what looked like the town of Soweto. Knowing Andries, he was using it to blackmail someone. There was also a video of a local district meeting and one of a traffic jam at a busy Johannesburg intersection. Then I gasped.

He'd recorded us fucking. I glared at the small screen and watched him cuff my wrists and ankles together. He laid me on my side and screwed me from behind. If I wasn't so angry, I might have enjoyed it. But there were two more videos documenting different sexual encounters, and I furiously removed the memory card and smashed it with the iron provided by the hotel.

I didn't know whether he'd recorded us because he wanted a memento of our time together or because he'd planned to blackmail me, too. It didn't matter. He was dead. I flushed the smashed pieces down the toilet, thinking humankind sucked and I needed a drink.

There it was again.

Foreign sounds seeped into my half-consciousness. I floated in a warm mist. A hazy spray of millions of minuscule water droplets surrounded me. The pain evaporated into the swirling fog. A warm hand caressed mine.

Mikel?

Mikel?

This time the fog slowly dissipated and I moved my lips.

"Mikel?"

My eyes fluttered open and I squeezed them shut. *Light.* Bright light bore down on me.

The light!

I blinked and blinked again and the world gradually came into focus.

"Nubiti?" I rasped.

Liberation

"Praise Allah," she said softly. She gently caressed my forehead, her eyes welling with tears. "You will be okay, Haley. You are safe."

"Nubiti?"

She was there. She wasn't a mirage or a hallucination. She was *real.*

"Haley! I am so sorry…so sorry…"

I turned my head and Momed clutched my other hand.

"I did not know. I never thought. I am sorry, so sorry…"

"Momed," I whispered. My voice sounded rough, gravelly. My mouth was dry and infused with a nasty metallic taste. "Thirsty."

I licked my lips and slid my tongue over a cherry-flavored salve. My eyes rolled around the room and stopped at an IV bag hanging on a coatrack. I followed the clear tube to where it was inserted into my forearm. I was in a bedroom, a woman's bedroom with flowery purple-and-white lace curtains. The quilt that covered me matched the curtains. There was a purple stuffed camel staring at me from a white upholstered chair set in the corner.

"Here. Not too much," said Nubiti.

She held a small teacup in her palm. Momed helped me sit up. The water was cool, delicious. I greedily gulped it up in three swallows.

"More," I croaked.

"Soon, Haley, and some soup, too," she replied.

"Thank you." I smiled weakly and closed my eyes, a dull pain pulsating in my left buttock.

My throat constricted.

The cellar.

I'd survived the darkness, the silence and Baba's torture.

"What day is it?" Tears streamed down my cheeks.

Nubiti squeezed my hand reassuringly. "It is Friday. Mohammed and Mohammed found you on Wednesday."

Five days. I'd been locked in the cellar for five days.

"It was terrible, Haley. We could not find you," Momed cried. "We went to meet you at the fruit stand, but you were not there. We thought you got lost or went to the wrong stand. We searched the whole old city. We waited for you at the hotel. You disappeared. I am so sorry, Haley, so sorry."

"It's okay, Momed."

He looked exhausted, disheveled, his exquisite charcoal eyes rimmed with dark circles. A hint of sympathy simmered inside me, an emotion I hadn't felt in a long time.

"Don't blame yourself. You found me."

"I never thought Baba—"

I cringed at the mention of him. Momed noticed and lowered his head. I reached for his hand. "How did you find me?"

"Me and Mohammed, I mean Hammed, posted your picture on the missing person's website. There are a lot of missing people now because of the revolution, but we thought we would try."

The protests had turned into a revolution. I was missing the revolution, the reason I'd come to Egypt, yet I was too weak to care, too shattered, the fire gone.

"We were frantic. Then I saw Ba—my father going into the

storeroom. He did not have anything with him and he did not come out with anything. I became suspicious, and two days later, he went in there with my uncle, Mohammed's father."

Hazy images of four, loafer-clad feet flashed through my mind. They'd been real. I wasn't hallucinating.

"That is when we found you. You were very sick and kept calling me 'Mikel.'"

Mikel. The memories of him had comforted me. His taste. His smell. His love. I'd spent all those years trying to forget him, erase him from my memory, yet it was him I summoned in the darkness when I'd thought I would die.

Momed caressed my hand. "I am ashamed by what my father did to you," he said.

Whatever I'd been given that dripped from the IV bag into my veins dulled the pain but not the memories. I retracted my hand and slid it beneath the sheets, trailing my fingers along the small bandages between my thighs and on my genitals.

My stomach roiled, remembering the smell of burnt flesh. The image of the angry vein pounding on Baba's forehead made my skin crawl. I closed my eyes. The fatigue washed over me. I had more questions and needed to contact my parents, but I couldn't summon the energy. Sleep beckoned and I let it take me.

The soft drone of sounds became voices. I opened my eyes. Nubiti was sitting in the same chair at my bedside and Hammed stood behind her, a hand resting intimately on her shoulder. Another woman wearing a red "No Mubarak" t-shirt and a white headscarf lingered by the window and nervously toyed with the lace curtains.

"Good, you are awake." Nubiti smiled. "This is my cousin, Dalila. She is a nurse and needs to examine your wounds. First, some water."

Feeling stronger and more alert, I pushed myself upright, gripped the teacup and gulped the cool water. If they would have let me, I could have easily guzzled a gallon of it. I couldn't believe I'd lasted five days without water.

I should be dead. The fact that I wasn't should have overjoyed me. I'd prevailed against Baba and his sick revenge. He'd broken me, but I didn't give him the satisfaction of killing me. Yet once fully conscious, I felt anxious and disconnected, sad and frightened. As if everything around me was really a dream and I would wake up back in the cellar.

"I will go," Hammed said. He briefly glanced at me and lowered his head.

My eyes welled with tears. Hammed had seen me naked plenty of times and he'd seen what Baba had done to me. He couldn't look at me. I was disgusting. *Damaged.*

Dalila grasped my shoulder. I flinched and eyed her warily. She said something in Arabic to Nubiti and Nubiti translated. "She needs to change the bandages." She gazed worriedly at me, her expression filled with pity.

I hated that look. I didn't want people to feel sorry for me. "Okay, sorry," I muttered.

Dalila drew the covers to the bottom of the bed. I was wearing a pink nightgown and she grabbed the hem and rolled it up to my breasts.

A large lump formed in my throat. Besides the bandages that covered the burns, my body was covered with dark purple-and-yellowish bruises. I looked like I'd lost ten pounds or more. I couldn't hold back the tears.

Nubiti clutched my hand and squeezed hard. "Do not worry, Haley, you will heal," she soothed.

I nodded, but I didn't believe it. My body would heal, but my spirit was shattered. Still, her tenderness was calming, standing between me and insanity. I wiped my wet cheeks and smiled weakly.

"Is this your bedroom?" I asked.

The question was an attempt to distract myself from a profound helplessness gnawing at my gut, threatening to overwhelm me. I hated it. I hated being a blubbering wimp, especially since I was alive and should be celebrating.

"Yes. We wanted to take you to hospital, but they are all overcrowded with injured revolutionaries. Dalila stole the medicine you need. You have a bad infection and are severely dehydrated."

"Thank you, Dalila, thank you both."

Dalila smiled and removed the bandages one by one, gently rolling me onto my side to remove the big one on my buttock. She applied a salve on each wound before replacing the dressings. When she finished, she handed Nubiti three pill bottles, rattling off instructions in Arabic. Then she removed the IV line from my arm, grabbed the half-empty IV bag from the coatrack and unceremoniously left.

"Dalila said you are well enough to start eating. She left you antibiotics, and you must take them all and complete the treatment. There are pain killers, too, and hydration tablets. Your wounds are healing and she left bandages for three days changing. You have a cracked rib, but it will heal on its own. You also need to get out of bed and walk soon."

"Can I brush my teeth?"

Nubiti's sweet, melodic giggle rippled through the room. My stomach twisted enviously, doubting I would ever laugh again, ever feel normal again.

Hammed returned carrying a simmering bowl of soup. Momed trailed behind him dressed in fresh clothes. He enthusiastically bounded around to the other side of the bed, grasped my hand and lightly kissed my cheek. "Haley, you look better!"

I involuntarily flinched again. He grimaced, visibly hurt by my reaction.

"Momed, I–"

"Here, have some soup." Nubiti interrupted, glaring irritably at him.

Steam wafted from the bowl. Tomato and garlic teased my nostrils and my stomach rumbled. I forgot about Momed and grabbed the spoon, my hunger primal. I took a taste, savoring the delicious creaminess on my tongue. Then I greedily shoved spoonful after spoonful into my mouth, not stopping until there were only a few drops left, which I summarily gulped from the bowl.

I wiped my mouth with the back of my hand and Nubiti giggled again.

"That was delicious, thank you," I said.

Momed's enthusiastic grin was back and Hammed smirked, reminding me of before. Sadness pricked at the edge of my soul. I lowered my eyes, wondering if I would forever look at my life as before and after the cellar.

"Maybe you should get out of bed now," Nubiti suggested softly.

I held back the tears. Considering she barely knew me, her nurturing was remarkable.

"Okay, but, um, I need to call my parents." My throat tightened.

I wasn't ready to talk about the cellar, didn't know whether I'd ever be able to talk about it. But I was sure they were worried and consoled myself with the fact that at least they didn't have to mourn over their mutilated daughter's dead body or wonder where I'd disappeared to for the rest of their lives.

An uncomfortable silence fell over the room. The three of them glanced uneasily at each other.

Momed spoke first. "The government has shut down internet and cellphone service."

"Some landlines have been shut down, too," Hammed added.

"The country is in chaos, Haley, but we will find a way," Momed said.

On the one hand I was relieved, the wait giving me time to gather my thoughts and compose myself. But I also felt a powerful need to connect with my parents, a little girl longing for her Mommy and Daddy, longing for their love.

The Mohammeds helped me out of bed. I stood shakily. I hadn't been on two legs for several days and my muscles felt like jelly. The memory of waking up on the putrid mattress lying in my own shit resurfaced. The Mohammeds must have seen the mess and smelled my rotting feces. Humiliated all over again, it suddenly became important, *essential*, I recover quickly and leave the country.

I hated Egypt.

I put one trembling foot in front of the other. They guided me across the hall into a small bathroom where they left me with Nubiti. Her sweet face turned grim. When I looked in the mirror, I understood why.

A large knot protruded from my forehead. My eyes were sunken and ghostly, hair tangled and greasy and skin ashen. I quickly looked away and braced my hands on the sink. A strangled sob caught in my throat, remembering all the men I'd been with over the years. Their undisguised desire and appreciation of my beauty had sustained me, made me feel whole and wanted. I'd taken it for granted.

"Here is a new toothbrush. If you feel strong enough, I will wash your hair," Nubiti said. "Do not worry, Haley, you will be back to normal soon."

Normal. I didn't know what normal was anymore. Using the little strength I had, I furiously brushed my teeth until Nubiti gently grasped my wrist and pried the brush from my fingers.

"Sorry," I muttered. I washed my face, averting my eyes from the stranger reflecting back at me in the mirror. When I was done, Nubiti tenderly rubbed a lavender-scented moisturizer on my skin. As I knelt over the tub and she shampooed my hair, an irrational feeling of dread simmered inside me. I shook it off and asked, "Where's the rest of your family?"

"My father and mother are at the Square. They bring food to the young people who camp there. They are very angry at what happened to you and do not like how women are treated in Egypt. They believe nothing will change unless Mubarak is overthrown and there are real elections. They stay all day at the square and come back to sleep at night. My brother is in the army and he has not been home for three days. He believes the military will support the cause. I hope it is true."

If only for her sake, I hoped so, too. I was starting to like her and hadn't made a new friend in a long time, which had been by choice— *before.*

She rinsed off my hair and pulled me upright. I braced a hand on the wall to steady myself while she dried it. Exhausted, the Mohammeds guided me back to bed. A strawberry aroma wafted from my scalp, the scent comforting. After a small bowl of applesauce, a vanilla pudding cup and more water spiked with hydration tablets, I closed my eyes and drifted into a deep sleep.

~~~~~~†~~~~~~

He spun around and smiled broadly. I stopped in my tracks, gaping. Danel's brother was Mikel Garro…

I could smell his unique scent and taste his delicious skin. Then I panicked. My eyes shot open only to be faced with the darkness and silence.

No, no, no! It wasn't a dream. It wasn't! The Mohammeds rescued me. I saw Nubiti's bedroom. It was real. It had to be real…

"No!" I screamed. I bolted upright and *really* opened my eyes, trembling and breathing heavily. A sliver of hazy moonlight filtered through a slit in the curtains and the nightmare waned and faded. I recognized Nubiti's bedroom and burst into tears.

"Haley?" The light came on and Nubiti was at my side in a flash. She wrapped her arms around me and cooed soothing words.

"I dreamed, I dreamed I was back in the c-c-cellar," I sobbed.

"You are safe, Haley, you are safe…"

Nubiti's parents came to the room and stopped in the doorway. They were dressed in long silky bathrobes, their hair disheveled and eyes sleepy. They looked mortified.

"Sorry," I choked guiltily.

"Do not worry, darling girl." Nubiti's mother glided gracefully to the bed and sat next to her daughter. She was beautiful, an older version of Nubiti. "My name is Kissa and Nassor is my husband," she said in lilting, British-accented English. She affectionately clasped my hand and gently brushed the tears from my face. "You are welcome in our home and no one can hurt you here."

"Thank you. I'm sorry I woke you up."

The panic slowly receded. I smiled weakly at Nassor, who thankfully remained in the doorway, an irrational fear bubbling inside me. I couldn't deal with a strange man hovering too close, although he seemed harmless enough. Nerdy-looking with a wiry build, a shiny bald oval spot on top of his head and glasses perched on the tip of his nose. Still, I didn't want him there, watching him from the corner of an eye as the women fussed over me and brought me a cold chicken sandwich and glass of milk.

The sandwich was the first solid food I'd eaten in days. I devoured it. Kissa seemed pleased, her eyes twinkling happily. When she was satisfied I could sleep again, she embraced me like one of her own and whispered in my ear. "Darling girl, you did not deserve what Mohammed's father did to you."

My heart lurched and eyes moistened again. I wanted my Mom, but Nubiti's mother was a good substitute. As if reading my mind, she said, "A friend will come tomorrow with his cellphone. He works for the stock exchange and has service. You can call your parents."

I burst out crying again and she held me tightly. I hated being weak, blubbering at the drop of the hat, but I'd completely lost my self-control, a trait which I'd coveted and guarded before. The cellar had indeed broken me, and I wondered if I would ever feel normal again.

Kissa and Nassor stayed until I was calm. As they retreated to their room, he lovingly wrapped an arm around her waist. Nubiti stayed behind and asked, "Do you want me to sit with you?"

"Will you stay with me?"

She smiled sweetly. "Yes, of course, Haley."

She stood and moved to turn off the light. My stomach clenched anxiously. The panic mushroomed. "Please, leave it on," I begged.

"Yes, of course."

I lifted the covers and she slid into bed beside me. "Thank you, Nubiti," I murmured, snuggling close.

Although she wasn't Jillian, she was a good substitute, too. My last thought before I fell asleep was I would be better tomorrow and stop crying. I'd survived the cellar and I hated being pitied.

I woke the next morning to bright sunshine streaming through the window. I was safe in Nubiti's bedroom and wasn't dreaming. A tiny spark of hope ignited within me. I swung my legs over the edge of the bed, ignored the spasm in my side from the broken rib and cautiously stood.

"Good morning, Haley," Nubiti greeted brightly. "I have clothes for you. I hope they fit. Would you like me to bring breakfast to you or would you like to eat in the kitchen?"

I felt stronger, the pain minor, my stomach growling hungrily. "The kitchen. Thanks Nubiti, thanks for everything."

She helped me take a quick shower and change the bandages. I counted the burns. Besides the one that had become infected on my left buttock, there were seven more round open blisters. Two on my pubic area, three between my thighs close to my sex and two on my hips.

The helplessness and disconnect rumbled through me. I swallowed down tears. I didn't remember the last two or three times Baba had used my flesh as an ashtray. I wondered how many more times he'd smoked and jerked off while I lay unconscious, trembling at the thought.

"Haley?"

"Nothing, it's nothing," I said quickly.

I grabbed the panties she'd given me and scrambled into them. I slipped on the jeans next and they hung on me. She dashed back to the bedroom and returned with a long blue skirt and a safety pin. The bra was too small, so I went without one, grateful the flowery, long-sleeved cotton shirt hid the pucker of my nipples.

I didn't want to be provocative or sexy. The idea of a man touching me was terrifying. Yet I didn't need to worry. Bruised, burned and ghostly, no man would give me a second look. Still, I didn't want to deal with that side of me, my sexual desires switched off like the lightbulb on the ceiling in the cellar.

I didn't know myself anymore, an unease and powerlessness gnawing at me as I followed Nubiti to the kitchen. Her home was small, smaller than most hotel suites I'd stayed in. It made me uncomfortable and nervous.

There were three bedrooms, the bathroom, a cozy living room and a kitchen, which was the largest room in the flat. It contained a rectangular dining table that sat eight. I slid onto a chair at the end of it and looked at my bare feet. The sandals she'd provided didn't fit either. I didn't fit.

Nubiti fried eggs and reheated a bowl of fava beans, chattering about the revolution in her melodic voice. When the doorbell rang, I flinched, suddenly panicked. I inhaled deeply. Once, twice, three times. Nubiti was too busy making breakfast to notice, and then Momed and Hammed bounded into the room.

"Haley, you are better!" Momed cried enthusiastically. He didn't lunge to kiss my cheek this time, kneeling before me and tenderly kissing the back of my hand instead. "I have left Ba—my father. Hammed and I, we rented an apartment. It is wonderful!"

His gusto at that moment reminded me of Mikel. My heart clenched, a deep sadness engulfing me. But it was better than the insipid anxiousness that threatened to overwhelm me. I grinned weakly, watching Hammed embrace Nubiti and kiss her passionately. When they broke away from each other, she smiled brightly and blushed.

A rush of guilt sliced through me and I lowered my eyes. For the first time since Mikel, I saw myself as before. *Before the cellar.*

Insensitive. Oblivious to the consequences of my incessant desires. I'd become a coldhearted bitch, and I was certain if Nubiti knew I'd fucked Hammed, I wouldn't be enjoying her loving care.

"I cannot look at him now. I will not obey him. I am free!"

Momed danced around the kitchen and the doorbell rang again.

Nubiti glanced at the clock on the stove. "Edfu is here," she announced. She lovingly nuzzled her head against Hammed's arm before scampering to the door.

"I moved everything while he is at the Square. My bed, too," Momed said.

I cringed. My pulsed raced. The panic ballooned and my eyes welled with tears. Nubiti returned with an older man dressed in a suit and tie. He handed me a phone and the panic spiked. I shakily took it.

"Haley, this is Edfu. You can call your parents."

I couldn't acknowledge the favor. His presence terrified me. It was only after the four of them disappeared into the living room that I stopped holding my breath.

I glared at the phone, gulping air. A big lump formed in my throat, my pulse raced wildly. I desperately wanted to connect with my parents, feel their love, but I didn't know what to say. I don't know how long I sat there, imagining our conversation in my head. If Nubiti hadn't poked her nose into the kitchen, her brows creased worriedly, I might have never punched in the number. But I did. My mother answered after the first ring, her "hello" tinged with anguish.

"Mom."

"Haley, honey, we've been so worried!"

I heard my father in the background order "put her on speaker." His voice quivered. "Are you okay?"

I burst into tears.

"Honey, what happened?" Mom asked anxiously.

"Are you still in Egypt?" Dad asked.

"We've been watching the news. Your Dad contacted the State Department, but they're useless. They said they evacuated all the Americans who wanted to leave and closed the embassy. Please, honey, what happened?"

"I'm okay, I'm okay," I choked between sobs.

"Are you hurt?" Dad asked. I could hear the fear in his voice.

I gulped back tears, wanting to reassure him, wanting to get it over with. "I'm still in Egypt, but I'm fine. I had some tr-trouble..."

"What kind of trouble, honey?"

"I'll tell you when I see you. It's-it's a long story."

"You're coming home?" Dad asked hopefully.

"Yes, as soon as I can."

The image of Baba slamming my camera against the stone wall in the cellar popped into my head. Because of my arrest in Madrid, I always carried my passport and I'd stuck it in the camera case that day. Without the American embassy's help, I didn't know how I would escape Egypt, the promise to my parents an empty one.

The helplessness took over again and I swallowed hard. Then it hit me. "I have to go. I borrowed a phone to call you. The government shut down most service, but some friends are helping me. I had to call. I knew you'd be worried."

"Oh, honey, we won't stop worrying until we see you again. Please, come home soon."

"I want to, Mom." My voice cracked. The tears threatened. "I'll call you and let you know my plans. I love you."

"We love you, too," they said in unison.

I hung up and quickly dialed another number, one that was easy to remember because it corresponded to a significant date in the life of someone I loved.

"Jack?"

I hadn't spoken to Jack Luck since I'd left the yacht more than three years earlier. He knew right away something bad had happened to me and immediately took charge.

It would be a few days before he solidified a plan. I used the time to regain my strength and return to the hotel. I didn't want to leave the apartment, but I needed some clothes and my credit card. And just as Momed had said, the country was in chaos.

So was I.

Irritable, jumpy. Disconnected from the people around me one minute and in full panic mode the next. As soon as I stepped outside, the dread and anxiety boiled to the surface.

I almost turned back, seeking the relative safety of the apartment and Nubiti's tender care. But I needed money. Most of all, I wouldn't leave Egypt without the Garro top. Once a symbol of betrayal and lost love, it had become a comfort and an irrational obsession, festering and growing, the memories of him dulling the constant edginess.

The Mohammeds waited in the white SUV. I put one foot in front of the other and focused on getting to them. What should have been a forty-five minute trip from Nubiti's apartment to Tahrir Square took three hours. Protesters blocked streets, military tanks were everywhere and the air was filled with nervous expectation Mubarak would soon relinquish control.

We walked the last two miles to the hotel. I anxiously trudged with my head lowered, hiding my blue eyes and blending in with the headscarf and long skirt Nubiti had given me. Hammed and Momed stuck by my side, growling at anyone who dared come too close.

When we arrived at the hotel, armed security guarded the building. A diligent young guard stopped me from entering, insisting I provide identification. My blonde hair and blue eyes were the only proof I possessed, and I removed the headscarf. They were proof I was a foreigner and probably a hotel guest, and the Mohammeds cajoled the man into allowing me inside.

As it had been the day I left, the lobby was filled with media personalities and their crews. I'd wanted to get in and out quickly and avoid attention, but a Sky News producer immediately approached and began badgering me about where I'd been for the last week.

The producer's acknowledgement confirmed my identity, which was enough for the guard. He quickly returned to his post. My heart pounded wildly. I don't recall what I said to the pesky woman or how I finally ended up in the suite, but once there I dropped onto the bed and wept uncontrollably.

It was then I knew I needed to confide in someone. I was going crazy, the trauma I'd experienced in the cellar too much for me to handle alone and too difficult to hide. But I would need to wait. The only people I knew in Egypt were the Mohammeds and Nubiti and her parents. I couldn't open up to them, a part of me hating them.

They were Egyptians.

I haphazardly stuffed clothes into the carry-on, tossed toiletries and makeup into a pile on the bed and grabbed the backpack. The pack was the only item that had remained in my possession since I'd started out on my own, a reminder of a time when I was happy, carefree and excited to be alive. For a brief moment I remembered that feeling.

The moment was brief. I pulled the Garro top from the bottom of the bag and pressed it to my nose. I inhaled deeply and imagined his scent. *Fabric softener and oranges.* I quickly stripped off the flowery shirt, slipped on the tank top and put the shirt back on.

Just knowing the Garro top was next to my skin and near my heart alleviated some of my anxiety. I opened the wall safe, grabbed the credit card and rushed from the room, leaving behind a closet full of designer clothes and shoes. I didn't want them anymore, unable to imagine why I would ever need them.

I left Egypt the next day. The Mohammeds picked me up at Nubiti's apartment at seven in the morning. After a hearty breakfast and tearful goodbyes from Nubiti and her parents, which I couldn't reciprocate, a surreal haze descended over me, panic simmering in my gut.

Hammed headed east and stopped at a Mosque on the edge of the city. Jack was concerned about my safety and had somehow commandeered a mid-level military officer to accompany me. He was waiting for us in the parking lot, another stranger, an Egyptian. The panic spiked.

An older man in his forties, he was dressed in tan fatigues, black boots and a green helmet. He carried a rifle, which was at once unnerving and comforting. The Mohammeds jumped out to greet him and I waited in the car, anxious to be on our way.

If the plan went without a hitch, I would be back in the United States in less than a day. The government suddenly turned on internet and cellphone access in the middle of the night and I'd called my parents and Jillian. The relief in their voices was ominous. I couldn't get it out of my head that they were bound to be disappointed.

I wasn't me anymore.

The officer hopped into the car and sat up front with Hammed. Momed scooted into the back with me. Then I saw him and froze.

Baba.

He walked out of the Mosque dressed in the same long white robe and turban. His beard and mustache were neatly trimmed and graying. His eyes were black and he glared sadistically at me, a vein pounding on his forehead.

My body quivered. My head pounded. "No, no, no," I whimpered.

"Haley, what is it?"

Momed's words barely registered. I was back in the cellar lying on the mattress in my filth. The harsh yellow lightbulb on the ceiling illuminated my naked body. Baba pressed the hot cherry on the cigarette into my flesh.

"Haley!"

Baba gripped my arms and shook me, but he wasn't Baba. He was Momed.

"Haley, please, what is it?"

"Baba..." My eyes followed the man in the robe.

"No, Haley, no. He is not Baba. It is not him."

The man in the robe turned a corner and disappeared. Choking back tears, I snapped back to reality. The Mohammeds and the soldier gazed uncomfortably at me.

The barren Eastern Desert lulled me into a state of disassociation. Men talked in low voices. A cadence of Arabic syllables echoed in my head. When the world came into focus again, Jack was there.

I rushed into his outstretched arms. I didn't remember crossing the Sinai Peninsula and the border into Israel. I didn't know if I'd thanked the Mohammeds for delivering me safely, or if I even said goodbye to them.

The last I saw of them was Momed waving enthusiastically at me from the other side of the fence in Taba, Egypt. I waved back, hoping he would find a nice girl to love, one who would appreciate his sweet exuberance for life. In typical fashion, Hammed watched stoically. My gut clenched affectionately.

Seconds later I was in a helicopter. Jack didn't speak or ask questions during the short hop to Tel Aviv. When I was settled in his private jet and we were in the air, he grinned and clasped my hand.

"It's good to see you again, kid," he said.

Tears welled in my throat. "You can't imagine how good it is to see you. Thank you for helping me."

"Would you like a drink? Are you hungry?" he asked.

I was always thirsty and hungry. "Yes, water, please, and something to eat would be great."

He eyed me curiously, probably wondering why I didn't order a martini or a different cocktail. I hadn't drunk a bit of alcohol for almost two weeks, and I didn't miss it. My body craved water instead. When the flight attendant, who thankfully wasn't the hunk I'd fucked three years before but an attractive woman, placed a glass of ice water on the table, I gulped it down and asked for more.

Jack grinned and said, "Celine says hello. She wanted to come, but I thought it would be better if it was only me."

I fought back the emotions. Jack Luck was an extraordinary man. He had an uncanny ability to read people, and despite the fact that he didn't know the details of my ordeal, he intuitively knew I wouldn't be comfortable with Celine's prying. Plus, he'd come to my rescue when I desperately needed him, no questions asked.

The flight attendant placed another glass of water before me and a plate with lobster tail, a juicy filet mignon, scalloped potatoes and fresh broccoli. I'd had nothing to eat or drink during the five-and-a-half-hour drive across Egypt, and after days of eating fava beans, pita bread and kebab, my mouth watered. I waited impatiently for her to serve Jack and open a bottle of red wine.

"To you, kid, and to a bright future." Jack smiled his rare smile and lifted his glass for a toast.

I forced a weak smile, dubious about my future. Unease and panic nipped at the edges of my being, a constant reminder of the cellar. But I felt better, more alert, and I politely clinked my glass against his and took a small taste of the wine.

We ate in silence. I devoured every tantalizing morsel, drank two more glasses of water and occasionally sipped some wine. Dessert was mint chocolate ice cream with a crunchy Oreo cookie crust. Jack's brows arched with surprise when I requested a glass of milk to go with it.

He skipped the dessert and watched me gobble every crumb between big swigs of milk. When the plates were cleared, he reached across the table and affectionately clasped my hand, his expression turning serious.

"I've been following your career, kid, and I knew something was wrong when you stopped posting photos of the revolution on your website."

I lowered my eyes. The fact that Jack Luck had kept track of me should've made me ecstatic, but I couldn't summon the emotion.

"Look at me, Haley," he ordered softly. I complied and gazed warily at him. The panic bubbled and threatened. "I'm not going to ask you to tell me what happened," he continued, "but you're a strong young lady and I'm sure you'll get past it. You must, Haley. The world needs you and your talent. Your photographs are not simply pictures. They tell a story. They arouse emotions and provoke dialogue.

"Celine and I were entertaining some ambassadors and dignitaries the day your photo of the woman being molested in Tahrir Square was published. It caused quite a stir. The imagery of that moment caught us all off guard and many of us were forced to reevaluate our positions.

"That's one example. The portrait you took of Celine and me is another. She still gets sentimental when she looks at it."

He paused for a moment, eyes kind and warm and searching for acknowledgement I was hearing him.

My pulse raced. The panic mushroomed. I nodded slightly.

"My point is that no matter what happened to you, you mustn't give up your talent. Take some time. Heal. Then get back on the horse. You're the spunkiest and most determined young lady I've ever met. You're Haley's Comet and we need you on earth."

Unlike him, I'd never thought about myself as a shooting star. After Mikel, I rolled where the gusts of wind sent me—a tumbleweed. A dry shrub, rootless and rambling, the relentless quest for money shots and sex turning me into someone I didn't recognize, someone I'd never imagined I would be.

I pushed down the panic. A big lump formed in my throat. His heartfelt assessment of my talent was gratifying but also terrifying. After the cellar, I'd landed between a garbage bin of rotting food and a brick wall, stuck in limbo, the fire in my belly gone. Haley's Comet had burnt out.

Second Chance

We arrived at Teterboro Airport at seven at night. As the jet taxied toward the terminal, I stared at my reflection in the bathroom mirror. I was beautiful again. My eyes were clear and skin glowed, and the rest of my body was mending quickly, the blisters mutating into scabs, the bruises disappearing and the pain in my rib just a twinge now and then.

I'd gained back a few pounds, too, although considering how much I was eating I'd thought it would be more. From the outside I look the same as before the cellar, and I was thankful my parents would see me as I'd been.

Expecting to stop to refuel and spend an hour in the VIP airport lounge before continuing to the Midwest, I was shocked to see them and Jillian waiting for me at the bottom of the boarding stairs.

"Haley!" Dad shouted.

He held out his arms for me. The helplessness and grief and fear I'd felt for days collided and burst to the surface. I bounded down the steps and flew into them. "Daddy," I sobbed.

"It's going to be okay, it's going to be okay," he soothed.

Mom embraced me and then Jillian. I was wrapped in their love and couldn't believe it. I'd been dreading the reunion, my head clouded with crazy thoughts they'd somehow know I was bad and not love me anymore. But they were crazy thoughts. They had to be, because they cried with me, cried tears of happiness and relief, and so did I.

"We love you, Haley," Dad said. He kissed the top of my head and peered over my shoulder at Jack. "Thank you, Jack, thank you for bringing my little girl home."

He released me and went to Jack, shaking his hand and hugging him gratefully. Seeing the two of them together made me uncomfortable. The memory of the two-way mirror and decadent sex on the yacht flashed through my mind. It had been three-and-a-half years since I began my descent into depravity with Jack and Celine, and I doubted my father would've been as appreciative if he'd known the famous Jack Luck had fucked me.

"We knew you'd want to see Jillian, too," Mom said. "She has to work, so we flew out here to meet you. We'll all stay at her apartment. Oh, honey, it's good to see you. We were so worried."

Jillian grasped my hand and gave me one of her "we'll talk later" looks. I choked back more tears. I'd planned to spend a couple of days with my parents and then go straight to her. Tell her everything, not only the sketchy details I'd reveal to them, but *everything*, the anguish and self-loathing eating away at my soul with every passing hour. It was a relief to know it would happen sooner than I'd expected.

A shiny black limousine pulled up. Jack drew me into his arms and hugged me hard. "Remember what I said, kid. I want to see you back in action again soon. Take care of yourself, and if you need anything, anything at all, you let me know."

"Thanks, Jack," I replied softly.

The fog threatened to close in on me again. I slid into the limo and inhaled deeply. While we made our way to Jillian's apartment in Brooklyn, my mother chattered nervously about the weather, Kyle's new girlfriend and other innocuous matters. It reminded me of the day I'd left home. But instead of rolling past lush green hills and cornfields, tall steel buildings loomed on busy streets and I wasn't her carefree, adventurous young daughter anymore.

The driver parked in front of a three-story, walk-up apartment. Jillian clutched my elbow and guided me to the top floor. I forgot about myself for a moment, proud of my best friend. She'd done well, graduating mid-year and immediately hired by a well-established New York security software company.

"This is home, roomy" she grinned.

The apartment was a small two bedroom, six hundred square feet at the most. But it was laid out well with the kitchen opening to the living area and the bedrooms and bathroom in the back, and she'd decorated it with a vintage sofa, chairs and accessories.

It was my apartment, too, although I'd never been there. Her first roommate had turned out to be a closet heroin addict and Jillian kicked her out after two weeks. When she'd grumbled to me about her decision to rent a two bedroom flat instead of a one bedroom, I told her I'd be her roommate and stay there when I was in New York.

And there I was, pulse racing, the panic escalating. Jillian opened a bottle of wine and Mom drew me to an antique upholstered settee to sit beside her.

"I didn't know you knew Jack Luck," she said. "How did you meet him?" My throat constricted. There was a lot she didn't know about me. "Oh, honey, please, tell us what's going on. I can tell you're hurting. Let us help you."

Eyes flickering worriedly, Jillian set a glass of wine on the end table next to me and settled beside Dad on the sofa.

"Can-can I have some water, please," I stammered.

She jumped up and quickly brought me a cold bottle of water. I shakily took a sip.

"If you're not ready, Haley, you don't have to say anything," Dad said. "But I hope you know you can tell us anything. We love you no matter what."

That did it and I burst into tears.

Mom wrapped her arms around me and I sobbed through the story, most of which was true. Instead of revealing I was in the middle of a ménage à trois with both the Mohammeds, I said I was having sex with just Momed when Baba showed up. And I couldn't bring myself to tell them the burns were concentrated around my genitals, so I simply told them he'd burned me several times with cigarettes.

"Fucking animal," Jillian spit. "Isn't there something we can do? He should be in jail."

Her reaction was as I'd expected, as was Dad's, who choked back his own tears, and Mom's, who calmly soothed me with encouraging words.

I felt better saying it out loud, the anxiety and fear waning. After pizza and more wine, which I barely touched, we went to bed.

~~~~~~†~~~~~~

When we were alone in Jillian's bedroom, her eyes moistened and she pulled me into her arms.

"Fuck, Hales, you almost died." She held me close and stroked my hair. "I don't know what I'd do without my best friend."

"Jills, it was, it was…"

"I know, I know…"

"No you don't, not really. A part of me believes I deserved it…"

She stepped back, gripped my arms and pursed her lips angrily. "That's bullshit! No one deserves to be kidnapped and tortured and left to die. Why would you think you deserved it?"

My bottom lip quivered and I muttered, "You don't know me, don't know what I've done or what I've become."

"What are you talking about? Of course I know you! Shit, Hales…"

My stomach roiled. I wanted to believe I didn't deserve it, didn't deserve what Baba had done to me, but she didn't know. She didn't know what my real life was like before the cellar.

"I-I-wasn't fucking just Momed," I croaked. "I was fucking both of them when Baba showed up. And it wasn't the first time I fucked two men. I've fucked so many men I've lost count. A few women, too." I hurriedly stripped off my jeans and panties and pointed to the scabs on my genitals, shaking with trepidation. "He wanted to teach me a lesson. He wanted me to know I was bad…"

Jillian glared at the wounds for a second. "Christ, Haley," she muttered.

She picked up the panties and handed them to me. I could tell by her expression she was surprised, mortified, confused, but being Jillian it didn't stop her from comforting me.

"Just because you're sexually active, experimenting, doesn't mean–"

"Experimenting?" I grimaced. "Maybe at first, but then it was all I thought about. I didn't care if the men were married or nice. I didn't care about them at all, as long as they gave me what I wanted, what I craved. Like a drug. If I didn't get some, bring them to their knees–"

"Okay, I get it," she interrupted, "but it still doesn't mean you deserved it, Hales. What consenting adults do behind closed–"

"That's not all, that's not all…" I wriggled back into the panties, dropped onto the bed and hung my head, trembling.

"Fuck, Hales," she sighed. She sat next to me and grasped my hand. "What do you think you did that could ever justify what that sadistic bastard did to you?"

My eyes welled with tears and I stammered, "You-you know the little girl who was buried in the rubble in Chile?"

"Yes, the photos are amazing."

"Oh, God, Jillian…"

I'd prepared myself for death in the cellar, revisiting my decadent past and seeking answers as to how I'd lost my way so I could die in peace. At that moment I wished I'd died. Jillian would surely hate me for what I'd done.

"Tell me, Haley." She squeezed my hand reassuringly.

"Okay." My heart beat wildly. "The little girl's mother…she begged me to help her remove the wooden beam…the beam that was crushing the kid's leg…trapping her. I ignored her. All I wanted was the perfect shot. I circled the girl, zooming in and out, taking close-ups and then backing up and taking wide-angle shots.

"The woman screamed and screamed at me to help her, but I swear I couldn't hear her. I was obsessed. Then some men from town arrived to help and I just walked away. I walked away and remember feeling excited, *thrilled,* because I knew one of those photos would be great and I'd be even more famous."

Jillian slowly withdrew her hand from mine. "That doesn't sound like you at all."

There it was. The disappointment. The disapproval. My heart sank. Raw, intense shame flooded through me. Along with the helplessness and anxiety, it had been festering in my gut. Once it surfaced, I couldn't tamp it down. I had to tell her everything.

"I also blackmailed a man," I stated somberly.

"Fuck, Haley."

"And the stampede in Africa, the photo of the guy from Parliament? I was fucking him for months and he saved my life…" She didn't respond, didn't look at me. "Oh, God, Jills…"

"Tell me, Haley," she replied softly.

The shame and guilt were overwhelming. I swallowed hard. "He-he covered me with his body, and when the stampede was over, I crawled out from under him and he was dead. Then-then I took photos of him and the rest of the people and walked away…"

The silence was deafening, worse than the silence in the cellar. I cried softly and whimpered, "I–I don't know how it happened, how I became so cold. After Mikel, I didn't care. It crept up on me, Jills. Please don't hate me…"

Jillian sighed and grasped my hand once more.

"I don't hate you, Haley, I'm just surprised. And no matter what you did, you didn't deserve what Baba did to you. Damn Mikel. I wished you'd never met him."

My throat tightened. "It's not his fault," I croaked. "I did it to myself. I thought I was prepared for anything, but I didn't plan on falling in love and being rejected like that. I didn't know how to deal with it. I guess I closed down and focused on my career and the sex because it made me feel better. I don't want to be that person anymore. I don't…"

"Oh, Hales, of course you don't, and now you have a second chance."

I rested my head on her shoulder. We sat like that for a long time. There was nothing I could do but move forward and make the best of it—*my second chance*. A tinge of hope sparked inside me. I didn't know whether I'd find happiness again, but I would try, and I would be a better person. *I would*.

Grinning conspiratorially, she patted my hand. "There's never a dull moment with you anymore," she teased.

I giggled a genuine "that's funny giggle." It was the first time in years I truly laughed instead of faking it because I was supposed to. My heart swelled with love, grateful for her friendship.

She changed into a pajama top and shorts and slipped into bed. I stripped off my long-sleeved cotton shirt and joined her wearing my panties and the Garro tank top.

"Shit, Hales, you still have that old thing," she grumbled. "And you're wearing it?"

"Yes." I snuggled against her warm body. "I know it sounds weird, but when I was locked in the cellar, I thought about Mikel all the time. The memories were comforting."

"After what he did to you? Fucking unbelievable…"

"Yeah," I sighed. I understood her reticence, but I wouldn't suppress my feelings for him anymore. "I know it's crazy, but a part of me still loves him and always will."

"Well, if you're going to sleep in it, you're going to have to wash it. It smells gamey."

"Okay," I giggled.

"Shit, I'm just happy you're back safe. I love you, Hales."

"I love you, too, Jills."

~~~~~~†~~~~~~

Mom and Dad stayed for a few more days. I didn't want to leave the apartment, so while Jillian was at work, we played card games and dominos and watched TV. They showered me with love and encouragement, and then they were gone.

I had nightmares about the cellar, but with the help of a therapist the anxiousness and bouts of fogginess slowly faded. I settled into a routine cleaning and cooking, much to Jillian's amazement, and I wandered around New York taking the subway to Central Park, museums and the tourist sites.

The months passed. When May rolled around, I was stronger and more confident, enjoying the simple life. I even ventured out at night with Jillian sometimes, seeing a Broadway show or going to a gallery opening, but never the nightclubs. That part of my life over. The thought of drinking and flirting with strangers disgusted me.

It was mid-May when the doorbell rang. I was chopping vegetables for a new soup recipe and jumped, startled, not used to visitors during the day.

"Delivery from Jack Luck," a man's voice announced over the intercom.

I groaned, wanting to leave the past in the past. Yet remembering Jack's last words I wasn't surprised. I knew if he didn't see new photos on my website he'd eventually contact me. I stomped down the stairs, picked up the package and discerned right away what was inside.

A camera with a note that read "I'm waiting, kid."

When I returned to the apartment, I hesitantly opened the box and pulled out the camera. My pulse raced erratically. I caressed it and checked the megapixels and ISO. The black hole beckoned and I hastily put it back in the box. What had once been a second appendage like an artist's paintbrush or a footballer's soccer ball suddenly frightened me.

"Hales?"

I jumped again and stared at Jillian, my mind muddled in the past.

The cellar, the faceless men, Andries' blank stare and Mikel's crooked grin.

"What are you doing here?" I choked.

"What do you mean? It's Saturday. What's that?" She immediately keyed in on the camera box. My gut knotted. "Fuck, Haley, it's a camera!"

"I know. It's from Jack."

"I officially love that man. So?"

"So what?"

"Christ, Hales, don't you think it's time?" I hung my head and shifted uncomfortably. The panic that had disappeared weeks ago threatened to resurface. "Come on, Haley, you can't hide here forever. You're meant for more. You know it. You've proved it."

I was safe in the small Brooklyn apartment with her, no longer a tumbleweed and relatively happy. And I'd come to terms with the fact that Haley's Comet had burnt out. "I—I thought I'd go to culinary school…"

"Shit, Hales, you're a lousy cook."

My brows creased with bewilderment. She gave me a "you know what I'm saying" look and I dissolved into a fit of laughter.

She laughed with me. I was transported back in time before I'd set out on my own and we'd huddled together and tittered uncontrollably about one thing or another in our bedrooms back home.

"Just take some fucking pictures, Hales," she said, gasping for breath. "You don't have to take off to South America or Africa or wherever. You know you want to…"

I stored the camera in my bedroom closet. When I shuffled into the kitchen for coffee the next morning, the box was on the counter next to the coffee pot. I smiled and rolled my eyes. Jillian had snuck into my room before I woke, determined as always. Yet the trepidation would not go away. I returned the camera to the closet. When she strolled into the apartment carrying fresh cinnamon rolls for breakfast, I pretended nothing had happened.

The camera was on the kitchen counter the next morning, only this time Jillian had taken it out of the box. Plus, the three lens attachments were set next to it along with a sticky note that read "I won't give up, Hales. Don't you."

I should've known she wouldn't stop badgering me until she got what she wanted. She was dogged when she truly cared and she cared about me. Still, I was torn. My repressed talent begged to be set free and the dark depravity hoped I'd succumb.

From the moment the camera was delivered it taunted me, just as Jack knew it would. My pragmatic, rational side told me I was being foolish. There was no harm in taking a few pictures. And like Jillian had said, I didn't need to fly off to the far corners of the earth to do it.

But my emotional side was still too fragile, associating a camera with all the bad memories from my life as Haley's Comet. I was afraid to head down that black hole again.

It was Jillian's doggedness that turned the tide. After she left for work, I headed to Central Park and took the camera with me. From that point on I truly began to heal and love myself again.

I photographed everything, the New York streets offering a plethora of images. Uniformed doormen, intricate carvings on the sides of old buildings, sunsets from the top of the Empire State Building. I spent an entire afternoon at an outdoor café surreptitiously photographing people walking their dogs as they passed by. Jillian loved the collection, creating funny names for each person and pet, and we dissolved into laughter.

I didn't post the photos on my website. Fame no longer interested me and I had plenty of money. Then one hot July day I wandered around Harlem photographing the Apollo Theatre marquee and the famous Lenox Lounge. I witnessed an overzealous cop kill a black kid during a stop and frisk and photographed the event from beginning to end. And instead of feeling nothing like I had in the past, adrenaline shot through my veins.

I hadn't felt such excitement since the protests in Cairo. I raced back to the apartment. In the back of my mind I knew I was tempting fate, the fire in my belly back and not knowing where it would lead me, but I was lured forward by the prospect of redemption.

I ran out of the subway, down the two blocks to the flat and up the three flights of stairs. When I reached the top, I stopped to catch my breath and immediately smelled a scent I'd never forgotten. *Fabric softener and oranges.* I froze.

"Aley! You safe, gracias a dios!"

"Mikel?" His name stuck in my throat. My heart pounded furiously. The blood rushed to my head and I gripped the handrail, the fog closing in.

He rushed to my side and wrapped an arm around my waist, steadying me. Stomach roiling, I took several deep breaths, unable to believe he was really there. Yet I smelled his unique scent and felt his strong arm holding me up.

"Mikel?" I squeaked breathlessly.

"It me, cariño. Please, come, you must sit."

He gently led me to the door and I robotically unlocked it. The heat radiated from him, sending hot electricity up my spine. As we entered the apartment, he lightly touched the small of my back, the intimate gesture multiplying the effect.

"I sorry, Aley, I wrong." He guided me to the sofa and gently took the camera from my hand, set it on an end table and drew me down to sit beside him.

I peeked at him, my entire body trembling. His luscious chocolate eyes flickered with a myriad of emotions—remorse, nervous anticipation, longing. He looked the same except his floppy hair was cut short and his exuberance was muted.

He was beautiful.

"Aley, please, we talk, sí?"

I should have been angry, should have immediately slapped him across the face for hurting me and betraying our love. But seeing him, smelling him, turned me into mush. Besides, I'd already forgiven him. It was the memories of him that had comforted me in the dark silent cellar, and since the day I'd left him I'd always hoped he'd come back to me.

And there he was, contrite, solemn and so very handsome and seductive.

The world stopped.

"I very worry. I see no photo by you for long time. I very worry."

I let him clasp my hand and gazed into his sultry brown eyes. My insides churned anxiously and throat welled with tears. "Why?" I croaked.

I'd been desperate for an answer to that question for years, and it had been almost four years to the day since I'd arrived in Pamplona and fell in love with him. Yet suddenly I wasn't sure I wanted the answer. I didn't believe any reason would be satisfactory enough to mend my broken heart.

"I think it more good for you," he replied softly, peering solemnly at me.

I gaped, heart hammering. "Good for me?" I understood the words but not the meaning. His betrayal was in no way *good for me*.

"Sí, mi amor, you got dream, you got talent. You must go out to world and take picture, but I want to keep you with me. Near. All time. I love you 'ard, but mama say I selfish." My heart skipped a beat. He'd talked to Ysenia about me? "I sad you go to Barcelona. Very sad. And Mama say we too young. You got career and I got career. I must give you free. It more good for you, for us."

"So-so you thought it would be better for me...for-for us if you set me free?" I stammered.

"Sí, mi amor. You say you go and come back, go and come back, but it not good. You say it okay, but I know you doubt. I keep you down. Mama say you give up dream for me and I know it true. I love you and want you 'appy."

"Oh, God, Mikel..."

A warm glow ignited within me. He'd sensed my doubt and asked about it a couple of times, and until I was alone on the train to Barcelona I hadn't decided what to do. But as soon as I got on that train I altered my plan, hoping I could have both him and my career. I'd been willing to sacrifice my independence for his love, but I'd never had the chance to tell him. Maybe if I had, all the unnecessary heartache and lonely years could have been avoided. I *knew* he loved me as much as I loved him.

Yet even if I'd gotten that chance, I wondered if it would have really mattered, especially with Ysenia advising him. I couldn't fault her reasoning. Mikel and I *were* really young back then, and my career would have certainly turned out a lot differently if I'd stayed with him. And in the end I fell in love with him because of his sweetness and guilelessness, so I shouldn't be surprised he was worried about my happiness.

I wished I'd confronted him, wished I'd asked for an explanation, but I was too hurt, too devastated by the last scene in the bedroom, which I still didn't understand. "But-but why the woman? Why couldn't we just talk about it?"

He anxiously raked a hand through his hair, his handsome face etched with shame and beautiful eyes laced with sorrow. "I sorry, mi amor, I do bad, very bad. I want to be nice, kiss you goodbye and be friends, but Danel say you not go. 'e say you try to change my mind and I fold cards because I love you. Fast break more good. That why she there. I do it so you go. I also very, very sad. She make me feel more good, make me forget."

His butchering of the English language was as endearing as ever, his explanation sincere. I sighed softly and my stomach unknotted. Danel had been right. I would have tried to talk Mikel out of it. Reassure him. And deep down I understood his need for solace, although I wished he would have trusted our love, wished he would have found a less cruel way to break up with me.

"But Danel not care for you. 'e worry for me. 'e worry for my name and business. After you go, I 'ear Danel and Carlos talk. Danel want me with Spain girl. Basque girl. 'e say it more good for me…"

My breath caught in my throat and gut clenched angrily. I remembered the day I'd left for Barcelona and the argument between them. Of course the closing act had been Danel's idea.

He'd been unhappy about the bad press surrounding Mikel's choice of girlfriends. Mikel couldn't have cared less about the controversy, but Danel did. He'd found a way to make it disappear, make *me* disappear, for good. And he'd encouraged Mikel to make it happen in the nastiest of ways. Mikel would have trusted his brother, as he had all his life. If Danel hadn't butted in, I was sure our parting would have been much different.

"I very mad at hermano. I mad at me. I know I 'urt you bad and want to say I sorry, but you gone. You leave phone with 'ouse. I not know where you go. I want to email you but do not find right word to say. Every day I look at website for picture. Two week and I see cave. Then more picture and I know I right to give you free.

"But I not 'appy. I see many woman and look for new mi amor, but it no good. I love you. I miss you. I 'ang bull painting in bedroom. Every day I look at website. You do good. Famous photographer, Aley Comet, and I proud, very proud.

"Then I see Playboy. You very bonita. You my cariño, mi amor, but you not mine. Every day after you go, I look at website. Then one month, no new picture. Two month, nada. Three month, nada. I worry and very scare for you. Four month, nada. I think you dead and I pay man to look for you. 'e find you and say you good. Send me you picture, but I worry. I know in 'eart there bad for you and I must come."

I couldn't believe it. Just like Jack Luck, Mikel had been following me through my website. The warm glow mushroomed. My heart burst with joy. Despite the miles between us, despite the long and tortuous separation, he knew I'd been suffering, knew I'd been hurt.

And after what he'd done, he had the courage to face me and ask for forgiveness. Because he still loved me. Mikel Garro still loved me. The floodgates opened.

He abruptly stood, shifted uncomfortably and hung his head, his beautiful brown eyes wounded and sad. "I sorry, Aley, I love you and no want 'urt you more. I go."

"No," I choked. "No!"

I jumped up, threw my arms around his neck and buried my nose in his throat, sobbing uncontrollably. With each teardrop the heartache and despair melted away. He relaxed against me and drew me close, resting his chin on the top of my head. "Mi amor, mi amor..." he murmured.

"I love you, too," I managed to croak between sobs.

He gasped and held me tighter. Every synapse in my body ignited with sweet anticipation, savoring his special Mikel scent. For the first time in months my libido awakened.

"Aley, I very sorry, very stupid. I not do again. I love you and I very 'appy you love me also." A crooked smile lit his face and he swept me off my feet and swung me around, laughing jubilantly. I laughed, too, a cathartic, hopeful, refreshing laugh.

When he set me on my feet, he kissed me softly, reverently, his sensuous chocolate eyes locking onto mine. "You not 'urt? I very worry. I know you very nosy. Get trouble," he teased.

I loved his playfulness and grinned. If I hadn't been to therapy and learned I didn't deserve Baba's sadistic punishment, I might have reacted differently. But I'd come to terms with those dark days in the cellar, and it was true. My nosiness, or rather my desires had *definitely* gotten me into trouble.

I didn't flinch, didn't hesitate. I needed to tell him about my life as a tumbleweed, certain he'd understand and wouldn't forsake me again. If I was wrong, if he didn't want me anymore, then our love wasn't true, but I needed to tell him. Tell him about the cellar. Tell him about the lonely years without him. Only then could we move forward, because when I woke in the middle of the night next to him trembling and sweating from another nightmare, I wouldn't pretend it was simply a silly bad dream.

His eyes never left mine. A host of emotions flickered in them—jealously, shock, anguish. When I finished, he hung his head and muttered, "It because I bad. I sorry, Aley."

For a long time I blamed him, too. But during those dark and silent hours in the cellar, I'd accepted the fact that when I left home at eighteen I wasn't as mature or as prepared for life as I'd thought. I could have chosen a different path.

I cupped his face and eyed him solemnly. "I did it to myself, mi amor, but it's over now. I missed you so much."

His soft lips touched mine. A delicious tingle crawled over my skin. He kissed me tenderly, passionately, hands roaming beneath the simple white t-shirt I'd donned that morning. His lips left mine long enough to peel the tee over my head, and he cupped my ass, pressed close and leisurely rubbed the hard bulge beneath his jeans against my belly.

All the exquisite feelings he'd induced in the past flooded to the surface. The dormant ache between my legs sparked. A primal desire took over, and I fumbled with the buttons on his shirt and hastily popped them open one by one. I tugged the tear-drenched garment over his shoulders and planted my mouth on his rock hard chest, sliding my tongue along the rippling muscles, tasting him, smelling him, bathed in the heat radiating from his bare flesh.

Growling contentedly, he reached for the button on my jeans. I froze, panicked, suddenly self-conscious. I'd forgotten about the ugly scars on my genitals. I hadn't groomed my pubic hair. No one had seen down there since Jillian.

Mikel tensed, brows furrowing. "What, Aley?"

"I, um, where Baba, um, it's ugly…"

His beautiful brown eyes flashed guiltily. "It okay, mi amor. You magnífico."

He gently brushed an index finger along my cheek. I smiled weakly, stomach churning. He stepped back and quickly stripped off his jeans and jockeys, his eyes twinkling mischievously.

Gaping, I leered at his naked sculpted form and swollen cock standing at attention.

"I scar also," he grinned sexily. He pointed to an inch-long one on his knee and one on his calf. He flipped around, bent slightly and brushed a finger over a small welt on his buttock. Then pivoting to face me, he stretched out his arms, lips curving into an exuberant smile, brows lifted expectantly.

I flew into them, heart fluttering happily. "I love you, Mikel Garro."

He swung me around and kissed me hard, our fate sealed with that one, long feverish kiss. Then he hungrily devoured me, deftly removing my bra and greedily latching on to my nipples, sucking and licking and molding my tits with his hands. He drew me down to the floor and stretched over me, unhurriedly continuing the assault and moving downward. When he reached the apex of my sex, he peeked at me as he slowly peeled off my jeans and panties and sneakers and set them aside.

My nipples hardened, my pussy burned, yet it wasn't enough to distract me from the hideous marks between my legs. I leaned on my elbows and nervously watched his lips graze my inner thighs and land on a deep scar.

He didn't cringe or gasp. He found the most visible ones and leisurely kissed and nipped at them. He rolled me over and licked the big round one on my buttock. Then he slithered up my back, his thick cock skimming over my naked flesh, and he buried his nose in the back of my throat. "You bonita, cariño, I miss you very bad," he murmured huskily.

All my worries and all my woes disappeared. It was me and Mikel and the hot sensations made more intense because I loved him. When he plunged into me and moaned with pleasure, I moaned with him, my body shuddering excitedly.

He took his time, thrusting slowly, deeply, savoring each stroke and hitting my sweet spots. He kissed me tenderly, his tongue matching the rhythm of mine. My muscles tightened, an orgasm coming for me. I held it back, wanting more, wanting the moment to last forever. He stopped kissing me and pressed his forehead against mine, thrusting faster. His warm breath danced on my lips. I wrapped my legs around his hips and bowed into him.

"Mi amor," he groaned.

He grinded and pounded, abandoning all restraint and pushing me to the brink. I let go. The hot ache erupted and spread through every sinew in my body, rocking me, shattering me, bathing me in sweet love.

He came with me, exhaling heavily and gently slumping on top of me. There were no words, no need for words. We'd made it back to each other, the world was righted and I wasn't broken. Baba didn't win. I was excited, hopeful, my blood pumping with a joy I hadn't felt in a very long time.

I rested my cheek against his and sighed contentedly, listening to him breathe. Steady, even puffs tickled the skin on my neck. Smiling, I remembered how he liked to tease me by pretending to fall asleep. I nudged him with my hip, thinking we should retreat to my bedroom before Jillian returned from work. Then the door opened and she breezed into the room.

Gaping, she stopped in her tracks. "What the fuck?"

I bolted upright. Mikel opened his eyes, grinned crookedly and wrapped an arm around my naked waist.

"Hi, Jills, um, this is Mikel…"

ABOUT THE AUTHOR

From the author of the erotic romance series *The Vitamin D Treatment and Side Effects, The Vitamin D Treatment Finale*, Julia Bramer tells an uncompromising story of a woman coming of age in a sometimes brutal world in *Tumbleweed*.

Julia lives in Colorado with her husband and an old, spoiled cat. She enjoys football and soccer, barbecues and books. She's been fortunate to be able to travel the world, which has shaped her perspective on life. She writes love stories with a naughty edge and often weaves in scenes of places and people she's encountered during her travels.

Her other books include the twisted tale of love and revenge in *TwiSted TWo-SteP* and the romantic thriller *Sugar Daddy's Baby*.